AWAKENING

ROBERT M. KERNS

KNIGHTSFALL PRESS

* * *

Published by Knightsfall Press
PO Box 280
Mineral Wells, WV 26150

ABOUT THIS BOOK

Gavin Cross is a young man in an unfamiliar city with no knowledge of how he came to be there. A desperate choice awakens a power he must learn to control, or it will kill him.

Marcus is an ancient master, possessing countless secrets of forgotten lore. He trivializes workings of magic anyone else would say is impossible.

Gavin becomes Marcus's first apprentice in uncounted years and must thread his way through a society where people who've never met him regard him with unease at best or outright fear at worst. But when he discovers a plot to destabilize and overthrow that society, Gavin must make another choice.

Option One: a society's leadership who would prefer Gavin dead. Option Two: a traitor who actively seeks Gavin's death. Hmmm, looks like it's time to make Option Three...

I find myself thinking about one of my classes today. The class in question was a study of the ancient epics, but there was one precocious soul who decided to venture into more recent history. She looked up at me from her seat, all earnest and curious, and asked what truly started the cascade of events that led to the second Godswar.

I smiled as politely as I could and corrected her that scholars refer to the late unpleasantness as the War of Darkness. I also pointed out that the class was intended to study the ancient epics, not my current work in progress. However, I indulged her, saying, "If I had to pick one event that started us on the path of no return, I would have to say it was the arrival of Gavin Cross in this world. Without doubt, tensions were already building to another conflict, but Gavin put a spark to the tinder."

To this day, I cannot imagine how he withstood all the temptations he faced. So many times, during those years, the entire world hovered over the abyss, and whether we fell rested solely on Gavin's shoulders.

—An excerpt from Journal #57
Declan deHavand, Headmaster
The Bardic College *Skuv Ir Nathene*
circa 6099 PG (Post Godswar)

CHAPTER 1

Kiri stood atop one of the many rolling hills in the grasslands of Mivar Province, her destination in sight at last. The sun from a cloudless sky warmed her face, the soft breeze brushing her nose with a hint of the salty sea air from the south. She placed her sack on the ground beside her, taking a moment to stretch her fatigued body. Her stretches complete, Kiri retrieved a water skin from her sack and took a drink, taking care to slosh the cool liquid around her mouth before swallowing.

The unpleasant itch in her left shoulder flared, and Kiri sighed. She reached up with her right hand to massage the shoulder and, not for the first time, wished she could cover the brand there in some way. The brand proclaimed her status to all who saw her. With one last sigh, wishing for something she could never have, Kiri retrieved her sack and resumed walking to the city sprawling across the river valley below.

Tel Mivar was more than a province capital; it also served as the capital for the entire Kingdom of Tel, and like its sister cities in the other provinces, Tel Mivar was a relic of ancient times. Kirloth and his Apprentices, wielding incredible power unheard of in the modern age, raised the city from the very bones of the earth and transmuted its structures into a marble-shaded stone immune to the ravages of weather and time.

That is not to say the city remained unchanged, however. As the world's population rebounded in the wake of the Godswar, Tel Mivar found itself at maximum capacity in less than three centuries. Wooden construction soon started springing up outside the city's walls, and over time, Tel Mivar became one of the most prosperous and populous trading ports in the world, its population divided among the old city and the new.

No walls surrounded the wooden construction that had grown up outside Tel Mivar, though building some had been discussed down through the centuries, and Kiri strolled past homes and shops whose architecture elicited strong memories of her homeland. In Vushaar, the land of her birth, almost all construction was wood; only affluent people could afford brick, and only royalty could afford stone.

The nostalgia lasted just until Kiri came within sight of the West Gate, and she relied upon the training of her youth to hide her nervousness.

"Well...look here!" the youngest guard said as Kiri approached. "We have ourselves a rather fine-looking slave. Where's your owner?"

Kiri squared her mental shoulders and met the guard's lecherous gaze eye for eye, before lowering her eyes in submission. She hoped word of her escape had not preceded her arrival.

"My master has sent me to Tel Mivar to visit the spice merchant," Kiri said. "May this slave please pass?"

One of the other guards sauntered over.

"Well now, I don't know," the newest guard said. "It seems to me we ought to help ourselves to the goods before we allow you to enter the city."

Kiri shuddered in the depths of her mind and prayed she kept it from being seen. Something about the second guard spiked her fear. She took a couple slow breaths before responding.

"If that is what you wish, this slave will strive to please and hopes my master approves," Kiri said, keeping her eyes downcast. "Baron Kalinor does not usually like anyone touching his property without permission."

The two guards almost jumped back. A close friend of the king, Baron Kalinor's reputation as a petty and vindictive soul was known far and wide. He wasn't well acquainted with forgiveness, either.

"G-g-go on t-t-through," the young guard said, his former brazenness now fled.

Kiri kept the smile lighting her heart from showing on her face as she resumed her walk into the city.

THE MOMENT she passed through the gatehouse and into the city proper, the itch Kiri had endured the last two years flared into an almost-burning sensation. Kiri remembered hearing other slaves at her master's estate talking of this, and they said it was because the various protections, conjurations, and other magical effects built into the city created an ambiance of magic that resonated with the power maintaining the brand.

A sudden pain in her midriff dropped Kiri to her knees, and she struggled to pull the sack off her back. Shaking hands worked to untie the knots in the sack's drawstring, and her movements were jerking and frantic as she rummaged through the sack for what she sought. She seemed to find everything but the object of her search; jerky and nuts, extra clothing even if they were simple homespun garments, and pieces of flint were but a few of the items she pushed aside.

As the pain began to build, Kiri sighed her relief as she pulled a partially-empty vial from the sack. Not trusting her shaking hands, Kiri pulled out the cork stopper with her teeth and spat it into the gutter before downing the contents of the vial in one, large swallow. The mixture was off-blue with hints of purple, and it was a vile-tasting brew, bitter and chalky. Within a few heartbeats, the pain was gone, and Kiri sagged against a convenient lamppost.

Not content with the papers that declared her his property or the brand on her left shoulder, Baron Kalinor laced Kiri's meals with a poison that concentrated in the lining of her stomach. Should Kiri ever fail to imbibe the foul-tasting swill in the vials within a few moments of the pain's onset, the poison would deliver a slow, agonizing death, and no cure for it existed in nature.

With one last deep breath, Kiri pulled the drawstrings on her sack tight and draped it over her shoulder once more. She added an apothecary visit to her mental itinerary; only three more vials remained in the sack. She would need more within a day or so.

Kiri sighed as she pushed herself to her feet. She wasn't proud that she'd stolen two coin-pouches from Kalinor's estate; her parents didn't raise her to be a thief, but she hadn't seen any other way to fund her trip home.

Two MAIN STREETS crossed Tel Mivar—one north to south and the other east to west. They divided the city equally, and they intersected at Market Plaza. Kiri turned south onto a secondary avenue that ran north to south about halfway between West Gate and Market Plaza. Kiri had no wish to stay on the main thoroughfare, though; she attracted far too much attention.

The average Vushaari possessed a complexion that was just noticeably darker than the fairer-skinned people of Tel, with blond or red hair almost unheard of, and Vushaari were not an uncommon sight in Tel, either, given their culture of being sea traders. No...Kiri attracted too much attention because she had been 'graced' with the kind of looks that turned heads across rooms: well-proportioned features, wavy hair the color of glossy anthracite, an hourglass figure, and a smile that could put even most disagreeable person at ease. Kiri had grown into one of those women who drew attention no matter how much she wanted to be unnoticed.

Even the secondary avenue seemed crowded with people; Kiri had never seen the like before. Despite having spent both time in the Vushaari capital and the port city of Birsha—Vushaar's most populated city—Kiri was unprepared for the sheer hordes of people congesting the streets of Tel Mivar.

Kiri was behaving like a unlettered rube as she walked south along the avenue. The way she gawked, turning her head this way and that, one would think she'd never seen a city before.

Kiri should've kept her attention focused on her direction of travel. She was looking back the way she came—not watching where she was going—when she bumped into someone. She back-pedaled and turned to apologize to the person but froze, mouth opened to speak. Standing in front of her was an unwashed man with greasy brown hair, wearing worn leather armor...and he carried a handbill.

Kiri could only watch in stunned silence as the slaver lifted the handbill to read it, his eyes flicking from the parchment to Kiri and back. At last, he turned it for Kiri to see.

Wanted!

One week ago, a Vushaari slave escaped from the Kalinor manse.

She has shoulder-length, wavy hair the color of lustrous black and the Vushaari olive complexion.

The slave is to be taken alive, unharmed, and unmarked...for which Baron Kalinor will pay a sizeable reward.

For several moments, Kiri stood frozen, staring at the handbill. Word of her escape had preceded her, and her hopes of freedom dispersed like mist before a breeze. She considered surrender; yes, the Baron would find some creative way to punish her, but there wouldn't be any lasting injury. He prided himself on owning such a slave. Kiri resolved herself long ago to the likelihood of never seeing home again, and this attempt to run was nothing but a fool's errand at best.

It was her thoughts of home and family, more than anything else, that re-ignited the fire of rebellion. Kiri saw the slaver recognize her fire for what it was, but he was too slow. A half-step carried her close enough, and her right knee was a blacksmith's hammer striking the anvil of the slaver's groin.

The slaver's eyes bulged as he croaked in a breath, and Kiri turned to run. The strings she used to drape the sack across her back went taut, the slaver clutching the sack even as he collapsed to his knees, and Kiri struggled in vain to pull herself free.

* * *

HE WALKED through the people that crowded the street, unremarked and unnoticed. His average build, brown hair, clean-shaven face, and simple clothes ensured no one noted his passage, for he was a member of an order dating back to the Godswar that went unmentioned in every history text. He was enjoying the pleasant, sunny day, because his order's liege had informed the local chapterhouse that a female Vushaari slave would arrive in the city today, and she was to reach whatever destination she chose undisturbed...and unaware of her protection.

A slight commotion caught his eye, and he saw the object of his search facing a very unclean man and started drifting their way. He was close enough to see the Vushaari knee the man and his collapse to his knees in response. His eyes narrowed upon seeing the man clutching the Vushaari woman's sack.

Without missing a step, he drew a short dagger from the folds of his clothes and stepped close to the unwashed man. He clamped his left hand over the unwashed man's mouth and nose as he stabbed the dagger into the base of his skull. The unwashed man went limp, including the hand clutching the Vushaari's sack.

The Vushaari dashed toward a nearby alley without a backward glance, and the man gave the dagger a savage twist and jerked it free of the corpse's skull. Lowering the corpse to the ground, the man threw the dagger into a nearby storm drain and disappeared into the crowd once more.

* * *

KIRI DIDN'T GIVE it a second thought when the slaver released his hold. She pushed her way through the crowd and headed for the nearest alley as quickly as she could. Within moments, she was out of the bustling crowd of people.

Kiri lost track of how many twists and turns she had taken as she stumbled her way through the alleys of Tel Mivar. She didn't think she had crossed any streets, but it didn't matter all that much if she had. Kiri turned a corner to avoid what looked like a street ahead and found herself in a cul-de-sac.

Walking to the end of the short passageway, Kiri collapsed on a mostly clean section of pavement and leaned her back against the wall. She didn't know how far the slaver was behind her, but she was winded from her flight. A few minutes' rest wouldn't hurt that much.

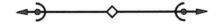

CHAPTER 2

Rough stone heated his cheek and torso. Then, he realized the sun heated his back, neck, and arms. It was strange. Almost as if he were waking from a deep sleep, awareness and consciousness returned at a crawling pace. He became more aware of himself and his surroundings, a throbbing ache permeating every fiber of his being. The breeze trying to cool him smelled of the sea, and coastal birds cawed in the distance.

"Well, now, I'd say you had yourself a drunk to remember, son," a voice said. The voice was seasoned and worn.

He rolled over and blinked his eyes. The sun stabbed his head, and he raised his left arm to block it. An old man stood over him. His full head of white hair was unkempt to say the least, but 'in wild disarray' would also apply. The full beard—also snow white—only served to complement the hair. The old man wore gray robes, tattered and frayed around the hem at his ankles, and he leaned upon a balsa-wood staff worn with age and use. A strong feeling of grandfatherly regard belied the old man's outlandish appearance.

"I say, boy, are you well?" The old man punctuated his question by prodding the boy. "What's your name, anyway?"

"My name is Gavin Cross," he croaked. His voice was scratchy and parched, and using it produced a momentary cough.

The old man smiled and turned his head as if listening to something on his right side, but he soon returned his attention to Gavin. "Yes, my boy, of course it is. Now, give me your hand; let's get you up."

Gavin extended his right hand, and the old man hoisted him to his feet with no apparent effort. Gavin saw now that the old man wasn't too tall; he barely reached Gavin's shoulders. Gavin also saw that he was standing in a seedy alleyway wearing no shirt or shoes; garbage lined one side of the alley, and something not too far away smelled rather foul.

The old man gave Gavin an appraising look before nodding, a satisfied grin curling one side of his mouth. "Yes, indeed, my boy, you will do fine...just fine." He looked away again, squinting his eyes just a bit. "All right, son, it's time to be on your way. You want to go that way..." He pointed behind him down the alley.

"Now, just wait a moment," Gavin said as the old man put a hand on his back and started ushering him down the alley. "Where am I, and for that matter, who are you?"

The old man stopped and regarded Gavin as a patient parent regards a petulant child. The grin returned as he said, "Well, you're here when you should be over there a ways, and as for who I am, think of me as an old friend who's trying to help you on your way. But we don't have time for this. I'll catch up to you later maybe, and we can talk then. Now, shoo! You have somewhere you need to be."

What a crazy, old codger... Gavin thought as he started off down the alley. About every fifth or sixth step, something squished under his feet, and Gavin vowed he would spend half a day in the shower, as soon as he found one.

The alley ended not too far away, intersecting another, and Gavin looked over his shoulder, saying, "Which way-"

Gavin found no trace of the old man; it was as if he had never been there. Gavin frowned and examined the alley for signs of a door that the old man might have entered, but he could find none, not even footprints in the filth.

With a sigh, Gavin turned and resumed his consideration of which way to go. Not seeing any difference to either choice, Gavin turned left and followed the alley.

Gavin found himself in a maze of twisting turns. The alley wasn't more than three feet wide, for the most part, but every so often, it widened to five or six for a stretch. As he walked, Gavin considered his situation. He had no money; his dark-tan, homespun pants had no pockets. In fact, his pants were frayed and tattered around the ankles, not unlike the old man's robes, and his belt was a length of hemp rope.

The bone-deep, throbbing ache was gone, replaced by a tingling sensation that was fast becoming unsettling; every nerve in his body felt like it was crackling fire. What's more, the tingling seemed to ebb and flow much like a peaceful but active sea.

I'M 'SUPPOSED to be over there a ways,' am I? Well, how am I supposed to know when I get there if I don't know where I'm going? I should probably be going home...

Gavin froze in mid-step and looked all around him, though for what he didn't know.

I don't know where 'home' is. How can I not remember where home is? Or what I do? Or who my family is? What happened to all my memories? I can't even remember my parents.

Gavin resumed walking, and he never noticed his pace was quicker than it had been.

I'll bet that old man knows. He told me I needed to head this way. Why would he say that if he didn't know me? Do I-

Gavin didn't give a second thought to the semi-liquid goo he was placing his left foot upon, and his foot shot forward as quick as a skate on wet ice. Gavin lost his balance just as his legs were starting to resemble a wide A-frame. The collision with the alley floor drove the breath from his lungs, and for a moment, Gavin just lay there.

Gavin rolled onto his left side and started pushing himself to his feet. As he rose, he noticed something chiseled into the wall. A circle enclosed a ring of runes he didn't understand. Inside the runes, another circle enclosed a single, large rune. The single rune looked like an arrow pointing up that only had the angled line on the left, and half-way down the shaft, a horizontal line extended right with two, vertical lines extending up from that horizontal line.

The whole engraving was covered in places with grime across uncounted years, and Gavin reached out to wipe some of it away for a better look. The stone just above the outer circle was rough, and a small piece about the size of a pencil's tip jabbed into the meat of his hand and tore a line across the pad.

Gavin jerked his hand back with an "Ow!" His hand started to bleed, and Gavin saw he'd left some blood on the wall, as well. The blood began running down the stony surface, but Gavin wasn't paying it much attention while he focused on staunching the crimson that pooled in his palm.

The moment his blood touched the outer circle of the engraving, the entire design erupted in ruby-colored radiance that burned away the grime covering it, and Gavin lost all interest in his bleeding hand. The tingling sensation throughout Gavin's body flared to new heights, and the radiance began to pulse. It was several moments before Gavin realized the radiance was pulsing in perfect time with his own heartbeat.

Now, the tingling Gavin had felt since awakening exploded into an inferno. Gavin felt overwhelmed by what seemed to be a new sense, an awareness of power all around him just waiting to be manipulated. Gavin recognized at last that the radiance pulsing from the etching was in fact power bleeding into the natural world, and it strengthened into a bright fire, bringing with it an agony across his entire body unlike anything Gavin had ever imagined. Every muscle in his body went rigid, even those that allowed him to breathe, and Gavin felt a word being burned into his mind.

In an instant, it was over, and Gavin almost collapsed to his knees in relief. Gasping for breath, he considered the word he now knew. He didn't know any other words like it; of that, he was certain, and yet, Gavin knew how to pronounce the word without error. He didn't, though…didn't even try a part of it. That word was somehow a key to the vast power Gavin felt all around him, ebbing and flowing like the currents of a vast, peaceful lake.

More than a little unsettled by his most recent experience, Gavin shook his head to clear his thoughts and turned from the strange etching in the wall—now dormant once more.

* * *

SOME TIME LATER, Gavin found himself at yet another intersection. Off to his left, Gavin saw a busy thoroughfare, but something about that moving mass of people didn't feel right. He turned right instead. A short distance ahead, what looked to be another alley came in from the left.

Gavin made the turn himself, stopping cold as his eyes widened. He found himself in a cul-de-sac and sitting at the far end was the most beautiful woman Gavin had ever seen: wavy hair that glistened in the sun that was now overhead; an olive complexion; and soft, feminine curves. Not even the strange mark branded into her shoulder could mar her beauty. Arms crossed across her midriff held a linen sack closed by drawstrings.

Gavin gazed upon her, his lips quirking into a slight smile of appreciation, and he didn't even notice when she lifted her head and looked at him.

DESPITE HER WEARINESS, Kiri sensed the presence of another nearby. She didn't know how, but she knew someone had arrived. All she wanted to do was lay her head back against the wall in peace, but she was her father's daughter. She would meet this new arrival unbowed.

She lifted her head, opening her eyes…and used all her willpower to keep from smiling at the sight. A young man stood at the end of the alley. He wore only trousers, made of simple home-spun at that, but there was a health, a vitality, about him unlike anything she had ever seen in a peasant before. How he stared amused her the most; it had been a long time since she had seen such innocence.

Her eyes drifting over his body, Kiri was struck by how handsome the young man was. Sandy blond hair cropped shorter than was common, clean-shaven, and a slender, proportionate form…she had no trouble picturing him dressed in the finest courtly attire, trading pleasant conversation with the elite of nobility.

Desire flared within her for the first time in oh so long, but with desire came the pain of the last two years. She couldn't stop the memories, and she clamped her eyes shut, turning her head from side to side as she tried to push away those unwelcome thoughts.

THE WOMAN'S motion jerked Gavin out of his reverie. He had no idea how long he'd been standing there, letting his eyes roam over her form, and he felt the flush of his embarrassment rise in his cheeks.

He crossed the short distance to the woman and knelt in front of her.

"Are you okay?" Gavin said.

The young woman opened her eyes and frowned as she said, "What do you mean? What is that word?"

Now, it was Gavin's turn to frown. "What is what word?"

"*Okay*," the woman said, and her speech made the word sound alien to Gavin. "I have not heard its like before."

"Oh. Uhm. I was asking if you're well."

"I am well enough, thank you," she said.

"Is there anything I can do to help you?"

"Do you know where the Vushaari embassy is?"

Gavin couldn't keep from chuckling. "I don't even know where *I* am. I woke up in an alley not too far from here, but I don't remember anything about myself or this place."

Before the young woman could respond, the sound of footfalls filled the cul-de-sac. The woman's eyes darted to look past Gavin, and she paled. Gavin turned to look as well.

Three men stood at the entrance to the cul-de-sac. Their leather garb was worn in places, but Gavin focused on the metal rod the man on his right was holding. Even from his distance, Gavin could see its grip on one end, with a ring of metal around a wavy line on the opposite end.

Gavin's eyes narrowed on the rod for a moment, before he turned back to look at the woman's left shoulder. The mark she bore was a solid circle enclosing a horizontal, wavy line—like an elongated 'S' turned on its side; a bar crossed the line diagonally from right to left through one of the troughs of the line.

Gavin shifted his eyes from the mark to the woman's eyes, saying, "Slavers?"

"Yes," the woman said, jerking her head in a brief nod. Her voice was little more than a whimper.

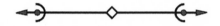

CHAPTER 3

Gavin stood and took a few steps toward the men, placing himself between the woman and them. The idea that these men would capture, brutalize, and hunt the woman behind him made Gavin seethe, and he was not prepared at all for the side effect of his anger. The moment Gavin started getting angry, the tingling sensation that had been with him since he awoke flared into a burning sensation that seemed fit to consume his very soul…and it was growing stronger.

The three men smiled in satisfaction, and the center man spoke.

"Well, look here, boys. We have a two-for-one, and the fresh meat looks like he still has some fight in him! Roderick, be a good man, and add him to our collection."

The man holding the rod started approaching Gavin at a measured pace. Gavin was confused, though; the brand wasn't red-hot, so how did those guys think they could brand him?

"Don't let him touch you!" the woman said, her voice a terrified whisper.

But Gavin didn't think he had a choice. The burning sensation within him wanted to reach out to the rod in the man's hand, straining to grasp and consume it. The man didn't seem to feel any of it, however, maintaining his measured pace toward Gavin; as he neared, the man even lifted the rod and held it out from him like a short sword, ready to jab the brand against Gavin.

When the man was as close to Gavin as he wanted to be, a feral grin crossed his expression as he thrust the brand toward Gavin. Gavin lifted his right hand to grasp the incoming brand, taking the wavy line right on the palm of his hand and wrapping his fingers around the metal ring.

For the briefest of moments, a physical heat built against Gavin's palm and in his left shoulder, but that sensation didn't last for more than a heartbeat. The burning sensation Gavin had been feeling within himself erupted into an unchecked conflagration. It was so intense that Gavin broke into a sweat. The inferno raced down his right arm and slammed into the brand he held. For the briefest of moments, the inferno bashed against some form of resistance, but that resistance shattered almost as quickly as Gavin sensed it.

It was at that moment the feral grin on the slaver's face vanished. He paled as his eyes widened. "No…no…please…"

But it was too late. Gavin didn't understand what was happening as he felt the inferno within race down his arm, through the rod, and into the slaver. Without warning, the slaver threw his head back and screamed in terrible agony. Eldritch fire, the flames shifting colors like a kaleidoscope, erupted from the man's mouth and eyes.

After what seemed like an eternity, the screaming stopped all at once. The eldritch fire puffed out, and the body fell backward to lay eyes and mouth wide open, the face twisted in agony. A strange mark was now burned into the corpse's forehead, and the remaining slavers seemed to recognize it…at least their pale complexions and the new puddle at the center man's feet suggested they recognized the mark. The first part looked like two sickles with one inverted over the other and their points merging to create a solid line. To the right of that was a greater-than symbol with a dot inside it.

Gavin, though, no longer paid the slavers much attention. What-ever had killed the slaver left Gavin feeling weak as a child and unable to stand. He dropped the rod—now a blackened, twisted thing—and staggered toward the wall of the cul-de-sac.

Gavin slumped against the alley wall, trying to regain his strength. The woman sat in terrified tension, staring at the remaining slavers, and those slavers stood in wide-eyed terror of Gavin, no longer seeming to realize the woman existed.

The tableau was broken at last by the arrival of another group of slavers, three more in total.

"What in Lornithar's Abyss is going on here?" the lead woman of the new arrivals asked.

The center man pointed down the cul-de-sac, saying, "H-he killed Roderick! Look!"

The woman walked over to look at the slaver's corpse and gasped at the sight of the mark on the man's forehead. She cast a skeptical glance at Gavin before returning to her people.

"Well, you have swords, don't you? Get in there, and use them. Kill them both."

"But-"

The woman walked over and pushed the center man toward Gavin, giving him a kick on the rump once he was moving.

"Get in there, and do it, or I'll kill you myself," she said, gesturing at the remaining slaver from the first group. "You, too; go help him."

Gavin watched the men approach, and even though their swords danced in their shaking hands, he knew they could still kill him and the woman.

I will not be slaughtered like an animal, Gavin thought as he pressed the palm of his hand against his knee and made himself stand. It took all of his effort to keep from wobbling—both while rising and once he was on his feet—but Gavin was not about to show anymore weakness in front of these slavers.

"I will not allow you to harm myself or the woman," Gavin said, forcing his voice to be strong and commanding. "If you leave of your own accord and do not pursue us, I will consider the matter closed."

"You think we're just going to leave our property?" the slaver woman asked, stepping up to join her fellows closer to Gavin.

The slavers were backing Gavin into a corner...in both the figurative and literal senses. With the slavers unwilling to see reason and not knowing any other way to end the confrontation, Gavin focused his mind on the word that had been burned into him not so long ago. He closed his eyes and began taking slow, deep breaths.

When Gavin opened his eyes once more, he saw a slaver was almost close enough to use his sword, and Gavin drew in his breath to speak.

"He's gonna cast! Move!" one of the slavers in the rear shouted, and the three slavers closest to Gavin darted aside. Gavin heard a *TWANG!* at the same time something slammed into his right shoulder. The force of the impact partially spun him around, and Gavin collapsed to one knee, his eyes clamped tight as he grimaced. His shoulder had sprouted a crossbow quarrel.

I can't let them hurt her. I must stop the slavers... That was the last thought in his mind as he lifted his head to face the slavers and spoke the Word, "*Thraxys.*"

The tingling sensation once more erupted into an inferno, raging throughout Gavin and searing every part of his soul. Eldritch fire licked out around the crossbow quarrel and consumed the blood running down his chest. But the slavers never noticed, for they fell to the ground dead the moment Gavin invoked the Word.

Unprecedented levels of agony followed in the wake of Gavin's blood burning. It started with infinite needles heated to an infinite temperature piercing his flesh and soul at an infinitesimal rate. The needles gradually transitioned to the sensation of the layers of his flesh being forcibly separated at an agonizing rate, and just as an infinite number of maggots began feeding on him—both within his body and without, Gavin passed into blissful unconsciousness.

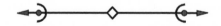

CHAPTER 4

A massive, marble edifice, the Temple of Valthon had stood in the northeast quarter of the city since the Founding following the Godswar. To the right of the main entrance, a greeter sat behind a desk. The temple's greeter was always an acolyte in training to become a cleric, usually new to the temple and very inexperienced. Marcus paid the child no mind as he topped the steps and proceeded into the Hall of the Gods.

The Hall of the Gods was, perhaps, the largest vestibule known to exist, and it was named so for the statues that lined each wall. Every person who had chosen to accept the mantle of divinity following the Godswar had a statue here: Bellos, Kalthor, Marin, Xanta, and Irikos...among several others. Each statue was angled a bit, so that if one stood on the proper spot all the statues appeared to be facing the person.

Marcus stood in silence a few moments, taking the time to look upon each marble face. Finally, he sighed and lowered his head, saying, "I miss you all, my friends." Then, Marcus took a deep breath and proceeded to his destination: the shrine of Valthon. He was almost late.

. . .

OVIR THATCHERSON, Royal Priest of Tel, stood near the altar in the shrine. A little shy of six feet tall, he still possessed the physique of the young cleric who had earned membership in the Warpriests of Valthon some thirty-odd years before. He kept his graying hair trimmed close, and his ease with authority shone through in every movement and mannerism. He wore the gray robes that were typical of Valthon's clergy.

Ovir looked up at the sound of the shrine's door opening, and he couldn't keep from smiling. In the doorway stood a man that was easily the shadow to his light. Black robes hung from a tall, muscular frame, and the gold runes on the sleeve-cuffs seemed almost to glow. His white hair and Vandyke beard were well-trimmed and maintained, and his piercing, blue eyes held the weight of a soul that had seen too much. A silver medallion—like those worn by all wizards—rested atop the man's sternum, but unlike every other medallion Ovir had ever seen, this man's medallion bore no House glyph in the recessed center.

"Marcus, I'm sorry. I completely forgot we were meeting for lunch today," Ovir said as the black-robed man approached. An acolyte rushed up with a piece of parchment. Ovir scanned it and shook his head. "No, send the warpriests to search the alleys and docks; they can handle the toughs that frequent those areas. Send the clerics, priests, and senior acolytes into the markets and more public areas where the town guard can assist if they're in trouble."

The acolyte nodded and hastily scribbled the corrections on the parchment before he scampered out.

"Ovir, I've not seen the temple in such a state for quite some time. Whatever is the matter?"

Ovir sighed and leaned against a pew. "Valthon visited me last night. I don't know if it was a dream or if he actually took me somewhere, but we were standing in a void. He told me that the man who would stand unyielding against the forces of Skullkeep would arrive in the city today. He told me the Lornithrasa are active once again and aware of the arrival, and he said when I find him, I'm to deliver him to you...to be trained as only you can."

Marcus sighed, shaking his head. "Ovir, you've kicked the entire clergy into an uproar over this; do you even know whom you-"

Marcus stopped mid-sentence, staggering. He turned to look over his left shoulder for a few heartbeats before turning back to Ovir, saying, "City map…now."

Ovir grabbed one of the shrine's attendants and sent him off at a sprint. He turned back to his old friend, saying, "Marcus, what is it? Are you-"

Marcus lifted his hand to forestall Ovir's questions and closed his eyes, angling his head slightly in the direction he had stared. The attendant returned with the map, gasping for air, and Ovir laid it out on the altar. Marcus walked up and pointed to a spot in the southwestern warrens, near the docks.

"Send the warpriests there, Ovir," Marcus said, "but warn them to be careful. The wizard they find might be more powerful than me."

Marcus fell silent and leaned heavily against the altar. He took several deep breaths and rolled his shoulders to stretch.

"Marcus, are you well? Is there anything I can do?"

"Whoever is there just invoked a massive Interation effect. If I had to guess, the warpriests will find at least one dead body." Marcus took one more deep breath before he stood and shook himself. "Ovir, I've not felt such power in ages, but it was just a raw blast…like the wizard didn't understand what he or she was doing."

"A first casting, maybe?" Ovir asked.

Marcus shook his head. "I don't see how. Only a Word of Power could have produced such a resonance, and even then, there are no wizards now who are strong enough to cause what I felt. I have to be there, Ovir. I alone am equipped to protect the city from whoever this is."

Marcus stepped back and said, "*Paedryx*," invoking the Word of Transmutation that formed the basis for the modern teleportation spell. A sapphire haze that crackled with power rose out of the floor and took on the form of an arched gateway.

"You're not going alone, my friend," Ovir said as he stepped through the gateway first.

* * *

KIRI STARED in sheer terror at the bodies lying on the ground. The young man was alive yet unconscious, but the slavers were dead. Growing up in her homeland, she'd heard stories of magic powerful enough to kill outright, but she'd never seen such a thing until now. It terrified her more than the slavers themselves had. She drew her knees to her chest and wrapped her arms around her knees, unable to stop the oncoming sobs.

"THERE, THERE," an aged and weathered voice said. "What's the matter, young lady?"

Kiri looked up, her eyes full of terror. She saw an old man on one knee in front of her, a gnarled staff leaning against the building to her right. His wild, snow-white hair swayed with the slight breeze like the trees of a forest. She took in his gray robe that was tattered around the hem and the feeling of grandfatherly warmth he radiated, and she knew she should recognize him. Somewhere, she'd met this old man before.

"They're...they're dead," she sobbed. "He just killed them."

"Well, in his defense, they were trying to kill the both of you. Some would say he did you a service."

Kiri shook her head and tightened her arms around her knees. "The Cavaliers back home are right; magic is evil."

The old man sighed and rolled himself into a sitting position beside Kiri, putting his left arm around her and pulling her close to him. "No, child, don't you ever think that. Magic is what we make of it. Yes, it can be one of the ghastliest things in the world...but only because vile people make it so. That young man did the one thing he could to protect the both of you. He had no sword, no armor, and no martial training at all. What was he supposed to do?"

The woman relaxed a bit and leaned into the old man. There was something about him that comforted her on every level of her soul, and with him there, the world didn't seem like such a bad place.

A short time later, the old man lifted his head and looked toward the northeast, nodding a couple times before he said, "I'm sorry, my dear, but I'm afraid I can't stay."

"Why-"

"Sssh, now," he said, patting her right shoulder with his right hand, "you've no need to fear. I know these two very well, and one is an old friend. You will be safe."

The old man extricated himself and climbed to his feet. He took his staff and began making his way out of the cul-de-sac. Kiri watched him go, and a nagging feeling crept into the back of her mind that something was just not right. She never realized that, though he had been sitting in the muck and grime of the alley with her, the old man's tattered robe looked as clean as if it had been freshly laundered.

The old man had just turned the corner when an archway of sapphire energy rose out of the cobblestones.

OVIR STEPPED through the gateway and rushed to the bodies on the cobblestones. He found only the young woman and man still lived, and then, he was aware of Marcus arriving behind him and the gateway closing.

"He said I'd be safe with you," the woman said.

Ovir looked up from the unconscious young man and asked, "Who said that, dear?"

"The old man that just left."

At hearing this, Marcus pivoted on his left heel, striding to the end of the cul-de-sac. He started to look left first, but the undeniable presence he felt made him turn right. Standing not fifteen feet away, Marcus saw whom he'd expected: the old man with wild hair in a tattered, gray robe.

"It's been a long time, old friend," Marcus said as he stepped beyond the cul-de-sac's opening.

The old man chuckled. "Yes...well, we all have our work to do, and yours is lying back there unconscious. Give him a chance, and I think even you will be surprised by what you find. Oh, by the way, his name is Gavin Cross." He winked impishly at Marcus and faded away like mist on the wind.

"Meddling again, are we?" Marcus said as he scanned the space the old man occupied just moments before, his voice dropping to little more than a whisper. "The last time you did that, it kicked off the Godswar."

WHILE MARCUS LEFT in search of the old man, Ovir knelt beside the young man who still lived. Blood tried to ooze from the wound around the crossbow bolt, but to Ovir's experienced eye, the wound looked like it had been cauterized around the projectile somehow.

"Is he going to be okay?" the young woman asked.

Ovir nodded. "Oh, yes. He'll be fine. I don't see any injuries beyond the bolt through his shoulder. In a way, it's a small blessing he's unconscious; otherwise, this might hurt a bit."

Ovir grasped the crossbow bolt protruding from the back of Gavin's shoulder and, with a sharp motion, snapped off the barbed tip. He then removed the bolt with a jerk; Gavin didn't even stir. Normally, Ovir wouldn't even give the broken bolt a second glance, but the wound channel it left in its wake was sufficiently cauterized that blood and tissue did not start filling the passage; Ovir could see sunlight through the hole in Gavin's shoulder. Faced with that unprecedented sight, he couldn't keep from looking down at the bolt he still held in his hand.

"By the gods!"

Marcus arrived at Ovir's side, saying, "What is it, Ovir?"

"Marcus, look at this!" Ovir said, holding up the bolt for Marcus to see. "Have you ever seen anything like it?"

Across a span that matched the depth of Gavin's shoulder, the shaft of the bolt was blackened and charred, as if it had been on fire.

Marcus's eyes narrowed at seeing the bolt, and he said, "Yes, Ovir, I have seen something like it before."

With no further explanation, the old wizard began searching the surroundings with his eyes, and he soon found the blackened and twisted remains of the slavers' brand. He crouched down and picked it up, turning it over in his hands a couple times before he returned it to the ground and started searching once more. It was then Marcus looked at the slaver corpse lying flat on its back, eyes and mouth wide and a strange mark or symbol burned into its forehead.

"Ovir, did you see this corpse right behind you?"

"Well, no. I saw the boy still lived, so I-"

"Turn around, and have a look at the forehead."

Ovir pushed himself to his feet and turned around, eyes widening. "Marcus, that's...what does all this mean? Where have you seen this before?"

Marcus turned to face his long-time friend. "Ovir, the consequence of a slaver trying to brand a wizard directly relates to the inherent power of the wizard the slaver attempts to brand. If someone tried to brand...oh, say...Torval Mivar's son, the most that slaver would have to fear would be a small scar on the palm of his hand, and it certainly wouldn't kill him."

Now, Marcus turned to the young woman, asking, "That's what killed him, yes? He tried to brand the unconscious young man there?"

The young woman nodded, saying, "It was ghastly. Right before the slaver died, he was screaming, and weird-colored flames were shooting out his eyes and mouth."

Marcus nodded and said, "That's what would happen if someone tried to brand a wizard of *my* power. Mark and all."

"Marcus, that's not just some random mark," Ovir said. "That's your House's glyph!"

The old wizard nodded as he said, "Yes. That way, the Houses would know which family the slaver was dumb enough to attack. But we have more pressing matters."

"Yes," Ovir said, turning back to the people behind them. "I am getting on in years, but I'm pretty sure I should not be able to see daylight through his shoulder. Give me your hand also, young lady; I think you're rather ill."

The young woman reached out and took Ovir's right hand in

hers, while he placed his left hand on Gavin's injured shoulder. He bowed his head and recited the prayer for healing he had learned so many years before.

Ovir felt the warm glow of his god's power build within him and pass down his arms, through his hands, and into the two people he touched. If the cleric were strong enough and in sufficient favor with his or her deity, there would usually be some sort of glow or nimbus around the cleric and person(s) being healed. The bright, white glow that filled the cul-de-sac was so bright anyone nearby would turn away, lest she or he be blinded for a time.

Within moments, the glow faded, and Ovir looked down to see a snow-white, perfect circle where the young man's wound had been.

The young woman frowned as she rubbed her stomach, saying, "I don't feel the poison anymore. Thank you! How did you know?"

"I've seen it used before. It produces a slight discoloration around the eyes," Ovir said as he pushed himself to his feet. "But don't thank me, my dear. Valthon did all the work; I simply asked for a few moments of His time."

Now, she looked at Gavin's unconscious form. "What about him?"

"He's breathing strong enough," Ovir said. "At this point, I'd say his unconsciousness is related to his first use of the Art, instead of some specific injury."

"He put himself between me and the slavers," she said, her voice soft and almost vulnerable. "It's been a long time since anyone has cared that much about me."

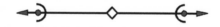

CHAPTER 5

H e heard it just as his feet touched the main floor of the Tower. "Marcus, I need a word."

The old wizard looked to his left and saw Valera, the Magister of Divination and the Collegiate Justice, standing a short distance away. Valera was Vushaari, and while her skin was weathered and wrinkled with her age, she shared the olive complexion for which her people were known. The curly hair that had once been a lustrous anthracite was now mostly gray, but she bore it well. She wore the white robe that announced her philosophy toward the Art as protection or defending others, and the amethyst runes on her sleeves proclaimed her status as Magister, the amethyst color signifying her specialization in Divination.

Her brow was furrowed, her lips pursed.

"You're worried, Valera," Marcus said. "I haven't seen you like this in years."

"Of course, I'm worried. We have a problem, but we shouldn't discuss it here."

. . .

Marcus sat in one of the chairs facing Valera across her desk and leaned back against it. It was almost as comfortable as his favorite chair in the suite upstairs.

"All right. This is private. What has you so worried?"

"Two days ago, a wizard killed 53 slavers across the southwestern warrens in a massive Interation effect."

"Yes, Valera, I know."

"You know? What happened? Did you have to kill him?"

Marcus chuckled. "No. He's unconscious in the sick rooms of the Temple right now. It was his first invocation. How did you learn of this?"

"The town guard consulted the Magister of Interation, who consulted me. Marcus, the slavers are screaming for justice; they're making noises about going to the King!"

Marcus scoffed. "Let them. If that feckless wonder wearing the crown so much as looks in the direction of the College, I'll reduce the entire palace compound to molten rock."

Valera blanched. "Marcus, you can't do that!"

"Why not? I built it."

"Yes, I know…but nobody else does. Besides, who would rule Tel?"

"The Constitution has provisions for that. The Conclave of the Great Houses would appoint a regent, assuming Bellos didn't wake up and decide to name an Archmagister."

Valera closed her eyes and took deep breaths for several moments, finally saying, "Marcus, I have to tell the Magister of Interation what I know. That boy killed 53 people."

"That boy, Valera, is of my House. You will do no such thing. He is too valuable to be executed, especially for what should be considered a public service."

"Marcus-"

Marcus stood. "No, Valera. The old man is meddling again, which means the others won't be far behind. He told me I'm to train the boy as only I can."

"I can't believe you're going to train a murderer in the Art, Marcus!"

"It's only murder when there's prior intent. Besides, Valera, you know who I am, which means you have a better idea than most about what I've done or ordered to be done. That boy certainly isn't the first killer to be trained in the Art, and I daresay he won't be the last."

"I suppose you're right."

"I usually am. I trust I don't need to discuss the consequences of interfering."

Valera sighed, saying, "I can't say I like being threatened, Marcus…even by implication…but I'm not about to interfere. You're quite correct; I do know better than most what you're capable of."

Without a further word, Marcus turned and left the office.

* * *

VALERA SAT in her office in silence, still shaken by the exchange with Marcus. It was the first time he had ever threatened her. But that wasn't all that was on her mind. She opened the top, right-hand drawer of her desk and withdrew a piece of parchment. It bore only one statement, and that statement was all Valera had been able to remember of her first vision in more than twenty years. Oh, yes… she knew the boy who killed 53 slavers with one Word was a son of Marcus's House; she knew it the instant she learned what had happened.

The death of slavers shall herald the return of Kirloth to this world, and the Apprentices shall be drawn unto him.

* * *

MARCUS STRODE through the halls of the sick rooms at the Temple of Valthon, an often-overlooked area, except by those who needed it. Like the rest of the structure and the city as well, the sick rooms were made of marble-shaded stone. Unlike the rest of the temple, the sick rooms carried an ambiance of illness and fear.

Marcus entered the room that was his destination and could not restrain a smile. The slave girl sat at Gavin's bedside, holding his right hand in both of hers.

"Hello," Marcus said, and she started, dropping Gavin's hand in the process. "I would speak with you...outside."

KIRI FOUND Marcus in the hallway, leaning against the wall opposite Gavin's door, when she emerged. She kept her head bowed and moved like a woman intent on avoiding the attention of others.

"Close the door," Marcus said. "Should he awaken, I would not have him hear this."

Kiri felt the color drain from her face as she closed the door. She wanted more than anything to cast off the brand and be herself again, but the mannerisms of the past two years were too familiar. She kept her head bowed as she turned to Marcus.

"Look at me. I do not speak to the top of people's heads."

"But I am a slave," she said.

Marcus snorted. "You're no more a slave than I am, especially here."

"B-but the brand-"

"It means nothing to me...Princess."

She lifted her head in a jerk, meeting Marcus's eyes at last. "You know?"

A smirk curled one side of Marcus's lips, and he allowed himself a mirthless chuckle, before saying, "Child, I have lived far longer than you would believe. While there are a great many things I do not *know*, there is very little I cannot *learn*."

Now, she worked her lower lip between her teeth. She didn't bow her head, but she did look away. "Will you tell him, when he wakes?"

"I haven't decided," Marcus replied, "but that is not why I called you out here. I will have the name of the one who claims you."

She took a deep breath and answered. "Baron Kalinor."

Marcus's eyes narrowed a bit, and she thought she saw a hint of a sneer cross his expression. "Very well."

She watched Marcus turn to leave and couldn't keep from asking, "Why did you want to know?"

"You may eventually find out," Marcus said over his shoulder as he walked away.

* * *

THE KALINOR ESTATE was a massive edifice of hewn stone and wood, surrounded by a manor wall of mortar and hewn stone. The estate held several huts or shacks that served to house the various professions any estate would need, such as a blacksmith and baker. Unlike the walls created by Kirloth and the Apprentices around the estates of the Dukes and Duchesses, Kalinor's manor wall had guard towers on either side of the gate and at each of the four corners.

THE GUARDS in the towers closest to the gate cried out in surprise and shock when an arch-shaped sapphire gateway rose out of the earth, allowing a tall man in black robes entrance to the grounds. They fired their crossbows as warning shots, and the man lowered his eyes to regard the quarrels sticking out of the earth at his feet before turning to face them.

"I have come to speak with Kalinor," he said. "You may call me 'Marcus.' I have no wish to fight, but neither do I mind killing every one of you if you force the issue."

The men in the guard towers put down their crossbows as the estate's steward arrived with three guards trailing him. Marcus turned to face the steward and nodded. The steward was a man a bit past middle age, though his hazel eyes still possessed the sparkle of cunning and intelligence. The guards behind him were bewildered.

"You've caused a bit of stir inside the house," the steward said.

Marcus shrugged. "I usually do. I've come to speak with your 'master.'"

"Very well. He's in the study." The steward turned and led the guards and Marcus to the estate.

BARON KALINOR LOOKED up from his desk as the doors to his study opened. Surprise and anger colored his expression, for he'd left instructions not to be disturbed. He was a slim man, approaching middle age, and his brow and the corners of his mouth were lined.

The desk itself was a massive mahogany construction, stained to bring out the grain of the wood. Armchairs sat on the opposite side of the desk from Kalinor, and they were upholstered in a checkered design in the orange and black that were the family's colors.

"Who do you think you are, barging in here?" the Baron said as he pushed up out of his chair. "I'll have that worthless steward strapped for this!"

"You'll do no such thing, Kalinor," Marcus said as he walked across the study and sat in one of the chairs facing the Baron's desk. "If you so much as speak harshly to anyone on your staff regarding my arrival, the next time you see me, I won't be so pleasant."

"How dare you! The King shall hear of this!"

"That worthless toad can roast on a fiery spit in Lornithar's Abyss for all I care," Marcus said, "and you may feel free to tell him I said so."

Kalinor sputtered in rage but said nothing coherent.

"Some days ago, a Vushaari slave escaped from this estate," Marcus said. "You will transfer ownership of her to me and cancel the handbill advertising a reward for her return."

"That one is the finest slave to be found in Tel. Why in the name of the gods would you believe I'd just give her away?"

Marcus lifted his right hand and cupped it as if he were holding an apple or orange. A slight tightening around his eyes was the only indication of his effort. A small pinprick of light appeared in the air above his right palm, and within a few moments, an orb of roiling, seething power the color of gold hovered in the air.

"You'll do it because it's in your own best interests," Marcus said. "You should consider these family names: Koska, Layfarn, Gwidell, Pertalla...just to name four."

"Who?" Kalinor said, frowning. "I've never heard of those families."

"Exactly."

Kalinor snorted and sat in his chair, leaning forward. "You would have me believe you wiped them out? Over what? Slaves?"

Marcus allowed the orb of power to dissipate, and he leaned back in the armchair. "No, of course not. The royal family had not yet reinstituted the abhorrent practice when those families met their demise. Koska was a wizard House shortly before the death of Bellock Vanlon; the matriarch was advancing a plot to destroy the Great Houses of Tel. Layfarn was a merchant family of some moderate success, about a hundred years after Bellock's death, until they decided to branch out into kidnapping for hire and took a contract on a mage's child. Gwidell was...well, let's say they were a rather depraved bunch and had the poor taste to start stealing children because of those tastes; that was...oh...about a thousand years before the death of Bellock Vanlon. The Pertalla Family...they tried to destroy the Compact of Dakkor and would not see reason; that was only three-hundred-fifty years ago or so.

"Kalinor, you will write out a Transfer of Ownership of the Vushaari slave known as Kiri, and you will leave the new owner's name blank. I shall see to that. You will do it now, and you will speak to no one of our discussion."

Kalinor leaned back in his own chair for several moments before leaning forward once again. When he spoke, he tapped his finger on his desk for emphasis. "You're a daft fool if you think I'm going to sign over ownership of my finest piece because you walked in the door and spouted off some random nonsense."

A dark smile curled Marcus's lips. "I was hoping you'd see things my way, Kalinor. You see, personally, I'd just as soon kill you and be done with it, but I will be training a new apprentice soon. As I must be a role-model for him, I'm no longer free to go about the country-side doing as I wish."

Marcus lifted his left hand and snapped his fingers. The study's door opened, and the steward entered. "You called, milord?"

"Yes," Marcus said. "Kalinor has seen fit to reject my offer of life. Gather those of the household you're willing to vouch for and take them away. Any who are direct blood relation to the baron are exempt from my pardon. I will complete my business here and meet you in Tel Mivar."

"Now, see here!" Kalinor said. "You can't just-"

Marcus turned to face him and said, "Be silent. You lost all say in this when you rejected my request."

"Who do you think-"

Marcus invoked a Word, "*Khraexar.*" Kalinor froze mid-speech. His eyes moved, and he still breathed, but he was paralyzed otherwise.

"Much better," Marcus said, turning to the steward. "Do you understand your instructions?"

"Yes, milord."

"Very well then," Marcus said. "Be quick. This estate has little time left."

The steward turned and reached for the door latch with his left hand. Doing so drew back the sleeve on that arm and revealed a strange tattoo at the man's wrist. Marcus smiled as he remembered the day he had designed it.

Marcus stood and approached Kalinor's desk. He rifled through the drawers until he found parchment of suitable quality and laid it atop the desk. Marcus then took the pen and dipped it in the inkwell before holding it over the parchment and tapping the pen to litter drops of ink across the parchment. That done, Marcus tossed the pen aside.

He took a deep breath and placed his hand on Kalinor's brow, just before he invoked another Word, "*Zyrhaek.*" Unlike the Word that paralyzed Kalinor, this was a Transmutation. Kalinor's eyes widened as he watched the ink on the parchment squirm and shift into words...words in his own hand no less!

I hereby transfer ownership
Of
the Vushaari slave known as Kiri
To
Gavin Cross
In the interests of clearing a great debt.

Signed by my hand, this 3ʳᵈ Day of Bilfar
In the 6080ᵗʰ year of our victory in the Godswar

Kalinor, Baron of Tel

MARCUS NODDED his satisfaction at the result and picked up some sealing wax, dribbling a little bit below the words 'Kalinor, Baron of Tel.' It was then a simple matter to remove Kalinor's signet from his hand, place it on his own finger, and press it into the cooling wax.

"And we're done," Marcus said as he folded the document and slipped it inside his robe. He walked around Kalinor's desk and approached the study's door. As he grasped the door latch, Marcus turned to face the room's other occupant.

"Kalinor, as much as I once would have preferred to leave you alive and paralyzed to experience firsthand the flames that will soon consume your estate, I am no longer that cruel…despite what some would say of me. Besides, I've grown to detest the practice of burning people alive. After you've done it a few times, you never want to do it again."

Marcus invoked two Words at once, blending them together to create a composite effect, *"Rhosed-Thraxys."* The first invocation dispelled the paralysis; the second killed Kalinor outright. Marcus turned and left the study. The sound of the heavy oak door closing coincided with the dull *thud* of Kalinor's head hitting the desk.

Marcus left the manor and walked across the yard. He noticed all the guard towers within sight were still manned; the steward must not have thought much of Kalinor's soldiers. Without stopping or saying a word to the guards above the gate, Marcus opened the gate and walked through, not bothering to close it behind him. The guards shouted something, but Marcus paid them no mind.

Marcus stopped some fifty yards from the estate and turned. He had spent his walk clearing his mind of all but his intent. When he turned, Marcus took a deep breath and invoked two Words of Power, "*Thraxys-Idluhn,*" blending them together to create another composite effect. The first Word killed everyone still on the estate where they stood; the second set fire to the estate, a blue fire so hot it would melt stone.

Nodding his satisfaction at the white flames licking the stone structures around the estate, Marcus invoked another Word, causing a sapphire archway to rise out of the ground. He stepped through it and was gone.

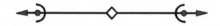

CHAPTER 6

Gavin swam back up to the world from a sea of total darkness, and as he returned to awareness, the first thing he noticed was his right hand being held by two soft hands. Then, he realized the tingling sensation was part of him. He was lying on something soft and comfortable.

Gavin opened his eyes just a bit. The slave woman was sitting by his bed, her hands holding his. He didn't know how long he'd been unconscious, but it had been long enough to change into less revealing attire. She wore a dress of simple homespun cloth; its colors were green with blue highlights and trim. Despite the simplicity of the garment, Gavin admired how it complimented her, but he didn't like how it left her shoulders bare, displaying the slave-mark for all the world to see. Her dark hair was combed and coiffed. It was at that moment she turned back and found Gavin looking at her.

"Oh! You're awake!"

"Where are we?"

Gavin forced himself to pull his eyes away from the woman to take in his surroundings. It was a simple room with the chair in which the woman sat as well as a lounge that looked slept in. The bed linens were simple but well-made, and sconces whose flames neither consumed fuel nor radiated heat lit the room.

"We're in one of the sick rooms at the temple. Ovir and Marcus brought us here."

"I'm sorry," Gavin said. "In all the excitement around the alley, I never introduced myself."

The woman smiled and lowered her eyes, saying, "My name is Kiri."

"Kiri...I like that. My name is Gavin Cross."

If he hadn't been looking at her, Gavin would've missed the flicker of recognition before Kiri closed her expression. *She knows me*, Gavin thought, *or at least, she knows of me.*

"You mentioned an Ovir and Marcus," Gavin said. "Who are they?"

"Ovir is a priest of Valthon. He arrived in the alley with a wizard named Marcus. They appear to be good friends. Ovir healed us."

"Nonsense, child," a new voice said. "I told you in the alley. Valthon did all the work; I just asked for a moment of His time."

An older man with the barrel chest and slim build of a military life stepped into the room and stood at the foot of Gavin's bed. He wore his gray hair cut short, and his green eyes shone with mirth and warm welcome.

"Glad to see you're awake," the older man said. "Forgive the intrusion, but I was already stopping by to check on you. I am Ovir Thatcherson, Royal Priest of Tel."

Gavin started to rise but Ovir motioned for him to lay still. "Thank you for your care. I don't know what resources I have to call upon, but I would like to pay you for your trouble in some way."

Ovir waved that notion away, shaking his head. "Nonsense, my boy. First of all, the temple's sickrooms are available to all, free of charge. Secondly, even if they were not, you're blood-kin to a very good friend."

Gavin's eyes shot wide. "You know my family? Do you know me? Where I'm from?"

"Slow down there, son," Ovir said, stepping outside long

enough to pull in another chair and move it to the left side of Gavin's bed, seating himself. "Let's just say I know your…distant… family. Remember the slaver who tried to brand you?"

"I don't know if I'll ever forget that," Gavin said.

"Remember the mark that was burned into the man's forehead?"

Gavin nodded.

"That mark is your family's House glyph. Think of it like the coats of arms the commoner nobility use. Every glyph is unique, and they're crafted or decided upon in a way I don't understand. But the short of it is that you don't have to know your family for your blood to carry your House's glyph. Don't ask me how that works, though; I've never understood or known anyone who does."

"What can you tell me about my family?"

Ovir smiled and shrugged. "Oh, I'm sure I could tell you quite a bit, but I think that might be best left to the fellow who will be training you."

"Aren't I a little old to be going back to school?" Gavin asked.

"No," a new voice said from the direction of the door. The voice was deep, full of confidence and authority, and Gavin blinked in surprise as he felt a momentary flicker of recognition upon looking at the man standing in the doorway. He looked familiar somehow.

He was tall but possessed of wiry, powerful frame. His head almost touched the top of the doorframe. His white hair and beard were trimmed close, and his piercing, blue eyes carried the weight of a man who had seen too much. He wore a black robe with gold-colored runes running around the cuffs of the sleeves, and a silver medallion rested over his heart, hanging from his neck by a simple chain. The medallion had a blank recessed center, and runes too small for Gavin to see well encircled that recessed center.

"I am known in this time and place as Marcus, and I will be your instructor in the Art, what many today call magic."

"I'm getting the feeling that I don't have much choice in the matter," Gavin said, looking at Marcus.

The old wizard shook his head, saying, "No, I'm afraid you don't. You invoked a Word of Power, and that invocation started you down a path you cannot leave. If you don't learn to master the power within you, it will begin to cascade until it kills you. Trust me; that would not be a pleasant death."

Gavin sighed, before saying, "I see." His eyes fell upon Kiri. "What happens to her?"

Marcus shrugged. "Does it matter?"

"I did not almost die trying to save her life, just to cast her back out into the world that harmed her so."

For just a moment, no longer than the blink of an eye, Gavin thought he saw approval flicker across Marcus's expression.

"The only way for you to continue to safeguard her is for the world at large to believe she is your property, but be warned. Slavery, like all domestic policies, has its supporters and its opponents. As wizards, we are members of the Society of the Arcane, and the Society as a whole tends to frown upon the practice of slavery."

"Are you saying slavery is illegal within the Society?"

Marcus shook his head. "No, but you will find few friends at the College if you are believed to own a slave."

Gavin pulled his eyes away from Marcus to look at Kiri. She held her head low, not making eye contact, but Gavin saw her hands trembling. He shifted his attention back to Marcus.

"Is there any way to remove the slave-mark?" Gavin asked.

"Many have tried," Marcus said, "but none have succeeded thus far."

"Then, she's coming with us. I won't cast her back into that hell, and I don't really care what the Society at large thinks of me."

Again, the ghost of approval flickered across Marcus's face.

"Then, you will need this," Marcus said, as he reached into his robe and withdrew a folded piece of parchment, tossing it to land on Gavin's lap.

Gavin unfolded the parchment and read the document, his eyes widening. "Kalinor gave her to me?"

Kiri's head shot up, and she stared at Gavin, her eyes wide and jaw slack.

"I can be persuasive when I have to be," Marcus said.

The expression Marcus directed at Gavin shifted to one of

appraisal, and he lifted his arms to cross them against his chest. "I have a test for you. No…that's not quite right; let's call it a diagnostic."

The old wizard lifted his right hand and cupped it as if he were holding a sphere. Only a slight tension around his eyes showed the concentration he exerted, but a pinpoint of light formed, hovering just above his palm. Over the next few moments, that pinpoint grew into an orb of gold-colored power about the size of an apple.

The tingling Gavin had been feeling since waking up in the alley went wild mere heartbeats after the pinpoint formed, and it intensified as the orb grew. The tingling seemed to take on a resonance, though. Gavin felt a resonance with the orb, but he felt a strong resonance with Marcus as well. Gavin also felt a weaker resonance with what seemed to be the world around him, so faint it almost didn't warrant the label of 'resonance.'

"All wizards have a connection to the ambient magic. We can feel workings of the Art, and even the presence of other wizards. We call this sense our *skathos*," Marcus said, holding the orb above his palm. "Now, tell me what this feels like to you."

"Ever since I woke up in the alley, I've felt a strange tingling across my entire body. That makes it worse."

Marcus nodded, smiling just a bit. "Good." He released the orb, and it faded into wisps of light before disappearing completely. "Now, I want you to try it. Focus on that tingling you feel; it is the physical manifestation of your *skathos* and your connection to the power all wizards manipulate. You should find a core of it in the pit of your chest. Focus on that, and gather it in your arm. Then, push it out through your hand and hold it just above your palm. Force it to take the shape of an orb."

"Okay. I'll try." Gavin closed his eyes and focused on that tingling sensation. He immersed himself in it and followed its flow and ebb. Sure enough, there was a core of seething power at what felt like the very center of his soul. Gavin reached for that core and pulled it out of its resting place, wrapped all the tingling in his body around it and pushed it down his right arm.

The moment that core of power seemed near the surface of his body, Gavin felt his awareness explode. Through his *skathos*, he saw Marcus as a roiling, seething font of power similar to his own. Ovir...Ovir was different; he saw Ovir more as a window through which his god's power shone like the rays of a bright, cloudless day. He then became aware of something not too far over his right shoulder that blazed like a sun. All of this, Gavin felt he could draw into him and use toward creating the orb; he chose not to do so.

Okay, I have it in my arm...now, just to push it out through my hand and make an orb. Whew, this is rough, Gavin thought.

Gavin frowned as he exerted his focus and concentration on pushing the tingling ball of seething power down his arm and out through his hand. He felt it flow out of his hand and start to join the ambient magic; it took *a lot* of effort to hold it above his hand and force it into an orb. Gavin could feel himself breaking into a sweat.

MARCUS STOOD in silence as he watched the orb of power form over Gavin's hand. He watched Gavin start sweating from the effort, and he watched as that roiling, seething orb rolled into an egg-shaped oval on occasion. It was then that things turned interesting.

The flames above the sconces flared in brightness for a moment before fading down to half their former light, and those flames angled toward the orb like plants growing toward the sun. Soon, the room began losing its warmth, and Marcus felt the orb reaching out toward the ambient magics that were woven throughout the city.

Gavin's orb started about the size of an orange that would shift into an egg every so often as it spun. When the sconces flared and faded, that orange exploded to the size of a honeydew. When the room started taking on the chill of mid-Spring outside, that honeydew exploded into an over-sized watermelon.

Ovir and Kiri gaped at the orb of power and kept directing concerned glances to Marcus each time it changed.

Marcus couldn't contain his pride any longer. "Gavin, my boy, open your eyes! Don't lose your focus, but open your eyes!"

. . .

GAVIN OPENED HIS EYES, and the shock of what he saw almost caused his will to slip. A roiling mass of incandescence seethed six inches above the palm of his hand. In mere heartbeats, Gavin saw every color of the rainbow and then some shift through the orb.

"My god, Marcus, what is this?"

"That, my boy, is power...raw power. That is what wizards manipulate to create the effects the Words of Power produce. It is the source of that tingling you feel." Marcus's expression became that of a child faced with a feast of sweets. "By the gods, Gavin, it's going to be fun training you. There hasn't been a wizard like you in thousands of years."

"Uhm, Marcus?"

"Yes, my boy?" Marcus's gaze was still intent upon the orb.

"How do I stop it?"

Marcus laughed. "Yes, that could seem a bit tricky. Search through the sphere; find the core of your power, and pull it back to you. Then, tell me what all you feel connected to you."

Gavin closed his eyes and concentrated on the sphere. It was difficult to tell the difference between his core of power and what he had drawn in, but he did indeed find it. Extricating it from the seething fury without a catastrophic collapse took a bit of work, but within a few moments, Gavin had that tingling sensation across his body once more...though the tingling was very strong in the right side of his torso. The sphere collapsed in on itself, shrinking almost to one-third its former size.

"Okay, okay...what do I still feel connected? I feel something... it's a little weird...it feels almost like a mesh or a blanket or a weave that extends throughout the whole city. I don't know why, but I think it's defensive or protective somehow. I feel...I feel something under the temple, deep under the temple; it seems to run through the substrata of this whole region, like a river or lake. There's something not too far southwest of here that blazes like the sun and another high above it."

Marcus blinked and tore his gaze away from the orb. "What did you say, boy? What was that last part?"

"There's a source of power not too far southwest of us that

blazes like a sun, and there's another high above it. The one high above, though, feels distant like it's hidden somehow."

Marcus blanched. "You're sensing the Citadel; that's not possible." Marcus then shook his head, as if to clear it, and continued, "Never mind that. In your mind, focus on spreading the power you've drawn across that mesh you felt. Then, concentrate, and release the power."

The sphere above Gavin's hand unfolded from itself, becoming a mesh and looking much like a fishing net, and dissipated. The sconces returned to their normal brightness, and the room's warmth returned.

"Gavin, do you remember the mark that burned itself into the slaver's forehead when he tried to brand you?" Marcus asked.

Gavin nodded, saying, "Yes, I do."

"Gavin, the mark that was burned into the slaver's forehead was your family's House glyph. It also happens to be *my* House glyph. I have no idea how, but there is no doubt we are related."

Gavin lay on the bed, gaping at Marcus. "I…how…is there any way to learn how we're related?"

"We have a few different methods available to us, but in my view, the 'how' is not nearly as important as the fact that we are. Over the years, it's been said my greatest flaw is that I put too much faith and trust in family, but since I know we're blood, there are things I will teach you I would never mention to another soul, things I feel you will need to know and understand."

Gavin nodded, saying, "I see."

"Ovir, will you stand as witness?" Marcus asked.

The old priest smiled and nodded once, as he said, "Of course, old friend."

"With the Royal Priest of Tel to serve as witness," Marcus said, his tone formal, "I hereby take Gavin Cross as my apprentice…as was in the old ways. Further, as we have unassailable proof of his blood relation to me, I hereby name Gavin Cross to be my full heir, with all the rights, responsibilities, and privileges thereof."

Gavin stared wide-eyed at the old wizard, almost gaping. "Are you sure you want to do that? I mean, you know nothing about me."

"I know you are my blood, however that may have happened. Besides, an old friend vouched for you," Marcus said. "Do you feel up to leaving?"

Gavin nodded. "I think so. Where are we going?"

"The only place to train a wizard is the College of the Arcane, in the center of the city. Besides, I think we've abused Ovir's hospitality enough."

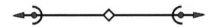

CHAPTER 7

T he markets of Tel Mivar occupied a large swath of territory around the center of the city, where the College of the Arcane was located. There were eight markets, each with their own specific functions: northwest market, north-central market, northeast market, east-central market, southeast, south-central, southwest, and west-central markets. While there was mostly an order to which shops were in which markets, the occasional oddity did exist...such as the rare book dealer of the south-central market nestled in with the brothels and taverns that made their money off the docks.

If one possessed sufficient determination, almost anything could be found in the markets of Tel Mivar. Trade-ships from Vushaar (a human kingdom to the south), the halfling and gnome lands far across the sea to the west, and various ports along the western coast of Tel all off-loaded goods in the capital city. The only other port city with markets to rival Tel Mivar was Kyndrath, the primary port and shipping-head for the Minotaur lands beyond the gnomes and halflings.

Occupying a little over fifty acres at the center of Tel Mivar stood the College of the Arcane. While there were various basic schools throughout the world where one could learn minor magics, anyone who desired sufficient mastery of the Art to be called an arcanist traveled to the College for study and training. Four massive obelisks rose high above a slate-gray, crenelated wall a short distance off the corners of a tower, and they served as the residences of the students studying at the College. The tower, almost small and squat in comparison to the four obelisks around it, looked every inch the classic square-ish keep with crenelated battlements and stood not quite half the height of the obelisks. This keep held the classrooms, the Chamber of the Council of Magisters, laboratories, the most extensive library of works on the arcane in the known world, rooms for visiting arcanists, and suites for the magisters when the Council was in session, and it was known as the Tower of the Council.

GAVIN LOOKED—ALMOST gawked—at the city around them, while Marcus walked slowly by his side, and Kiri walked two paces behind him off his right shoulder. The streets were paved with a smooth stone Gavin couldn't identify, and there were wide sidewalks for pedestrians. Marcus, however, seemed to ignore the convention of using the sidewalks, and for whatever reason, the drovers and horsemen made way for the old wizard. Gavin assumed it had something to do with the old man's black robes.

"Wow," Gavin whispered as they broke past the many stalls of the north market. "That is…that is…I've never seen anything like it."

A slate-gray, crenelated wall made of stone Gavin didn't recognize surrounded the College grounds, and there was only one gate, facing due north.

"This is the most amazing…" Gavin said as he ran his hand over the surface of the College's wall. "How was it made?"

Marcus chuckled, and since Gavin was focused on the wall, he missed the old wizard's smile of pride. "Kirloth and his apprentices raised the wall and obelisks from the earth, forming and shaping them with the Art. No mortal tool has ever touched them. The

Tower of the Council had been the keep of a local warlord who was quite willing to give up his territory for the construction of the city."

"Kirloth…" Gavin said, his voice trailing off. "Hmmm…sounds sort of imposing."

"He was acknowledged as the greatest master of the Art in his day. Would-be arcanists risked life and limb to seek him out and beg him to train them in the ways of the Art. When the rebellion against the evil gods arose, the leaders of the Army of Valthon approached him to lead the arcanist contingent. They say he faced Milthas alone during the siege of the elf-god's fortress in Arundel. Well, not quite alone…after all, Valthon imparted just enough divine power for Kirloth and Milthas to be on even terms."

"How does one go about learning the Art?" Gavin asked as they walked toward the gates of the College.

Marcus shrugged. "Learning the Art isn't something for which one can set a specific process. With mages, it is, but we'll discuss wizardry…since we're both wizards. Wizardry is as much a part of the wizard as it is a thing of the Art; the same spell from two different wizards might look or sound different but will always feel the same."

"Feel? I'm not sure I understand."

"All wizards perceive the use of the Art within a certain radius that is based upon the strength of that wizard's power. For instance, a minor wizard might have problems noticing a spell from the next room, whereas I can sense a simple light spell across the city."

By that time, they had reached the gates of the College, and Gavin saw two people stood at the gate, one on each side. They wore brown, plain robes, and the young woman on the western side of the gate wore a silver medallion that rested over her heart. He also noticed that, while managing not to move a hair from her post, the young woman seemed to flinch away from the pair of men.

The two gate attendants hurriedly opened the gates without even a challenge, and Marcus led his apprentice onto the College's grounds. Once they were mostly out of earshot from the gate, Marcus turned to Gavin as they walked.

"Did you notice the young woman at the gate? How she reacted to you?"

"I thought it was you," Gavin said.

"Oh, no, my young man," Marcus replied, a sly grin curling one corner of his lips. "From me, she sensed an old man comfortable in his power. You are a raging storm that sears everything around you." Marcus fell silent a moment. "Hmmm…the more I think about it, it seems to me your first lesson should be constructing your own shroud."

"I don't understand."

"It never hurts for others to underestimate you," Marcus replied as he opened one of the double doors they now faced. "It can save you trouble or allow you the element of surprise when trouble is inevitable. But we can discuss all this later; let's get you settled in."

An open staircase occupied the center of the tower, and Marcus led Gavin up six flights of stairs before he stepped into a hallway. Marcus turned right and led Gavin down that hallway to the second door on the left and stopped. Unlike every other door Gavin had seen so far, the door in front of Marcus did not possess a traditional latch. Where every other door had a latch handle and keyhole, this door had only a handle and a metal plate.

Marcus removed his medallion and pressed it to the plate. Gavin both heard and felt a click, and then, Marcus swung the door wide and entered.

Gavin followed Marcus into the suite and smiled. The center room was divided in half, the half closest the door possessing a dining table and chairs with the far half a sort of living room. The far wall held a hearth. The table and chairs were wooden and of exquisite craftsmanship. The two armchairs by the hearth were upholstered in a pleasant, very artistic style. A tapestry depicting a battle Gavin couldn't recognize hung above the hearth.

"This first door to the left is the bathroom. The far door to the left is my bedroom," Marcus said, indicating each door with a gesture. "The first door to the right is the library, and the far room on this side will be your bedroom. We'll conduct our studies here in the main room. Any questions so far?"

"Where will Kiri sleep?" Gavin asked.

"There are only two beds in the suite," Marcus said, "and she's not sleeping with me."

"I...I see," Gavin said. "I want to thank you for helping me, Marcus."

"You're welcome," Marcus said. "However, if you truly wish to thank me, take what you learn, and make it a part of you. Don't just use the Art; live it. At that point, you will have repaid any kindness by me and then some."

Marcus turned and walked over to the armchair on the left side of the hearth. He sat and removed his medallion once more. He pressed it to the metal plate on the lid, and Gavin heard the tell-tale click, much like that of the door. Marcus lifted the lid and reached inside. He soon withdrew a silver amulet on a chain.

This medallion looked almost identical to the one Marcus wore. Gavin thought the runes that circled the center, recessed area looked pretty much the same as those on Marcus's. Unlike Marcus's medallion, however, this one had a glyph in the recessed center, and it was the same symbol that had been burned into the slaver's forehead in the alley.

"This would've been my daughter's, had she lived, but I think it will suit you also."

Gavin accepted the medallion and put his head through the chain. When Gavin first put it around his neck, the medallion rested just below the bottom of his sternum. In a moment, Gavin felt the chain begin to shrink and shift until the medallion rested atop his heart.

"If you don't mind, I'd like to wash up a bit," Gavin said. "I think I sweated the bed wet at the temple while I was unconscious."

Marcus gestured toward the bathroom and pulled a brown-leather-bound volume from the chest.

. . .

MARCUS LOOKED up from the volume as Gavin exited the bathroom and nodded. "If you like, take a quick walk-through of your room, and let me know if there's anything specific it's missing for you."

Gavin walked over and opened the door to his room. The room was about fifteen feet by twenty, and it was well-lit. The bed was in the far corner, and a wardrobe faced it. The wall in which the door was mounted had a writing desk with a comfortable-seeming chair.

"Everything seems to be in order," Gavin said. "Kiri and I will probably need a set of clothes at some point, but I think I'm good to get started."

Marcus looked up from the volume on his knee and nodded. "Give me a few moments to finish collecting my thoughts, and we'll be off to the tailor I use."

Gavin took a seat at the table and became lost in his thoughts to the accompaniment of a quill scratching at the pages of a journal.

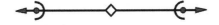

CHAPTER 8

Later that evening, Gavin was turning down the bed, not even thinking about the sleeping arrangements when he heard the door close behind him. Gavin finished placing the pillows where they belonged before he turned, but when he did turn, Gavin froze.

Kiri stood in front of the closed door. She held her head down, not looking at Gavin, and her dress lay discarded by her feet. She wore nothing underneath.

Gavin's mind stopped. It was as if his train of thought stopped against a large tree laid across its tracks. A part of him wanted nothing more than to stand there and enjoy the sight of the young woman now standing nude in front of him, for she was beyond pretty. But the rest of him didn't understand. Why would she do this? They'd only just met, and…then, it clicked.

I own her now. She thinks I'm going to…oh, no. Hell, no.

Gavin cast about for something—anything—he could use to cover Kiri, and he eyed a linen robe hanging on one side of the armoire. He grabbed it off the hook and turned to approach Kiri.

At his first step, Gavin saw sudden tension in her shoulders, arms, and torso; she was fighting to keep from trembling. *Oh, damn…is she afraid of me?*

Another step, and Kiri flinched. She tried to control it, but Gavin saw it. *I can't do this. Whatever possessed me to think I could do this?*

Another step, and Kiri's hands started to clench and then stopped. *Maybe Marcus would let me sleep in the library. Surely, he'd understand, right?*

Gavin took the last step to bring him to Kiri, and in one swift motion, he swept the robe behind her and dropped it to hang on her shoulders. He was very proud that he'd managed it without any part of him touching any part of Kiri. Then, he stepped back until his legs met the edge of the bed.

"Kiri, I'd like to talk, but I'd rather not talk to the top of your head."

Kiri lifted her head, and even though she pointed her face toward Gavin, she still did not make eye contact with him.

Gavin wanted to sigh, but he was concerned how Kiri would interpret that.

"Kiri…" He didn't know what to say. He didn't know how to ask the question he feared she'd answer with a 'yes.'

"Do I displease you, sir?" Kiri asked, her voice little more than a whisper.

"No, you do not displease me," Gavin said as his mind churned. *How can I prove to her that I'm not like the men who've assaulted her? What kind of people would just accept living around someone so terrified of them? I know I couldn't live like this, day in and day out. Why, why, why did this have to happen now? All I want to do is go to sleep, but no…the most stunning woman I've ever seen is sharing my bedroom, and she thinks I'm going to rape her. I so did not need this tonight. Heck with it…there must be extra blankets around here somewhere; this can be tomorrow's problem.*

Gavin turned to the armoire and pulled open the drawers in the bottom. There were four extra blankets folded in the bottom drawer. Gavin took one and unfolded it until it was as long as the bed but only as wide as one person and laid it on the floor. Then, he did the same with a second. He grabbed one of the two pillows on the bed and dropped it on the blankets by the head of the bed and took a third blanket from the drawer and closed it. Gavin turned and found Kiri looking at what he'd done, her brow furrowed.

"Kiri, I am not about to touch you without your permission. I realize it will take time for you to relax around me, and I hope you'll see me as a friend someday. I will not treat you like I think you've been treated in the past. The bed is yours."

Kiri stared at Gavin as though no part of her world made sense anymore. Her jaw worked like she was about to speak as she frowned, relaxed, and frowned again.

"Kiri, I do not have the words to communicate how deeply I abhor the concept of slavery. If I had my way, that mark would vanish from your shoulder, and you'd be free to live your life as you see fit. I don't know if that's possible; just because Marcus said no one's figured out how to remove a slave brand yet doesn't mean it can't be done. So, until I can deliver your freedom to you, I want you to live as though you were. Do what you want. Go where you want. Now…I am going to bed."

Gavin lay down on the blankets and covered himself with the third. Within moments, he was fading off to sleep.

MARCUS LOOKED up from his journal at the sound of the bedroom door opening. He forced himself not to react to the sight of Kiri striding from the room, the robe about her shoulders flowing almost like a cloak, even though his reaction would've been a satisfied chuckle at the evidence he was right about Gavin. She stopped at the armchair in which she'd sat not too long ago, and she clutched the back of that chair as if it were an anchor.

"What do I do?"

Now, Marcus quirked his left eyebrow. "With respect to what?"

"He laid blankets on the floor beside the bed and went to sleep. He said the bed was mine. What do I do?"

Marcus sat, looking into her eyes, and he couldn't help but remember her as she was before she left Vushaar, her homeland. He remembered the strong-willed, compassionate, young woman who was learning to rule her father's country once he was gone. He remembered all the time and effort he'd spent watching over the Muran family for countless centuries…protecting them, mentoring them, and sometimes avenging them. It took all of Marcus's incredible will to keep himself from unraveling that slave mark with a composite effect right there and then.

Oh, yes. He knew precisely how to remove the mark…with no threat whatsoever to Kiri's life. For that matter, Marcus knew how to eradicate slavery across the world; he'd always known. But ending slavery was not his task to achieve.

Instead, Marcus restricted himself to words, saying, "Kiri, you are the daughter of the oldest dynasty in the world, and you were raised by one of the greatest men that dynasty has ever produced. What do you *want* to do?"

"I—I want to go to sleep."

"Kalinor and those who chose to serve him will never trouble you again, girl; I promise you that. You've been in a very dark and evil place, these last two years, enduring all kinds of depravity and viciousness no one should ever have to experience. But you're safe now. No one will harm you here. Go to sleep."

Kiri stood silent for a few moments before she turned and walked back to the bedroom, closing the door behind her.

Marcus waited in his chair for several minutes before he, too, went to bed.

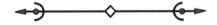

CHAPTER 9

Gavin stepped out of the bathroom just in time to see Kiri walk out of the bedroom. She didn't seem as timid as she had the night before. Gavin knew one night or a hundred wouldn't erase everything she had endured, but he hoped the day would come when she faced him with her shoulders squared and her head held high.

"May I visit the temple?" Kiri asked.

Gavin replied by crossing his arms and quirking one eyebrow upward, saying, "That's not the right way to say that."

Kiri frowned, and her eyes shifted side to side like she was thinking about Gavin's statement. After a few moments, she lifted her eyes back to Gavin and said, "Master-"

"Nope. I'm certainly not going listen to *that* word. Have you forgotten what I said last night before I went to sleep?"

Silence extended between them until a faint smile crossed Kiri's lips almost too fast for Gavin to notice, and she said, "I want to visit the temple today."

"Better," Gavin said, smiling as he uncrossed his arms, "and I see no reason why you can't. My only worry is whether you'll be harassed as you travel. Marcus, what do you think?"

The old wizard looked up from his journal. "Yes? What was the question?"

Gavin was quite sure Marcus knew exactly what he'd asked, but he humored the old wizard all the same. "I was asking your opinion of whether Kiri would be harassed if she went to the temple."

"I suppose there is that possibility if she's traveling alone. Kalinor and his amusements are no longer in a position to protect her. So, we shall have to provide another threat. You said you were hungry, and I imagine the young lady is as well. I recommend visiting the dining hall to address that, and while you're on the main floor, step outside to the garden and bring me a stone about the size of your palm. The closer it is to a disc in shape, the better."

ABOUT AN HOUR LATER, Gavin and Kiri returned to the suite. Gavin was about to knock when he remembered how Marcus opened the door. He lifted his medallion from where it hung around his neck and placed the face of it against the smooth panel beside the door. He both heard and felt the latching mechanism release and pushed the door open.

Marcus stood at the table, a book lying open in front of him, and he looked up at the sound of the door.

"Ah, good! I was hoping you'd remember how to unlock the door. Did you bring the stone?"

Gavin nodded. "Yes, I did. I have it here." He held up a smooth river rock the size of the cup of his palm. It was the shade of gray that seems only to be found in stone and striped with strands of black.

"Excellent, my boy. Lay it on the table here." Gavin did so as Marcus went to the library and returned with a small knife. "Now, what we're about to do is create an amulet for Kiri that will ensure everyone knows whom they will face if they harm her. It will also serve as a key to the door, so she can come and go as she pleases. First, Gavin, I need you to prick your thumb or finger just enough to draw some blood, and then, drip a couple drops on the stone."

Gavin did as Marcus instructed and wrapped his thumb in a small rag the old wizard handed him.

"Now, Kiri, you must do the same."

"Me? Why me?"

"The power in the door will respond to Gavin's blood as if it were his medallion, but that would create a skeleton key anyone could use to enter any location protected so. By incorporating your blood as well, I will tie this amulet to you and you alone. Even if someone were to steal it, it would not open the suite or anywhere else for them."

Gavin frowned and quickly lowered his head, hoping Marcus wouldn't notice. *I wonder what other doors my medallion will open...*

Kiri sighed and held out her hand. Marcus gave her the knife and she winced as she drew some blood from her thumb. After dripping a couple drops onto the stone, Kiri accepted a rag from Marcus and stepped back.

Marcus pulled a leather cord from a pocket of his robe and, placing the stone in his palm, laid the cord on his fingers in a small coil.

"Gavin, this may hurt a bit."

Taking a couple deep breaths, Marcus closed his eyes and invoked two Words of Power, blending them together to create a composite effect, "*Uhnrys-Sykhurhos.*"

Gavin felt the power take hold in the form of a savage concussion to his soul and that ever-present tingling sensation erupting into a raging torrent. The experience almost knocked the wind from Gavin's lungs, and he felt his knees weaken. But that didn't stop him from watching what was happening in Marcus's left hand.

The old man's left hand and forearm developed an aura of gold-colored power, and waves of that power began flowing into the stone and leather cord. The stone absorbed the blood as the glyph in the center of Gavin's medallion etched itself into the stone. A hole formed at the top of the stone, and the leather cord threaded itself through that hole before the ends joined to form an unbroken circle of leather.

"By the gods..." Kiri said, her eyes wide. "I've never seen anything like that!"

By that point, the aura faded, leaving an amulet bearing Gavin's House Glyph, and Marcus extended his hand toward Kiri.

"Take it, and wear it always. The leather will not break or decay."

Kiri accepted the new necklace and lifted it over her head to hang around her neck. At first, the amulet rested on the fabric of her dress atop her sternum, but the leather cord began to shrink, drawing the stone up until it rested just below where her collar bones met.

"Gavin isn't in a position yet to be the threat behind the warning that glyph represents, but you have my word that anyone who dares lay a hand on you will spend what time they have left alive in unimaginable agony."

"T-The amulet can do that?" Kiri asked.

"No, of course not...but *I* can."

Gavin's eyes never left the old wizard, and something in Marcus's eyes suggested to Gavin he knew quite a bit about inflicting agony on others.

Kiri gave a faint nod before walking to the door. Just as she grasped the handle to pull open the door, she stopped and turned back to the two wizards, saying, "Gavin, would you mind walking with me?"

"I wouldn't mind a bit, Kiri."

THE MARKETS SURROUNDING the College of the Arcane were just as busy as the day before.

"Where do all these people come from?" Gavin asked as he and Kiri threaded their way through the crowd.

"Many of them are from right here in Tel Mivar," Kiri said as they walked. "It's one of the largest cities in the world, even if you don't count the fifty acres of the College at the city's center. There's also a fair amount of barge traffic on the Vischaene between here and Tel Cothos, so I'm sure that's also part of it…not to mention wagon convoys from Tel Roshan and Tel Wygoth and many smaller settlements in between."

"What's Vushaar like, Kiri?"

"Vushaar is a beautiful country. Nearest the Inner Sea, it's a land of jungles and rain forests, even though Thartan Province is more like the grasslands and rolling hills of Mivar Province. As you move farther south, the terrain shifts to grasslands and plains, before becoming tundra and snow caps in the deep, deep south. There are places in southern Vushaar where the snow and ice never melt."

"That does sound beautiful. Which part of Vushaar are you from?"

"I grew up in the capital city. It's located in a natural basin formed by the northern edge of the Sarnath Hills. It's right where the jungles and rain forests give way to the grasslands. But my mother was from Thartan Province, and we'd go to her family's home sometimes. How about you? Where do you call home?"

Gavin shrugged. "I wish I knew. My earliest memory is waking up in an alley, not too long before I found you, and I woke up knowing only my name. I know basic stuff, like two plus two equals four and the new year always starts in the winter."

Kiri stopped and looked at Gavin, frowning. "No, it doesn't. Ever since the Godswar, we've started our years the day after we won the final battle of the war…in high summer. Each new year starts on the first day of Andoven."

Now, Gavin frowned. "That's not right. The new year starts on the first day of…of…" Gavin *knew* the word he wanted was right on the tip of his tongue. It was *right there*, but the gray mists that always seemed to be on the edge of his consciousness swirled through his mind. The word was lost to him.

"Damn it!" Gavin said, clenching his hands into fists. "I *know* this! Why can't I think of it? I know all kinds of useless information, like water is a polar molecule made up of one atom of oxygen and two atoms of hydrogen. I know the air we breathe isn't a pure substance; it's actually a mixture of nitrogen, oxygen, and a few other trace elements. Why—by all that's holy—can't I remember the name of the first month of the year?"

"Gavin?" Kiri asked, her voice soft.

"Yes, Kiri?"

"That strange word you used…what is an *atom?*"

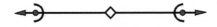

CHAPTER 10

Marcus watched Gavin and Kiri leave the suite, and he couldn't keep from smiling. It was early yet, almost too early in fact, but he thought those two would work out very well indeed...once Kiri worked through the traumas of the past two years.

Still, there was too much to do to sit there speculating about the future. Marcus levered himself to his feet and went to the library. He retrieved a few pieces of parchment from a drawer and returned to the suite's main table with a quill and a bottle of ink as well.

He was just about to sit and begin working out his plan for training Gavin when a column of flame that neither burned or radiated heat erupted from the floor on the other side of the table. The column of flame was short-lived and left a purple-robed figure standing in its wake. The cowl of the robe's hood and the cuffs of its sleeves bore runes embroidered in gold thread, and the new arrival's face was obscured beneath the hood in impenetrable shadow. All that could be seen were his eyes; they glowed the color of open flame, and the pupils were vertical slits.

Marcus smiled. "Nathrac, it has been too long. How are you?"

"I am well, old friend," the purple-robed figure said in a voice that resonated against Marcus's bones. "Forgive my intrusion, but He would speak with you."

Marcus nodded. There was only one who could use Nathrac as a messenger, and Marcus knew just where to find him. Marcus put the cork stopper back in the ink bottle and stepped back from the table.

"Then, I suppose we shouldn't keep my former apprentice waiting."

Nathrac left the suite the same way he arrived, and Marcus strode to the door. He walked the short distance to the Grand Stair, the staircase that went to every floor of the Tower, and started ascending.

The very last landing before the roof access had an arch built into the stone wall—with no door—but it was Marcus's destination nonetheless. As the old wizard approached the landing, a blue phantom faded into view. Phantoms can take almost any form, ghosts that they are, but this phantom bore the shape of a man. He wore a chain shirt over studded leather armor, with studded leather gauntlets and greaves. A short sword hung on his left side, and he held a halberd in his right hand.

"It has been some time since last thou stood before me, milord. Dost thou require access to thy Citadel?"

"Yes, I do, old friend. My former apprentice desires a word."

The phantom turned to his left and reached into the wall with his left hand. Marcus felt—much more than heard—a lock release, and the space within the archway began shimmering. The stone blocks within the archway faded away, and the arch became a doorway to a carpeted corridor.

Marcus stepped through the archway, and it vanished behind him. Marcus walked the short distance to the end of the corridor and took a moment to admire the space. Intricate tapestries hung on the walls, and sconces whose flames neither consumed fuel nor radiated heat lit the space.

The Citadel had been Marcus's first real home in a long, long time, and if Marcus were honest with himself, he missed it a great deal. A part of him wanted to regret leaving it to his successors, but they'd needed a refuge of their own, too.

Marcus took a deep breath and turned to his right. His former apprentice was waiting, and he no longer wished to relive memories of so long ago.

MARCUS ENTERED a small sitting room a short distance from where he'd entered the Citadel. It was a comfortable, intimate space, possessing two armchairs near a hearth with a small stand for drinks between them. One chair was already occupied, and its occupant stood as Marcus opened the door.

He looked to be a young man whose hair and Vandyke beard were the color of caramel. He wore gold robes, and the gold wizard's medallion resting atop his chest was shaped like a dragon's head. Careful inspection of the dragon-head medallion would reveal the Wygoth Glyph engraved on a scale between the dragon's eyes.

He smiled as Marcus entered the room and took the few steps necessary to meet him.

"It's been a long time, master," Bellos said.

Marcus chuckled. "I'm no more your master than you're my apprentice anymore, not since you agreed to become the God of Magic, but it has been a long time. Nathrac said you wanted to speak with me."

"How have you been?"

Bellos led Marcus to the chairs, and they took their seats.

"I'm tired. I've been alive far too long, but we've discussed this before."

Bellos nodded. "Yes, I suppose we have."

"Why do you want to see me after all these years?"

"I wanted to discuss your new apprentice."

"Gavin? Who is he to you? For that matter, who is he to me? He's a member of my House, and I don't see how that's possible."

"Don't you, Marcus?" Bellos grimaced as if tasting something foul. "I never did like that name, you know. You really could have chosen something else, but I digress. There's one branch of your family about which you know nothing."

Marcus's nostrils flared. His jaw clenched for a moment before saying, "Gerrus...the traitor."

"That's not fair, and you know it. If your family had not been murdered by Lornithar's Temple Guardsmen, would you have been so quick to join the war? Gerrus wanted his family safe more than anything. It tore his heart to leave you and Marin, but he couldn't bring himself to risk his wife and children."

"So, who is Gavin?"

Bellos sighed. "Gavin is Gerrus's grandson...many, many times removed. I know you've never forgiven Gerrus for saving his family by joining those who fled the Godswar, but I *also* know how much you regret never locating the refugee world to reconcile with him. Part of that is my fault; the people needed you during the Founding. Don't hate Gavin for your brother's choice; perhaps, this is the multiverse's way of giving you a chance to make peace with him."

Marcus snorted. "I don't believe that for a moment, but the old man is an incorrigible meddler. He never did like my reaction to Gerrus's choice."

Silence reigned for several moments, until Marcus took a deep breath and released it as a heavy sigh.

"Do you know anything of his life after he left here?"

"The refugees came to look to him for leadership and guidance. He did not want that, but they didn't give him much of a choice. They were not alone in the world Nesta found for them, and the refugees would've died, were it not for Gerrus and the other wizards. They defended the refugees with the knowledge Gerrus learned at your father's laboratory until they could build fortifications. He was very old when he died, and it was a peaceful passing. His wife was by his side, and they were surrounded by children, grandchildren, and great-grandchildren."

Marcus nodded as he stared into flames in the hearth.

After a time, Marcus shifted his gaze to Bellos and asked, "Was Gavin's pedigree all that you wished to discuss?"

"I know the old man said Gavin should be trained as only you can, but I wanted to clarify that. I ask that you train him like you trained us, for I fear he will have need of all the knowledge you possess and then some."

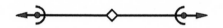

CHAPTER 11

Gavin stared up at the Temple of Valthon. The sick rooms were in the basement, and he was too busy looking at the city to notice the Temple when he left yesterday. Like every other building in the 'Old City,' the temple looked to be one, solid piece of marble. This included the columns supporting the massive portico that stretched out in front of the main entrance. The columns themselves were fluted cylinders, stretching up to plain, square capitals, and about twenty-five feet back from the columns, the main building began. Two sets of massive, double doors were set at equidistant locations from the edges of the face, and a young woman sat behind a simple desk at the right set of doors.

Gavin realized Kiri was leaving him, approaching the young woman, and he tore himself away from his inspection of one of the columns. Words floated through his mind like *Doric* and *Ionic*, but he couldn't piece together what those words meant or why he would think of them when he was looking at columns. He decided those words were simply other pieces of the huge mystery of who he was.

"I have come to speak with the Royal Priest," Kiri said as she reached the young woman.

Gavin turned just in time to see the young woman do a double take, and she just stared at Kiri, her mouth gaping open.

"Is there a problem?" Gavin asked as he approached.

The young woman shifted her attention to Gavin, and as if by reflex, her eyes lowered to the silver disc resting atop his heart. Gavin watched her eyes widen as some of the color left her cheeks, and her mouth snapped shut. The woman then looked back at the small amulet hanging around Kiri's neck before looking back at Gavin's medallion again. Her jaw worked as if to speak, but no sound escaped her lips.

"Are you okay?" Gavin asked.

Kiri leaned close to Gavin and whispered, "Well."

Gavin nodded and said, "Are you well?"

The young woman shook herself, and she bowed her head as she spoke, "Forgive me, milord. I wasn't aware any of your House yet lived. I bid thee welcome to the Temple of Valthon. I am Acolyte Laila, honored to serve as the Temple Greeter today."

Gavin longed to ask her what she knew about his House, but he was afraid that would mean they'd never get in for Kiri to speak with Ovir.

"It's nice to meet you, Laila," Gavin said, "and I don't see there's any harm done. I'm Gavin Cross. My friend did ask to speak with Ovir, though. Is he available?"

The young woman glanced at the time piece sitting on the corner of her desk and pursed her lips. "He should be finished with the morning service by now, milord, but he runs long from time to time. You might be able to catch him in Valthon's shrine. If he isn't there, one of the attending clerics will be able to help you."

"I hope the day is good to you, Laila," Gavin said. "Thank you for your help."

Stepping through the open, double doors, Gavin passed through one of the archways allowing entrance to a statuary, and a deep warmth of welcome suffused his entire being.

The space was an open-air atrium supported by arches, and statues stood on each side of the space, separated by columns that supported the arches. Four statues occupied the left, with five on the right. In the center of the space, a dais—shin-high at most (depending on the shin)—held a final statue.

The first statue on the left depicted a tall, broad-shouldered man in plate armor. The hilts of two swords rose above each shoulder, while a mace hung at his left side and a double-headed hammer at his right. His arms crossed his chest, and his expression seemed to say, *I'm ready for this; are you?* A plaque on the statue's base read, "Kalthor, God of War."

The second statue depicted a woman in a flowing dress. Her long hair was gathered with a bow and hung in front of her left shoulder. She reached out with her right hand as if to say, *Come; let me help you.* The plaque beneath her statue read, "Padola, Goddess of Healing and Life."

The third statue on the left depicted a man. He stood about Gavin's height and had none of Kalthor's bulk. He wore a robe, and a dragon-head medallion rested atop his heart. His left hand held an open book, and his head leaned forward as if he'd just been reading. He had a Vandyke beard. His expression said, *Oh, hello; how long have you been there?* His plaque read, "Bellos, God of Magic."

The fourth statue on the left depicted a man also wearing a robe, and he too wore a medallion. Gavin froze as he looked at the medallion and then swept his off to hold it up for comparison; the glyphs in the center of each medallion matched. This statue had no specific posture or expression; he simply stood with his fingers interlaced at his navel. The plaque beneath this statue read, "Marin, God of the Sea."

The fifth statue on the right depicted a tall, willowy woman in traveling clothes. A knapsack with a bedroll tied across the bottom sat at her feet, and a lute hung on her back. Her hair was shoulder-length, and her arms were folded across her midriff, her left arm against her and her right hand holding her left elbow. Her head angled down just a bit as she frowned at the statue in the center of space, and her expression said, *What has that rapscallion done now?* Her plaque read, "Nesta, Goddess of Travelers and Bards."

The fourth statue on the right depicted a man wearing a robe with its hood pulled over his head. He wore a somber expression, and his arms folded across his midriff with each hand inside the other sleeve. This plaque read, "Lilkan, God of Death and the Underworld."

The third statue on the right depicted a stocky man, barely taller than Gavin's waist. His beard touched his chest, and his mustache was two braids that extended as far as his beard. Thick gloves extended three-fourths of the way up his forearms, and he wore a blacksmith's apron over plate armor. A double-edged axe with a haft that reached his waist leaned against his left leg. This plaque read, "Irikos, God of the Forge."

The second statue on the right showed a woman half a head shorter than Nesta and twice as willowy. Curly hair cascaded below her shoulders, and she wore a hooded jerkin over belted trousers. A full quiver of arrows was strapped to her right thigh, and she wore a bow diagonally across her torso, string in front. Her ears were pointed. Her plaque read, "Xanta, Goddess of Nature."

The first statue on the right, across from Kalthor, depicted a man. The statue was angled to stand partially turned away from the entrance to the space, and the man looked back over his shoulder toward the door. His arms were folded across his midriff like Nesta's. He bore a pencil-thin mustache and a ring in his left earlobe. His left eyebrow quirked upward, and his lips curled in a cocky smirk as if to say, *I just cut your coin-purse and danced with your wife, but I'll still shake your hand.* This plaque read, "Dakkor, God of Thieves."

At last, Gavin turned to the statue that stood in the center of the space. It depicted a short man barely tall enough to reach Gavin's shoulder, and his unkempt hair was in wild disarray to match his scraggily beard. He wore a robe that was tattered and frayed at the hem. His fingers were laced over his navel, too, and his impish grin and uplifted eyebrow seemed to say, *Who, me?* His plaque read, "Valthon, God of Time and Change."

"What is this place?" Gavin asked, turning to face Kiri who stood by the entrance.

"It's the Hall of the Gods. Except for Valthon and Nesta, all those you see before you accepted the mantle of divinity at the end of the Godswar."

Gavin turned back to look at the statue of Valthon. "When I woke up in that alley, there was a crazy, old man standing over me who looked a lot like this." Gavin stood staring at the statue for several more moments before he shook himself. "Which way to Valthon's shrine?"

"My ma…I mean, Baron Kalinor…brought me here on occasion," Kiri said as she started walking to the far side of the room. "It's this way."

Leaving the Hall of the Gods, they entered a curving hallway shaped like a horseshoe. For whatever reason, Kiri led them right, and soon, they stood in an open space about fifty yards on each side, and a meandering stream of people entered the open space from a set of doors on their left that led to the space between the sides of the horseshoe.

They walked over to the doors, and the stream of people shifted to one side, so they could enter. Valthon's shrine was a large, oval-shaped room with several rows of pews filling the two-thirds of the space closest the door, with a wide center aisle and narrower aisles along each curving wall. The space was devoid of smells, without even incense, and the cloth draped across the altar was a simple gray.

Gavin saw Ovir standing near the shrine, speaking with two much younger people. They all wore gray robes, and the younger man and woman nodded as Ovir spoke.

As Kiri and Gavin walked up the center aisle, their movement attracted Ovir's attention, and he smiled.

"Kiri! Gavin! Good to see you! Give me just a moment to finish here, and then, we can talk." Ovir turned his attention back to the younger people and spoke for a few more moments before nodding their dismissal.

As the younger people wearing gray robes hustled out of the shrine, Ovir approached Gavin and Kiri.

"How are you feeling, Gavin?"

"I'm well, thank you. A good night's sleep seems to have removed the last trace of weariness I felt when we left yesterday."

Ovir nodded. "Good. I'm glad to hear it, and how are you, Kiri?"

If Kiri felt uncomfortable at being addressed directly by the Royal Priest of Tel, it didn't show.

"I am well, sir, and thank you for asking."

"So, what brings the two of you here? How can I help?"

Gavin smiled. "Well, Kiri was the one who wanted to speak with you. I just tagged along to see her safely here. I'll find some way to pass the time while the two of you talk, if you have the time for it."

"Of course. If you like, I'll introduce you to the Temple's library. I'm sure you could find something interesting to read in there."

Ovir led them back out of the shrine and said, "This is the concourse. Most of these doors you see lead to small shrines of one god or another. The administration offices for the clergy of Valthon, along with the library and my residence, are on the upper floor. As you already know, the floors below house sickrooms."

Ovir turned to his right and led them to a stairwell with stairs going up and down and headed up to the second floor. Upon exiting the stairwell, Ovir pointed to a set of double doors a short distance to their left.

"You'll find the library through there. It's open to all. Kiri and I will be in the residence if you need us; anyone you see can direct you there."

"Thanks," Gavin said and headed for the indicated doors.

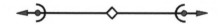

CHAPTER 12

The doors closed behind Gavin with a heavy *clack*. The Temple's library looked to be five times the size of Marcus's library in the suite, so it was fifty feet wide by seventy-five feet long. A thirty-foot square in the center of the room held reading tables, and bookshelves filled the rest of the space. What struck Gavin first was that the space didn't smell like it was full of old books. A floral scent Gavin didn't recognize filled the place, and the scent helped Gavin relax.

I have no idea how long Kiri is going to be with Ovir, but I'm certainly not going to joggle her elbow. There must be something here worth reading.

Gavin started exploring the shelves of the library, his steps slow. Most of the texts bore titles that gave Gavin the impression of religious treatises and the like. Gavin was about to explore a different section of the library when he found a book horizontally stuffed into a shelf atop the spines of the other books; it was the first book Gavin had seen placed thus. He removed it from its place with care and turned it to read the cover, "The Registry of Houses, Volume 4573."

Gavin smiled and took the book to the nearest reading table. Placing the book on the table, Gavin measured it with his left index finger and saw it was about three-quarters of it in thickness. *How many Houses are there for the Registry of them to be this thick?*

Opening the front cover, he saw a line at the bottom of the title page that read, "Published: 22 Nesnae 4572."

What year did they say it is? 6080? 6081? That would make this book fifteen hundred years old, give or take. That would make me wonder if I'd find my House in here, but since I seem to be related to the God of the Sea too, I feel safe I'll find it. I just hope I have enough time to find it before Kiri is ready to leave.

Turning past the title page, Gavin found the table of contents, and his shoulders tensed. *Oh, shit...no House Glyphs.*

Gavin picked a name at random, House Alcor, and flipped to that page. He sighed as he leaned back against the chair. An illustration of what could only be Alcor's House Glyph occupied the top quarter of the page; it was a simple Glyph with two diagonal lines almost touching to form an A-frame. The diagonal line on the left was just slightly below the line on the right, and a second diagonal line was below the one on the left, which stopped a little past the upper-left line's start.

Gavin took off his medallion and laid it beside the Alcor glyph. *Nope, not even close. Hmmm...maybe there's an index at the back.*

Returning his medallion to his neck, Gavin closed the tome and turned it over to rest on its front cover. He opened the back cover and, skipping the blank page at the very back, found himself looking at the entry for House Zynvis. The Zynvis Glyph was a vertical line with a diagonal line bisecting it from left to right; at the point of bisection, the image of a sickle was attached by the tip of its haft.

Well, I'm not House Zynvis, either. Gavin sighed. *This will take a while...*

He swept his medallion off his neck once more and laid it on the table beside the book and started turning the pages with care, scanning the House Glyphs as he went.

The first name he recognized was Wygoth, one of Kirloth's apprentices during the Godswar and now one of the Great Houses of Tel. The Wygoth Glyph was two diagonal lines going up from left to right with an underlined caret beneath them.

Nope. Not mine.

A few minutes later, he found an entry for House Roshan, the next name he recognized which was also one of Kirloth's apprentices and now a Great House of Tel. The House Glyph was two horizontal lines with a single dot centered beneath them. Below the dot were two vertical lines centered along the horizontal lines above.

I'm not House Roshan, either.

The next page that caught Gavin's eye did so not for the House's name or its Glyph but where it was from. The wizard members of the royal family of Vushaar made up House Muran; its House Glyph was a dot in the upper-third, with a horizontal line coming in from the left and stopping at the edge of the dot in the middle-third. The lower-third of the Glyph looked like a letter T that had been rotated eighty-five degrees to the left.

Huh...I wonder if Kiri knows anyone from House Muran. She said she grew up in the capital city.

A few pages later, Gavin found the entry for House Mivar, the city and province's namesake. He wasn't House Mivar, either. Mivar's Glyph, like that of Gavin's House, was divided into left-, middle-, and right-thirds...unlike the upper-, middle-, and lower-thirds Gavin had seen so far. The left-third of the Mivar Glyph was a vertical line that turned left in a right angle at the overall mid-point of the Glyph and, then, turned back to a diagonal line. The middle-third was a dot in the center. The right-third looked like a capital E made with four lines and points at the line intersections instead of the usual block style.

Close...well, the dot in the middle is similar. Still, though...not me.

The L's yielded no results, either. Halfway through the K's, Gavin found what he sought, and a shiver ran down his spine.

The Glyph on the left page had a left-, middle-, and right-third. The left-third looked like two sickles with one inverted over the other and their points merging to create a solid line. The middle-third was a single dot in the middle of the space, and the right-third was a greater-than symbol with a wider angle than normal.

House Kirloth...I'm House Kirloth.

* * *

OVIR OFFERED KIRI a seat in the parlor of his suite of rooms, and he chose the chair opposite hers.

"Would you like some refreshment?"

"No, thank you, sir."

"So, how can I help you, Your Highness?"

Kiri's jaw dropped just a bit. "You know?"

"I didn't recognize you right away in the alley, Your Highness, but one of the times I visited Gavin's room in our infirmary, you turned your head in such a way you were the spitting image of your mother. I don't make it home often, but I do remember seeing the Crown Prince, his wife, and their newborn daughter. This was several years ago, you understand...before your father became King."

"Why did you keep my secret in the shrine?"

"The rebellion that has been coming for several years finally started last month, and two years ago, your homeland mourned your loss along with the *Sprite*. If your father's enemies knew you were alive, you'd make a very potent weapon against him in the civil war, so I think it's in everyone's best interests if—for the time being —I forget you'll be my Queen someday."

"I'll never be Queen; I'm a slave."

"Do you honestly think your father—or our people—would care about that? Besides, I have information you don't."

"Really? What is it?"

Ovir stared into the flames glowing in the hearth for several moments before he returned his attention to Kiri.

"About three thousand years ago, there was a seer who gave a number of prophecies, and there was a set—sometimes called a sequence—of prophecies that made absolutely no sense to me or anyone else who had ever read them...until I realized who you were. Those prophecies foretell the rise to power of the Slave Queen, she who will rebuild the country from the ashes of the Vushaari Civil War."

Kiri sat back in her armchair, staring at Ovir with her jaw slack. "The Slave Queen? Really?"

"Oh, yes, but I somehow doubt you came to discuss historical prophecies."

Kiri couldn't keep from grinning. "Well, in a way, I did."

Ovir frowned. "Please, explain."

Kiri took a deep breath and let it out as a slow sigh. "I've never told anyone this, not even my father. Honestly, a part of me wasn't sure if it was real or not. The night before I was to leave for Tel Mivar, I went to the shrine in the palace to pray for the well-being of my father and homeland. When I arrived, I met a strange, old man who told me that, if I truly wanted to ensure my father's safety and that of my homeland, all I had to do was find a young man named Gavin Cross."

Now, Ovir's jaw dropped. "Are you certain of that name?"

"Yes, Ovir, I am. Despite everything that has happened since I left my home, I remember that exchange very, very well. Before that moment, I had never heard a name like 'Gavin Cross' before."

Ovir leaned back in his chair and stared at the ceiling in silence for several moments. After a time, he returned his attention to his guest and saw the discomfort in her expression.

"Is this what you wanted to discuss?"

"In a way. All the nights I've woken up wanting to scream and slit my throat, the one thing that kept me from doing it was that I had to find Gavin Cross to keep my family safe. And now? I've found him, only he's not some awe-inspiring general or leader of the people. He's maybe five years older than I am, and he has no idea who he is or where he's from…or anything really beyond his name! How is he supposed to save my homeland? It makes it seem like everything I endured, everything I survived, was for nothing. I…I just don't understand." Kiri put her elbows on her knees and rested her head in her hands. "I just don't understand."

Ovir watched the young woman sitting across from him, and the distress she radiated was palpable, almost a third presence in the room.

"I don't have the answer you seek. I wish I did. All I can say is that I have faith events will unfold as they should. You're free of the world Kalinor and his ilk have created, and I personally feel you should learn to enjoy life again. Who knows what you may find if you do?"

"I'm not sure I'll ever understand how to enjoy life again." Kiri took a deep breath and shook herself. "Thank you, Ovir. I appreciate your time today and hope I have not imposed on you too much."

"Not at all, child. You're welcome here anytime."

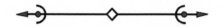

CHAPTER 13

Kiri didn't say a word as she left the temple at Gavin's side. Gavin wanted to ask if she'd found the answers she sought, but Kiri seemed so focused on her thoughts that he didn't feel he should intrude.

In truth, Gavin struggled with his own thoughts. The library at the Temple felt small, but it was well-stocked. In a book that seemed to lay forgotten on a back shelf, Gavin found one piece of information he wanted: the meaning of the glyph at the center of his medallion.

House Kirloth. Now, Gavin understood all the weird looks from the people in town and the nervous fear he provoked in the Temple's greeter. The book Gavin read insisted House Kirloth died out eighty-two years after the Godswar. And yet, Marcus had said the medallion Gavin now wore had been intended for his daughter. What did that mean? Was the historian wrong? Was Marcus lying to him? If Gavin truly was House Kirloth, what relation was Marcus?

"Gavin..."

The tone of Kiri's voice pulled him from his thoughts more than his name. He looked to her and saw she stared ahead of them, her olive skin pale. Gavin looked ahead and saw five people, two men and three women, blocking their way. They wore a mish-mash of leather armor that looked old and ill-used, and each bore a number of sheathed blades.

Soft footfalls behind drew Gavin's attention, and he saw four more people similar in garb move to block the way they'd come.

"We have no interest in you, girl," the man standing at the center of the line in front said. "Our interest is with him alone. Be on your way."

"What is he to you?" Kiri said, and Gavin blinked at the steel in her voice.

"That's none of your concern, slave," a woman to the first speaker's left said.

Gavin sighed, saying, "Somehow, I don't think you're inviting me over for tea and biscuits."

The man who'd spoken first smirked. "If you don't fight us, we'll make it quick."

"Let's make it quick anyway," Gavin said, giving the man his own smirk.

Gavin focused on the five in front and the four behind as he drew on the roiling, seething power deep inside him. Every part of his body started to tingle, and Gavin pushed all of that into the Word he'd used against the slavers, "*Thraxys.*"

The invocation slammed into Gavin and swept the breath from his lungs, driving him to his knees. His body felt like it was melting, but he did not lose consciousness. He watched the five in front collapse like puppets whose strings were cut.

"Gavin, run!" Kiri said, her voice almost a shout, but Gavin couldn't.

Invoking the Word of Power, even though it didn't knock him unconscious like the first time, drained Gavin. His awareness felt spongy, and his limbs moved as if mired in molasses.

Kiri grabbed Gavin's arm and helped him stand, but Gavin's vision spun, and he collapsed back to his knees.

A man stepped into sight from an alleyway behind them and

drew a blade unlike any Gavin had ever seen before. It was black. Not glossy black like obsidian or enameled metal, but a flat, matte black that seemed to draw in all light and color near it.

Kiri put herself between Gavin and the man, but it was a futile gesture. The man knocked her aside with a backhand blow, sending her to the ground.

The man grabbed Gavin by his hair and drew back his head, exposing Gavin's throat as he lifted his black blade.

"And so do I protect my master," the man whispered.

Something whistled by Gavin's head and struck the man with a wet *thud*. Two more objects whistled by Gavin to strike home in less than a heartbeat, and the grip on Gavin's hair weakened.

Gavin looked up, still a bit dazed himself, and saw three arrows sticking out of the man's chest. He looked down the street and saw a hooded woman with a bow and thigh quiver. Curly, blond hair escaped the hood, and she winked at Gavin before disappearing into the chaos of the street behind her.

Movement to his right attracted Gavin's attention as bodies landed on the street around him, jumping down from nearby rooftops. Hot pain erupted in Gavin's arm as he watched the strange blade rake the length of his right forearm in a wavy line, and just as quick as it erupted, the pain ended. The world around him faded to nothing.

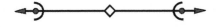

CHAPTER 14

It was not the first time Iosen of House Sivas stood at the gates of the royal palace in Tel Mivar. In fact, he and the king were old friends. The guards didn't even stop him for a pass as Iosen approached the main doors of the palace and hastened to open the doors for him. Iosen would normally have at least nodded his thanks, but it was most unlike Leuwyn to summon him so soon after one of their visits.

IOSEN THREADED his way through the palace until he found himself standing before the doors to the royal apartments. The guards standing at these doors recognized him as well, but unlike the men at the palace doors, these soldiers nodded their acknowledgement of Iosen and gestured for him to stop. The guard on Iosen's right rapped on the door with his knuckles before disappearing inside to announce Iosen's arrival. The guard soon opened the door wide and bade Iosen to enter, closing the door behind him as he left.

. . .

THE ROYAL APARTMENTS were decorated with only the most exquisite finery; tapestries, rugs, furniture…even the tea service would bring more than most families made in a year if it were sold. Iosen soon found his friend. The man was in his study, of all places. Calling Leuwyn, King of Tel, a scholar was about as honest as calling a career sailor a landsman.

Leuwyn's sandy hair topped a frame that would've been an average build, did it not look so emaciated. Iosen knew the palace staff kept him well-fed, or at least tried to do so, but in all the years Iosen had known him, Leuwyn always looked half-starved.

Leuwyn turned and gave Iosen a weak smile. "Ah, there you are, old friend. There is someone here who would meet you."

Iosen started to call out to his friend as he entered the study, but something held him back. He glanced off to his right and froze. A figure draped in a black, hooded robe stood by the window, seeming to gaze out over the city. The figure was so tall and broad-shouldered, the frame had to belong to a man; he held his hands behind him, his right hand gripping his left wrist, and Iosen saw no runes on the sleeves. The color drained from Iosen's face as the hair on the back of his neck stood on edge.

Iosen's eyes remained locked on the figure as it turned to face the room. Despite how the hood hung low over the man's face, the room was well lit enough for Iosen to make out some details. The man's skin looked…wrong…somehow. It was pasty white and desiccated, almost as if it had been dead for some time.

"This is the man who will deliver the Society to us?" he asked as he walked across the room. The voice sounded unnatural. The words were well formed, but there was an odd clicking every so often. Iosen placed the sound at last, and whatever color remained in his face fled then. The clicking was the sound of teeth striking together while forming certain words…because the man no longer had lips.

Iosen overcame his unease when he processed what the man had said. He shifted his eyes to Leuwyn and glared at his friend, saying, "You told him?"

"Told me?" the man said. "Do you honestly believe this king of yours developed so well-planned and cunning a stratagem? This imbecile needs servants to tell him which shoe goes on which foot."

Iosen waited for the explosion of royal wrath at such an insult, but it never came. He turned to look at his friend and almost gaped. Leuwyn was cringing like a whipped dog.

"Your friend has been mine for many years now, Sivas," the man said, drawing Iosen's attention back to him, "and it is time you joined him."

"But – but you're…"

"Yes?" the man said. "Do you think you recognize me?"

"Black robes without runes," Iosen said, staring at the man's wrists. "There's only one who wears black robes without runes."

The man chuckled. It was dark and held no mirth. "It took the cur hours to realize who I am, and he didn't believe it until I took him to the fortress. Now, say it. Who am I?"

"Y-you're-" Iosen stopped and took a deep breath, forcing himself to calm so he could speak in an even tone. "You're the Necromancer of Skullkeep."

"Very good, Sivas. Perhaps, *you* should be king." The Necromancer directed a look at Leuwyn who cringed even more, if that were possible. "Yes. That possibility merits some thought. At the very least, I wouldn't have to work so hard to explain what I wanted done."

The Necromancer turned back to Iosen and indicated the plush armchairs near the silent hearth.

"Let us sit, Sivas, and you can tell me of your preparations to replace the Council of Magisters with one more amenable to royal oversight."

The Necromancer took a few steps and helped himself to a seat, waiting for Iosen to do likewise. Iosen knew he had no choice and did as he was bidden. Just as Iosen was sitting in the armchair across from the Necromancer, the Black Robe turned his head toward Leuwyn and spoke.

"Be gone, cur; Sivas and I shall have no interruptions to our discussion."

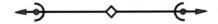

CHAPTER 15

Gavin found himself standing in a void. He could see nothing in any direction, and yet, he felt himself standing on *something*. As Gavin lifted his eyes from looking beneath his feet, he saw a man standing a short distance away; the man was not there a moment ago.

The man appeared young, maybe Gavin's age or a little older, and his attire seemed familiar to Gavin. The fabric making up the attire was navy blue with black pinstripes. There was a jacket with three buttons and a vest beneath the jacket. Gavin could see a white shirt beneath the vest with a line of buttons that disappeared under the vest, and the man wore shiny, black shoes with laces.

His dark hair was styled in a series of spikes that leaned forward.

"Hello, Gavin. I hope my attire makes you feel a little more at home."

"It seems familiar, but I can't remember from where."

"I see the old man took much from you. Greetings and well met. I am Lornithar, and I have a proposition for you."

"'Lornithar' doesn't mean anything to me."

Lornithar gave him a flat look and sighed, saying, "A long time ago, I was driven from my rightful place as ruler of this world by the old ones and those they uplifted, and I will see my place restored. All those who serve me will be rewarded. As for the rest…well… every society needs chattel. You have it within yourself to be one of my greatest lieutenants, and I would have you at my side."

"What of Kiri? Where does she fit into all this?"

"I'm afraid your slave and I—well, her family really—have unfinished business. There will be no such offers for her."

Gavin nodded. "You said you had a proposition for me."

"Yes. I can give you back all the old man took from you. Who you are, where you're from, your daughter…all this I can return to you. All you have to do is agree to serve me, agree to become my agent within the Society of the Arcane."

The ache, the yearning, to know who he was almost pushed Gavin into agreeing, yet a small voice in the back of his mind bade Gavin to wait.

"And what would you have me do, if I agreed to this proposition?"

"You would become my agent within the Society of the Arcane, as I said. Just sit back, bide your time, and collect information on the Society's weaknesses in preparation for our strike. After all, you owe them nothing."

It was a very tempting offer, but still, Gavin could not bring himself to say yes right then.

"You're correct. I don't owe the Society a thing, but I'm never one to make rash decisions. I'd like to consider the matter. Is there any way I can contact you?"

The man's eyes narrowed. The expression he directed to Gavin wasn't *quite* a glare, but it bore no welcome or warmth by any stretch of the imagination.

"There's something else you should know. The wound you sustained will kill you; it's the nature of the blade, you see. It drains life. If you agree to serve me, I can keep the blade at bay."

"I appreciate the information, but it changes nothing. I still need to consider the offer."

"Very well, but I'll give you proof of my good faith, a small piece of who you are. One of mine will contact you."

The man vanished, and Gavin's awareness faded.

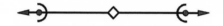

CHAPTER 16

Kiri once again stood in a sickroom beneath the Temple of Valthon, and once again, she watched over Gavin. Seeing him lying there on the cot, so pale…it twisted her guts. His right forearm wasn't pale, though. A rope-like scar curved its way from elbow to wrist, and it was blacker than the deepest night. Kiri had watched it slowly expand and contract several times, almost like the tides.

"Hello, Kiri."

Kiri turned and saw Ovir standing at the foot of Gavin's cot. She jerked her chin toward Gavin as she said, "What's wrong with his arm?"

"Think of it as a scar. Yes, it is an uncommon scar, but the weapon that made it is an uncommon blade. I fear Gavin is not long for this world."

"What? Why?"

"Out of the many instances in which that type of blade has been used, I know of no more than a handful in which the victim lived. Even those few who did survive…well…they were never quite the same afterward."

Movement darkened the room's door, and both Kiri and Ovir

turned to look. Marcus stood in the doorway. His eyes rested on Gavin for a time before he stepped inside and closed the door.

"How is he, Ovir?"

"His life-beat is strong, Marcus, but you can see for yourself the scar left by the Void-blade. He has not awoken yet."

Marcus scowled and crossed his arms. "This is my fault, Ovir. I thought we had more time."

"Marcus, you couldn't have known this would happen, especially so soon after we found him."

Kiri took the steps necessary to kneel at the left side of Gavin's cot. She took his left hand in hers and bowed her head, saying, "Please, come back to us, Gavin. Come back to me."

Everyone started when Gavin took a deep breath.

GAVIN OPENED HIS EYES. Ovir and Marcus stood at the foot of his bed, and Kiri knelt at his left side, his hand clutched in hers as her eyes shone with unshed tears.

Without any preamble, Marcus walked around the bed to approach Gavin from his right side. Nearing the head of the bed, Marcus reached out and pulled down the collar of Gavin's tunic to reveal the base of his neck and the area where his collarbones met. Marcus held the pose for several moments before nodding and returning to Ovir's side.

"What was that about?" Gavin asked.

"I was checking to see if you changed sides."

"And if I had?"

Marcus looked at Gavin in silence for a few moments before saying, "You wouldn't be alive to ask."

Silence took over the room, an awkward weight that settled like a dense, heavy fog.

"He...Lornithar...spoke with me."

Ovir's jaw dropped, but Marcus scoffed.

"I'm not surprised," the old wizard said. "What did he offer you?"

"Full restoration of my memories. He said something about how an old man took much from me. He returned memories of my daughter…as a good-faith gesture, he said."

"Why didn't you agree? I've seen how much you want to know who you are," Kiri said.

Gavin shifted his attention to Kiri, and now, he remained silent for several moments. At last, he said, "There was something about him. I just didn't have a good feeling about him."

Gavin almost mentioned how Lornithar had threatened Kiri's family, but he was torn. He didn't want to cause Kiri any undue worry, and Lornithar didn't seem all that capable of delivering on those threats just yet.

"He must not have been trying very hard with you, then," Marcus said. "Lornithar can be very *persuasive* when he chooses."

"Who is Lornithar anyway? He told me, but I'm not sure I trust him enough to believe what he told me."

Marcus exhaled heavily and said, "At some point in the distant past, before written history, Lornithar came to this world and set himself up as its ruler and god, and he chose lieutenants among each race to enforce his will and round out his 'pantheon.'" Marcus's eyes unfocused as he stared at the wall behind Gavin's head, looking at something only he could see. "Milthas was the first. He was an elf sentenced to death for despicable acts that would make Kiri's last two years seem like a garden party. Lornithar plucked him from the executioner's block and elevated him. It wasn't long until Milthas began styling himself the God of Magic. Lornithar chose eight or so more, and they terrorized this world for uncounted ages as our 'gods.' It wasn't until Valthon and Nesta found us and supported our fight that we had a chance. That was the beginning of the Godswar." Marcus blinked and scanned his surroundings, before shaking himself as if to push away old memories.

An awkward silence descended on the room. No one spoke or moved for several moments. At last, Gavin extracted his left hand from Kiri's grasp and, pushing back the blanket that covered him, swung his feet to the floor. Gavin pushed himself to his feet and swayed…but stayed upright.

"I feel far too weak, but I think I can return to the College."

"That weakness is due to the nature of the blade that wounded you," Marcus said. "Look at your right forearm."

Gavin lifted his right arm and almost gasped at the sight. A wavy line snaked from his elbow to his wrist. The quarter-inch at the center of the line was pure Void, lacking any color or light, but the black became a gradient for the eighth of an inch on either side of the line.

"Marcus! What is this? What happened?"

"You were touched by a Void-blade, a weapon unique to a group known as the Lornithrasa. I won't go into the full particulars right now, but if you were not a wizard, you would never have awoken. The Void-blade drains the life of its victims, consuming their souls, and it is only through the peculiarities of our nature that wizards survive the blade. Do you remember the diagnostic I had you perform? The orb of power?"

"Yes."

"Good. Do it now."

Gavin took a deep breath and closed his eyes. He focused on the seed of power at the pit of his soul and pushed it into his arm and down to his hand, willing it to manifest. Gavin felt the first pin-prick of light appear and began drawing from the ambient power that suffused all creation, feeding the pin-prick and growing it into a kaleidoscopic sphere about the size of a tennis ball.

"Open your eyes, and look at the scar on your arm."

Gavin opened his eyes and felt his eyes widen just a bit. The thick line was no more; the scar was just thick enough to distinguish, about twice the diameter of fine thread.

"How do you feel, Gavin?"

The orb of power wobbled a bit as Gavin took stock of himself, shifting to an oversized egg for a few moments.

"I feel normal. I'm not weak anymore."

"Yes, you do. The power that makes us what we are is anathema to the Void-blade and what it does. You will never be able to rid yourself of that scar or its effects, but you can mitigate it for brief periods. So...are you certain you're ready to return to the College?"

Gavin allowed the orb to dissipate and felt the weakness return. He was watching the scar when he released the orb and watched the wavy, black thread become the wavy, black rope he first saw.

"I had better be, don't you think? Especially if what I feel right now is my new 'normal?'"

Marcus smiled and nodded.

Gavin turned to Ovir and extended his hand, which Ovir accepted and gave a firm handshake, as he said, "Ovir, thank you for your hospitality once again. Don't take this the wrong way, but I hope it's quite some time before I see this part of the Temple again."

Ovir laughed. "I don't doubt it, and I agree!"

Gavin glanced over the room once more before he extended his left hand to Kiri. She seemed to hesitate a moment before she approached and accepted Gavin's invitation.

"Ovir, I'll see you for our weekly game," Marcus said, before leading Gavin and Kiri into the hallway.

* * *

By the time they approached the door to Marcus's suite, Kiri supported most of Gavin's weight, and the Void-scar enveloped most of Gavin's forearm. More than once as Gavin grew weaker and leaned more and more on Kiri, Marcus had tried to take some of the load, but she wouldn't have it.

Marcus opened the suite's door, and Kiri helped Gavin to the room they shared. She helped him reach the bed, where Gavin sat. Kiri saw how much effort it cost Gavin to hold himself sitting upright.

"Give me just a moment, Kiri, and I'll go to bed," Gavin said, his voice a soft shadow of its usual strength.

Kiri stepped past him and retrieved his pillow from the floor, placing it on the bed. "You're already there, Gavin."

"No…your bed."

"You nearly died yesterday, Gavin; there's no way I'm allowing you to sleep on the floor."

Kiri thought he would argue further, but Gavin's eyelids drooped. Kiri stepped close and guided him gently to lay on his right side, his head resting on the pillow. She stepped back and watched Gavin sleep, the slow rhythmic motion of his chest as he breathed. *Why couldn't you have found me when I washed up on that beach?*

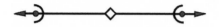

CHAPTER 17

Gavin's eyes opened with a jerk. *I'm wide awake. I'm never instantly wide awake, and what am I doing in Kiri's bed? Oh, damn...did I...did we....?*

A quick glance showed Gavin he was laying atop the blankets and covers, fully clothed. He left the bed as gently and quietly as he could and turned. Kiri lay sleeping on the other side of the bed, wrapped up in the covers. He lifted his right arm and saw the black, rope-like Void-scar; it was thinner than he remembered.

So, it wasn't just a bad dream. Gavin caught a whiff of himself as he examined the Void-scar and shook his head. *Woof...I need to buy Kiri something nice for letting such a foul-smelling soul borrow half of her bed.*

A SHORT TIME LATER, Gavin emerged from the washroom clean, dressed, and ready to face the day. He walked across the chambers to place his sleeping garments in his room and pull on socks and shoes before returning to sit in the armchair across from Marcus. It was several more minutes before Marcus closed the journal and laid both it and the quill aside.

"I'm sorry about making you wait, Gavin," Marcus said as he

stood and stretched. "I had a particularly compelling train of thought I wanted to record before it was lost to the day's events."

When Marcus remained standing, Gavin stood as well, as he said, "It's all right, Marcus. It gave me the opportunity to work the last bits of sleep out of my head. So…are we going to begin by studying geography today?"

Marcus shook his head as he started walking toward the suite's door. "While we could spend several weeks straight discussing only geography, I'm of the opinion the best learning environment is one that covers multiple subjects. From here on out, we'll follow a set schedule. Every morning will be devoted to your studies of the Art, but the afternoons will rotate through geography, history, politics, and current events."

On the ground floor, Marcus turned and led Gavin deep into the Tower's lower levels. They went past the two floors that served as storage halls and exited the staircase on the third underground floor. At specific intervals, they passed doors on either side of the well-lit hallway. These doors were engraved with all manner of runes Gavin didn't understand, and the whole area made him feel as if his blood were on fire.

"Where are we, Marcus?" Gavin asked as they made their third left turn and the floor started angling down. The walls shifted from the smooth, solid stone that made up most of the College's construction into a hewn-rock passageway, which made Gavin think they were entering a cave.

"We've just passed the summoning classrooms," Marcus said as he continued walking. "They're heavily protected to ensure that none of the class 'projects' escape into the College proper. The first rooms we passed are used to teach the basic summoning spells, whereas the protections in these last three or four are designed for the…well, no class ever summons anything that would require those rooms."

"Oh," Gavin said. "Those are the rooms for the powerful summoning spells?"

"Quite so."

The floor's angle of descent gradually steepened as they

progressed down its corkscrew path, though never becoming a dangerous grade, until it leveled and straightened without warning. Some thirty feet ahead Gavin saw a massive door with even more runes etched into its surface than the powerful summoning rooms they'd passed a short time ago.

As the pair approached the door, a man-shaped specter faded into view on the right-hand side of the door. The specter was just visible enough to see it 'wore' a kind of plate armor, with two swords strapped across its back.

The specter addressed Marcus, saying, "It has been some time since you last visited this place, milord. Have you come to request my duties as Master of the Field?"

"No, old friend, not today," Marcus said. "This young man is my apprentice, and the arena's the safest place available for a novice to practice Words of Power."

The specter bowed deeply at the waist before turning and reaching into the door. A massive *clack-thud* echoed all around them, and the door began to rise up into the ceiling.

GAVIN NOW FOUND himself standing in a massive cavern. Aside from the fifteen-foot-wide path that allowed individuals to enter the space, stone bleachers seven levels high stood in sections centered on what would be the site of the main event. The arena floor was loose dirt, though not so deep the bedrock beneath it couldn't be felt, and in the very center of the space a thirty-feet-wide copper ring was set into the floor with only an inch or so rising above the dirt.

"Wow, Marcus," Gavin said as he turned all around on his path toward the arena ring, "this is amazing. Who made this? No, wait… I'm guessing Kirloth and his apprentices were involved."

Marcus smiled a bit, nodding. "You're quite correct. Kirloth, Mivar, Roshan, Wygoth, and Cothos created the arena after the principal work on the city and College were complete. Up until then, all wizard duels took place about half a league from the city down the highway that became the Tel Roshan Road. Now, tell me what you sense with your *skathos*."

Gavin stopped and closed his eyes, concentrating on his new sense. "It feels about the same as our suite in the Tower. There's the general ambient 'noise' you told me was normal for Tel. I can tell we're under the city, but I can't gauge how far."

"Good. Now, step into the ring."

Gavin did as instructed and gasped. "Marcus, it all went away! It's quiet in here."

"The ring in the floor you crossed was imbued with powerful anti-magic effects. Those effects don't block magic; they simply ensure any effects created outside the ring will not affect anything inside the ring and vice versa."

Gavin grinned like a starving child presented with a feast. "I really like it here, Marcus. Can I live down here?"

"Gavin, you are not a dwarf," Marcus said, his tone severe for a moment before he broke into a small laugh. "It is peaceful down here, though."

A few moments of silence passed before Marcus shook himself.

"Now, as to your lesson today. Everything the College teaches today is based upon the old ways. The history classes teach that Kirloth and Bellos devised a new magic after the Godswar, something less dangerous than the Words of Power. That's utter rubbish. Kirloth, Bellos, and Mivar devised a new way of accessing the power the Words manipulate."

Marcus took a deep breath and, glancing around the arena, indicated for Gavin to follow him to one set of stone bleachers. He indicated Gavin to sit and began the lesson in earnest.

"Bellos received a number of insights upon his ascendance to the ranks of the divine. Among them was the knowledge that as the years progressed fewer wizards would be born, and those wizards who were born would gradually be weaker in the Art than those who came before. Now, as the new God of Magic, it was Bellos's responsibility to ensure magic did not fade from the world; there were multiple reasons why the loss of magic would be a very bad thing, but those reasons are a discussion for another time. Suffice it to say, Bellos needed a new source of magic-users.

"At that point in history, the only arcanists were wizards; no one ever considered that there might be another way of using magic. Bellos came to Tel Mivar to discuss the problem with his former mentor, and since Mivar had just completed the final volume of his Histories and was looking for a project, the three of them began work into devising a new system of magic."

"But I thought the College taught that Bellos and Kirloth devised the new system alone," Gavin said.

Marcus turned to face Gavin, frowning. "How did you hear that?"

Gavin shrugged. "I heard students talking in the dining hall. I gathered they were discussing homework assignments."

"Over the last four hundred years or so, there's been a rift slowly growing between the Council of Magisters and the Great Houses. The way they see it, Bellos is a god, and Kirloth is safely dead, but Mivars still exist. They see no reason to do or say anything that might give House Mivar any more of an advantage than it already has. The history curriculum here is a product of that, but as I was saying…

"Arcanists have always used eight of the nine Schools of Magic. The fruit of their labor is what modern scholars call the Circle System, with the addition of a ninth School: Thaumaturgy. Under the Circle System, spells are classified into one of five Circles based on the spell's power and required level of relative mastery. It's roughly an exponential progression; a Second Circle spell is about twice as powerful as a First, but a Third Circle spell is roughly three times as powerful as a Second. Now, many today believe that the Circle System is an evolution of magic into a safer and better system. That point of view is also utter rubbish. The Circle System is a dilution; there is no way a Fifth Circle evocation cast by a mage will ever be as powerful as the weakest Word of Evocation invoked by a competent wizard."

"I guess I don't understand magic well enough," Gavin said, "because I don't see how it's a dilution."

Marcus gave Gavin a small smile as he said, "The explanation of 'why' is the focus of today's lesson: the nature of wizards and wizardry. I explained this a little bit when we first met. Wizards have within them a core of power; it is something they are born with, and we have never been able to understand why we have it. There's no rhyme or reason to who will be born a wizard that I've been able to determine, either. I've seen children of two wizard parents born with no power whatsoever, and I've seen powerful wizards born to families that have no hint of power for generations. The Great Houses of Tel, at least, seem to have at least one wizard per generation, thankfully, though Andrin Mivar is a bit of an outlier. To make it even more difficult to understand, the strength of that core of power varies from wizard to wizard. All magic manipulates reality, whether you're a wizard, a mage, or one of Ovir's clerics, but arcanists manipulate reality at the most fundamental level."

Marcus fell silent for a time, and his face developed an expression Gavin didn't understand. After several moments, Marcus sighed.

"Gavin, I thought we would have more time. Ovir told me the Lornithrasa were active again when he first told me of your arrival in the city, but I underestimated the threat they posed. I had planned to start slowly and present small, concrete examples for each progression of learning. Now, I fear we must accelerate things a bit."

"How so, Marcus?"

"In my youth, it would have been unheard of for a mentor to discuss this next topic with an apprentice still so new to the Art: composite effects. A composite effect is created when a wizard invokes multiple Words at once, but to understand what that means, we must address the one, essential truth: the effect is shaped by the wizard's intent."

Marcus turned and, gesturing for Gavin to follow, strode across the arena to stand within the ring. He produced a scroll from within his robe and lifted it to shoulder level.

"This is a scroll of Fireball. Fireball is a Second Circle spell of the Evocation School, and it is woefully overused. It seems like every budding mage simply has to learn how to cast it."

Marcus took the scroll in both hands and unrolled it. He read the words scribed upon the parchment and, upon his successful completion, pointed his finger into the air. A single pin-point of light the color of classic, red-orange flame shot upward some forty feet and expanded into a thirty-foot sphere of flame.

"Every fireball cast by a mage is the same, because what you just saw is all that the spell can create. But what if a wizard wants a fireball?"

Marcus spoke a Word of Power and pointed once more with his finger. Gavin felt the invocation through his *skathos* as a sphere of red-orange fire the size of a peach pit flew into the air. It reached a point about fifty feet up and violently erupted into a solid sphere of flame before it dissipated.

"That," Marcus said, "was a wizard's fireball. Did you feel the difference?"

Gavin nodded. "The scroll felt like a small stone thrown into a pool. That felt like a boulder."

"Good. When I was a child, I slipped into the blacksmith's place at my father's estate and put a piece of copper in the forge. The heat was such the copper caught fire long before it reached the coals, but what fascinated me the most was that the flames produced by the burning copper were green. Watch."

Marcus spoke the Word once more and pointed up. Gavin felt Marcus's power slam against his *skathos* again and watched as another peach pit of fire flew upward and exploded in flame. This time, though, the flame was green. Gavin stared in silence.

"Some things produce blue flames when they burn," Marcus said and repeated the invocation to create a blue fireball, "but all this fire is making me a bit warm. How about some ice?"

Marcus repeated the exact same Word, only this time a thirty-foot sphere of ice was the result, which dissipated into a mist on its way down to the wizards.

"Marcus, that is amazing."

"A mage could not do what I've just done. This is the ultimate expression of the one, essential truth. We'll start with illusions; your first illusion will be a static image of a horse; everyone knows what a horse looks like."

As it turned out, Gavin didn't know what a horse looked like…

or maybe he was having trouble translating what he saw in his mind into the static illusion. His first attempt left him doubled over, hands on his knees and gasping. The image in front of Gavin was a most anorexic animal, barely more than a stick figure. Gavin did a decent job envisioning a horse's head, however, making the image even more absurd.

"Well," Marcus said as he scratched his beard, "I see we have some room for improvement."

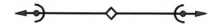

CHAPTER 18

Marcus stood on the quay overlooking Tel Mivar's harbor, and a stiff breeze blew down the river valley, slowing ships' progress into the harbor. Marcus's thoughts strayed to his apprentice back in the Tower, who was (hopefully) pursuing his studies. He almost regretted not asking Gavin to accompany him down to the docks, but then again, the boy was quick-witted. It was altogether possible Gavin would see enough to start assembling the pieces to puzzles he shouldn't even know exist yet.

A ship flying a Vushaari flag coasted into the harbor, towed by a longboat filled with strong oarsmen. The deck crew already had the fenders cast over the side to protect the ship and dock from each other, and Marcus watched the longboat's crew bring the ship within reach of the line-handlers on the dock. The ship's crew threw lines to the men waiting on the dock and removed the tow line supplied by the longboat. The longboat rowed out of the ship's path before returning to the harbor for the next ship as the line-men pulled the ship the last few yards into dock. Within moments, the gangplank was down and the passengers disembarking.

A man in simple traveling clothes walked off the ship in the middle of the small crowd. The crowd around him had chatty women, parents with children, and well-dressed businessmen and business-women. The man almost stood out in how unremarkable he seemed. He kept his dark hair well-trimmed, and a thin beard came down from his sideburns to run along the line of his jaw and circle his mouth. The clothes failed to conceal the man's muscular physique.

The instrument case in his right hand protected one of the finest lutes in the known world, and his left held the thick straps of the gray canvas duffel bag slung over that same shoulder. He scanned the area around him as he moved, and though his eyes found Marcus at once, his vigilance did not cease.

"What? No orange schooner?" Marcus asked as the man approached.

He shrugged through the weight of the duffel. "Well, milord, you did say you wanted me to be unrecognized. Declan the Dandy is off scouring the western archipelagos, looking for undiscovered accounts of events in some of the ancient epics. Everyone knows that; you should've seen the crowd on the docks of Birsha when he left." The man broke into a huge grin. "My brother takes such a child-like delight in portraying me; you should've seen his smile when I asked him to take the schooner to the archipelagos."

"You never disappoint me, Declan," Marcus said, gesturing for the man to walk with him. "That is why I had them summon you."

All trace of banter and joviality disappeared from Declan's demeanor as he fell into step with Marcus. "What's the mission, sir?"

"Oh, no need to be so formal as all that. I have a new apprentice-"

"A new apprentice? Really?" Declan asked, turning his head to show Marcus his right eyebrow quirking upward. "I seem to recall you having a rather specific opinion on the idea of taking any new apprentices."

"Yes...well...he came highly recommended by an old friend," Marcus said. "In fact, my apprentice is why you are here. It is my intent for you to earn his trust and become an associate. It is not an infiltration but a protection detail hiding in plain sight. While you're working on that, I would appreciate it if you would assist me in rounding out his training. There are many aspects of the world you have seen that I have not, and I feel the knowledge those experiences have given you would be of value to Gavin at some point in his life.

"I had not intended to bring you into this quite so soon, but I'm afraid the Lornithrasa forced my hand. They attacked a few days after Gavin arrived, and were it not for the intervention of an as-yet-unknown archer, the local Wraiths would not have had time to respond."

"I see, milord," Declan said as they walked, head lowered in thought and stepping aside for a crew of longshoreman moving toward the ship Declan had just departed. "Do you have any specifics in mind for my training curriculum?"

"Show him the weak points of the Art," Marcus said, taking effort to avoid a coil of rope another longshoreman was preparing for a ship being towed in by another longboat. Fortunately, they were close to leaving the docks. "He also has a slave. I think learning your style of blade-work will be asset in the future...to both of them. That's all that comes to mind right now. I leave the rest up to you. Oh, and I have arranged your usual quarters at the College."

* * *

"Gavin?"

Gavin pulled his eyes away from the tome Marcus had set him to reading and saw Kiri standing at the edge of the table. He sat at the center of the long edge with his back to the library door. He could see her working her lower lip between her teeth and how her fingers fidgeted at her waist. *She's nervous about something.*

"Yes, Kiri?"

"Can we...I mean, am I disturbing you?"

Kiri wore one of the dresses the tailor had made. It was green with silver trim and hugged almost every curve Kiri possessed. Fabric went up her chest and back to join at her neck where a clasp secured them; her shoulders and arms were bare, and the skirt fell to mid-shin from where it gathered at her hips.

"Not at all," Gavin said, closing the book before him and gesturing to the unoccupied chairs around the table. "Is something wrong?"

"No," Kiri said, taking a seat at the end of the table. "I just wanted to thank you for protecting me. I'm sure it's not easy having your peers think you are the kind of person who condones slavery and consorts with those who perpetuate it."

"Well, you are certainly welcome. I meant what I said about not throwing you back into the world that harmed you. Besides, I'd say they're far more unsettled by me being House Kirloth; I doubt they're even aware of you."

"Oh, no; they're aware of me. You wouldn't believe how many pairs of eyes watch me whenever I go anywhere unaccompanied."

Gavin's eyes narrowed just a bit. "Has anyone-"

"No...not a one...but that doesn't mean they can't look at me."

They were both silent for a time. Gavin gazed into her eyes and found he didn't want to look away.

"Yes, well...I can't honestly hold that against them. I can't deny enjoying the sight of you in motion; you possess a grace and poise most uncommon for most people I've seen." Gavin's breath caught in his throat as he realized what he'd just said, and he suppressed a cough. "Forgive me; I don't want to make you uncomfortable. I don't know why I admitted that."

Kiri lowered her eyes to the table, where she fidgeted with her fingers. "I can see how hard you work at giving me space, at not being like all the other men I've known these past two years. It means more to me than you know."

Gavin didn't know what to say to that, whether he should say she was welcome, so he nodded in acknowledgement. He watched her fidget with her fingers in silence, determined not to direct the conversation or push her to say more than she wanted.

"I was betrothed when my father sent me away, and my father wouldn't let him come with me. As the ship pulled away from the dock, I wanted to hate my father; I thought we were so in love.

Given how events unfolded, I'm relieved; he would be dead or worse…"

"Do you miss him?"

"Miss him specifically? No…but I do miss my innocence, my uncomplicated view of the world. Back then, the only men I knew were my father and those he chose to associate with; they were all good people, upstanding citizens. I thought I was so in love and so lucky; I thought I'd found what my parents had. Looking back on it now, I don't see how I could possibly have been in love. I was such a child, no matter how much of a woman I looked."

Kiri fell silent again for a time, and Gavin didn't want to say or do anything that might make her leave.

"You said Lornithar returned memories of your daughter."

"That's right. I-"

"Tell me about her?"

"I'm not sure what all there is to tell, really. I was twenty when she was born, and I was so happy. Whoever started the tradition of calling babies 'little bundles of joy' certainly knew what they were talking about. We named her Jennifer Anne, the middle names of our mothers, but don't ask me which one was 'Anne' or which one was 'Jennifer.' I don't see how I could lose the memory of her taking her first steps or the first time she looked up at me and said, 'Da-da.' She'll be turning thirteen soon, wherever she is; at least, I think she will be. The last memory I have about her is choosing a pendant for her thirteenth birthday in a jewelry store; it was a silver angel-wing pendant with a ruby in the center."

"You don't seem thirty-three to me; you don't look that old."

Gavin chuckled. "Thanks, I guess."

"I'd love to have what you have."

"What? A daughter?"

"The lack of memories."

The wistfulness Gavin felt was gone in a finger-snap, and he shook his head as he lifted his eyes to meet Kiri's. "No, you don't… not one bit. Look, I understand the last two years were bad; I'll never understand just how bad they were, but I realize they were bad. No matter how bad they were, though, you have no idea what it's like to live with a void where your sense of self should be, a hole that should be filled with all the experiences of your life that made you who you are. You don't want this, Kiri; no matter how bad you think your life is, you don't want this."

Just then, the solid *click* of the suite's lock releasing echoed through the common room, and Gavin and Kiri watched the door swing wide. Marcus entered the suite, trailed by a man in earth-toned traveling clothes. The old wizard smiled at seeing Gavin and Kiri together.

"Ah, there you both are," he said as he stepped aside to allow the other to enter the room. "It saves me from having to track down one of you. Gavin, Kiri, I would like to introduce Declan deHavand-"

Kiri gasped, her hand flying to her mouth.

Marcus stopped speaking and focused on her, saying, "Yes? Do you have something to say?"

"I always heard that Declan the Dandy's real name was Declan deHavand," Kiri said, her voice almost a whisper.

"People hear a lot of things, young lady," Marcus said. "It's always a challenging task to separate fact from fiction."

Gavin's eyes narrowed on his mentor. "You didn't say she was wrong, Marcus."

"He's got you there, old friend," the man introduced as Declan said overtop a chuckle. "Yes, the lady is quite correct. To the world at large, I am the bard known as Declan the Dandy. However, I have much older allegiances than the Traditions and *Skuv Ir Nathene*, and I am here in response to those. It would be best that you ask nothing further on the matter, as I won't answer, and the asking could precipitate an unpleasant situation, depending on who hears the question."

Gavin and Kiri both nodded, while Kiri swallowed a bit hard.

Marcus sighed, saying, "Yes, well...as I was saying, Declan will be joining your training curriculum, Gavin, and I would also appreciate it if you kept him with you whenever you or you and Kiri should go into the city."

"Aren't I a little old to have a chaperone, Marcus?" Gavin asked.

"Nonsense. I would never insult Declan by having him be a

chaperone. Gavin, the Lornithrasa have already attempted to kill you once, and they did manage to scar you with a Void-blade. I am not prepared to risk your life by allowing illusions of privacy outside the grounds of the College. From here on out, we will split your academic studies to allow you time to train with him. Kiri, given that your schedule is a bit more open, you shall train with Declan every morning."

"But it is a capital offense for a slave to possess a blade," Kiri said.

"How quaint, child; you think I care about the royal laws," Marcus replied. "Even if some poor sod became aware of the training you will be receiving *and* managed to gain entrance to the college grounds, the individual would then face me. Besides, I have no interest in provoking a confrontation with the worthless sot who currently wears the crown or his sycophants; you will not possess a blade outside College grounds. Do you have any further objections?"

Kiri shook her head and lowered her eyes.

"Very well," Marcus said. "We shall begin the new training schedule next week."

* * *

AT THE APPOINTED TIME, Declan came to Marcus's suite to collect Gavin. Gavin looked up from the book that was the current focus of his attention and had to force himself not to stare. When Gavin first met him, Declan wore earth-toned clothing and looked so unremarkable no one would've thought to pay him any mind in a crowd of more than four people. Declan was no longer nondescript.

Declan stood just inside the door of Marcus's suite, though it was anyone's guess how he'd opened it with no medallion. He wore leather armor that was a matte midnight black, blacker even than the dye typically used to produce black leather, and Gavin thought he counted no less than eight dagger hilts in his cursory examination.

"How many do you see?" Declan asked.

"Eight," Gavin said.

"Better than most," Declan said as he flexed and stretched his fingers, "but you're still low."

Kiri stepped out of the room she and Gavin shared. She'd returned from her first session with Declan a short time before lunch, and she moved like she was *very* sore.

"Do you mind if I come with you?" Kiri asked. "I'd like to watch."

"I have no objections," Declan said. "Gavin?"

"Something tells me I shouldn't be so willing to have an audience for my first session with you," Gavin said with a shrug, "but why not?"

DECLAN AND GAVIN stood just inside the arena ring but on opposite sides, and Kiri sat on the third row of a section of stone bleachers. Declan held a training dagger in his hand, and Gavin was unarmed, save for what he knew.

"So, what Words have you learned, Gavin?" Declan asked.

"Uhm…well, I know a Word of Interation."

Declan lifted his left hand in a 'stop' gesture. "Let's stay away from death magic, Gavin; I'd just as soon live to a ripe, old age. What else?"

"The only Words Marcus taught me to use are those of Illusion, but I've picked up a Word of Conjuration and a Word of Transmutation on my own."

"Conjuration," Declan said. "Can you use that to duplicate the mage spell Light?"

"I don't know," Gavin said. "What does the mage spell Light do?"

"It creates a palm-sized sphere of white light within a foot of the mage. The mage has some limited control over the sphere, but nothing significant. Most mages use it in place of a reading lamp."

"Oh! Yes, I can duplicate that."

Declan smiled. "Excellent. Gavin, I want you to create a sphere of light on the tip of my nose. Begin whenever you're ready."

"Uhm, Declan? Are you sure about this?" Gavin asked. "Anything I create will probably be rather bright. I don't want to hurt you."

"I'll take my chances."

Okay…he asked for this, Gavin thought. He was much better at clearing his mind of all distractions than he had once been, and it took very little time at all to form a mental picture of a sphere of white light on the tip of Declan's nose. Gavin drew in a breath to speak and invoked the Word of Conjuration, saying, "*Nythraex.*"

Declan waited until Gavin opened his mouth to speak. He then simply took one step back, which carried him outside the arena ring, but his eyes widened and his jaw slackened when a bright, white haze formed in the air just in front of him and hung there for a heartbeat—at most—before it dissipated.

"Hey!" Gavin said. "You cheated!"

"No, Gavin; I did not," Declan said, schooling his features back to neutral. "The only objective in a fight to the death is to win. If we had been in such a fight, I would've been at a severe disadvantage at any range beyond arm's reach…especially if you used the Word of Interation you know. That's the second rule of killing a wizard: be within arm's reach."

Gavin felt a chill go through him. "What's the first rule?"

"Don't let the wizard know you're a threat…until it's too late."

"Okay," Gavin said, swallowing hard. "Is there a third?"

"No," Declan said. "If you fail at the first and then fail at the second, you won't live long enough for a third to be of any help."

Declan stepped back into the arena ring, continuing to speak. "Did you see what I did? I used the environment against you. You must always be aware of where you are and what's around you; you never know when something that is insignificant to everyone else just might save your life. Now, let's do it again. Put a sphere of light on the tip of my nose."

He's not going to pull that on me a second time. I'm close enough to this side of the ring that I can take a step back and be outside it, too. I just need to hold my focus and the invocation together while I take the step; I've never done that before.

Declan was only the periphery of Gavin's focus as he cleared his mind and drew breath to speak, so when Gavin perceived movement across the ring, he took a step to the side, which carried him outside the ring...just in time to catch a soft tomato full in the face. Gavin squawked and fell backward, his arms wind milling until he landed on his backside in the mixture of sawdust and dirt. A small cloud of dust rose around him, and Gavin wiped away the remains of the tomato to the accompaniment of Kiri's laughter.

When Gavin finished raking tomato off his face and out of his eyes, he found Declan standing over him. Gavin fully expected to see the bard laughing along with Kiri and was surprised to find him serious.

"Never be so focused on what you're doing that you lose sight of what the other guy's doing," Declan said as he held out a hand to Gavin.

Gavin accepted the hand and allowed Declan to help him to his feet.

"Have any other vegetables hidden somewhere?" Gavin asked, his tone only half teasing.

"Tomatoes are fruits, and let's hope you don't need to find out," Declan said as he turned and started walking for the door. "Come! We're going to walk the grounds. We will divide the grounds into eighths, focusing on an eighth each session, and you will compile a list of any innocuous objects that could be used to shift the advantage of a fight to your favor."

"What about Kiri?" Gavin asked as he hastened to catch Declan.

"She compiled her list for the section we'll be visiting this morning. I'm looking forward to seeing how—or even if—yours compares to hers."

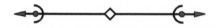

CHAPTER 19

G avin's days settled into a familiar routine. Each morning, Marcus exposed Gavin to complex concepts of arcane theory he said even the Council of Magisters would be hard-pressed to understand; Gavin doubted that assertion, but there was no denying his increased facility with the Art. Some three weeks into his studies, Gavin remained standing through an invocation, a feat Marcus assured him most wizards of his power would not do at his stage of experience.

Gavin spent the bulk of his afternoons studying the topic of the day, whether that was geography, history, or current events, but no matter what the afternoon topic, there was still time set aside for Gavin to study with Declan.

GAVIN LEFT the bedroom he shared with Kiri intent on washing up before the morning studies with Marcus, and he found his mentor sitting in his favorite armchair and gazing into the hearth. Something in the old man's demeanor pulled at Gavin's attention, and he stopped.

"Is something wrong, Marcus?"

Silence reigned over the space for several moments before Marcus lifted his eyes to look at Gavin.

"Wrong? No...I wouldn't say it's wrong." Marcus held up a folded piece of parchment. "I received a request this morning that changes my timetable yet again for our studies. Normally, I would reject the request out of hand, for it truly is an absurd waste of your time. And yet...despite it being a waste, there may be some merit to the idea." Marcus nodded his head toward the bathroom. "Go wash up. We'll begin the day once you're finished."

GAVIN EXITED the bathroom to find Marcus sitting at the table. He saw the folded parchment off to Marcus's left, while Marcus held two sheets of parchment yellowed with age.

"Sit, Gavin," Marcus said, pointing to the chair across the table from him. Once Gavin was seated, Marcus extended one of the two old pieces of parchment. "Read that, please."

Gavin accepted the parchment and looked at it. The ink was faded, almost to the point of illegibility in places, but enough remained that Gavin could discern the words.

"'We cannot...begin to discuss...the world-changing event... that has become known as the Godswar...without discussing...one of its most...central figures: the arcanist known only as Kirloth.'" Gavin looked up from the parchment. "Marcus, I've read this before. It's part of the introduction to Mivar's Histories."

Marcus extended the second aged piece of parchment in silence.

Gavin accepted it and found the ink was just as faded as the first.

"'Master, I compose this missive to inform you of my coming works. I feel compelled to chronicle the horrors we have survived, lest we make some future choice in ignorance that would undo all we have fought to achieve. I cannot in good conscience choose what parts to include, and many of the events do not paint you in a kind light. It is not my intent to anger or defame you, but I could not publish my work without you being aware of its content. Your apprentice and friend, Mivar.'"

Gavin looked up from the parchment to see Marcus holding his medallion, rubbing his thumb across its surface.

"Gavin, have you noticed anything odd about the people you encounter after donning that medallion?"

Gavin nodded. "I don't understand why, but something about this medallion makes people uncomfortable...if not outright afraid. I saw it at the Temple when I walked there with Kiri. I saw it before we reached the Temple, too, just walking through the crowds in the markets; people stepped away from us when they saw me."

"Do you know why?"

Gavin shook his head.

Marcus stopped rubbing his medallion and let it fall to rest against his chest once more. Gavin felt his eyes widen at the sight of it. The recessed center was no longer blank; it now bore the same glyph as Gavin's medallion.

"The people are uneasy around you...because of me. I am Kirloth, and one day, you will be Kirloth. Today, we're going to discuss what that means."

"Surely, you don't mean that you're *this* Kirloth," Gavin said, lifting the old pieces of parchment as example. "You'd have to be... what...six thousand years old?"

"I am in truth 6,138 years old, Gavin. I was born the eldest of three brothers; my given name is Amdar. My brothers are—or were —Gerrus and Marin. Gerrus was your grandfather, a great many times removed, and you probably saw Marin's statue in the Hall of the Gods. That is why you are House Kirloth."

Gavin sat staring at the pieces of parchment. He had not a thought in the world of how to respond.

"It is an incredible weight to process, I know," Marcus said.

"Does anyone else know you're Kirloth? I mean, *the* Kirloth?"

"Valera, the Magister of Divination, does...and probably Ovir."

"Why do you hide it?"

"Think about how people react to your medallion, Gavin."

Gavin thought back to all the uncomfortable glances, the people shying away, and nodded.

"Now, picture the reactions they'd have to the man who built that reputation in the first place, the man who founded this country. I was the first Archmagister, Gavin, the first to wear the gold robes. The people are so fed up with the king and the state of Tel that there would be riots, mass uprisings demanding I take the throne as Archmagister once more. There would be a civil war, and I would have to kill a great many people to end it. The world cannot afford for Tel to endure that upheaval just now; too many events are coming together."

Gavin frowned. "So, if I'm Gerrus's descendant…I'm from the Refugee World? That's where I was born?"

"Yes. I never completed my studies in cross-planar scrying or teleportation, so I have no way—at present—of returning you home."

"I'm not sure I'd want to go home not remembering who I am or who my family is. Why did Valthon take my memories?"

"What makes you say He did?"

Gavin sighed. "Lornithar said something about 'an old man took much from me.' I don't really remember the conversation, but that part stuck. The only 'old man' I imagine Lornithar would even discuss is Valthon."

Marcus nodded. "Perhaps, you are right, but Valthon wouldn't *take* your memories. Hide them? Certainly, but never take them. Those memories and the experiences they represent are what made you who you are. No. If He did anything, He hid them for a time. As for why…the only reason that comes to mind is that something about those memories and experiences would have affected how you view and interact with this world. He must have wanted you able to approach all this with a clean slate, as it were."

"I guess I can understand that. It doesn't make it fun to be on the receiving end, though."

"No," Marcus said with a slight chuckle, "I don't imagine it would. Gavin, for all the long years since our victory in the Godswar, I have been what some have called 'the Instrument Outside of Time.' I have moved through the background of the world, ensuring everything we built during the Founding is protected and handling any extraordinary situations that arise, usually in a manner that makes a point. Take Kalinor, for example."

"Who? Oh…you mean the guy who used to own Kiri?"

"Yes."

"I'm still amazed that you were able to convince him to turn her over to me. Kiri is…well…she's striking; I can't imagine it was easy."

"Gavin, I never convinced Kalinor to turn Kiri over to you. He was of the same opinion you are and felt there was nothing for him in giving her up."

"Then, how…?"

Marcus invoked a Word of Power, "*Klaepos.*" Gavin felt the power slam into him, but it didn't hurt as much as he was expecting. A circular area in the air just above the table's surface began rippling like the surface of a pond into which a stone has been thrown. The rippling increased until the circle flashed a bright, white light.

Gavin found himself looking over a patch of ground near a road somewhere. Round protrusions of what might have once been stone drew out a rough design of an estate with a manor wall and various outbuildings plus the manor house. Inside the rectangular line of the manor wall, the ground was charred and blackened. There was no grass. There were no trees.

"Marcus, what is this?"

"What you see is all that remains of Kalinor's estate. The man's majordomo was in truth one of my agents…had been for some time. When I approached Kalinor with a very generous offer, he chose to decline it. My agent spirited away all those he felt could be saved or were innocent, and I laid waste to the rest."

Gavin stared at the circular image. His jaw worked for some time before he spoke.

"Marcus, how could you do that? How many people were still there?"

"I don't know. I trust my man, though. He had been there for the better part of three years and knew everyone on that estate better than they knew themselves. If he felt that only the kitchen staff and their families should escape, you can rest assured no innocents died there. This, Gavin…this is what it means to be Kirloth. We do what must be done to safeguard the world."

"No! I don't care what you say, Marcus. I would *never* d-do…*that*!"

"In a way, you already have. Do you remember when you met Kiri? The slavers who attacked you?"

"What of them?"

"Do you know what happened when you invoked that Word? Do you even know what Word you invoked?"

Gavin felt a sinking feeling in the pit of his stomach. He didn't remember much from his first invocation, but he did remember the Word. He had yet to ask Marcus what it did, and now, it seemed asking was no longer his choice to make.

Marcus accepted Gavin's silence for an answer. "You were focused on the slavers when you invoked the Word, yes?"

"You know I was."

"The Word you used was one of the fundamental Words of Interation, Gavin, one of the most powerful. Fifty-three slavers throughout the southwestern warrens died that day, and only three people know the truth. Well…four, now."

Gavin collapsed against the chair. His skin felt cold, clammy. His breath came in short, ragged gasps, and he couldn't quite process what Marcus was telling him.

"The town guard consulted the Magister of Interation, and he confirmed it was an Interation effect, but he wasn't able to tell them anymore than that. The effect was beyond his capability to duplicate; he's a mage, you see."

"You said four people know, now. You and I are two; who are the others?"

"Ovir and Valera. I don't believe you've had the occasion to meet Valera yet. As I mentioned earlier, she's the Magister of Divination, but she's also the Collegiate Justice, overseeing all offenses at the College."

"Why am I not in jail for murder?"

"Honestly? Because I don't really give a damn about slavers. I abhor the entire institution, and if I had my preferences, the entire group would be dead. You're far too valuable as a wizard to spend a brief time in the city dungeon before visiting the headsman's block. Besides, an old friend said to train you as only I can, which tells me you have more yet ahead of you."

Gavin sighed.

"But fifty-three people, Marcus! They were someone's sons and daughters!"

Marcus shook his head, frowning. "Gavin, everyone dies; it's just a question of when, how, and what we do with the time we have. They certainly were not making much of theirs."

"So that makes it okay? It's perfectly fine just to sit back and decide who lives and who dies...all because of which family we're born into?"

"When the situation calls for it, yes. That's what Kirloth does, Gavin: make the hard choices no one else can face. It makes for a lonely life at times, but I have no problems sleeping at night, especially considering some of the situations I've prevented.

"Now, the reason I decided it was time to have this discussion is that Valera asked to speak with you. The new class is starting in a few weeks, and the College always assigns mentors to the new students for their first year. For the life of me, I can't see why she wants you for the task; you're not an enrolled student, but she wants to discuss it with you all the same. If you choose to do it, it will come from your personal time; I refuse to take time away from your studies. She's in her office right now, if you want to see if she's available for that discussion."

"The Magisters' offices are on the second floor, right? The floor right below us?"

"Yes, they are, but Valera works out of the Office of the Collegiate Justice on the main floor. It's the first door on the north side of the west hall."

"I'll try to speak with her now." Gavin pushed the parchment across the table to Marcus and stood.

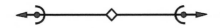

CHAPTER 20

Gavin followed Marcus's directions to the main floor and soon found himself standing in front of a door labeled, "Office of the Collegiate Justice." He took a deep breath and opened the door, stepping inside.

Gavin's eyes first landed on a petite brunette sitting behind a desk in the center of the room. She looked up when Gavin entered, and he saw her eyes were a strong, vibrant green. She wore white robes with vermillion runes on the cuffs of her sleeves, and Gavin remembered from a recent lesson that the robe color indicated a person's philosophy toward the Art, while the color of the sleeve runes indicated the person's specialization…if any.

Gavin wasn't familiar enough with the runes yet to know the young woman's rank, for the runes themselves proclaimed the person's rank within the Society of the Arcane, but he did know white robes meant the person felt the Art should be used to protect others. Vermillion runes meant a specialist in Tutation, the School of Magic dedicated to the study and advancement of protective effects, such as wards, shields, etc.

The young woman was giving Gavin a scrutiny of her own, and her eyes locked on his medallion, as everyone's eyes so often did. Her eyes widened just a little bit, and she inhaled a deep breath.

"You're him," she said, almost a whisper.

"Him who?" Gavin asked.

A deep, rosy red flushed the young woman's face, and Gavin guessed she hadn't realized she'd spoken aloud. She dropped her eyes to the top of her desk and fidgeted with her hands.

"I...well...it's just that several of the College's summer staff have seen Marcus with a young man wearing the medallion of House Kirloth, and my friend in the House Registry told me that Marcus registered a Gavin Cross as the heir to House Kirloth a few weeks ago."

Gavin could see that the young lady's embarrassment showed no signs of abating anytime soon, and he walked the four or so strides necessary to bring him to her desk, extending his hand.

"Hi, I'm Gavin Cross. I was told the Magister wanted to see me."

The young lady still didn't look up, but she did stand. Mumbling a "Please, wait a moment, milord," she moved to the inner door, knocked once, and stepped inside.

VALERA LOOKED up from the book she studied at the sound of a knock, followed by the door opening. She saw her assistant, Sera, step into the office and close the door behind her...even going so far as to lean against the door as if blockading it.

"He's here!" she said, though—for all its urgency—her voice barely rose above a whisper.

"Who's here, child?"

"Lord Kirloth!"

"Who? Oh...do you mean Gavin Cross?"

"Yes!" Sera nodded with such force Valera feared for the young girl's neck.

"Calm yourself, child. I'm sure he's a very nice young man. Do please show him in."

Sera opened the door just enough to slide back out to the reception area, and once the door closed, Valera shook her head, sighing. Being on the far side of sixty, she couldn't remember the last time a young man bothered her as much as this Gavin Cross seemed to bother young Sera. Though to be fair, it wasn't every day a newly-discovered son of one of Tel's oldest Houses appeared in the College, either.

THE SOUND of a door opening drew Gavin's attention from the bookshelf whose spines he was examining. Half the reception area served as a waiting space with comfortable chairs, while the other half was a working office containing books and records. Gavin didn't open any of the cabinets, but he saw no reason he couldn't spend the time he waited, examining the books.

Now, though, he turned, finding the young assistant still refusing to face him, and he bit back a sigh. This was by far the most pronounced reaction to his medallion Gavin had seen so far, and he found himself even more unsettled by it than he was by people's wide eyes and stepping out of his way.

"The Magister will see you now," the assistant said and turned back to the door.

Gavin followed the assistant into the inner office.

The office Gavin entered was a tasteful, comfortable mix between a sitting room and an office. Doilies dotted the landscape, and a silver tea service rested atop an end table on one side of the room. A large, mahogany desk dominated the room.

What grabbed Gavin's attention, though, was the older woman in a white robe rising to her feet behind the desk. Her long, wavy hair was the same color as Kiri's, glossy black, though hers was streaked with gray, and she was about Kiri's height, maybe just a touch shorter. Though a tad weathered by the years, her skin reminded Gavin very much of Kiri in its olive tone. What sealed the resemblance, though, were the green eyes that didn't hide her intelligence or her zest for life. It was uncanny how much she resembled Kiri.

Gavin pushed those thoughts out of his mind as he approached the desk and extended his hand, saying, "Gavin Cross, ma'am. My mentor said you wanted a word."

Valera gave Gavin a firm handshake, which allowed Gavin to notice amethyst runes on the sleeve of the woman's robe. Those runes confirmed Marcus's statement that she was the Magister of Divination, and from the robe's sleeve, Gavin's eyes went to the silver medallion that rested atop her heart. He froze. He recognized the House Glyph from the book in the Temple's library. It was a dot in the upper-third, with a horizontal line coming in from the left and stopping at the edge of the dot in the middle-third. The lower-third of the Glyph looked like a letter T that had been rotated eighty-five degrees to the left.

Muran…she's House Muran, the royal family of Vushaar!

Gavin realized he was staring and broke the handshake, saying, "I apologize. I didn't mean to stare."

"It's quite all right, Gavin; my House Glyph is almost as rare as yours," Valera said, indicating the chairs between which Gavin stood. "Please, make yourself comfortable."

Gavin accepted her invitation and chose the chair to Valera's right.

"Did your mentor mention why I wanted a word?" Valera asked as she resumed her seat.

Gavin nodded. "He did, ma'am."

"I've known your mentor a great many years, and I very much doubt he stopped there."

"No, ma'am. He also gave me his opinion of the topic."

Valera sat silent for a few moments before saying, "May I ask what that opinion was?"

"He said he couldn't see why you wanted me, ma'am, since I'm not an actual enrolled student…and he implied it was a waste of my time."

Valera chuckled. "I'm not surprised. He has continually rebuffed all my attempts to put him in a classroom crammed full of our wizard students. He says what he has to teach is not for the faint of heart."

Images of charred earth and molten rock, along with the words 'fifty-three people,' flashed through Gavin's mind, and he met Valera's eyes with his own, saying, "And I would agree with him, ma'am."

"Yes. Perhaps, you would."

Silence ruled the room for several moments.

"What I want to discuss," Valera said, "is for you to be one of this year's mentors. Each year, I find older students who I feel can serve as a positive influence and help the new students through the first year here. It's nothing so formal as the Mentor/Apprentice arrangement outlined in the Arcanists' Code; I just borrowed the term."

"But Marcus is right, ma'am; I'm not a student. I don't know what classes are like here. I don't know anything about the student culture here at the College or whom to see if a student has a specific problem. How can I possibly be a mentor to these people?"

"Gavin, I hope and pray with all my heart that none of our students will *ever* have to face the situations you've faced in the short time you've been with us. Still, I fear it is all too possible that they will. Would it not be better to present them a potential role model who has faced those challenges and correctly responded?"

Gavin sat silent for several moments. At last, he said, "How can you say that, Valera? How can you sit there and tell me that the deaths of fifty-three people was the correct response?"

"He told you about that, did he? A wizard's first invocation is always the most uncontrolled use of his or her power that the world will ever see, and your first invocation was one of the most fundamental Words of Interation known to exist. In its use, you called forth incredible power; a lesser wizard would have died. You didn't choose to kill fifty-three people; you were defending yourself and another. What other method did you have for doing so?"

Gavin sighed. "None, really."

"Remember that. Now, about being a mentor…"

"I'll do it."

"Excellent. I'll send Sera with a schedule of the Mentor Training and Orientation sessions."

"Who?"

"My assistant. The young lady you met."

"Oh. I didn't really meet her, ma'am. She never introduced herself, but she certainly seemed to know who I am."

Valera delivered a slight smile. "Yes, well, it's not every day that a new wizard is discovered, let alone one of such a prestigious House as Kirloth."

"Are you sure you don't mean 'notorious' or 'infamous,' ma'am?"

"It is often the case that the most prestigious families have certain aspects to their history that do not bear scrutiny well, and I daresay your mentor made more of those aspects than most."

Gavin's thoughts stopped on Valera's last sentence. "Ma'am, Marcus told me something just before I came to see you that I'm having trouble believing."

"I'm not surprised in the least. If I may ask, what was it?"

"He told me he is Kirloth…as in *the* Kirloth, the one that dueled Milthas during the Godswar."

When Valera didn't jump to dissuade Gavin from that, he felt a gaping pit forming in his stomach.

"Yes, Gavin, he is. Your mentor is the man many scholars throughout the last six thousand years have heralded as the greatest wizard of all time. He takes more for granted about the Art than most of us will ever experience or even suspect might be possible."

Gavin leaned back against his chair and stared at the top of Valera's desk.

"Were you hoping I would tell you he is not who he claims to be?"

"A little bit," Gavin said, adding a few slight nods, "yeah."

"Don't try relating to him as Kirloth. So much of who Kirloth was or wasn't is bound up in traditions and history. Learn who he is now, and you may find that man far more approachable."

"Thank you, ma'am. I'll try. Is there anything else? I'm probably already late for my studies."

Valera smiled. "No. I think we have discussed all that needs discussion for now."

"Thank you, ma'am." Gavin stood and left.

. . .

VALERA LOOKED at the closed door for several moments before she opened the center drawer of the desk. Inside it lay a folded piece of parchment, and she withdrew it, unfolding it to rest atop her desk.

The writing on the parchment was harsh, jerky…as if the writer had been in a bit of a rush. Several places, the ink had dripped or run, but none of blemishes precluded reading the words:

THE DEATH of slavers shall herald the return of Kirloth to this world, and the Apprentices shall be drawn unto him.

VALERA STILL REMEMBERED the night her first vision in twenty years had awoken her. The images of the vision had passed too quickly for her to retain them, but the words—these words—still resonated within her mind.

Valera stared at the parchment as she considered the new students who would be arriving in less than three weeks. Oh, yes… she knew exactly which students Gavin would mentor.

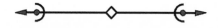

CHAPTER 21

S tanding between two young men she'd known all her life, Lillian Mivar was the only child of House Mivar. She stood on the taller edge of the average height for a woman with a lithe figure and auburn hair that hung to her shoulders in natural curls. Her bright green eyes shone in the morning sun and did nothing to hide her intelligence.

The young man on Lillian's right was a veritable giant, though not actually a member of that race. Braden Wygoth stood head-and-shoulders over everyone around him—with a stout, muscular physique—but his open, welcoming demeanor made him approach-able. His hair was dark, almost raven black like his mother's, and kept well-trimmed.

Wynn Roshan stood on Lillian's left, and he was the opposite of Braden. Short and wiry, he exuded a nervous energy. Tapping a foot, snapping fingers…he was always moving. His blonde hair was a touch longer than was normal for men, but Wynn didn't seem to notice.

Lillian drew comfort from her friends beside her as she scanned the courtyard. There were a great many faces she'd never seen before. As someone who would be Duchess Mivar one day, not to mention being seventeen years old, Lillian knew she shouldn't have the anxiety that was tying her guts into knots, but she had never been comfortable at the dinner parties her grandfather—the Duke Mivar—hosted, either.

A massive hand enclosed Lillian's left shoulder, and she felt an oak-tree-sized arm against her back.

"You can do this, Lillian," Braden said in his deep, rumbling voice. "We're right here with you."

"Yep, yep," Wynn said, his tenor voice seeming to carry his energy with it. "Haven't-you-always-heard-that-the-Great-Houses-stand-together?" This last came out in a rush; Lillian wasn't sure Wynn ever took a breath when he started speaking until he completed *all* of what he wanted to say.

Lillian smiled at the two people she felt closest to in all the world, after her own family. "I wish I had the words to say how grateful I am you're here with me. This would be much more daunting were I alone."

"Oh, nonsense, Lillian," Braden said. "You have a strength in you; all you need do is realize it."

A group approached, and they turned to find an older lady in white robes approaching with Torval Mivar, Lillian's grandfather; Sypara Wygoth, Braden's mother; and Carth Roshan, Wynn's father. Lillian's eyes lit up as she realized who the older lady must be.

"Greetings," the older lady said, "My name is Valera, and I am the Magister of Divination. It is good to see you here, especially together."

Lillian couldn't hold it in any longer. She stepped forward and said, "Ma'am, I am Lillian Mivar, and it's an honor to meet you! I have wanted to specialize in Divination ever since I started planning for the College."

"That's very kind of you, Lady Mivar," Valera said with a respectful nod, "but students cannot choose to specialize until they reach Third Tier. The Society has felt for some time—and I agree —that students should be exposed to everything the Art has to offer before making the decision to specialize, let alone choosing a specific School. Third Tier is quite some distance in your future at this point, and there's always the chance that something will cause you to change your mind."

"Don't be so sure, Valera," Torval said. "Lillian has spoken of nothing else since she was old enough to start reading my spellbooks."

Lillian fought her blush at her grandfather's words. Normally, a new student's parents would be attending the day's festivities with the student, but Andrin Mivar—Lillian's father—was not a wizard. Besides, he much preferred managing the Mivar family's business interests and serving as his father's adjutant in managing the Mivar Province. As Lillian was the next true-born wizard of the family, she would inherit the Duchy and leadership of House Mivar, not her father.

For many families as steeped in the Art as House Mivar, a son—especially an only child—would have been ostracized for something that wasn't the child's fault. Torval Mivar loved his son as much as any father could, and he had given Andrin the choice of pursuing studies as a mage. Andrin, however, couldn't bear the thought of being a Mivar arcanist who was not a wizard, and he had chosen instead to assist his father with the civil side of House Mivar's duties.

Torval Mivar stood just above Valera's height, and the only hair he possessed was a thick band of curly, white hair that ran from sideburn to sideburn around the back of his head. His weathered skin held every year of his life for all to see, but his eyes sparkled with an energy and zest for life that belied his age. Torval wore green robes with amber runes.

Standing to his right was a man of average height, who possessed ginger hair streaked with gray. Carth Roshan was the eldest of two brothers, his sibling having risen to command the Battle-mages of Tel, and he seemed to possess none of his son's nervous energy. Amber runes ringed the sleeve cuffs of Carth's crimson robes.

Sypara Wygoth stood to Torval's left, and she made Torval look tall. Everyone who met the Head of House Wygoth marveled that such a small woman had produced a son the size of Braden. Her hair was almost pure black—despite being shot with gray, and her bright, blue eyes carried an impish, mischievous glint. Her lips having the slight curl of an ever-present grin, Sypara presented the impression of an adult rascal who felt no impetus to 'grow up.' Her white robes gleamed in the morning sun, and the vermilion runes at the cuffs of her sleeve served to accent the robes' color.

"So, who are you assigning as our children's mentor, Valera?" Carth Roshan asked.

"Now, Carth, that's bad form, and you know it!" Sypara said before Valera could respond. "We have no business 'interfering' in the management of the College."

"'Interfering,' is it? I've heard rumors of upper-Tier students hazing the new ones, and I just wanted to make it clear I won't stand for that where Wynn is concerned."

Sypara gathered herself to respond, but Valera lifted her hand, bidding Sypara to hold a moment.

"Carth, I've heard the same rumors you have—for several years now—and I regret that I've not been able to confirm or deny those rumors through evidence. That being said, I feel a recent addition to this year's roster of mentors will help curtail that."

Carth scoffed. "I fail to see how one student will make any difference if the problem is as wide-spread and ingrained as I've heard."

Lillian wanted to speak up, but she was torn. She had spent many the hour talking with Mariana Cothos, who was five years older, about what the College would be like, and from what Mariana had said, hazing had always been a part of the College.

Just then, Valera angled her head a bit to the side, looking beyond the group, and smiled; Lillian turned her head and saw a young man walking around the path leading to the Tower's main door from the gardens. Valera waved to get his attention and motioned for him to approach them.

"Well, Carth," Valera said, "it just so happens that the young man I was planning to assign to your children is right there. Let me introduce him, and you can make up your mind."

The young man approaching them wore the brown robes of a student, and everyone could see he wore a wizard's medallion. But he walked with his head slightly bowed and his right index finger tapped his jaw, which blocked view of the medallion's glyph. Otherwise, he wore his light brown hair cropped close, and there were hints of facial hair that might grow into a Vandyke beard one day.

He approached the group, still lost in thought, and stopped at Valera's side. All at once, he seemed to realize everyone was looking at him.

"Oh, I'm sorry, Valera," he said. "Marcus gave me a puzzle a little while ago, and I'm still working my way through it. How can I help you?"

As he straightened, the young man bared the medallion to view, and the others standing with Valera drew back.

"Gavin Cross of House Kirloth, I would introduce you to Carth of House Roshan, Torval of House Mivar, and Sypara of House Wygoth. These are their respective children who will be starting this term: Wynn, Lillian, and Braden. Well, Lillian is in truth Torval's granddaughter, but that's a matter for another time."

Gavin smiled, saying, "Hello. It's nice to meet you."

After handshakes had been exchanged all around, Carth said, "So, tell us, Gavin; what do you enjoy most about being a student at the College?"

"Oh, I'm not a student," Gavin said. "I'm Marcus's apprentice."

Valera showed commendable restraint in maintaining her non-expression as it seemed like everyone else's jaw dropped.

"Excuse me," Torval said, "but did you say you are Marcus's apprentice?"

"Yes. When he named me his apprentice, he said something about 'as was in the old ways.'"

"Tell me, Gavin," Carth said, "what's your opinion of hazing?"

Gavin considered the matter for several moments, before

returning his eyes to Carth. "Sir, I cannot imagine a case in which hazing—even with the best of intentions—is anything other than bullying, and I despise bullies. Valera has asked me to be a mentor for a few students of the new class, and no one will be hazing my group if I have anything to say about it."

Carth turned to Valera, saying, "He'll do."

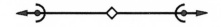

CHAPTER 22

A soft knock at the door pulled Valera from her musings. Her steward entered, saying, "Commander Roshan is here, ma'am."

"Send him in at once, please," Valera said, "and stay until I've offered the commander refreshment."

The steward nodded and left.

While she waited, Valera scanned the space with her eyes and sighed. The space was comfortable, but it was not home. She still remembered her father's expression, his exact words, his enraged tone of voice, when she announced her intention to remain in Tel and pursue her studies in Divination. Her father disowned her and had even gone so far as to have all records of her existence removed from the family genealogy. It didn't often bother Valera these days. It was a pain long since past. Still, old hurts sometimes stealthed out of the shadows in her mind to ambush her.

The door opened once more to admit the steward followed by Garris Roshan. A man of average height with a bulky, muscular build, he wore a burgundy mantle atop his red robe with silver runes that proclaimed him a *magus* within the Society. The mantle bore the color of the Battle-mages of Tel, and a wizard's medallion bearing the glyph of House Roshan rested atop his heart. He kept his hair trimmed close, and the intelligence in his hazel eyes belied his brutish appearance.

"It's been some time since we've spoken, Valera," Garris said as he stood beside the available armchair.

"Please sit," Valera said, indicating the chair at his side. "May I offer you refreshment? Tea, perhaps?"

The man eased his bulk into the offered chair, and he directed a rueful smile toward Valera. "You know me too well. Do you, by chance, have any of that tea you served last time…the Vushaari blend?"

"Of course, Garris," Valera said and looked to her steward. "Please, prepare a pot."

Garris Roshan was seven years into his command of the Battle-mages, and the weight of the post showed. Sixteen years ago, Garris possessed a spring in his step…no gray hair, no weathered skin. Looking at him now, one might have believed twice as long had passed since Valera tutored him in Divination.

Though nominally a unit of Tel's Army, the Battle-mages in truth answered to the Archmagister and Society of the Arcane…in that order. Given the cold feud between King Leuwyn and the Society at the time, however, no one pushed the matter, but few people doubted where the unit's loyalties were.

"I hope the purpose of your summons does not relate to my nephew or sister," Garris said, as they waited for the tea. "That's the only reason why you would ask for some of my time that came to mind."

Valera waved her hand. "Oh, no. Wynn and Bella are just fine. No, I asked to speak with you because I need something, something I fear we all need more than we realize."

"Oh? What's that?"

"I need you to re-assign Mariana Cothos to the College until further notice. If she forces an explanation from you, tell her the College is preparing a committee to evaluate the efficacy of the Battle-mage program here."

Garris frowned, saying, "Why would you want-" His eyes widened when his mind found the one explanation that fit. "The others are already here, aren't they? If Wynn started this term, then Lillian and Braden are also here, being about the same age, and I've heard rumors of a young wizard of House Kirloth roaming the grounds. Have they met him yet?"

"Yes, they have, and his name is Gavin Cross. They met him their very first day here, in fact."

"Do tell."

"It's nothing particularly glamourous or exciting. Your brother wanted to know who his son's mentor would be; well, he phrased it in such a way it was plain he saw no reason Wynn and the others should be separated. Sypara pounced on him at once for interfering with the administration of the College."

Garris lost all trace of composure, erupting into deep, full-throated laughter. "That's Carth! He never was bashful about giving his opinion." After another round of mirth, Garris sobered and lifted his eyes to meet Valera's. "Tell me why you want her, aside from the obvious."

"My first vision in twenty years woke me in the middle of the night, not even a week before Marcus and Ovir found Gavin. I wrote down as much of it as I could, but the central sense of it was this. *'The death of slavers shall herald the return of Kirloth to this world, and the Apprentices shall be drawn unto him.'* The same day he awoke in this world, Gavin killed fifty-three slavers in an unfocused invocation, and as of right now, Cothos is the only Great House of Tel unrepresented at the College."

A polite knock announced the steward's return with the tea service. Garris inhaled the pleasant aroma, smiling, before returning his attention to the matter at hand.

"I'll give the order the moment I return," Garris said and proceeded to watch the steward pour tea.

* * *

GAVIN LEANED against the desk at the front of the empty classroom as he waited on the students he would be mentoring to arrive. Made of oak, if Gavin was any judge, its solid, well-maintained construction lent an understated gravitas to the space. The classroom was a standard lecture hall with stadium-style seating and a large, center aisle with smaller aisles on each flank. A small current of Conjuration permeated the space, and Gavin suspected it was an embedded effect to project speakers' voices throughout the hall.

It wouldn't be so bad to spend my life in classrooms, Gavin thought as his eyes roamed over the empty seats of the hall, but then, his thoughts drifted back to his discussion with Marcus about what it means to be Kirloth. *But somehow, I think Marcus would say it was wasting my life.*

The classroom's only door opened, cutting short Gavin's thoughts, and he saw the young girl of House Mivar he met a few days before. *What was her name?* Then, a tall, stocky boy followed her, and Gavin smiled. *Lillian. Her name is Lillian; his name is Braden, and that means...* Short, wiry Wynn Roshan followed Braden Wygoth into the space.

Lillian led her friends down the center aisle to sit in the first three seats of the front row. Braden squeezed himself into the aisle seat, Lillian beside him and Wynn on Lillian's right.

"Don't worry, Braden. I don't plan on us always meeting here," Gavin said. "It's far too large a space for just nine people."

Over the next few minutes, five more people—three young women and two men—entered the hall, and none of them were wizards. They approached close enough to see the glyph in Gavin's medallion, and almost as one, their eyes dropped to the three students in the front row. They glanced around and quickly found seats in rows about half-way between the door and Gavin.

Gavin watched the scene play out, and he started to let it pass. Then, he remembered Valera's presentation at the start of the mentor orientation, and Gavin knew that 'let it pass' he could not.

"Yes, I am House Kirloth," Gavin said, "and as the medallion also announces, I am a wizard. And yes, these three are Heirs of the Great Houses of Tel. Do we intimidate you?"

The five students glanced at each other. Gavin feared they would remain silent, but one of the young women spoke.

"Yes, milord. The whole campus is buzzing about the first wizard of House Kirloth in no one knows how long."

"My name is Gavin, and I don't want to hear 'milord' ever again; that's not who I am." Gavin fell silent as he looked up at the ceiling, searching his memories for the quote. When he found it, Gavin smiled. "'...for I tell you now that I will brook no bias within your ranks. These people so desire to study and wield the Art that they propose to do so through sheer force of will, embodied as countless hours of study, and I will not have them be second-class members of the Society. You are all brothers and sisters in the Art before me.'"

Lillian sat in the front row with a huge grin on her face, but the new arrivals couldn't see that.

"Do you recognize the quote?" Gavin asked.

When no one answered for some time, Lillian's hand shot up.

"This isn't a formal class, Lillian; you don't have to raise your hand and be recognized."

"The quote...it was part of Bellos's address to the assembled Society of the Arcane when the first mage students came to the College. I love that part of the Histories."

Gavin nodded. "It is pretty good. I read it for the first time a few days ago." He directed his attention back to the prospective mages in the row above. "Please, join us."

The students glanced at each other before standing and moving down to the front row. They sat on the opposite side of the aisle from Lillian, Braden, and Wynn. Gavin took it as progress.

"Thank you," Gavin said and scanned the students present before continuing. "This program is intended to help new students transition to life at the College, and some of you may question why all first-years are required to participate. The thing is, even if you yourself don't need the support this program is intended to provide, there's always the chance that you can help provide it to others. We are indeed all brothers and sisters in the Art, and none of us is as strong as all of us. It is my hope that you will come to me...whether you have questions or need help or just need to talk…but I understand that such trust and rapport takes time to build. Let's proceed with the introductions."

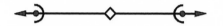

CHAPTER 23

Marcus drove Gavin's training at a relentless pace. Though Gavin's studies focused on developing mastery of the Art, traditional, academic studies were not exempt.

It was a cool evening as the region teetered just on the cusp of autumn. The slight breeze carried the complex potpourri of scents one only found in the College's gardens. Herbs, flowers, rare plants for the alchemy classes...all these scents and more wafted through the air.

Gavin strolled through the gardens, head bent as he wrestled with a matter that had plagued him for some time. What it meant to be Kirloth. Everything Marcus told him still circled through his mind. How could he be Kirloth anyway...*that* Kirloth, at least? Sure, he said he was over six thousand years old, but anyone could *say* that.

The sound of metal striking stone drew Gavin's attention, and a short distance to his left, Gavin saw what seemed a very unlikely sight. Valera, Magister of Divination, knelt over a flower bed, her arms smeared to the elbows with soil and fertilizer. The flower bed was one of the few such that were level to the path; most were built up as large planters surrounded by bench-sized walls. Naturally, of course, Valera was working with the flowers because she chose to do so, but the image was so unexpected, Gavin decided to walk over and say hello.

Valera looked up as a shadow crossed her flower bed and smiled at seeing Gavin. "Hello, Gavin. How has life been treating you?"

"I'd have to say 'well' if restricted to one word," Gavin said. "How are the new students doing?"

Valera smiled again. "They seem to be settling in quite well. A few told me they'd received an incident or two of hazing during the first week or so, but that stopped for some reason...quite suddenly in fact."

"I might as well get some use out of this medallion," Gavin said, shrugging. "I must admit, ma'am, I never expected to see the Magister of Divination working in a flower bed."

Valera laughed outright as she shifted into a sitting position and gestured toward a spot of path free of planting soil and fertilizer. Gavin accepted the invitation to sit as Valera said, "When I was a little girl, I always helped my mother with our flower beds. She died when I was barely a woman, but I guess working with flowers will always be special to me. I doubt you stopped by to chat, though. What's on your mind?"

"Honestly, I just saw you over here and felt like saying hello, but now that you mention it, I have been wrestling with something."

Valera gave Gavin an encouraging smile. "Well, as long as it's not forgotten secrets of the Art, I might be able to offer a different viewpoint if you feel up to discussing it."

"Marcus told me something that I'm having trouble reconciling."

"I see. Why don't you help an old woman with a rock and tell me what's on your mind?"

Gavin stood and removed his initiate's robe, revealing a plain, short-sleeved tunic and pants beneath; they were a light tan, the color of loose dirt long desiccated by the sun, and brought the strange word *khaki* to Gavin's mind. He carefully folded the robe and placed it on a nearby planter before kneeling beside Valera.

"The problem stone," Valera said, as she gestured toward the soil in front of her, "is that big rock there. I've tried digging around it, and I can see it's way too big for my old bones to move."

Gavin looked at what he could see of the rock. Its edges were at most as thick as the length of Gavin's index finger from the tip to the first knuckle, but clearing away some of the dirt beneath it, he saw that the rock thickened at a very steep angle. He took hold as best he could and tried to lift the exposed portion; the rock didn't budge, and neither did any of the dirt on top.

"So, what did Marcus say that has you in such turmoil?" Valera asked while Gavin considered the rock.

Gavin pursed his lips and looked away. "How long have you known he was Kirloth…as in the Kirloth that built this city and wrote the Arcanists' Code?"

"I've known ever since I took my Test of Mastery to become the Magister of Divination. The Test of Mastery is different for each School, and for Divination, it's a scrying that's a form of true sight. If the arcanist succeeds in casting it, she—or he—sees everyone for who they truly are while the effect is active. Marcus made the mistake of being present, and I saw Kirloth. Bellos asked me to keep that knowledge to myself until Marcus himself chose to speak of it. But somehow, I don't think that's what has you so troubled."

"No, ma'am, not really."

Gavin shifted his position so that he could place direct leverage on the rock. He stood right at its edge, crouched down, and dug his hands as far under the stone as he could. Then, he stood, lifting with his legs. His efforts just barely shifted the topsoil above the rock.

"Before he told me that you wanted me to be a mentor, he spent some time explaining what it means to be Kirloth. He gave me examples and said I would be Kirloth someday and that it would fall to me to carry on. In a way, I'm almost glad he's out and about right now; it gives me time to sort through this," Gavin said.

"Out and about?"

"Yes. The other morning, I found a note on the table in our

common room; it said he was going to be away for a little while, hopefully no more than two weeks, and that I was to continue my studies without him," Gavin said, before sighing and turning to Valera. "Ma'am-"

"Dear boy, you're helping me in my flower bed; call me Valera."

"Ma—Valera, I'm not sure this rock is moving without some major excavation. Would you be opposed to a little magic?"

Valera frowned. "Under normal circumstances, I wouldn't even consider it; it can be very refreshing to accomplish something without bending creation to your will, but these bulbs require a certain depth. Besides that, I've already loosened the dirt with a little Transmutation. What do you have in mind?"

Gavin sorted through all the various Words flitting around his head. The Word of Transmutation Gavin chose was the ancient forebear to the modern teleportation spell, which just happened to be a Fifth Circle spell. Gavin had stumbled across that particular Word reading one of Mivar's Histories about the period after the Godswar known as the Founding.

Gavin reached out with his right index finger and placed it against the rock. He closed his eyes and directed all his mind to forming a picture of the rock being on the path beside him. When Gavin felt confident his focus was sufficient, he took a deep breath and invoked the Word, "*Paedryx.*"

Even for such a minor working of the Art, pain savaged Gavin's guts, feeling like he'd been sliced open with liberal amounts of acid poured inside. The result, however, was undeniable. The rock vanished from its place beneath the topsoil to reappear on the path beside Gavin, between the flower bed and the planter upon which Gavin had leaned earlier. It was an oblong rock, nearly a foot thick at its thickest point and a rough two feet on each 'side.' The teleportation effect took hold so quickly, Gavin and Valera were able to watch an impressive area of topsoil collapse into the space where the rock had been.

"Gavin," Valera said, her voice barely above a whisper, "was a Word of Power really necessary to move that rock?"

Gavin shrugged. "I'm sorry, Valera, but I don't know any spells.

I learned that particular Word from the volume of Mivar's Histories that covered the Founding."

Valera blinked and turned to face Gavin, her expression beyond confused. "Gavin, I've read all of Mivar's works. Mivar didn't mention any Words of Power in them."

"It was in the chapter where he discussed Kirloth calling the Judgment of Valthon against the kings, but it wasn't part of the main text. It was like the script was a watermark on the page."

Valera shook her head, her expression a mixture of wonder and bemusement. "Most, if not all, of Mivar's histories possess an aura of power about them. Our scholars have always assumed Mivar placed powerful protections on the volumes so they'd withstand the test of time. Matter of fact, it's been the assumption for so long, any works considered important are copied into protected tomes. I wonder how many books in our library contain hidden Words of Power..."

The statement didn't seem to be directed at Gavin in its entirety, so he chose to remain silent. After a few moments, Valera shook off her mood and smiled. "As for your other problem, remember that you—and you alone—determine how you live your life. What Marcus told you is what it means to be Kirloth to *him*, and unfortunately, we have needed that Kirloth from time to time. Yes, you will indeed be Kirloth someday, but when that day comes, it will be you —and you alone—who determines what it means to be Kirloth."

"Thank you, Valera," Gavin said as he cleaned his hands and reached for his robe. "What would you like me to do with the rock?"

"Oh, don't bother yourself anymore," Valera said. "I'll have one of the grounds staff deal with it."

Gavin nodded and was starting to stand when he felt an Enchantment effect ripple across his *skathos*. The effect felt like it occurred somewhere in the hedge maze at the center of the gardens, but what piqued Gavin's interest the most was that the effect felt almost the same as the paralysis effect he'd practiced in the arena a few days before.

"Valera," Gavin said, his eyes closed as he concentrated on the direction of the effect.

"Yes, Gavin?"

"Is there any reason someone should be casting a paralysis effect somewhere in the hedge maze?"

"What? What made you ask that?"

"I just felt an Enchantment effect from over there," Gavin said, eyes still closed and pointing with his left hand, "and it felt like the paralysis effect Marcus had me try right before he left."

"Gavin, I need you to go to the fourth floor of the Tower and knock on room N4. The Inquisitor assigned to the College will answer the door; her name is Reyna. Tell her everything you just told me."

Gavin opened his eyes and turned to Valera. "Shouldn't I go into the hedge maze?"

"You're an apprentice, Gavin; it's not your place."

Valera pushed herself to her feet, and Gavin stepped to block her path.

"Valera, I'm not saying you're incapable of handling this yourself. I just believe I'm better equipped to defend myself if there's something bad happening in there."

"Oh? Better equipped than a Magister?"

"When was the last time you used a Word of Interation, Valera?"

Valera looked at Gavin in silence. At last, she said, "I'll get Reyna. Go."

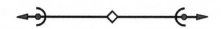

CHAPTER 24

The College's gardens had a small area devoted to a hedge maze, about an acre in total, and Gavin's concern grew when he traced the Enchantment effect to its entrance. Since leaving Valera, Gavin wracked his mind, trying to determine how casting a paralysis could be of scholarly value inside the maze, and he could think of none...especially on a day with no formal classes scheduled.

The hedge maze was designed to occupy a day's effort to reach the center, and if one were to become lost, the maze possessed a 'safe word' that would open a path from the speaker direct to the maze's entrance. Gavin remembered reading about the collaboration between the Council and the druids of the Sylvan Synod when the maze was constructed, some fifteen hundred years before. It was also through his voracious reading that Gavin knew the short-cut to the maze's center, and he took that path, guessing the location of the paralysis effect's source.

A SHORT TIME LATER, Gavin stepped around the final curve of the path and stopped cold. A young woman lay across the block of stone at the maze's center, partially obscured by a young man. A small pile of fabric already lay on the ground just to the side of the stone block.

"I just couldn't help myself," Gavin heard the young man say. "I've seen you around the College, these past few weeks, and you're irresistible, just like all the others. I'm rather pleased with myself that I waited this long before arranging our little meeting. Too bad you probably won't enjoy this as much as I will."

The young man dropped his trousers and moved toward the young woman.

"Hello, there!" Gavin called out as he took off at a jog. As he moved, Gavin shucked off his robe and draped it over his left arm.

The young man let out a little screech and looked over his shoulder as he bent to pull up his trousers. Alas, he moved with too much haste and smacked the side of his head against the stone block. The impact dazed him, and he fell backward with his trousers just above his knees.

Gavin was drawing close to the stone block now. He saw that the young woman's clothes were cut open and spread beneath her like a tablecloth, and she lay atop the stone with her arms and legs spread-eagled, held by the paralysis effect that had led Gavin here. The coloring of her skin was just slightly pale, as though she didn't spend much time in the sun. What hair Gavin could see was the auburn hue he thought made Lillian Mivar so pretty. Then, Gavin closed enough to see the woman's face, and he froze. It *was* Lillian.

Gavin's path took him near the would-be attacker, who was starting to recover his wits, and Gavin directed a casual kick to the side of young man's head as he passed, intent on keeping the young man diverted a few moments longer.

Reaching the stone, Gavin draped his robe across Lillian before he turned to the young man lying on the ground behind him. He didn't recognize the young man, nor the House Glyph on his medallion. Like Roshan's Glyph, this one had a horizontal line and centered dot in the upper- and middle-thirds, respectively. Unlike Roshan, though, two diagonal lines on the right side made up the lower third of this Glyph.

"The paralysis, how long does it last?" Gavin asked.

"You didn't have to kick me," the young man said, his speech slurred just a bit.

Rage slipped Gavin's control, and it seemed to color his vision. He watched his right hand reach down and clamp onto the young man's throat. The young man let out a garbled sound as Gavin hauled him to his feet, his trousers falling back around his ankles.

"Answer my question, you worthless cur," Gavin said, "or my boot will be the least of your worries."

"...can't...speak..." the young man said, gasping out the words.

Gavin released the young man's throat with a slight push backward. The young man let the momentum get the better of him, and he fell again. Gavin left the young man to sort himself out and turned back to Lillian. During his studies, there were mentions of Words that dispelled active effects as well as spells that duplicated that utility, but Gavin had yet to learn any of those Words.

Gavin closed his eyes and concentrated on his *skathos*, observing the ambient magic and the effects of the paralysis spell upon the ambient. The spell didn't seem to be all that well anchored from what Gavin could sense. Gavin remembered Marcus saying at one point how wizards were fundamentally a part of the power they wielded, and he hit upon an experimental plan.

Stepping around to Lillian's side, Gavin took her left hand in his and extended his right hand toward the sky. He closed his eyes and started drawing a small amount of the ambient power, just to start the process, and then focused his draw exclusively on the paralysis effect. To keep from building a dangerous accumulation of power he would have to expend in a very unpleasant invocation of the Art, Gavin pushed the power he drew through him and expelled it out his right hand to return to the ambient.

At first, it seemed like nothing was going to happen. Then, all of a sudden, Gavin felt the resistance of the paralysis spell break, and its power began flowing through him. A kaleidoscopic flame erupted from his right palm and lit up the area brighter than the noon-day sun. The longer the transfer occurred, the hotter Gavin felt, and he soon soaked his tunic and trousers in sweat. After an eternity that only lasted for five minutes or so, the paralysis effect dissipated, and Gavin leaned against the stone block, exhausted.

"That was amazing, Gavin," a voice said from behind Gavin.

Gavin turned to find Valera, a grim-faced woman in the black robes with crimson trim that signified the Inquisitors, and a blond-haired woman wearing the burgundy mantle of the Battle-mages of Tel and a medallion bearing the glyph of House Cothos; they were standing about fifteen feet past the end of the maze. The blond-haired woman looked at Gavin with undisguised wonder on her face, while Valera's expression held a smile and general expression of pride. The grim-faced woman glared in silence.

The young man on the ground shifted to look behind him and gasped, "Thank the gods! I found him trying to harm this woman, and I was afraid he was going to kill me."

The Inquisitor approached the young man and looked down at him, her expression best fit for some form of excrement to be scraped from one's shoe.

"If that is truly the case," the Inquisitor asked, "why is he fully clothed while you are on the ground with your trousers around your ankles?"

The young man swallowed hard and remained silent.

Gavin, meanwhile, turned to Lillian and helped her stand, making sure his robe stayed in place. Once Lillian was standing and her face visible, the blond-haired woman let out a startled cry and rushed to her side.

"Are you okay?" the blond-haired woman asked as she threw her arms around Lillian.

Lillian nodded. She took a couple deep breaths and looked to the Inquisitor. "Don't believe what he said; Gavin saved me. The one on the ground lured me here, claiming that someone was hurt and needed help. Before I could react, he pulled a scroll and used it to keep me immobile and unresisting."

The Inquisitor displayed an emotion other than contempt for the first time since her arrival. Her expression softened into an almost-smile. "Of course, he did. No one could take all this in and think otherwise. Besides, Gavin Cross is building a bit of a reputation among certain circles; attacking you like this would be most unlike that reputation. Do you wish to file a formal complaint?"

Lillian nodded. "What do I need to do to file the complaint?"

"Since he's a student and not a full member of the Society, the necessary forms are in the Collegiate Justice's office," the Inquisitor said, before turning to haul the young man to his feet. "Pull up your trousers, and place your hands behind you."

The young man complied, and the Inquisitor secured his wrists with a binding that dampened magic. Gavin moved to gather the various clothes lying around, but the Inquisitor stopped him with a gesture.

"This is now a crime scene," the Inquisitor said. "I will task a couple of my fellows to collect and document everything to be retrieved in this area; disturb as little as possible."

* * *

GAVIN ENTERED the suite he and Kiri shared with Marcus, after having left Lillian in the infirmary in the care of her friend, the battle-mage of House Cothos. Events had run a little fast, and no one had introduced themselves. Still, wizards' medallions were—in a way—all the introduction one needed.

"Gavin, is something wrong?"

Gavin looked up to see Kiri facing him, her brow furrowed.

"Yes, Kiri, something is wrong. One of the students in my mentor group was attacked tonight. I believe I managed to stop the attacker before he did anything truly heinous, but the idea that there are people who would use the Art for such purposes has left a rather foul taste in my mouth."

"Oh, that poor girl…how is she?" Kiri asked.

"She seemed well enough. She's in the infirmary right now with one of her friends."

"Gavin," Kiri said, her tone almost reproving, "I can assure you —no matter how she may seem—she is *not* 'well enough.'" Kiri stood in silence for a few moments as she worked her lower lip between her teeth. "I want to see her. I've already survived what she's facing now; perhaps, I can help her through it."

"Are you sure you want to do that? I mean, re-live all that?"

Kiri held Gavin's gaze for several moments before she lowered her eyes. "Gavin, I 're-live all that' every time I close my eyes."

THE INFIRMARY AT the College of the Arcane occupied half of the fifth floor, two floors above the floor where the suites of the Great Houses of Tel and the magisters were located. The waiting and triage areas were open and welcoming, featuring tall windows for either fresh air or natural sunlight. Doors led out of the waiting area to different sections of rooms, depending on the duration of the patient's stay or the type of illness/injury involved.

Gavin led Kiri past the reception desk to the hallway for the observation patients; Lillian's room was Number 5 of that ward.

"Mari, you don't have to sit with me. I'm fine." Lillian's voice was strong and clear as Gavin and Kiri approached her room in the infirmary.

Gavin rapped his knuckles on the doorframe and stepped into view. He saw the blond-haired battle-mage from the gardens sitting beside Lillian's bed. The moment Gavin rapped his knuckles on the doorframe, he saw Lillian's back go ramrod straight and her eyes widen a bit. When Lillian shifted her attention to the door and saw him, Gavin watched the tension leave her. Kiri was right; Lillian was not fine.

"Gavin," Lillian said, letting her head lay back into the pillow once more, "this is Mariana Cothos. Mari, this is Gavin; he's the mentor assigned to the group Wynn, Braden, and I attend."

"Some would say stopping a rapist goes a bit beyond the territory of mentor," the blond-haired woman said, her eyes locked on Gavin's medallion.

"Yes, well…it seemed like the thing to do at the time," Gavin replied with a self-deprecating shrug. "Lillian, my friend would like to speak with you if you feel up to it. She thinks her experience may be of some use to you."

"Who-" Lillian started to ask, but Gavin stepped aside to reveal Kiri. Lillian's question died a sudden death as her eyes widened.

"Hello. My name is Kiri. I'm here if you'd like to talk."

Gavin made eye contact with the blond-haired woman and motioned for her to follow him. He turned and left the room. When the woman followed him into the hall, Gavin pulled the door shut behind them.

"Why did you do that?" the woman asked.

"Why did I do what?"

"Pull me out of there. I was sitting with her tonight in case that guy Reyna took out of the gardens comes for her."

Gavin chuckled. "Oh, I daresay if he does, he'll have far more of a nasty surprise than he ever bargained for. Kiri isn't defenseless; she just doesn't carry a blade. Besides, Lillian was being strong for you. If you had stayed, I doubt Kiri would be able to get her to face what she's feeling."

"What makes you think she was faking being strong?"

"Didn't you see how she tensed when I knocked on the door-frame? Kiri will help her. Come on. We'll sit in the waiting area at the end of the hall."

The blond-haired woman extended her right hand, saying, "Thank you for saving Lillian; she's almost a little sister to me."

Gavin shook her hand. "It was my pleasure. No one should use the Art to prey on others as he did."

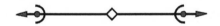

CHAPTER 25

L illian crossed her arms over her midriff as she looked at the slave. *Stop that; her name is Kiri. Why did Gavin have to take Mari-ana? It was so much easier to be strong for her.*

"I'm fine, Kiri," Lillian said, forcing her voice to be level and strong.

Kiri nodded, saying, "Very well," as she walked around the bed to sit in the chair Mariana had just vacated. Lillian watched Kiri work her lower lip between her teeth for a few moments before lifting her eyes to meet Lillian's.

"It was a little over two years ago when my father sent me away to Tel. The reasons are immaterial, at this point, but the ship sank. I don't know how I survived, but I did. I washed ashore on a piece of driftwood, barely alive and bewildered that I hadn't drowned.

"I was still getting my feet under me when a group of people found me. I thought they would help me; I was supposed to meet friends of my father in Tel Mivar, who would've paid them for their assistance I'm sure. Instead, they branded me...and spent the night taking turns with me. The women in their party even helped them hold me down. They didn't have a scroll of paralysis, you see."

"H—h—how did you know about that?"

"Gavin told me. Are you sure you don't want to talk about it?"

Lillian's resolve shattered, and the tears came. "I couldn't stop him, Kiri! I tried, but I c-c-couldn't! He asked for my help; he said one of his friends was hurt in the maze. I should've known something was wrong; I-I should have."

Kiri reached out and took Lillian's right hand in hers. Almost before Kiri realized what was happening, Lillian pulled her into a tight embrace and sobbed into her shoulder.

* * *

GAVIN AWOKE WITH A START, slamming his right elbow into the back of the wooden bench, and grimaced. He didn't know what had woken him, but the way the Void-scar on his forearm pulsed in time with his heartbeat, he felt he had a pretty good idea.

"I've never seen one of those scars before," Mariana said from her seat across the waiting room. "Read about them, yes…but never seen one."

"What time is it?" Gavin asked as he rubbed his face and yawned.

"Not quite daybreak. You can just see the first rays of daylight creeping over the horizon."

Gavin pushed himself into a sitting position and yawned again. "Did we spend the night in the waiting area?"

Mariana nodded and extended a cup to Gavin. "I thought about going down to my family's suite, but you were already sleeping. I didn't feel right leaving you here alone."

"On one side, I appreciate that, but on the other, one of us could have had a good night's sleep. Do you know if Kiri left Lillian's room at any point?"

Mariana shook her head. "I don't think so."

"I see." Gavin sighed. "Well, that's either good news or bad news. Do you-"

The main doors of the infirmary flew open and banged against their stops. A man in a tunic and trousers strode into the room. Though the clothing was simple in design, Gavin now knew enough about tailoring to recognize the quality (and therefore expense) of the work. He stopped just inside the doorway and scanned the room, his green eyes taking in everything.

"Mariana? I thought the Battle-mages were going on training maneuvers near Hope's Pass."

"They are, Andrin," Mariana said, "but Commander Roshan re-assigned me to the College until further notice."

"Where's Lillian? Do you know what happened?"

"I know the rough overview, but you'd be better off speaking to Gavin here. He stopped the attacker."

The man Mariana addressed as Andrin turned to Gavin, and his eyes dropped to Gavin's medallion. Gavin watched Andrin's eyes widen just enough to notice as his pallor paled, again just enough to notice.

"I-I wasn't aware any descendants of Kirloth remained," Andrin said.

Gavin shrugged. "If it makes you feel any better, I didn't either. I have reason to believe I'm from someplace called the Refugee World."

Andrin nodded, his eyes still locked on Gavin's medallion as he said, "Ah...Gerrus's line, then."

"That's what I'm told."

"So, Mariana says you stopped the attacker."

"He was a wizard, but I haven't learned all the various House Glyphs yet. He had Lillian laid out on the stone block at the center of the maze, and he had used a paralysis scroll on her. It was the use of the scroll that attracted my attention."

"How?" Mariana asked. "Scrolls are undetectable."

Gavin frowned as he shifted his attention to Mariana. "No, they're not. I felt the Enchantment effect very clearly. Granted, it was a little faint...but more than strong enough to identify."

Mariana drew breath, but Andrin spoke first.

"I've read that the sensitivity of a wizard's *skathos* is related to the strength of the wizard."

"At any rate," Gavin said, "I found him standing over Lillian and prevented him from concluding his intent, while Valera brought the nearest Inquisitor."

Just then, Torval Mivar entered the waiting area. His eyes locked on Mariana, and he approached the group.

"Mari, dear girl, it's good to see you," Torval said as he pulled the young battle-mage into a fierce embrace. "Thanks for being here for Lilli, and I'm glad you're here. I'm calling a Conclave to discuss what happened."

"A Conclave, sir? Is that really necessary?"

"No matter whether this was just some pervert having some fun or part of an orchestrated plan, it was an attack on the Great Houses of Tel, and I feel we need to discuss our position and response."

Mariana nodded, saying, "In that case, sir, I should probably introduce you to Gavin."

"No need, Mari; the lad and I are already acquainted," Torval said, stepping around his son and extending his right hand to Gavin. "I appreciate what you did; not many would've done it. Come to think of it, you'd also better come with us. We won't be able to convene the Conclave without you. But enough of that for now... where's my girl?"

"She's in Room 5, at the end of the observation hall."

With Mariana on his left, Gavin led the two elder men down the hallway of the observation rooms and found the door to Room 5 was still closed. Not even thinking about it, Gavin tapped Mariana's shoulder and pointed to the door, and Mariana walked ahead of the men. Mariana approached the door and rapped two, quiet knocks before edging the door open and peering inside. Within moments, Kiri came to the doorway.

"How is she?" Mariana asked, her voice a whisper.

Kiri looked over her shoulder to the sleeping form partially hidden beneath the covers as she said, "I think she's through the worst of it now. It will haunt her for years, but I don't think it will be anything more than a bad memory. We talked most of the night, and she only just went to sleep a short time ago."

"Her father and grandfather are here. They came to get her."

Kiri motioned for Mariana to back out of the doorway, and she followed Mariana to the hallway, closing the door behind her as she moved.

"Gentlemen, this is Kiri," Gavin said as Kiri stepped into the hallway. "She's been helping Lillian process what happened. Kiri, this is Torval Mivar and his son Andrin, Lillian's grandfather and father respectively."

If the older men thought it odd a slave would be taking care of Lillian, they didn't show it.

"How is she, miss?" Torval asked.

"She's sleeping. We were up most of the night talking, once I broke through her determination to be strong about it. You need to understand that this will be with her for quite a while. I think she'll come to terms with it in time, but it's still raw now. I spent the time after she went to sleep thanking the Gods that Gavin found her when he did; as bad as it was for her, it would've been far worse if that student had finished what he intended."

"We've come to take her to our estate, here in the city," Torval said. "I'm calling a Conclave of the Great Houses to discuss this attack. As Heir to House Mivar, Lillian is part of the Conclave."

Kiri shook her head. "That's not a good idea at all. Yes, she needs to talk about what happened, but it needs to be in an environment where she feels safe and has no pressure. Being your Heir is an incredible weight on her, and right now, she's still wrestling with the truth that what happened wasn't her fault or her failure."

"Are you calling my daughter broken? I don't like some *slave* saying my daughter is broken," Andrin said, taking a step toward Kiri.

Within the span of a finger-snap, Gavin stood between Kiri and Andrin. His back to was to Kiri; he gave Andrin his best glare.

"And I don't like your tone," Gavin said. "Now, back off, and apologize."

Andrin stepped closer to Gavin, returning the glare. "You think I'm afraid of some waif wearing Kirloth's glyph?"

For some people, having a man whose family had the stature of House Mivar so close would have been intimidating. In that moment, Gavin realized he was *not* most people. In that moment, everything Marcus had tried to tell him about what it means to be Kirloth snapped into perfect clarity. Gavin still didn't agree with Marcus's methods, and he certainly didn't believe the ends justified the means. Still, though, Gavin was not going to be someone who didn't hold to his convictions in the face of adversity.

"I don't really know what you're afraid of," Gavin said, "nor do I care all that much. Right now, you're angry and afraid for your daughter. You want nothing more than to put your hands around the neck of the filth who attacked her, but you can't do that. So, you're lashing out, except the person you happen to be lashing out against is under *my* protection.

"I'll admit I haven't been aware that I'm House Kirloth for all that long, but part of what I've learned over the last several weeks is that House Kirloth takes care of its own...whether anyone else realizes that or not. I don't like the turn this conversation has taken, but I'm not about to permit you to demean or browbeat anyone I name 'friend.' This conversation will end only one of two ways, and you will determine what path we take next. Now, choose."

Gavin took a half-step to his left so that Andrin could make eye contact with Kiri.

"Let's all just take a step back for a moment," Torval said.

Gavin's eyes never left Andrin as he said, "Sir, with all due respect, you're not the one who has made an ass of himself. This isn't your affair."

The silence extended past the point of awkward until Andrin sighed and bowed his head. When he lifted his eyes to Kiri once more, Andrin said, "Miss, I apologize."

The thick blanket of tension covering the hallway evaporated like a fog bank before the morning sun.

Kiri smiled and said, "I forgive you. How could I refuse to forgive a man who loves his daughter as much as you clearly do?"

"Miss-" Torval said.

"Please, call me Kiri."

Torval cleared his throat and resumed, "Kiri, do I understand that you believe it to be unwise to have Lillian recount what happened before the Conclave?"

"Is this Conclave made up of people she looks up to or whose good opinion she values?"

"Yes," Mariana said, before Torval could speak. "Lillian has felt like she has something to prove for several years now. She doesn't feel like she has what it takes to follow in her grandfather's footsteps."

Kiri closed her eyes and shook her head. "Sir, I don't feel anything good will come of making her recount what happened. She feels weak, vulnerable. One of the things she said last night is that what happened would never have happened to Mariana."

"That's not true!" Mariana said, her voice rising. "It could just as easily have happened to me!"

"I know that," Kiri said, "and you know that. Lillian is still developing her understanding and awareness of that." Kiri turned her attention back to Torval. "The conversation we had last night was very good for her, but this isn't the kind of thing one conversation will mend. Mariana, tell them how Lillian was before Gavin brought me to the room."

Torval and Andrin looked to her, and Mariana said, "She seemed fine. She was laughing and happy. I saw her lying naked on that stone block, unable to move, but you would never have known anything had happened, interacting with her last night."

Kiri nodded, saying, "I think the only reason she is talking with me is that I've survived what she's been through and worse. Is there any way to have your Conclave without forcing her attendance?"

Torval took a deep breath and looked up at the ceiling for several moments.

"Well…her presence would not be required to convene the Conclave if Mivar did not summon the Conclave, but I still feel the other Houses need to know what happened."

"What if I *want* to go?"

Gavin, Kiri, and Mariana spun to face the door to Lillian's room as Andrin and Torval shifted their attention. Lillian stood in the open doorway, a pastel blue dressing gown wrapped around her and matching slippers on her feet.

"Lillian-"

"I know, Kiri; you're worried for me. I heard. What I want most right now is to hide under the covers and curl up in a ball, and that's exactly why I can't. Even if I were not a student here at the College, I have responsibilities as Heir of House Mivar. I'm not saying I'm some pillar of strength, for I'd feel ever so much better if you went to the Conclave with me. But I should go."

Kiri turned to look at Torval. "Am I allowed to attend the Conclave?"

"I don't see why not," Torval said, before his eyes developed a mischievous gleam and his mouth curled into an impish grin, "and if any of the others don't like it, they can speak with Gavin."

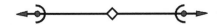

CHAPTER 26

Torval, Gavin, and the rest stopped on the third floor of the Tower to collect Wynn and Braden, as they were the Heirs of their respective Houses, before making their way down to the Tower's entrance.

As the group exited the Tower, they encountered a group of six upper-Tier students starting to enter. Their eyes locked on Lillian, and each displayed a predatory smile.

"There she is," the student in the front said, as he led the group over to Gavin and the others. "We've been looking all over for you. We want to speak with you about those slanderous lies about our friend you passed off as truth."

Before anyone else could react, Gavin stepped to the front of his group and approached the student who had spoken.

"The fact that you call such dishonorable filth as Rolf Sivas 'friend' tells me more about your collective character than I want to know, but that's not really germane to the discussion. You should know that Lillian Mivar is under my protection; if you would 'speak' with her, you must first face me."

"You're a brave fool, standing in front of all these people," the student said, "and there's six of us. You can't be with her all the time."

"You tell him, Van!" a student in the back said.

Another said, "We'll get her eventually; we always do."

"My mentor spent some time a while back telling me what it means to be Kirloth, and I'll be honest that I don't really approve of the methods and conduct he said was necessary as Kirloth. That being said, you boys need to think long and hard about whether this is a box you really want to open."

"Who do you think you are?" the student in front said. "You're only one guy."

Gavin stepped closer and spoke in a lower, though firm, voice, "I think I'm the guy who killed fifty-three slavers with just one Word, and there aren't that many of you. Now, make your move…or be somewhere else."

Gavin held eye contact with the student in front of the other five, waiting for him to do something stupid. In the end, though, the student displayed a slight glimmer of intelligence.

"Come on, guys," he said, backing away from Gavin. "There will be another day."

"There better not be," Gavin said, his voice almost a whisper.

Gavin and the others stood on the steps of the Tower, watching the six students disappear down the path to the gardens. Once they were out of sight, Gavin and company started walking to the College's gate.

"Would you have killed them just now?" Torval asked as he walked beside Gavin.

Gavin shrugged. "What matters is that they believed I would."

* * *

DURING THE FOUNDING, Kirloth and the First Council divided what became the Kingdom of Tel into four duchies. Despite a great deal of resistance to the idea, Kirloth installed his four former apprentices as dukes of these provinces, even going so far as writing their families' continued reign over these provinces into the new constitution, and since that time, Mivar, Roshan, Cothos, and Wygoth joined Kirloth to become known as the Great Houses of Tel.

The Mivar Estate occupied a place in the northwest quadrant of the city. Like the College and city, a manor wall untouched by mortal tools surrounded the space. Within the estate's grounds, several outbuildings stood, housing the various trades an estate required, such as a blacksmith, stables, and carpenter.

The manor house was a subdued, three-story mansion, possessing an ancient character. Marble columns supported a portico, and the house's walls looked to be of similar construction to the manor-wall. What astonished Gavin the most were the many protections built into the manor-wall. Reaching out with his *skathos*, Gavin could feel all of them but only recognize one or two.

Large, wrought iron gates barred entry to the estate grounds, and a rope hung outside the wall from a bell mounted just beside the right-hand gate. As Torval approached within seven or so feet of the gates, the *click!* of a massive latch unlocking echoed across the estate, and the gates swung wide on silent hinges.

"You grew up here?" Gavin asked Lillian as they walked to the house from the main gate.

"Yes, this is home."

"It's a very nice home," Gavin said.

Lillian smiled and said, "Thank you."

As THEY APPROACHED the doors of the manor house, those very doors opened to permit an older woman to step onto the portico. She was just below average height, and her hair ranged from silver to white in colored strands. She wore a simple, though well-crafted, dress—spring green in hue—and smiled with ease.

Lillian broke through the group and ran to her, each throwing her arms around the other in a fierce embrace. After several moments, they broke the embrace, and the older woman held Lillian at her arms' length, her hands on Lillian's shoulders.

"Oh, Lilli-girl, I was so worried when we heard. How are you?"

"I'm not harmed, Nanna," Lillian said. "The rest will take a while, but I'll heal. Kiri helped me."

"Kiri?"

By this time, the group reached the portico.

"She's Gavin's friend, Nanna," Lillian said and waded into the group to pull Gavin forward. "Gavin, I want to introduce Adelaide Mivar, my grandmother. Nanna, this is Gavin; he stopped t – the attack."

Adelaide turned to Gavin, and her eyes went straight to his medallion. Her eyes did indeed widen just enough to notice, but she showed no nervousness or unease. Instead, she smiled.

"Well, upon my word…it has been many the age since a wizard of House Kirloth openly walked across the world. Our family owes you a debt for what you did for Lilli."

"Nonsense," Gavin said. "I'll hear no talk of debts. What he was doing was *wrong*, and I wasn't about to allow it to happen. If anyone owes a debt, it's Rolf of House Sivas; something he said leads me to believe Lillian wasn't the first."

Torval moved up to stand beside his wife, saying, "Have the others arrived yet, Addie?"

"Yes," she said, "and Lyssa's buzzing about Kirloth's glyph being lit. Sypara apparently twisted Carth's arm; they have been letting Lyssa stew on it."

"Sypara has always been a rascal," Torval said. "We probably shouldn't keep them waiting."

Torval turned and led everyone into the house. The hardwood floors were varnished and polished to a high sheen, and a faint scent of something flowery hung in the air. Staircases curved up to the second-floor landing before curling back around to rise to the third. Gavin could see a set of closed, double doors just behind the stairs.

"You have a beautiful home," Gavin said.

"Thank you," Adelaide said and favored Gavin with an impish smile. "It's nice to have a man in the house who appreciates the work I do."

"Oh, now, Addie," Torval said, "you know I-" He stopped

speaking when he saw the impish smile and gleam in his wife's eyes. "Okay, you got me."

"Go on, then," Adelaide said, giving her husband a shooing gesture.

Torval laughed and led Gavin, Lillian, Kiri, Wynn, Braden, Mariana, and Andrin past the staircase to a set of double doors. He opened them and stepped through, allowing the others to enter before he closed the doors behind them. The room was a large meeting hall, lit by sconces that neither burned fuel nor radiated heat.

A large circular table occupied the very center of the room. The tabletop almost resembled a wizard's medallion, in that there was center section that bore the Mivar Glyph. A circle surrounded that section, and engraved lines spurred off from the circle, dividing the table into fifths. Each fifth had a Glyph engraved into the tabletop and two chairs—a large, prominent chair and a smaller one— except for one. The section that bore Kirloth's Glyph possessed only the larger, prominent chair.

Three people stood together talking, and they turned to face the new arrivals. Gavin recognized Carth Roshan and Sypara Wygoth. The person he didn't recognize was a striking, middle-aged woman whose copper hair was laced with strands of gray; she wore the crimson-trimmed black robes of the Inquisitors with white rank runes on the sleeves.

"Torval," the black-robed woman said as the group approached, "what's going on with the table? Kirloth's glyph has never lit up before."

"That's because a wizard of House Kirloth has never attended a Conclave before, Lyssa," Torval said.

"How could one? That family died out with the first Archmagister," the black-robed woman said.

Torval chuckled. "Apparently not, Lyssa." He stepped aside and indicated Gavin. "Allow me to present Gavin Cross of House Kirloth."

Torval turned to Gavin and indicated the black-robed woman.

"Gavin, this is Lyssa Cothos, Duchess and Head of House Cothos. I believe you already know the others."

"The precedents are clear, Torval," Lyssa said. "Yes, he is very impressive, but he's a student and probably underage at that. He can't take his House's seat at the Conclave."

"Forgive me for interrupting," Gavin said, "but I'm not a student. I don't know how old I am, though."

Lyssa frowned, saying, "What do you mean you're not a student? You wear the brown robes."

"Yes, but Marcus said something about taking me as his apprentice as was in the old ways," Gavin said. "Ovir witnessed it…legally witnessed it, I mean."

Now, Lyssa paled.

"Marcus took you as his apprentice?" Lyssa asked, her voice a little shaky. Torval, Sypara, and Carth stood back and looked on. Given Sypara's pursed lips and the gleam in her eyes, she was enjoying Lyssa's discomfiture.

"Yes," Gavin said. "He's been training me, and…well…I've kind of been experimenting with things on my own."

"You practice in your suite at the Tower?" Lillian asked. "Gavin, that's dangerous."

"No. I practice and experiment in the arena. Marcus took me down there to teach me Words of Power and how to manipulate them, and ever since then, the spectral guard allows me to pass when I tell him I've come to practice."

Lyssa swallowed hard and turned to look at Torval, saying, "He can sit at the Conclave."

EVERYONE TOOK THEIR SEATS, with Kiri sitting beside Andrin against the wall of the room.

Torval rapped his knuckles on the table. "Unless there be any objections, I hereby call this Conclave of the Great Houses to order." After a short pause, Torval continued, "Last evening, around two hours before sunset, Lillian was attacked by Rolf of House

Sivas. As Gavin was responsible for interrupting the assault, I ask him to relay what he knows."

Lyssa, Carth, and Sypara turned to face Gavin, and he felt his ears heat again. He looked at Lillian and saw her staring at the table.

"Lillian?" Gavin asked. "Are you okay with this?"

Lillian lifted her head just enough to look at Gavin from the corner of her eyes, nodding. "Go ahead, Gavin; they need to know."

"Okay. I'm sorry," Gavin said before turning back to the group. "I had just finished speaking with Valera at one of her flowerbeds when I felt an Enchantment effect deeper in the gardens, in the general direction of the hedge maze. I followed the faint resonance, which led me to the maze. I made use of the shortcut to the maze's center and saw a young man standing over a woman lying on the stone block. I could see she was not wearing any clothes, but I couldn't see her face.

"The man was talking to her, talking about how he'd looked forward to this since he first saw her and other sick things like that. At one point, he made a reference to 'all the rest.'

"To make a long story short, I stopped him and saw the woman was Lillian; she was held with a paralysis effect. I covered her with my robe and subdued the guy until Valera, an Inquisitor, and Mariana arrived."

Lyssa turned to her daughter, asking, "How did you come to be involved?"

"Commander Roshan re-assigned me to the College to assist with updating the Battle-mage curriculum. You remember Reyna, my best friend when I was at the College? She's stationed at the College now, and I was visiting with her when Valera arrived, so I walked with her."

"As I understand the situation," Carth Roshan said, "this Rolf of House Sivas not only committed one of the most heinous offenses delineated in the Code, but he also attacked the Great Houses doing it. I don't have any idea when someone last attacked our Houses; does anyone?"

Lyssa looked to Mariana, who sighed and closed her eyes as she leaned her head back against the chair. After a very brief moment, she opened her eyes and lifted her head, saying, "3367 PG."

Carth grimaced. "Oh."

"I'm sorry," Gavin said, "but what happened in 3367?"

"A *Termagus* of House Throsk caused the death of the Head of House Wygoth at the time," Torval said. "A number of people died in wizards' duels, and circumstances spiraled to a hair's breadth of a civil war. It didn't help matters that the Archmagister at the time happened to be from House Roshan, and she took the matter rather poorly."

"I see," Gavin said. "That's not so good a precedent."

"No," Torval said, shaking his head.

"I know the Council was supposed to be in session this morning," Gavin said, "and I thought it was about the complaint that Lillian filed last night. Is there anything wrong with waiting to see what the Council chooses to do?"

Lyssa sneered. Carth sighed. Sypara scoffed.

Torval grimaced and said, "Gavin, the Council has become increasingly less of a friend toward the Great Houses in the past few years, and it doesn't help that the young man's father is a close friend of the king."

"What's that got to do with anything?" Gavin asked. "I thought the Constitution of Tel said that the king has authority only over the civil affairs of the Kingdom of Tel...and only during the times when there is no Archmagister."

"Gavin," Sypara said, "there have been rumors for quite some time now that the king is actively looking for an excuse to assault the College and bring the Society of the Arcane under his direct authority."

"But that makes no sense," Gavin said. "Moving against the Society would violate his oath and give the four of you just cause to depose him and declare a regent."

"It doesn't matter what authority we have," Lyssa said. "Right now, the king controls the bulk of the martial force in the city. He has subtly manipulated personnel assignments in the army to put people who favor him—if not outright support him—in the major command positions. Our information indicates that the army would sit and wait it out if the king orders the Royal Guard to assault the College."

"It wouldn't be so bad if there were anyone alive today who could activate the city's garrison," Carth said. "Twenty-five thousand spectral warriors would make even the king step back and reconsider things."

"How does one activate the garrison?" Gavin asked, a sinking feeling starting to form in the pit of his stomach.

"As long as you meet the criteria," Torval said, "you just go to one of the activation sigils scattered around the city and speak the command word, but that's the problem. I'm not sure if even Mariana knows what the criteria are. Kirloth never recorded them that I'm aware."

Mariana shook her head in silence.

"Torval," Lyssa said, "it's good that you called the Conclave. We all needed to know what happened, but as much as I would like to believe the Council will fail to handle this according to the Code, we should wait to be sure before we start formulating a course of action."

"Agreed," Carth said. "I, too, am glad you called the Conclave. I think the Council should see us together in the gallery when they get around to announcing their findings."

"Does anyone object to us adjourning until the Council makes its announcement?" Sypara asked.

When no one spoke, Torval rapped his knuckles on the table once more. "Under general acclamation, I declare this Conclave adjourned."

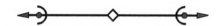

CHAPTER 27

Three days later, the Council of Magisters gave notice they would deliver their verdict. As with all meetings of the Council, the proceedings took place in the hall known as the Chamber of the Council. The space was set up like a series of tiered horseshoes, and the very center of the space was a recessed oval. At Gavin's right as he walked down a slight grade to the oval, an unoccupied throne sat on a raised dais just a few steps higher than the floor. It was a simple throne, more of a wooden chair with a padded seat and back and decorated with intricate carvings. Behind the throne, Gavin saw a door, and his sense of direction told him that door should open somehow into the Grand Stair.

Opposite the throne was a horseshoe-shaped table large enough to sit nine people in comfort, and today, every seat was occupied. Gavin saw almost every color robe represented, along with a wide variety of rune colors. The only color not present at the table was the black robe that signified a philosophy of the Art above all else.

On the one side of the oval, a statue stood atop a three-foot pedestal. The marble statue was a masterwork, depicting the person in intricate detail...everything from his pointed Van Dyke beard to the dragon-head medallion atop his sternum. He looked down upon the recessed oval, and his expression was one of wise consideration.

A spectator's gallery curved around the space at the door's level. It began on the left side of the walkway down from the door and curved all the way around to the edge of the statue's pedestal. It had five rows of benches in a stadium-seating configuration. A good fifteen feet above the level of the door, another gallery ran all the way around the room, having nearly ten rows of benches for even more seating. These galleries provided seating for anyone wishing to watch the Council's deliberations, and the Council was barred from forbidding access to them in the Arcanists' Code.

Gavin, Lillian, Wynn, Braden, and Mariana sat in the first row of the lower gallery. Kiri sat on the floor at Gavin's feet, no matter how hard Gavin tried to change her mind. Torval Mivar, Lyssa Cothos, Carth Roshan, and Sypara Wygoth sat in the second row. All nine Magisters occupied their respective seats at the table, including Valera and Tauron, and Rolf Sivas stood before the Council at the open end of the horseshoe.

In addition to serving as the Collegiate Justice and Magister of Divination, Valera also held the dubious honor of Eldest of the Council. The position was one of respect and an honorific at best, with no real power or authority beyond presiding over meetings for such things as calls to order, calls for votes, and adjournment.

"This meeting of the Council of Magisters of the Society of the Arcane is hereby called to order," Valera said, tapping a small square on the table near her left hand.

Images of each magister's School glyph appeared above the backs of their chairs, and red orbs appeared at the top corners of every doorway into the room.

"Tauron," Valera said, "will you begin, please?"

A man in red robes with silver runes ringing the cuffs of the sleeves stood. The glyph of Evocation above his chair brightened, indicating this magister now held the floor.

"In the matter of the Society of the Arcane vs. Rolf of House Sivas, the Council has determined that the matter be dropped."

Tauron resumed his seat, and the glyph of Divination brightened above Valera's chair.

"Does anyone have anything to say before the Council adjourns?"

Gavin stood, saying, "I have something to say."

"The Council recognizes Gavin Cross," Valera said. "Please, approach the Council."

Gavin moved to the stairs that led from the lower gallery to the Chamber's floor. The moment he stepped into the recessed area, the glyph of House Kirloth appeared above his head, and hushed whispers erupted from all around the galleries. Gavin walked to stand near Rolf to address the Council, guessing the room's embedded effects would carry his voice to everyone in attendance.

"I fail to understand how the Council—in its supposed wisdom— can vote to drop the matter we have come here to address. I caught him in the act of assaulting a woman who was bound by a paralysis effect, unable to resist or cry out for help, and statements I overheard indicate it was not the first time he's done something like this."

"Do you have any evidence that Rolf of House Sivas has done what he is alleged to have committed before?" Tauron asked, interrupting Gavin.

"Beyond the words I overheard, no," Gavin said. "However, it is an easy matter to verify; cast Divination of Truth on him."

"There has been no complaint filed against Rolf. With no formal complaint, there is no accusation of a crime, and it goes against the Arcanists' Code to cast Divination of Truth on anyone not accused of a crime," Kantar—the elven Magister of Tutation —said.

Gavin spoke, his voice savage, "I was one of three who witnessed Lillian Mivar sign the completed form in the office of the Collegiate Justice four days ago! What happened to that form?"

The Magister of Tutation turned to look at Tauron, saying, "As Chief Inquisitor, Tauron would be the one to answer that question."

Tauron shifted his eyes away and swallowed. "We're here to deliver a verdict, not answer questions, and that verdict is delivered.

I move we adjourn these proceedings and consider the matter closed."

"The Council cannot adjourn until all parties have yielded the floor," Valera said, her eyes on Gavin.

Gavin stood motionless, except for the slight shaking of his head as he worked through what he was hearing. What the Council was doing went against the very basis on which the Arcanists' Code was written.

"I will not stand by and allow the Council to do nothing about a piece of filth who has committed one of the most heinous violations of the Code possible, not to mention sullying the honor of wizardry and the Society as a whole," Gavin said, his teeth clenched. He pivoted on his heel to face Rolf. "Rolf of House Sivas, I myself witnessed you attempting to assault a woman held by a paralysis effect you yourself placed upon her, and before this assembly, I declare you a coward and beyond redemption." Gavin stepped within arms' reach and slapped Rolf across the face with the back of his left hand. "I hereby challenge you to a wizards' duel."

"Now, see here," Tauron said, "there's no call-"

"You're out of order," Gavin said, turning to look at the Magister of Evocation. "Nothing else matters until he accepts or declines."

It seemed like every eye in the room then turned to Rolf. The young man was pale, and rivers of sweat ran down his face. His eyes darted about like cornered prey.

"I – I accept," he said at last. "Name your terms."

"I see no reason to wait," Gavin said. "Let us visit the Arena once this hearing is concluded."

"Gavin," Valera said and cleared her throat, "it's been the custom for several decades to allow both parties to a duel some time…to make arrangements and that sort of thing."

Gavin turned to face Valera. "Very well. I can agree to two days, on the condition he is restricted to the College grounds for that period. I would hate to have to hunt him down like an animal; it would interrupt my studies."

Valera nodded. "Very well. Do you have anything further to say?"

"No. I yield the floor."

"Do we have any further business?" Valera asked, addressing the remark to the Council in general.

Tauron pulled away from glaring at Gavin to look at Valera. "I move we adjourn."

Kantar directed a speculative gaze toward Tauron for several heartbeats before he looked to Valera. "I second the motion."

"Any opposed?" Valera asked. When no one spoke, she said, "Then, I declare this meeting of the Council of Magisters adjourned." Valera once more tapped the small square beside her left hand. Both the glyphs above the magisters' chairs and the red orbs above the doors vanished.

Rolf darted for the nearest door, and Gavin watched him for a few moments before turning to join his friends. Just as he was reaching the steps that led to the lower gallery, he heard a voice behind him.

"Gavin, do you have a moment?"

Gavin turned to see Valera standing behind him. "Of course, Valera. What do you need?"

Valera glanced around the room. "May I have a word…in private?"

Gavin nodded and followed her.

VALERA LED GAVIN to an empty classroom not too far from the Council chambers. Such an occurrence was not all that odd, though; there were times throughout the week's class schedule where one or two lecture halls would be devoid of use. Valera leaned against the table beside the lectern.

"So, what's on your mind?" Gavin asked as he leaned against a desk in the front row.

Valera pursed her lips for a moment before she took a breath, saying, "I just wanted to be sure you've thought through this matter of a duel. Events seemed to happen rather fast in there."

Gavin shrugged. "I don't see what all there is to think through. He attacked my friend, and the Council is apparently incapable of doing its job of policing the Society. I will not allow him to walk these grounds a free man, knowing what he's done and what he's liable to do again. That leaves me with two choices: murder or a duel. One's legal; the other isn't."

"Gavin...he is the only son of a powerful family close to the king. No good can come from this."

"Valera, he was using the Art to paralyze women so that he could brutalize them with no resistance! How in the name of all the gods can you stand there and say no good will come of this?" Gavin turned and started to walk out, but he stopped after a few steps, his back ramrod straight, and turned slowly to face Valera once more. "Tell me you had nothing to do with Lillian's complaint disappearing."

"And if I did? Will you challenge me to a duel as well?"

The glare in Gavin's eyes softened as he sighed. "No, Valera; no, I won't. I will, however, be very disappointed and have nothing further to do with you."

A small—very small—smile curled Valera's lips. "You are both like and unlike your mentor, Gavin. He would've...well, no matter. I give you my word; I was not involved in the Council's capitulation to politics. Unlike the few who abstained, I voted 'Nay,' but it seems all Tau...*their*...scheming is for naught. My thoughts go with you, young man."

Valera walked past Gavin as she left the room, reaching a hand up to deliver a supporting squeeze to Gavin's shoulder as she passed.

GAVIN STOOD in silence for several moments, contemplating the exchange. He did not think Valera would've been the type to countenance such as what the Council tried to do. On the surface, he knew she could easily have been lying, but he didn't see that as likely. Marcus, after all, chose her for the post of Collegiate Justice, and he would not have chosen a compromiser.

· · ·

GAVIN TURNED to leave the classroom and stopped cold. A man stood in the doorway. He wore the brown robes of an initiate with no wizards' medallion. His sandy blond hair was well-groomed, as was his Van Dyke beard. Gavin had the unshakable feeling that he'd seen the man somewhere before.

"Do you have a moment?" the man asked.

Gavin shrugged. "I don't see why not. How can I help you?"

"I was attending the hearing, and I-"

"If you intend to threaten or coerce me to call off the duel," Gavin said, interrupting the man, "you might as well save your breath."

"No, no...not at all," the man said, moving over to sit at an empty seat near the door. "I merely wished to discuss the matter. It seems a dangerous route to take."

Gavin sighed and walked up the steps to a desk a couple levels below the man and turned its chair to face him before sitting. "That young man has done this before, and if left unchecked, he would do it again once he felt safe enough. There is a reason what he's done is clearly spelled out as a capital offense in the Code."

"Ah...so, you are a vigilante then, pursuing the cause of justice."

"No, not at all," Gavin said, shaking his head. "It's...well, it's like this. There is no doubt in my mind that what he did and was trying to do is wrong. I simply could not stand idly by and watch him walk away to do it again. Fortunately, our system provided me an option. I would hate to think what I might have done if all my options were illegal."

"I wouldn't worry about it," the man said, rising to his feet. "Be careful. There's no telling how this will spiral after you win your duel."

"How do you know I will win?" Gavin asked as he watched the man walk toward the door.

The man stopped in the doorway and looked over his shoulder, saying, "I know who trained him, and I know who trained you. There can be no other outcome."

"You're not a student here, are you?" Gavin asked.

The man stopped again and turned to face Gavin once more, a

small smile curling his lips as he said, "We are all students, Gavin; my first studies took a path very similar to yours...only many, many years ago."

With that, the man turned and disappeared around the edge of the doorway.

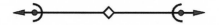

CHAPTER 28

The morning after the hearing, Gavin sat in the armchair by the hearth, writing in his journal, when a fierce pounding erupted on the suite's door. After setting aside his journal, ink, and stylus, Gavin went to the door and opened it, finding two Inquisitors standing in the hallway. They both looked imposing in their black robes trimmed in crimson, but the fact that one of them only came up to his fellow's shoulder added humor to the situation.

"What could possibly be so important that you make such a racket at this ungodly hour?" Gavin asked. "I'm not even sure the sun has risen yet."

"You're charged with gross violations of College policies," the taller Inquisitor said. "You will accompany us to the office of the Collegiate Justice."

Gavin frowned. "That makes no sense. Which policies am I accused of violating?"

"We are not privy to the actual complaint. The Chief Inquisitor instructed us to collect you."

"Oh, bother," Gavin said. "You guys might as well come inside while I wash and get dressed."

"Our orders are to bring you immediately," the shorter Inquisitor said.

Gavin shrugged. "Suit yourself. I'm not going to deal with the frustration produced by Tauron's stupidity without a quick wash and some fresh clothes. You're welcome to wait in a comfy chair or wait in the hallway, but you'll be waiting nonetheless."

The Inquisitors looked at each other for a moment. The shorter one shrugged.

The taller Inquisitor said, "we'll accept that offer of chairs."

THE WALK DOWNSTAIRS to Valera's office was quick but unhurried. The halls were vacant; not even the overachiever students had started moving yet. Gavin found the outer office where Valera's assistant Sera usually sat to be empty, and he stopped cold when he saw Tauron sitting behind Valera's desk.

"What took you so long?" Tauron asked, glaring at the two Inquisitors behind Gavin. "Have trouble finding him?"

"They interrupted me, Tauron," Gavin said, "and I told them I wasn't going anywhere without washing up and changing clothes. If you want to be mad that you weren't instantly obeyed, blame me."

Gavin watched Tauron's jaw tighten as he continued to glare at the Inquisitors.

"We'll discuss this later," Tauron said.

Gavin sighed. "I'd like to see a copy of the complaint filed against me."

"Well, you can't," Tauron snapped, transferring his scowl to Gavin.

"That's odd. I'm pretty sure anyone charged with violating the Code has to be provided full documentation of the charges."

Tauron's face and neck reddened. He slapped the desk with an open palm, saying, "I am the Chief Inquisitor of the Society of the Arcane, not to mention the Magister of Evocation! You do not lecture me on the Arcanists' Code!"

"He should when you're being a damned fool, Tauron," a new

voice said, and Gavin recognized it. He looked over his shoulder and saw Marcus standing in the doorway of Valera's private office. Marcus's arms were crossed in front of his chest, and he bestowed a most unfavorable scowl on Tauron, while the two Inquisitors started edging away from the door. "Does Valera know you're in her office?"

"This is not your concern, old man! Leave at once, or I'll have you named a renegade…as I should've done many years ago!"

Marcus continued to scowl at Tauron but uncrossed his arms, motioning for Gavin leave.

"If you walk out that door, boy, you'll be making a powerful enemy," Tauron said as Gavin started to rise.

Marcus approached Valera's desk, leaning forward to rest his palms flat on it as he said, "Tauron, if you so much as frown at my apprentice after today, I will challenge you to a duel on the spot. And when you accept, because your ego won't let you admit what a coward you are, I'll burn you down to ash where you stand. Gavin…we're leaving."

Marcus turned and walked behind Gavin as they left Tauron sputtering in rage, and Gavin started just a bit, surprised at seeing Declan leaning against the wall in the corridor outside. Marcus closed the outer door behind him without even looking back.

"Your note said you might be gone as long as two weeks, Marcus," Gavin said as they approached the Grand Stair. "Did you accomplish everything you need to do?"

"Not entirely, no. Declan contacted me when he saw those Inquisitors take you out of the suite and followed you to see where you were going. I know these old halls so well that I almost didn't need the teleportation marker in the vestibule here."

Marcus stopped at the base of the Grand Stair and sighed before saying, "I should be here for you, Gavin, but events are occurring elsewhere that also require my attention. See Bella in the library; she will be able to help you learn what you need to know about duels. I will return when I can."

Marcus stepped back and spoke a Word of Transmutation, "*Paedryx*."

Gavin felt the surge of his power take hold as a sapphire arch rose out of the floor. When the arch was just a bit taller than Marcus, it flashed and became a doorway to another place. Gavin saw structures that looked to be made of crystal and surrounded by trees, before Marcus stepped through the gateway. With Marcus's passage, the gateway vanished.

A FULL THREE floors of the Tower could only be accessed through a pair of massive double doors on the fifth floor. Those floors housed the College's library. While the library held copies of books and scrolls from a wide range of subjects, the library's primary purpose was to catalogue and house the finest collection of works on the Art in the known world. Scholars traveled from across the world to spend a day researching specific topics within the library's halls; none were turned away, and few were disappointed.

Gavin approached the library's circulation desk and found himself facing Mistress Bella Roshan, the Curator of the Library. Bella Roshan was a tall woman, her eyes nearly being even with Gavin's. Her golden blond hair was now predominantly gray, and age had wrinkled her features just a bit. Still, her sky-blue eyes sparkled with a zest and love of life uncommon even in people Gavin's age. The blue robe she wore indicated her philosophy toward the Art as being scholarly, but the embroidered runes ringing the cuffs of the sleeves were black, signifying she had never chosen to specialize in a specific School.

"Well, upon my word," Mistress Roshan said as Gavin approached, "I never expected to have a wizard of House Kirloth walk through my doors."

Gavin felt a slight flush of color heat his cheeks before he held out his hand and said, "I'm Gavin Cross."

Mistress Roshan accepted Gavin's hand and shook it. "I'm Bella Roshan, Curator of the Library. I hear you've been helping the newest class of students, my nephew among them."

"Oh, you're Wynn's aunt?" Gavin asked. "He hasn't mentioned he had family working at the College, but then, he doesn't really slow down for extended conversations."

"Yes, well…that's Wynn. What brings you to the library so early?"

"Marcus sent me," Gavin said. "He said you might help me learn what I need to know about duels."

"Ah, yes. You created quite the stir. It's all people have been talking about since yesterday afternoon. Come with me. I know just the book you need."

Bella stepped out from behind the massive curved desk and started walking toward a section of shelves on the main floor.

"You said everyone was talking about my duel. Is there anything you can tell me about what was being said?"

Bella looked over her shoulder for a moment as she led Gavin down the aisle between rows of bookshelves. "Well, as I said, a certain portion of the students aren't all that happy with you, but I know a great many more are. Whether anyone will admit it or not, that boy's depredations have been going on for far too long, and I know more than a few young ladies who are praying for you to carry the day."

"If everyone knows about this, why hasn't anything ever been done?"

Bella stopped and turned to face Gavin. "Gavin, there is a difference between knowing and proving, and given his family connections, there would have to be an incredible amount of proof."

"So, the signed statement of Lillian Mivar means nothing? I caught him trying to assault her; in some ways, I almost wish I'd killed him right there."

"Oh, no, young man. That would have been an altogether worse situation. Your mentor could have gotten away with it, but you? Killing him outright just might have sparked the civil war certain magisters are afraid of."

Gavin frowned as he looked at Bella. "I don't understand. Marcus has never said anything about a coming civil war in Tel."

"That's because he spends a lot of time and effort preventing it," Bella said.

Bella resumed walking. She passed one more bookshelf, before she turned down a row. She walked about half-way down the bookshelf and pulled a thin volume from among the many.

"Here you go," Bella said, extending the small book to Gavin. "There are reading desks right over there."

"Thank you," Gavin said as he started to walk past her but stopped. "What do you think? *Is* there a civil war brewing in Tel?"

"I hope not," Bella said with a sigh. "That has too many ways to go very wrong. A civil war in Tel would quite possibly splinter the Society as well, and if that splintering spiraled out to involve the other races, we could have a war on our hands unlike anything the world has seen since the Godswar. What's going on in Vushaar right now would look like an afternoon tea party."

Gavin frowned. "Is there something happening in Vushaar?"

"I'll say," Bella said. "Terris Muran has a civil war on his hands. Normally, I'd call it an uprising, but the opposing force is led by one of his own generals. I received a letter from a friend in the capital the other day, who said it looked like they were preparing to lay siege to the capital. Terris sent his daughter away to keep her safe, but her ship sank during a storm on the Inner Sea."

"Thanks again," Gavin said as he nodded and turned toward the reading desks.

"Not a problem, Gavin. Bring it up to the desk when you're done, and I'll have one of our student assistants re-shelve it."

Gavin found a reading desk that he thought would suit him, and the chair surprised him by being more comfortable than it looked. Gavin placed the book Bella had given him on the desk in front of him and began to read.

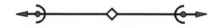

CHAPTER 29

At the appointed time, Gavin met Valera and Rolf at the main-floor landing of the Grand Stair. What surprised him most was the small horde of people gathered behind Valera.

"Uhm," Gavin said, his eyes a little wide, "I wasn't expecting the crowd."

Valera allowed herself a small smile. "Duels are public, Gavin. Besides, several people are interested in seeing the results first-hand."

Just then, Lillian, Wynn, Braden, and Mariana arrived from their families' suites. Gavin smiled just a bit at seeing his friends arrive, and Torval Mivar, Lyssa Cothos, Carth Roshan, and Sypara Wygoth walked through the main doors of the Tower and joined the group.

"Are you both ready to proceed?" Valera asked.

Rolf gave a choppy nod and stammered "Yes."

Gavin shrugged. "Why not? I don't see any reason to wait longer."

.   .   .

VALERA LED the group down into the deeper levels of the Tower. The route was second nature to Gavin, but the deeper they went, the more Rolf trembled, fidgeted, and gnawed at his lower lip.

About twenty minutes after leaving the main floor of the Tower, the group approached the massive door that allowed access to the arena. As they approached, the arena's spectral watchman faded into view.

"Ah, Young Kirloth," it said, addressing Gavin in its measured, wispy voice, "I perceive quite the crowd behind you; have you come to use my hall as a training venue?"

"I'm afraid not," Gavin said. "We come before you in need of your services as Master of the Field."

"Ah, I see. Very well; let us proceed."

The specter turned and pressed its right hand into the door, and the sound of massive locks releasing echoed up the cave-like walkway. A mere moment later, the door began its stately rise to allow entrance to the arena.

The other times Gavin had been here, the specter faded away once the door opened, but this time, it walked with Valera into the arena, stopping at the edge of the ring inset into the ground.

"Any spectators for this event are directed to find seats in the stands; this includes you also, Magister."

Once everyone migrated to the stands surrounding the arena, the specter turned to Gavin and Rolf and began speaking.

"Greetings. Today, I will be serving as Master of the Field," the specter said as it indicated the dueling ring. "The code governing wizards' duels is not complex. All duels are to the death, and once the duel begins, you must stay inside this ring until a victor is decided. If either participant steps outside the ring before the duel is concluded, that participant forfeits the duel and life. I will direct you to a mark on either side of the ring and direct you to take one step inside the ring. Once both parties are in the ring, I will declare the duel started, and you are free to do as you will. Do either of you have any questions before we begin?"

Gavin nodded once, saying, "Is the Rite of Holsgyng still part of the dueling protocols?"

The specter said, "Yes. It is."

"Then, I declare Rite of Holsgyng," Gavin said. "Should I win the duel, any and all property owned by my opponent shall be transferred to me."

"Let it be so recorded that the Rite of Holsgyng has been declared," the specter said before turning to Rolf. "Do you have any questions?"

Rolf shook his head 'no.'

"Very well. You will find marks on the opposite sides of the ring. Please, stand on one."

Gavin turned to his right and walked around to find a glowing mark on the ground that changed to his House glyph as he neared it. Gavin stood directly on the glyph, facing the ring. Rolf moved to stand on a spot across the ring from Gavin.

The specter moved to stand ninety degrees around the circle to Gavin's left, its back to the crowd.

"My oath requires me to ask if there is any way to settle peaceably whatever dispute brought you to this place," the specter said.

Gavin said, "That depends on him."

Rolf paled a bit and swallowed hard.

"Very well," the specter said. "I direct you to step inside the ring at this time."

Gavin and Rolf stepped into the ring.

"The duel has begun. May the gods have mercy upon you."

Gavin waited calmly to see what Rolf was going to do. Normally, that would be a very dangerous proposition, but Gavin was betting that Rolf had never received any training in Words of Power. Gavin won his bet. Rolf lifted his hands and began tracing spell-forms as he recited the words to a spell.

Gavin smiled and closed his eyes to concentrate on his *skathos*. As Rolf recited the words to the spell, the power for the spell built around him, and it created a pressure Gavin could sense...almost like humidity when it really needs to rain.

I guess the only way to know for sure is to let him cast, but I think he's casting an Evocation spell. I'm not curious enough, though, to wait and see.

From his reading the previous day, Gavin knew that there were no rules in wizards' duels…beyond staying inside the dueling ring. Literally, any tactic or device was valid to use in pursuit of victory. Given his feelings toward his opponent, Gavin wanted to be sure Rolf's death was both humiliating and memorable.

Gavin reached into his robe and withdrew a tomato. He took a couple steps forward, drew back his hand, and let fly. The tomato sailed across the fifty-odd feet separating Gavin and Rolf and struck the pride of House Sivas square on the bridge of his nose.

Rolf squawked as he lost his balance and his spell fizzled. Rolf fell backward, his arms wind milling, and he might have been able to save himself…except his heel caught on the metal ring. Within a heartbeat, Rolf lay sprawled in the sawdust that covered the arena floor, and he was outside the ring.

The specter soon stood over Rolf. It drew its sword and jabbed it into Rolf's heart. Rolf cried out, then lay still.

The specter said, "As Master of the Field, I declare this duel finished. Kirloth stands as victor with full rights to the loser's property."

The moment the specter declared him victor, Gavin turned and left the arena.

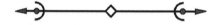

CHAPTER 30

T he sun was bright and high as Marcus walked down a
forgotten street in the slums of a forgotten city. Located in
the desert east of the Godswall Mountains, Vas Edrûn had
little to recommend it. Blocks of baked clay served as the primary
building material, and dust and sand were *everywhere*.

Marcus remembered a time when the verdant farmland of what
had become Mivar and Cothos Provinces extended all the way to
the sea on the far, eastern coast, but the creation of the Godswall
Mountains triggered a massive climate shift. The winds that carried
the rains west to east suddenly stopped coming. In some ways,
Marcus felt it wasn't fair to these people that they should have to live
with the consequences of their ancestors' decisions all those years
ago, but there wasn't much Marcus could do to change things.

Rumors had reached Marcus's ears that the people east of the
mountains were preparing to assault Skullkeep...or possibly rein-
force it...and he was here to investigate those rumors. In most cases,
Marcus would've left this to more capable people, but his intelligence network had never managed to infiltrate this society to any
great degree. Besides, his black robes were close enough to what was

worn by the clergy of Milthas, the fallen god of the elves and arcane magic, that Marcus could pass undisturbed through the streets.

Marcus was nearing his destination when he realized the street around him was devoid of life...no merchants, no beggars, not even any cut-purses. He glanced behind him, but the view was the same. When he turned to face in his direction of travel, however, the view was a bit different.

Nine people in worn leather armor stood in the street ahead of him. Some wore hoods, and some did not, but they all bore a blood-red symbol right at the base of their throats. Only one group used that symbol, and it was a symbol Marcus knew well.

"What...can't you find some little old lady or child to torment?" Marcus asked, adopting a posture and expression to display his contempt.

One of the group stepped forward. "We come for your charge, wizard; we have no quarrel with you. Return with us to Tel Mivar and give him to us, and you have my word his death will be as quick and painless as can be managed."

Marcus frowned. "My charge? What in the world can you possibly want with him?"

"We know who he is, old man, and what's more, we know who he will become. The order will not allow any threat to our master's return to remain. You have one last chance to reconsider."

Marcus laughed. "You're going to need a few more bodies. I've killed you bastards by the hundreds."

"Wizards may know how to kill us," the man said, "but we've learned how to kill wizards, too."

It was then Marcus heard the faintest shuffle behind his right side. Before he could turn or even truly process the sound, Marcus felt a sharp pain erupt in the neighborhood of his kidney. Marcus knew in that instant every moment counted, and he invoked the one Word of Transmutation he never thought he'd use.

The Word required no significant target like most Words did, and it affected the very fabric of time itself. In Marcus's youth, wizards never discussed this Word...never taught it, never wrote it down, even going great lengths to avoid admitting its existence.

Marcus saw as well as felt time slow to an infinitesimal crawl around him as the invocation took hold. He ordered his thoughts and invoked a composite effect, blending a series of Words into one long syllable.

The first part of the effect created a smoky-white glass sphere, causing it to appear hovering in the air in front of Marcus. Marcus said what he needed to say, and an Illusion component to the effect stored his image, his voice, and his words in the sphere. The final aspect of the composite effect, a Transmutation, teleported the sphere to the one soul Marcus knew he could trust without question.

At this point, the Transmutation effect slowing time around Marcus faded, and Marcus felt the blade driving deeper into his torso once more. The pain was excruciating, but Marcus had felt worse during his explorations of the Art.

Marcus couldn't resist a victorious laugh. "You fools have already failed; I've warned Gavin. Give your bastard master my regards."

The blade found Marcus's heart, and the old wizard felt his legs give way. The last thing he saw was an old friend slipping unseen through the alley toward him.

When the members of the deq finally turned from their discussion to collect their 'prize,' they froze. For several long moments, they stared at the pool of blood, now absent a corpse, and the deq's leader bellowed her rage to the heavens.

Beside the pool of blood, a dagger stood upright, its point embedded in the dirt. The hilt bore the symbol of Dakkor, god of thieves and Master of the Guild of Shadows during the Godswar.

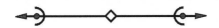

CHAPTER 31

As was often the case whenever Gavin planned to leave the College grounds, he found Declan sitting at the table in the common room, waiting to join him. Gavin long since gave up trying to understand how Declan kept entering their suite at will, especially since Marcus didn't seem all that bothered by it. Still, it was a puzzle, and Gavin wondered where else Declan could enter whenever he chose.

"So, I guess you're going with us?" Gavin asked as Kiri arrived at Gavin's side and Declan stood, pushing the chair under the table.

"You guess correctly," Declan said. "The old man asked me to keep an eye on you while he's traveling abroad."

"Have you heard anything from him?" Gavin asked as he led his friends to the suite's door.

Declan shook his head as they transitioned to the hallway. "No, but that's not uncommon. He'll turn up when he's ready."

By MID-DAY, the business at the property office was complete, and all Gavin needed to do was name an agent or agents to oversee the transfer of ownership; Gavin had already spoken with Mariana, who agreed to serve as agent and could call on some friends in the Battle-mages to assist her.

Gavin, Kiri, and Declan were discussing what do to for the mid-day meal when a column of flame that neither burned nor radiated heat erupted from the street in front of them. The flame vanished as fast as it arrived, and in its wake stood a person Gavin had never seen before.

The person standing before them wore a hooded, purple robe, with gold runes on the cuffs of the sleeve and cowl of the hood. Even in a place as well lit as a street at high sun, a deep, impenetrable shadow shrouded the person's face; only the eyes could be seen, and they were the red-orange color of open flame, the pupils vertical slits instead of circles.

"By the gods!" Kiri gasped. "Gavin, that's a Guardian!"

From his reading of Mivar's Histories, Gavin remembered the Guardians once served as the final line of protection for the Archmagister and, as such, had not been seen since the death of Bellock Vanlon...almost six hundred years before. The Guardians, as a whole, answered to the Chief of the Guard, the Archmagister, and Bellos and were utterly ambivalent to the existence of the Society of the Arcane or, for that matter, mortals in general.

"Gavin Cross," the person said, the voice a deep rumble Gavin felt in his very bones, "you will accompany me immediately to the Chamber of the Council."

Kiri held out her hand in a 'Stop!' gesture, saying, "He's not going anywhere without us."

The person turned its head to regard Kiri for a few heartbeats, before saying, "Your terms are acceptable, young one."

At that moment, the same type of flame that had delivered the purple-robed person consumed all four, and the street around them vanished.

GAVIN NOW FOUND himself standing in the Chamber of the Council, and despite the oddity of the situation, he couldn't stop the memory of challenging Rolf Sivas from rising to the forefront of his mind.

The Council of Magisters stood at their chairs around the table, and Gavin stood off to one side with Declan and Kiri beside him. Just a few steps away from Gavin stood Ovir, who looked just as bewildered as anyone else. The person in the purple robe with gold runes stood in the center of the space between the Council's table and the Archmagister's seat.

"This is outrageous," Tauron said. "How dare you abduct the Council of Magisters and invade the-"

The person in the purple robe turned his gaze to face Tauron. "You will be silent."

Tauron tried to maintain his ire but failed under the weight of that implacable gaze.

Once several moments of complete silence passed, the purple-robed person spoke. "I am Nathrac, Chief of the Citadel Guard and Commander of the Garrison for Tel Mivar, and it is my solemn duty to deliver this message."

Nathrac produced a smoky-white glass sphere from within his robe and held it at chest level. He spoke a word in the language of magic, and an image of Marcus appeared. A spike of fear tore at Gavin's soul.

"Be it known that this image and its message are my final wishes, and I have named Nathrac as executor," the image of Marcus said before his features softened into a smile. "Gavin, I would never have guessed I missed having an apprentice, needed one in fact, until I met you. There's no doubt in my mind you will be a wizard who brings honor to the title and the Society as a whole. For the record, I state that I named you my heir, with Ovir Thatcherson to serve as witness."

A stunned silence descended upon most of those present. Valera looked unsurprised, as did Ovir.

"Ovir, you have been a good friend these last few years," the image of Marcus said, "and I've cherished that friendship more than you know. Nathrac, what can I say to a friend and comrade who has stood with me across the ages? Know that I have counted you among my closest associates, and I regret I must say goodbye in this way. Old friend, I ask that you make certain individuals aware that Gavin is now Head of House Kirloth; I fear he will need them all too soon.

"Gavin, I would not have you grieve, because I've long awaited my reunion with my wife and daughter…but I suspect you'll do so regardless. Goodbye, my boy."

The image vanished the moment its message completed. Nathrac turned and approached Gavin; he held out his hands, one holding the glass sphere and the other a small piece of parchment.

"The parchment has two command words. The first will play the message you just saw, and the second will provide a silent, static image." Nathrac paused and seemed to sigh. "Gavin, you should know that you and your relationship with him meant more to Kirloth than anything I've seen in recent decades. His final request to me was that, once and only once, you may call upon me for aid if circumstances be dire enough. Bellos Himself approved this request, so agreeing to it does not violate the oaths I took upon assuming my current duties."

Gavin accepted the items from Nathrac, saying, "Thank you, Nathrac."

"He was hesitant about you knowing this last piece of information, but I cannot in good conscience keep it secret. The Lornithrasa murdered him when he would not deliver you to them. They will come for you again."

A column of flame that neither burned nor radiated heat surrounded Nathrac, and he was gone.

For several moments, silence dominated the room. Gavin realized that Kiri and Ovir must have placed a hand on each of his shoulders at some point, but he knew not when.

"I cannot believe that old man's audacity," a voice said, jerking Gavin out of his thoughts. Upon looking up, Gavin saw that Tauron was speaking. "Marcus has been a thorn in the side of the Council for as long as any of us can remember, and I-"

Gavin now stood in front of him, across the horseshoe table, and when he spoke, his voice was steady and almost calm. "If you finish those remarks, you shall face my challenge."

Tauron's face flushed an alarming shade of red, his eyes bulging and nostrils flared. He took a breath to speak, but before he could, Valera interjected. Her voice sounded much like a weary parent addressing a misbehaving child.

"Tauron," Valera said, "for once in your life, do the smart thing, and shut your damned mouth. Marcus was present at my Test of Mastery, and I saw him for who he truly was, just as I saw everyone else who was present. I've known he was Kirloth for nearly twenty years."

The flush left Tauron's face as he turned to look at Valera, saying, "And you never told us? How could-"

"During the divination that was the Test of Mastery, I also saw Bellos standing in place of that very statue," Valera said, pointing at the pedestal near the Archmagister's seat, "and he asked for my oath not to discuss what I now knew with another soul, living or dead, until Marcus spoke of it first. Would you have me go against His wishes?"

Tauron seemed to deflate in upon himself and stood in silence for several moments. He finally squared his shoulders and lifted his head to face Gavin. "I'm the Magister of Evocation and a former Battle-mage of Tel. Do you honestly think you can win a duel with me?"

Gavin said, "You're still just a mage, Tauron. If you lived more than three seconds, it would be by *my* choice."

Without awaiting a response, Gavin turned and strode from the room, leaving stunned silence in his wake.

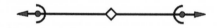

CHAPTER 32

G avin sat in the armchair beside the hearth, the chair he'd always used. He held a black robe in his hands. A messenger had just delivered it with a note from Valera saying that, as Gavin was Head of House Kirloth now, the Council had promoted him to *Magus* within the Society. *Magus* was the highest rank the Society had outside of Magister and Archmagister. The rank runes on the sleeves were white, indicating Gavin had no specialization.

This is really happening. Gavin thought as he rubbed the robe's fabric between his thumb and forefinger. *Marcus is really gone. I keep expecting the suite's door to open and see him walking in, asking where I am with my studies.*

The suite's door clicked and swung open on silent hinges. Gavin stared at the sight, frowning, until the door opened wide enough to reveal Declan standing outside, dressed in his matte, midnight black leather armor. He entered the suite and closed the door behind him.

"Gavin," Declan said, "there is a matter we must discuss, but you've been rather dead to the world the last few days. I couldn't bring myself to intrude upon you."

Kiri walked up to stand at Gavin's shoulder, smiling as she said, "Hi, Declan."

"Hello, Kiri," Declan said. "Gavin and I are going out for a while. There's something we need to discuss. Please, forgive me, but I'm afraid this discussion is for Gavin alone."

"That's okay, Declan," Kiri said. "I have plenty to do to keep myself busy."

"In that case, Gavin and I will leave as soon as he is properly attired."

Gavin frowned. "But I'm already dressed, Declan."

Declan pointedly looked at the black robe laying across the chair Marcus always used.

Gavin followed the direction of his friend's gaze and said, "Oh."

He switched robes, and they left.

DECLAN LED Gavin out of the College and into the western side of the city. As they walked, Gavin stopped and looked at something to his right. Declan turned, looking at Gavin with a quirked eyebrow and saying, "What is it, Gavin?"

"I think I know where we are. Do we have time? I mean, is it okay to make a quick detour? If I'm right, there's something I want to show you."

Declan shrugged. "We're not on a set schedule."

Gavin turned away from Declan and led him into an alley. About twenty-five yards into the alley, another alley met it. Gavin stopped and looked down that alley, grinning.

"Yes, that's it...so...we want to go this way."

Gavin pivoted on his right heel and resumed walking. At every right corner in the alley, Gavin stopped and examined the wall in front of him, usually saying, "No, that's not it."

They were ten minutes into their walk when Gavin approached a wall and stopped.

Chiseled into the stone of the building in front of them was a sigil. Gavin remembered it *very* well.

"Declan, do you happen to have a rag or something to wipe

away the muck on this wall?"

Declan examined his various pockets and produced a small piece of heavy canvas, which he offered to Gavin. Gavin accepted the canvas and wiped away all the muck and grime that still covered the sigil. Once he accomplished as much as he could, Gavin stepped back and pointed to the sigil, saying, "Do you know what that is?"

Declan stepped close and leaned down to be eye-level with the sigil. He spent several moments in silence before standing and facing Gavin. "I never thought I'd actually see one of these, Gavin. It's one of the activation sigils for Tel Mivar's garrison; from what I've read, there's probably twenty or thirty of them scattered all over the city. What made you bring us here?"

"The day I woke up in this city, I slipped and fell right here. To make a long story short, I cut my hand and bled on the wall. The sigil reacted to my blood; it lit up and glowed. The rune in the center glowed a ruby color…and that's when I learned the Word of Interation I know. My whole body went rigid, and it was like that Word was burned into my mind."

"Huh," Declan said as he looked at Gavin. "If I didn't know better, I'd say someone was meddling. I've never heard of that before…but…I haven't heard of *everything*." Declan turned his attention back to the activation sigil. "Do you think you can use that?"

"Why would I be able to use it?"

"There are two activation criteria: one, be the Archmagister or, two, be a true-born child of House Kirloth. I feel safe in saying you meet the second."

Gavin turned to the sigil and stepped close, crouching down to examine it.

Okay. Let's take this apart piece by piece. The core of it is an Interation effect, but that doesn't make any sense. Why would it…oh. The Master of the Field. He's part of the garrison, and they're all spirits. The Interation effect is necessary to draw the spirits into this realm. Now, here…these are Tutation runes. Protection? No; that doesn't seem right. Why would they need protection? Wards? Ah…bindings. These bind the spirits called forth to our reality, and those Conjuration runes give the spirits form and substance, at least some substance. There's nothing here, though, about using the sigil.

As he examined the sigil, Gavin reached out with his left hand and placed it on the sigil. The moment his hand touched it, the sigil began glowing. The Interation rune at the core glowed a ruby light. The Tutation runes glowed vermillion, and the Conjuration runes glowed aquamarine.

Gavin jerked his hand back, and the glow faded. He looked around, saying, "Do you see any blue specters outfitted for the Godswar?"

Declan looked around himself and shook his head. "No. We seem to be alone. Why?"

"I think that's what the garrison looks like. Blue...well, ghosts... with the arms and equipment of soldiers in the Army of Valthon during the Godswar."

"The arena's Master of the Field?" Declan asked, eyeing Gavin with his right eyebrow quirked upward.

Gavin nodded. "I think so. I think he's a member of Tel Mivar's garrison." Gavin stood and stepped away from the sigil, turning to Declan. "Thank you for indulging me on this detour. You originally wanted to take me somewhere?"

"I did, indeed. This way."

AFTER A TIME, they stopped at a structure just off a secondary thoroughfare in the southwestern warrens. Like all buildings in Tel Mivar's "Old City," this structure looked to be made of one solid piece of a marble-like stone. Unlike the other buildings around it, though, this building had no lock. There was a metal plate set into the wall beside the door, and the door had a simple handle.

Declan pulled back his left sleeve and pressed his wrist to the plate. Gavin both felt and heard the *click* as the latch released, and Declan pushed open the door, Gavin following.

The room Gavin entered looked about the size of a modest parlor. There was a hearth against one wall, but there was no firewood or any furniture. The doorway on the far side of the room was an open arch with a simple, black curtain hanging in it.

Declan secured the door through which they'd entered and led

Gavin across the room and through the curtain. Stepping through the curtain, Gavin found a room with a polished, metal staircase spiraling down. Declan didn't even slow as he continued to the staircase and began descending.

The floor below was well lit, still that marble-like stone of the floor above, and Gavin followed Declan in silence, curious as to their ultimate destination. Declan led him down a hallway and turned left into a short corridor that led to an archway with no doors, which in turn opened into a large room. Upon entering the large room, Gavin saw a large round table sitting in the center of the space, the room full of many people all wearing the same style leather armor Declan wore. They were all relaxed or outright lounging in chairs or on tables when Gavin first saw them, but the moment Gavin stepped into the room, everyone there shot to his or her feet and stood at attention.

Gavin was somewhat bewildered by their conduct, and he had not an idea in the world how he should respond. Words floated to the surface of his mind from somewhere deep in the gray fog, and he said, "It's okay. As you were."

They all relaxed, though none of them sat, and Declan stopped when he reached the table, turning to face Gavin.

Declan said, "I had hoped it would be many years before I had to tell you of us, but our hopes don't always come true. *We* are your final inheritance, Gavin. You now stand in the Tel Mivar chapterhouse of the Wraiths of Kirloth."

Gavin walked over and sat in a chair near Declan. Everyone else in the room returned to their seats, and Declan took the few steps necessary to lean against the table at Gavin's side.

"You have questions," Declan said, making it a statement.

"Of course, I do. For one thing, what do you people do?"

"Whatever you tell us to do," Declan said.

Gavin frowned, angling his head to one side just a bit as he looked at Declan. "That's not an answer. I'm serious, Declan; what is it you people do?"

"I was serious, also, Gavin. The Wraiths serve Kirloth without question. If you tell us to go out and kill every third left-handed person we find, we will go out and kill every third left-handed person we find…no questions asked. It's not normally so dire as that, though. By and large, we are Kirloth's eyes and ears throughout the world, and we have so many places infiltrated at so many levels that it is rare for us not to know something by the time the proper authorities do."

Declan stopped speaking long enough to look around the room, scanning faces. He settled on one person at last and waved him to approach. As the man approached, Gavin saw this new man was older; what hair he had left had long since turned gray, but he possessed an air of authority and efficiency most unlike anything Gavin had encountered.

"Take him, for example," Declan said. "His most recent infiltration was the estate of the man who turned out to own Kiri when you met her. He was the man's steward, but for him to be hired as the man's steward, a vacancy had to be created…if you take my meaning."

Gavin looked at the man standing a few feet away, and he couldn't help but get a sinking feeling in the pit of his stomach. "I guess that means you killed the previous steward."

"Personally? No, milord. I infiltrated the estate of an enemy and forged an order to pay for the steward's murder. I then took the order and posed as a butler tasked with delivering it and its accompanying payment—which I also stole from the enemy—to the Guild of Shadows, who were quite happy to carry out the contract. The disagreement between the two families was flaring up at the time already, so it was plausible that a kill order would be paid for by one side or the other."

Gavin leaned back in the chair, by all appearances working to assimilate this latest information. After a few moments, Gavin nodded his understanding, a slow, deliberate action.

"Thank you."

"Thank you, milord," the man said and gave one last nod before returning to his previous place in the room.

Declan scanned the faces again and smiled as his eyes found the face he sought. He gestured for someone else to step forward, and soon, a man stood in front of Gavin that Gavin would never have looked at twice in a crowd. His average build and brown hair was so 'everyman,' Gavin pictured him wearing many different outfits and roles with ease. What struck Gavin, though, was the man's vibrant, blue eyes.

"Some months back, the master—I mean, your mentor—notified us that an escaped Vushaari slave would be arriving in the city and tasked us to ensure she reached wherever she wanted to go unhindered. I found her on West Avenue, South, in the middle of being caught by a slaver. She was trying to run, but the slaver held her by her drawstring bag...despite just being kicked in the privates. I approached the slaver and ensured he would never harm another soul."

Escaped Vushaari slave...that had to be Kiri. "What made you think he'd just been kicked in his privates?"

"Milord, I have yet to meet a man who doesn't recognize the hunched-over, weak-kneed collapse of a man who's just been kicked...whether he saw the act done or not."

Gavin cocked his head to the right and nodded. "I can't really argue with that. Thank you for helping her. She's a friend."

"We know, Milord. She's free to travel the city as she wills. Anytime she leaves the College, no less than four of our number travel with her at all times."

"I'll encourage her to go for more walks, then." Gavin scanned the faces looking at him. "Thank you all for watching over her." Gavin turned to Declan, saying, "I agree; I'd just as soon not have inherited the Wraiths or anything else so soon. I think I'd like to go for a walk; I feel like I could use the time to think."

Gavin pushed himself to his feet and followed Declan out of the room. The moment Gavin stood, every person in the room snapped to their feet as well. Gavin stopped and nodded his acknowledgement before leaving.

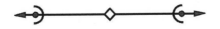

CHAPTER 33

T he smell of horse manure permeated the structure as if it were part of the air, and several students worked with stable-hands to muck out the stalls and transfer the fruits of their labor to the gardens for fertilizer. No more than a few heart-beats passed from Gavin's entry into the stables before a middle-aged man with a stocky, muscular frame approached him.

"Good day to you, sir," the man said. "I'm Robillard, the Master of the Stables."

"Well met," Gavin said, extending his hand. "I'm Gavin Cross."

"What brings you here today, sir?"

"Well, I have what I feel is an uncommon question. Who owns the horses of the stable? I imagine individual students or arcanists currently visiting the College?"

"Yes, there's a few here that match those descriptions, but by and large, the Society owns these fine animals. They're available for use to members of the Society."

"I see. How would one go about obtaining the use of one?"

"What you're doing right now…talking to me. Want to take one for a ride?"

Gavin nodded. "I do."

"Very well. Follow me." Robillard turned and led Gavin over to a door. Opening the door revealed an office, possessing only a couple chairs, a desk, and some file cabinets. Robillard waved Gavin to a chair and sat behind the desk.

"So…how much riding experience do you have? How comfortable are you in the saddle?"

Gavin frowned and shrugged. "Well, I don't really know. I can't say I ever remember riding a horse, but that doesn't mean I haven't. I only have memories for the past five to seven months, and I haven't ridden a horse in that time. Does it matter?"

"Knowing how to ride a horse will mean the difference between mildly sore and unbearably sore, depending on the distance of your ride. I can give you a few quick pointers if you're dead-set on heading out. If something should happen to the horse or its tack while in your care, it will be your responsibility to replace them. Beyond that, there's a fee per day that you have the horse signed out. Any problems so far?"

"No. I don't think so."

"I'll set you up with one of our older mares. She still has many good years in her, but she won't be as restive as one of the younger mounts would be. It'll make for a better ride."

"Thank you."

A BRIEF TIME LATER, Robillard led Gavin up to a horse whose back was level with Gavin's shoulders. Her coat was a tan color, and her mane and tail were white. The word *palomino* came to Gavin's mind unbidden.

Robillard stopped Gavin just outside the stall.

"Okay. Lesson 1: do not trust *any* horse. We don't think like they do; we don't see the world the same way they do, so you're not going to predict how they'll react. I've been working with horses since I was in short pants, and even I get surprised from time to time. Treat her with respect and kindness, and chances are, she'll return them."

"Lesson 2: do not stand directly behind *any* horse, especially unruly ones. Their kicks can kill you. How are we doing so far?"

Gavin nodded. "Everything so far seems fairly straightforward."

For the next hour, Robillard gave Gavin a crash-course in basic horsemanship and horse care while traveling, demonstrating all the necessary implements included in the over-sized saddlebags.

"That's about all I have for you," Robillard said. "Do you still want to proceed?"

"Yes, I do," Gavin said. "Oh...I have just one more question. What's her name?"

Robillard gave Gavin an approving smile before saying, "Jasmine."

Within a few minutes, Gavin led Jasmine out of the stables, saddled and ready to go, to the approving nods of Robillard.

"Not bad. I think you have handled horses before. This isn't really any of my business, but are you planning a long trip or something close?"

Gavin shrugged as he rubbed Jasmine's neck. "I haven't really given it much thought. I need to think and clear my head, and I thought seeing some unfamiliar places might help with that."

"In that case, you might want to stop by Hakamri's; it's on the way if you're heading to the West Gate, and it's the best emporium around for tents, bedrolls, and such. Tell Hakamri I sent you, and he'll take care of you."

Gavin nodded and pulled himself into the saddle, saying, "Thank you for your time, Master Robillard. I'll take care of Jasmine while she's with me."

A light touch of his heels to her sides prompted Jasmine to start off at a leisurely walk. The two gate attendants opened the gates at Gavin's approach, and they headed off for Hakamri's, Jasmine clip-clopping her way along the streets.

HAKAMRI'S WAS INDEED on the way to West Gate. The store fronted the main east-west street and was just beyond the secondary avenue that ran north-south through the western half of the city. From the outside, it looked like every other building in Tel Mivar—one solid piece of marble-like stone—except that it was fifty feet square; inside, the store was one large, open room. Racks of shelves were arranged in aisles and sections, the sections based on what type of merchandise one might find on its shelves.

Movement to the right drew Gavin's attention, and he saw a male standing beside him whose eye-level was just above Gavin's navel. His hair was coarse and gray; his beard was gathered into two braids the ends of which touched his chest, and his unkempt mane touched his shoulders. He gave Gavin an appraising look, his left eye squinted.

"And who be you?"

"I'm Gavin Cross. Robillard in the College stables said I should see Hakamri for traveling supplies."

"Is that so? Where be you off to?"

Gavin frowned. "Well, I'm not really sure. I just need some time away from the city…and maybe some clothes that aren't as conspicuous."

"What supplies have ye now?"

"A saddle, horse blanket, and saddlebags."

"Ye won't be going very far on that. Come wit' me, youngster."

A rough hand grabbed Gavin's right wrist, and he set off into the store at a brisk pace for such a short fellow.

"Hold on," Gavin said. "I'd at least like to meet Hakamri."

The oldster stopped and peered up at Gavin once more, saying, "Ye've been talking wit' him. Now…are ye coming or not?"

An hour later, Gavin left the store with a bedroll, tent, and ten days of travel rations, having paid for the goods by pressing his medallion into sealing wax at the bottom of a bill; the bill would be sent to the Bank of Tel, which would transfer the balance from House Kirloth's account to Hakamri's. Gavin wore traveling clothes designed to survive the rough conditions of the trail, his shirt a pleasant, forest green and his trousers the color of lightly-stained oak. His medallion lay against his chest, beneath his shirt.

Gavin placed his folded robe, linen shirt, and trousers in one of the saddlebags and secured the tent and bedroll behind the saddle. The travel rations went in the other saddlebag before Gavin hooked his left foot into the stirrup and heaved himself up to sit astride Jasmine. Gavin nudged Jasmine into the traffic flow heading toward West Gate and, soon, left Tel Mivar behind him.

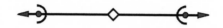

CHAPTER 34

K iri stared at the section of floor where Gavin had once slept, and not for the first time, she wished she knew where he was. It felt odd sleeping in this room—living in this suite—without Gavin, and she had not seen Gavin since the day after Nathrac delivered Marcus's will...almost a week and a half ago.

Walking out of the bedroom, Kiri stopped at the edge of the table in the common room, and her eyes fell on the shelves teeming with books and scrolls in the small room Marcus called his library. And there it was. Kiri knew what she would do now.

THE CURATOR of the Library was a middle-aged woman named Bella Roshan. Kiri remembered Gavin saying she was Wynn's aunt. As she approached the Curator's desk on the main floor of the Library, Kiri summoned all the interpersonal skills she learned in her youth, hoping she wouldn't be questioned too much.

Bella looked up from the documents on the desk in front of her as Kiri approached. Kiri saw both welcome and curiosity in the Curator's expression.

"Yes, child? How may I help you?"

Kiri mentally squared her shoulders and said, "My master, Gavin Cross, has sent me to see what records exist on the creation of the slave brands."

Bella remained silent, and Kiri felt like the woman's eyes were boring straight into her soul. She fought the urge to fidget and returned the elder woman's gaze with a carefully maintained non-expression of her own.

A smile so slight it could've been a smirk curled the left corner of Bella's mouth before she said, "Yes, my dear; I'm sure he did. The library does indeed possess those records, and they are secured in the Restricted Section. Access to the Restricted Section is normally limited to Magisters and the Conclave of the Great Houses."

"Normally?" Kiri asked, exerting effort to keep her voice level.

"My dear girl, we both know you're no wizard, but you're here on House Kirloth business...are you not? I see no reason to say Gavin himself must request you be allowed access. Follow me."

Kiri wanted nothing more than to breathe a heavy sigh of relief as Bella stood and led her to a spiral staircase leading up to the second level, but she forced herself to hold it in as Bella led her up the stairs and along the landing to a wooden door that was directly above the circulation desk.

The wooden door was a massive construct, secured to the wall by steel hinges larger than most swords. Runes were carved into the door's surface around every edge, matching runes chiseled into the stone doorway and floor. Each rune emanated a soft glow its own shade.

Bella produced a key from a pocket, and it had its own rune engraved on its shaft. Bella inserted the key into the lock and turned it all the way to the right. The glow faded.

"What would have happened if I had touched the door before you unlocked it?" Kiri asked.

Bella gripped the handle with both hands and planted her right foot against the wall near where it met the floor, while keeping her left foot angled back behind her to maintain balance. She leaned back just a bit and heaved with all her might on the door. Kiri heard a slight grunt as Bella exerted herself. The door began to swing open.

Bella stopped with the door at a 45° angle and looked at Kiri in silence for a moment before she shrugged, saying, "We might have found all your pieces...eventually."

"Oh."

Bella finished pushing the door open, and Kiri gaped as she saw the door was at least eight inches thick.

"You must keep those hinges well-oiled," Kiri said as she walked around Bella to enter the Restricted Section.

Bella smiled. "Of course not, dear." She pointed to one of the runes chiseled into the stone. It looked like a backwards F with the curly part of a question mark attached to the right side. "That rune holds an Illusion effect that silences the hinges. There's another that holds a Transmutation effect to prevent the hinges from degrading with time. I just wish whoever made this would've thought to include an effect that reduced the door's apparent weight; it's a chore to move. There's a cabinet on the far side with parchment, ink, and styluses."

Kiri stepped through the door and spun when Bella started pushing the door shut.

"Wait! How will I leave if you bring the protections back up?"

"They only affect the outside of the door. Anyone inside can leave whenever they choose. The records you seek occupy the middle three shelves of the bookcase against the right wall."

Kiri forced herself to remain impassive as Bella closed the door, but the heavy *thud* of the door stopping against the doorjamb felt all too much like the closing of a tomb. Kiri took a couple deep breaths and turned to survey her surroundings.

The entrance to the Restricted Section was several feet off-center, and an impressive, oaken table with chairs dominated the center of the room. The rest of the room was a maze of book-shelves, and everywhere Kiri looked, she saw full shelves.

Kiri turned to approach the bookcase Bella had indicated when another sight caught her attention. Against the wall opposite the door, there was a book stand that held a single volume. Kiri walked over to it and saw "Arcanists' Code, Volume II," embossed on the cover in silver lettering. "Arcanists' Code II" was embossed on the spine.

Kiri lifted the cover and read the first page, "'Volume II of the Arcanists' Code, containing Articles 35 through 50.'"

Kiri wanted to flip through the pages, but she didn't know how long it would be before Bella 'discovered' her subterfuge. Kiri closed the cover with care and walked to the indicated bookcase.

The first volume in the section was as thick as Kiri's index finger was long, and it weighed every bit as much as Kiri suspected. She carried it over to the table and—once seated—opened the front cover, reading, "'Constructing the Slave Brands: A Précis and Expanded Overview.'"

Kiri leaned back in her chair, staring at the tome. "This is just the introduction?" Her thoughts drifted back to the three shelves holding books, some of which twice as thick as this one or more. "This may take longer than I thought."

THE GROWLING OF Kiri's stomach pulled her attention away from the current book on the table in front of her. It was the fifth book she'd studied, and it described in detail how the slave brands and the magic they held were constructed. The sad part of it was, Kiri didn't understand a third of what she was reading. The words written in the common tongue were easy enough, but the diagrams detailing how the slave brand effect itself was created might as well have been obscure works of art for all Kiri was getting from them.

Kiri leaned back in the chair and stared at the book, saying, "I'm going to need some help."

* * *

KIRI STOOD before a door down the hall from the suite she and Gavin shared and knocked, and she didn't wait very long before the door swung open.

"Kiri!" Lillian stepped close and pulled Kiri into a friendly hug. "I wasn't expecting you until our usual dinner appointment tomorrow evening."

"I know. I'm hoping you might be able to help me," Kiri said as they broke the embrace.

"Whatever you need. Do you want to talk about it inside?"

"Mind coming to the library with me? I'm researching something, and I've reached the limit of my understanding."

Lillian stepped fully into the hallway and pulled the door shut, saying, "Let's go."

A BRIEF TIME LATER, Kiri approached Bella's desk again, this time with Lillian at her side. When Bella looked up from her work, her eyes narrowed in shrewd appraisal at seeing Lillian.

"Good afternoon, Lady Mivar," Bella said.

"Hello, ma'am."

Bella transferred her gaze to Kiri. "Back again, are we?"

"Yes, ma'am," Kiri said.

"And Gavin asked you to show Lady Mivar what you've found, I'm sure."

She knows! surged through Kiri's mind as she fought to keep her breathing and expression normal.

"No, ma'am. I asked Lillian to help me understand what I've found, before I take it to Gavin."

Bella stood and started to turn toward the staircase but stopped. She turned back to Kiri, and it took everything Kiri's father had taught her about strength of will to bear up under the weight of Bella's gaze.

"You're rather proficient. Just be sure you always use it for the right reasons," Bella said before resuming her walk to the staircase.

Oh, yes…she certainly knows, Kiri thought as she followed Bella.

ONCE LILLIAN and Kiri were inside the Restricted Section, Lillian turned to Kiri, asking, "What was all that about down there?"

"All what?" Kiri asked as she walked to the shelves containing the volume with all the diagrams about creating the slave brands.

"What was going on between you and Curator Roshan, Kiri?"

"Oh...uhm...well, I sort of told her Gavin asked me to investigate what records the Library had about the creation of the slave brands for him."

Lillian stopped cold. "Gavin doesn't know anything about this. Does he?"

Kiri held Lillian's gaze for a moment before looking away and shaking her head. "No. I haven't even seen Gavin in over a week... not since the announcement of Marcus's death."

"Oh, Kiri...what have you gotten me into?"

Kiri placed the thick tome on the table with a heavy *thud* and turned back to Lillian.

"Gavin won't care, Lillian. All will be well."

"That's easy for you to say. You didn't see what he did to those Fifth Tiers who were hazing the new students a couple months ago."

"Gavin is such a sweet guy. It couldn't have been that bad." Kiri opened the cabinet of writing supplies where she'd hidden all the notes she'd compiled so far. After placing the notes on the table, she returned to the cabinet to acquire more parchment and ink as well as a stylus.

"Not that bad? Kiri, he turned their loincloths into wreaths of holly branches...for a week, and that wasn't all."

"Where's the harm..." Then, Kiri remembered the needles on holly leaves. "Oh. Couldn't they have just not worn a loincloth for a week?"

"Yes, except they'd get hives all over their bodies if they didn't wear a loincloth, and Gavin said if the hives lasted for more than a day they'd be permanent."

Kiri worked her mouth to speak for several moments before the words finally came. "That's...that's almost cruel."

"The hazing stopped, though."

"I believe that."

Kiri stood in silence as she tried to reconcile what she'd just heard about Gavin with the Gavin she knew. She couldn't really picture Gavin doing something like that. Yes, he humiliated Rolf Sivas by killing him with a tomato, but Kiri didn't see that as the same thing.

"Kiri?" Lillian said.

Kiri blinked. "How long was I standing there?"

"Not too long. I don't think I have gray hair yet. So, what did you need my help with?"

Kiri opened the book on the table and turned its pages until she reached the first diagram and pointed at it.

"Can you help me understand that?"

Lillian pulled out a chair and eased into it as she pulled the book in front of her and traced the diagram with the fingers of her left hand. The diagram was a series of four circles, each circle enclosing runes which encircled a smaller circle enclosing still yet more runes all the way down to a core of five runes in the smallest circle.

At long last, Lillian spoke. "Kiri, this…this is very sophisticated work. I learned to read using my grandfather's spellbooks, and I've never seen anything like this." Kiri watched Lillian turn her head to face her. "This transcends even the best artificer work into the realm of artistry…no pun intended."

Kiri pulled out the chair beside Lillian and sat, watching her friend turn her attention back to the book. Now that the book was describing how the slave brands had been created (beyond the mere blacksmithing required to make the physical form), the book shifted into a different format. The left page contained notes and explanations of whatever diagram or magical equation that occupied the right page.

Lillian turned the page and smiled. "See here, Kiri? These next pages break down the diagram into its component parts, and it starts with those five Tutation runes at the core."

Lillian's voice trailed off, and Kiri assumed she was reading the text on the left page. Suddenly, she leaned back in her chair and shook her head.

"That crafty, old bastard."

"What?" Kiri asked.

Lillian pushed the book over to Kiri and tapped the left page, saying, "You didn't read far enough."

Kiri pulled the book closer to her and read, "'The work of creating the slave brands was a quagmire of defeat and desperation. The king was demanding a solution every day, and over fifty arcanists—so far—had lost their lives in mishaps trying to deliver what the king wanted. We had all but given up on there ever being the type of slave brand the king desired when the Black Robe wizard, Marcus, entered our laboratory. He placed a sheaf of papers on the table before us, saying, 'This will save still more of you from dying in attempts to bring that fool's dream to fruition.' He turned and left without another word. Everyone crowded in to see what Marcus had left, but I—as Project Leader—claimed the papers.

"'Immediately, I saw that it was a ritualized composite effect, which astounded me by itself, because I had never heard or read of anyone ever ritualizing a composite effect before. The core of the ritual was a powerful Tutation effect that I realized would protect all wizards from ever being branded as slaves, once I deciphered it. The other effects that would produce everything the king wanted the slave brands to do all depended upon that core.'"

Kiri didn't even examine the diagram of the core Tutation runes on the right page before turning the page to the read the next annotations.

"'We spent three weeks trying to deconstruct what Marcus gave us to remove that protection for wizards—as the king very much wanted to be able to brand wizards, too—but all our work was for naught. Somehow, Marcus had woven that core of Tutation throughout the entire ritual, and the ritual was wildly unstable without it. Kayla's hair being turned purple during one of our failed attempts was the least of the mishaps. Poor Bran's nose was upside down for four months, until the Magisters of Tutation and Transmutation finally managed to turn it right side up again, and I don't think the Magister of Divination ever located Darvis's right leg. It was the forceful and sudden relocation of Darvis's leg that convinced us we should leave well enough alone and use the ritual as it was.'"

Kiri pushed the book away and looked to Lillian. "So…Marcus made the slave brands."

"I wouldn't say that," Lillian said. "He just showed the team already working on it how to do so without anyone else dying."

"Do you think he knew how to remove the slave brand?"

Lillian nodded. "The man ritualized a composite effect to create the brand in the first place, Kiri; of course, he knew how to remove it."

"Then, why didn't he?" Kiri fought to hold back tears. "Why did he leave me like this?"

"We'll never know."

Kiri took several deep, calming breaths. She still felt almost betrayed somehow, but the shock of it was passing.

"Where do we go from here?"

Kiri watched Lillian, looking at her in silence as she waited for her friend to reply. Finally, Lillian shook her head.

"Kiri, I have no idea how to begin deciphering this diagram. Considering the source, I doubt the Magisters—or even my grand-father—could decipher it, either."

"Where does that leave us?"

Lillian sighed and shrugged, saying, "You're going to have to take it to Gavin. I can't think of anyone else who even stands a chance of making sense of this."

"Can we make a tracing of it?" Kiri asked. "Something you could take to study?"

Lillian looked at Kiri in silence for several moments. At last, she heaved a heavy sigh and nodded. "Please, don't get your hopes up, Kiri. I'll study this along, but please, don't focus all your hopes on the possibility that I'll suddenly have an epiphany."

Kiri nodded, saying, "Thank you."

Lillian retrieved some fresh parchment from the stack Kiri had placed on the table and started tracing.

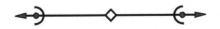

CHAPTER 35

Marcus made the slave brands. Kiri still didn't know what to make of that. *Yes, fine...he didn't make them himself, but he certainly enabled them to exist. Isn't that just as bad? And what does that mean for Gavin? People get nervous and wary at the mere mention of Kirloth; will people fear Gavin one day, too?*

The Slave Queen of Vushaar. The thought came out of nowhere and shouldered aside her turmoil over the brands. *Had Marcus known of those prophecies Ovir mentioned? Did he help the slave brands to exist, so that the prophecy of the Slave Queen might have a chance of coming true?*

A knock interrupted her thoughts, and for a moment, Kiri hoped Gavin was back...right up until she processed that Gavin wouldn't knock on his own door. She pushed herself to her feet and crossed the room. A slight tug opened the door to reveal Lillian.

Kiri smiled. "Hello."

"Is this a bad time?"

"No, of course not," Kiri said. "I was just thinking."

Kiri led Lillian into the suite and gestured to the armchairs in front of the hearth. Lillian sat in the chair on the right side, the same one Gavin always chose, and Kiri sat opposite her.

"You seemed pretty shaken by what we read in that book," Lillian said, as she folded her legs under her. "I just wanted to see how you were doing."

Kiri moved her eyes to the hearth and worked her lower lip between her teeth. Finally, she said, "I'm not really sure how I'm doing. That information about Marcus and the slave brands...well, it changed some things for me."

"How? It's not like Marcus was your best friend."

"Maybe he was, in his own way."

Lillian frowned. "Kiri, that doesn't make any sense."

"You told me once that you've wanted to study Divination since you were little."

"Yes. I don't know why, but it's always been what drew me to the Art."

"Ever read any prophecies...like old, old, old prophecies?"

"A few. My grandfather has a book in his library; it's kind of a primer on prophecy. He always said he inherited it from his great aunt or some such."

Kiri stared into the unlit hearth for several moments before she said, "Do the words 'Slave Queen of Vushaar' mean anything to you?"

Lillian frowned. "I think I remember something about that. I think it was mentioned as a classic example of a forked prophecy, something about only one path of the fork coming true. Why?"

Kiri wrung her hands as she stared at the lifeless hearth.

"Kiri, what's wrong?"

Kiri took a deep breath and brought her eyes back to meet Lillian's concern. "Lillian, I...my father is Terris Muran, King of Vushaar."

Kiri watched Lillian freeze. Her friend had become a statue.

"Wait," Lillian said at long last. "You're the crown princess who died at sea? I remember hearing about that. The ship...it was the diplomatic courier between Tel and Vushaar. Grandfather talked about it. Why can't I remember the ship's name?"

"It was the *Sprite*," Kiri said. Her voice was soft, vulnerable.

"Yes! The *Sprite!*" Kiri watched Lillian's eyes drift down and slightly to her left; she could almost feel Lillian's gaze burning into her shoulder. "You? You think you're the Slave Queen?"

Kiri shrugged, moving her eyes back to the hearth. "I don't want to be. I don't want to be Queen for a long, long time. Besides, I don't even know if my people would accept me."

Silence took over the room for several moments.

"Are you angry with me for not telling you?"

Lillian frowned. "What?"

"It's just that we've shared so much about ourselves, and I never told you who I am. You have a right to be angry."

"No, I don't. Not one little bit," Lillian said, adding emphasis by shaking her head side to side. "Kiri, learning to trust again isn't easy; I certainly don't look at men the same way anymore, even men I know I'm safe with. Besides, how could I be angry with you? You're my friend."

They sat in silence for a few moments before Kiri pulled her eyes away from the hearth and back to Lillian.

"I don't suppose you've heard any news of Vushaar?"

Lillian shook her head, saying, "No, I'm sorry. All I've heard is that things are very tense right now. There's an army preparing to besiege the capital, and no one knows on which side everyone else is. Nobody wears any colors."

Kiri nodded. "Ever since I heard what was happening, I've felt awful. I should be there with my father, helping him."

"Kiri, he sent you away from that to keep you safe."

"And just how well did that turn out?"

"Kiri...it's difficult to understand why things happen the way they do. It's difficult to believe that things will ever be better, especially after the last two years. You're alive. You're healthy, and I'd have to say you're safe. How many other people can say that?"

Kiri nodded. "I know; I know, and I feel like I'm where I'm supposed to be. It's just that I miss my father. I miss Q'Orval. I miss home."

"Well, of course you do. Who wouldn't?" Silence ruled the

space for several moments until Lillian spoke once more. "Say…are you hungry? Dinner starts in the dining hall shortly."

Kiri smiled and stood. "I should eat. Let's go."

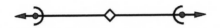

CHAPTER 36

A slight breeze blew through the gardens, carrying the scent of flowers and herbs. Lillian, Braden, and Wynn sat on one of the bench planters, and they awaited the arrival of their fellow classmates for the mentor session.

"So-" Braden said.

"Think-Gavin-will-be-here-today?" Wynn asked, cutting off Braden.

Lillian and Braden smiled. They were long used to that side of Wynn's nature.

"I don't know," Lillian said. "Kiri said she hasn't seen him in almost two weeks."

"I understand," Braden said. "I mean, when my father died, Mom and I were a mess. Aunt Kora stepped in and ran the Duchy while we got through the worst of it."

Lillian nodded. "Yes, it may be understandable, but if he's going to be out of touch for a long period of time, he should've notified Valera so she could assign us a new mentor."

"Do-we-really-need-a-mentor-now? Gavin-dealt-with-the-Fifth-Tiers-who-were-hazing-the-new-students."

"He certainly did," Braden said, adding a chuckle that sounded more like the rumble of distant thunder. "It will be a long time before I forget seeing those upperclassmen walk around with wreaths of holly leaves under their robes. Their expressions were priceless."

The other students of their mentor group approached.

"He didn't show again, did he?" the young lady asked.

Lillian shook her head.

"I'm so finished with this. If he doesn't care enough to show up, why should we be bothered to, either?"

The young lady turned and left, taking her fellows with her.

Lillian sighed, watching them go. She sat in silence for a few moments longer before turning to her friends.

"You guys go ahead and leave. I'm going see if Magister Valera is in her office."

* * *

"Hi, Sera," Lillian said as she entered Valera's outer office. "Is the Magister in?"

Sera smiled, saying, "Yes, she is. How much time do you need?"

"I don't know," Lillian said, fighting the urge to wring her hands. "I don't think too long."

Sera looked up at Lillian in silence a few moments before she stood and went to Valera's door. Knocking twice, she opened the door and slipped inside.

Moments later, Sera opened the door and motioned for Lillian to enter. Lillian started walking toward the door, and Sera stepped aside as Lillian entered Valera's office. Sera closed the door behind Lillian.

"And how can I help the Lady Mivar today?" Valera asked, gesturing for Lillian to sit.

Lillian chose the chair on her left and eased into it.

"Ma'am, I'm not comfortable bringing this matter to you, but I feel you should know."

"Know? Know what? Has someone approached you over the Rolf Sivas duel?"

"Oh, no…his so-called 'friends' made themselves *very* scarce following the duel. No, it's about the mentor sessions. Ma'am… well…no one has seen Gavin in two weeks."

Valera frowned. "Are you sure? Do you think there's been foul play?"

"No, I don't think so. Kiri said-"

Lillian watched the color drain from Valera's face in an instant as she collapsed against the back of the chair.

"Ma'am, what's wrong?"

"That name…who is it?"

"Kiri? She's Gavin's slave. Well, Gavin doesn't treat her like a slave. She ran away from her former owner, and Gavin found her in the warrens. The slavers attacked, and he defended her."

"You say her name is Kiri?"

"Yes-"

Now, Valera leaned forward in her seat, her eyes intent. "Is she Vushaari?"

"Yes. Ma'am, what is this about?"

Valera leaned back in her chair once more and, looking up at the ceiling, whispered, "She's alive. Thank the Gods she's alive."

After a few moments of silence, Valera sat upright once more, saying, "So, Gavin has been missing the mentor sessions? And Kiri doesn't know where he is, but you don't believe there's been foul play. Why is that?"

"Well, ma'am…I…I still have the initiate's robe he draped over me in the garden. I used it as a focus to scry him. When I did, I saw him sitting at a roadside camp somewhere making food over a campfire; he was wearing traveling clothes I've never seen him in before."

"Farscrying is a Third Circle spell," Valera said. "A First-Tier student shouldn't be able to cast it."

Now, Lillian looked away and wrung her hands. "It's in one of my grandfather's spellbooks, ma'am, and I've read them all."

The silence soon became awkward for Lillian, and she chanced a glance at Valera. The magister sat in her seat, looking at Lillian with a slight smile that seemed to convey a mixture of pride and amusement.

"Should I ask what other spells you cast on a regular basis?"

"Oh, no, ma'am! I only cast the scrying to see if Gavin was well. I know I'm not supposed to be casting yet."

Now, Valera did break out into a full-fledged smile. "Don't worry about it. Your secret is safe with me. I didn't exactly wait until the College to begin casting spells, either, but that's been a little while ago. Very well. Thank you for alerting me to the situation. I'll assign a new mentor and notify the group that I've done so."

"This won't get Gavin in trouble, will it? I didn't want that."

Valera smiled. "I regret that he didn't follow through, but I'm not going to say anything to him about it. Life has assaulted him with a great many changes lately. As for anyone else…well…even if Gavin's duel with Rolf wasn't so fresh in everyone's mind, I highly doubt anyone would brave confronting Kirloth over so minor a matter."

"Thank you, ma'am. I should be going." Lillian stood and left Valera's office.

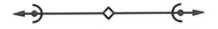

CHAPTER 37

Gavin stood on a small rise north of the Tel Roshan road, overlooking the remains of Kalinor's estate. What had once been stone structures had long since cooled, the masonry melted into solid blobs of stone, and the charred and blackened dirt extended five feet beyond what was once the manor wall.

"How hot does stone have to be before it melts?" Gavin said.

Jasmine snuffled and returned her attention to grazing.

"I'm sorry, Jasmine," Gavin said. "I don't understand Equine."

"It's just as well," a new voice said. "You'd never have a moment's peace."

Gavin spun to face behind him and saw a young man whose Vandyke beard and close-cropped hair were the color of caramel. He wore a black robe, and the rank runes on the cuffs of the robe's sleeves were white and proclaimed him a *Magus* within the Society. The silver wizard medallion bore the Glyph of Wygoth.

"The last time I saw you, you wore a brown initiate's robe with no medallion," Gavin said.

He shrugged, saying, "Yes, well, I don't normally wear a black robe, either."

"Why don't you show yourself for who you are, then? Why the masquerade?"

"Are you sure you want to know who I am, Gavin?"

"This is apparently the time of year for mental shocks to my system. Go ahead."

The black of the robe and silver of the medallion drained away like water-based paint in a rain storm. Gold remained in their wake, and the medallion shifted from its usual circle to the shape of a dragon's head. The Wygoth Glyph shrunk and shifted to occupy a scale between the dragon's eyes, and the rank runes on the sleeves were now black.

"That's what I thought," Gavin said. "You're Bellos."

"Yes, Gavin, I am."

"I can't imagine every arcanist receives a visit from you."

"No, they don't, but I thought you might benefit from a talk."

Gavin frowned, saying, "How so?"

"The man you knew as 'Marcus' was my friend, too."

"I can't believe he's gone," Gavin said, sighing. "I mean, sixty-one hundred years, and he just dies?"

"He didn't 'just die.' He was investigating some rumors the Wraiths could not, and he was cornered by the Lornithrasa. When he wouldn't surrender you, they killed him."

"That's the second time they've tried to get me. Why is that? What's so special about me that the Lornithrasa want me dead?"

"I'm not sure the time is right for you to know the answer to that question, Gavin. It's…well, it involves how the Godswar ended and one of the reasons my mentor was still alive after all this time."

"That wasn't cryptic at all."

Bellos chuckled. "Gavin, there are some things it's not time for you to know yet. When the time comes, though, we'll have another talk…or maybe you and the old man will."

"The old man?" Gavin asked. "You mean that crazy old codger in the alley when I woke up?"

Bellos outright laughed. "Oh, he's not as crazy as he puts on, but yes, that is who I mean."

"Who was he?"

"Are you sure-" Bellos cut off his question at Gavin's flat expression. "He was Valthon."

"Why did He take my memories?"

"He didn't take them, Gavin; like our mentor said, He merely hid them."

"Okay...why did He *hide* my memories?"

"I won't give you the whole answer, but we needed a wizard of House Kirloth, and you were...well...available. However, the memories you possessed would've interfered with learning what you need to know, and He made it so you could approach this world with an open mind."

"Can you restore my memories?"

"I'm sorry, Gavin. You still have more to learn. When the time comes, you will have your memories back; I promise you that."

Gavin sighed, saying, "Can you at least tell me if the memories of my daughter Lornithar restored are real or something He just planted there to tempt me?"

"You do indeed have a daughter named Jennifer Anne, Gavin, but she's older than you think."

"How old-" Gavin cut himself off and dropped his head. "Let me guess...it's not time for me to know that."

"I'm sorry, no."

Gavin took a deep breath and let it out as a long sigh. "Very well."

"There is something I want to discuss with you...something I'm not sure our mentor had time to discuss. If any of this sounds familiar, stop me."

Gavin nodded.

"Did he tell you about the origin of the Circle System?"

"Yes, he said you, Mivar, and he designed it after the Godswar. I inferred that it was designed so that mages could exist."

Bellos nodded. "You are quite correct. Let's sit."

Bellos gestured, and Gavin felt a strong—yet subtle—Conjuration effect as two plush armchairs appeared. Bellos gestured to the one closest to Gavin.

"Thank you," Gavin said as he sat.

"So…upon my ascension, I learned a great many things about how reality—for lack of a better term—works. Did you sense my creation of those chairs through your *skathos*?"

"Yes. It was a very pronounced Conjuration effect that somehow felt subtle at the same time, or maybe 'whispered' is the right word."

Bellos nodded. "What do you know about what led up to the Godswar?"

"I know that Lornithar and a group of elevated mortals he called his pantheon oppressed this world and its people until Valthon and Nesta sponsored a revolution. The revolution became known as the Godswar."

"That's good…as far as it goes. Valthon will be the first to tell you that He's not a god, and by implication, neither are my fellows who accepted ascension at the end of the Godswar. But if we're not gods, I almost shudder at the thought of meeting a real one.

"Valthon refers to Himself and Nesta as Ancients, and at a time so long ago the term 'pre-history' loses all meaning, there were many. Lornithar is also an Ancient. The Ancients were entrusted with the welfare and upkeep of the universe by the true gods, who created everything. For whatever reason—even Valthon doesn't remember why, or at least says He doesn't—Lornithar decided he wanted to be the *only* Ancient, and he proceeded to slaughter his way through their ranks, claiming their power for his own.

"Lornithar's first kill, though, brought with it an unexpected—and rather scary—side effect. Reality itself began to unravel, and arcane magic is but one expression of that unraveling."

Gavin stared at Bellos, his mouth agape and eyes just a bit wide.

"Yes, Gavin. Arcane magic did not exist prior to Lornithar's slaughter. The power that we call arcane magic is the binding that holds reality together. It is what forces Fire to coexist with Water and Air to coexist with Earth. It is what allows atoms and quarks and molecules and planets and suns and everything else to exist, and wizards are born with a connection to that power.

"That's not all, though. Arcanists have a symbiosis with that power. We both manipulate *and* perpetuate it. Had Lornithar not disrupted reality by killing his fellow Ancients, the separation between what makes reality exist and what you know as mortal existence would never have weakened...but because it did...arcanists became part of what keeps reality intact. And *that* is why I came to my mentor and Mivar to devise a new system of magic."

"Marcus said you foresaw that there would be fewer and fewer wizards born as time progressed. So, what you're saying is that—if you hadn't developed the Circle System or something like it—reality would've continued to unravel until everything ceased to exist?"

"That is *exactly* what I'm saying, Gavin."

"Do you know why fewer wizards were born over time?"

Bellos quirked his lips and shrugged.

"Ah, right. Not for me to know?"

"For the moment, yes, but that may change."

"How much of this did Marcus know?"

"Everything we've discussed so far...and a little more. But before you ask, he didn't know why fewer wizards were born."

"Is this why 'all arcanists are brothers and sisters in the Art?'"

"Yes, it is. Mages—for the most part—took over a very important role, simply by existing."

"Why did Valthon tell Marcus to train me?"

"The world needs a wizard of House Kirloth right now, Gavin, and no, our mentor didn't qualify...not since he stopped openly identifying his House. He *chose* that, by the way. Valthon and I certainly didn't require it of him."

"What do you need me to do?"

"Whatever you choose to do."

"What's to stop me from driving the Conclave to start a civil war?"

"Absolutely nothing...beyond your own conscience."

Gavin sighed, saying, "I'm not sure I have it within me to be the kind of man Marcus was."

"I don't *want* you to be the kind of man our mentor was," Bellos said. "Decades before the Godswar began, he came home to find his wife gang-raped and murdered and his six-year-old daughter dying. Temple Guardsmen from a nearby shrine to Lornithar had done the deed, and I highly doubt anyone will ever know the depths to which grief, hate, and rage drove him. You should be *very* grateful you did not witness the creation of the Wraiths first-hand. What he did to that captured Lornithrasa…'atrocity' doesn't even begin to describe it. Gavin, there is one person—and only one person—who can decide what it means to be Kirloth, and that person is you."

Gavin nodded. "I'll work on remembering that."

"Good. Now, I'm afraid I have other tasks requiring my attention. Take care of yourself." Bellos stood, and Gavin was quick to stand also.

In the blink of an eye, Bellos was gone, and his chairs vanished with him.

Gavin turned and looked out over the rounded masses of stone that had once been Kalinor's estate. He nodded slowly as he took a deep breath and eased it out again.

"I think it's time I left, too. Come on, Jasmine; let's go home." He gathered Jasmine's reins in his hand and, filling his mind with a clear picture of his intent, invoked a Word, "*Paedryx.*"

An archway made of sapphire energy rose out of the ground, and when it stood taller than Jasmine, it flashed and became a gateway to another place. Gavin led Jasmine through the gateway, returning to the College.

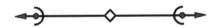

CHAPTER 38

The Dean of Residence unlocked the door with the master key and allowed Gavin, Declan, and Kiri entrance to the room. He took the time to specify any items in the room that were College property and left Gavin and the rest to their task.

Gavin intended to gather all of Rolf's property that was of any value and sell it off, the proceeds of the sale to be distributed between Rolf's victims Gavin could identify. Mariana had volunteered to lead the Battle-mages who would be notifying the property and tax office of the duel's outcome and securing any property in Rolf's name outside College grounds.

"Okay," Gavin said, as he scanned the room. "Let's take the linens off the bed and place the crates there. We can sort as we go. Any personal items that would have no worth in the sale may be set aside to be returned to his family."

OVER THE NEXT FEW HOURS, the three of them worked in near silence, only speaking when needing to ask a question or make a specific statement. Soon, they filled all five crates almost to their brims.

"Oh, no," Kiri said, her voice almost a whimper and drawing everyone's attention.

Gavin turned to see Kiri holding a box about the size of a plain, jewelry box. The lid stood open, Kiri's face pale as she stared at its contents.

"What is it, Kiri?" Gavin asked. "What have you found?"

"He kept a log, Gavin, but that's not all. He kept trophies, too."

Gavin walked over and took the box from Kiri. He sat on an unused corner of the bed and examined the box's contents for himself. Some papers with names and dates rested on the very top; all the names were female. Under the pages, Gavin found locks of hair bound by a small ribbon and labeled. Each name on the papers matched a labeled lock of hair.

Gavin adjusted the box so that Declan could see its contents, shaking his head as he said, "This guy must've been some kind of monster."

"It looks that way," Declan said.

THE PASSAGE of a few hours found Gavin leading the others out of the dormitory, carrying crates loaded with what was now Gavin's property; two more crates waited in the dorm room that was now spell-locked, thanks to a Word of Tutation Gavin had learned. Gavin wasn't sure how much could be sold, let alone what the items would bring, but he hoped there was enough revenue to provide some form of reparations to Rolf's victims.

"Gavin!"

A woman's voice pulled Gavin's attention from his thoughts, and he lifted his gaze to scan the area. He saw Mariana stepping down from a horse and hurrying to meet them.

"Hello, Mariana," Gavin said. "Have you had any difficulties securing the transfer of property?"

"One of the Battle-mages assisting me with the property transfer found something at Vischaene Vineyard you need to see, Gavin."

Gavin blinked. "Rolf had property outside Tel Mivar?"

"Yes," Mariana said. "There's a loophole a previous king slipped

into civil law that reduces the nobility's tax burden for any properties owned by the heir. Most noble families have put the bulk of
their assets in the heir's name these days, just to pay less taxes. I
imagine that practice will change soon, since House Sivas will be
almost destitute before the month is out."

Gavin blinked while he stared off into empty air. At last, he
pulled his focus back to Mariana, asking, "What all do I own now?"

Mariana produced a folded page from within her robe as she
said, "Here's a rough list. There may be a few other pieces buried in
the records office; I have people scouring the books right now,
assembling a complete list."

Gavin accepted the page and scanned it. Other than recognizing
the words, none of it meant anything to him. He held it so that Kiri
and Declan could read it.

"Do these places mean anything to either of you?" Gavin asked.

Declan gave a low whistle as he read over the list. "You own
Vischaene Vineyard? That's at least the second or third of the five
best wineries in the world. People have been trying to buy it for
hundreds of years. I never knew the Sivas family owned the Wygoth
Mines and Water Works, either."

When everyone looked at him, Declan said, "The Water Works
are a collection of watermills and sawmills on the River Cothos,
near the borders of Cothos and Mivar Provinces. The Mines are in
the nearby hills a few leagues farther into Wygoth Province."

Gavin handed the list to Declan, for he and Kiri to examine
further, and pulled Mariana off to the side, asking, "What did you
find?"

"You'll never believe me if I tell you, Gavin," Mariana said.
"The vineyard is only a couple hours north of the city. You should
see for yourself."

Gavin held her gaze, gauging how much he could press her for
details. Something about her expression gave Gavin the feeling that
he should let it go and ride north with her.

Something in his own expression must've given away his decision
to go with her, because Gavin saw Mariana relax. She took a deep

breath and exhaled a bit before she said, "It's...well, it's not good, Gavin. I don't know what to make of it, but I do know it's bad. Don't worry; I have people I trust securing the site as we speak."

"We need to move these crates to my suite in the Tower," Gavin said, glancing toward Kiri and Declan who were still marveling at the list of property Gavin now owned, "but there's no reason I can't leave with you right away."

* * *

THE PASSAGE of two hours found Mariana, Gavin, Kiri, and Declan approaching the gate of Vischaene Vineyard. Vischaene Vineyard was a sprawling estate dedicated to the production of some of the finest wines made by humans, and it was known the world over for those wines. The story went that a distant ancestor in House Sivas won the vineyard in a game of chance when it was little more than a grape farm, and over the years, the family built it into the successful enterprise it had become.

UPON THEIR ARRIVAL, the person Gavin thought to be the foreman started to approach them, but Mariana waved him off as she led Gavin and company not to the main house but to an outbuilding that looked to be little more than a shack attached to the stables.

"I'm certain Master Kirloth will have more than enough time to discuss the fate of the Vineyard, Ektor, but we have more pressing matters now," Mariana said, without even slowing. "Please, forgive me."

The outbuilding was indeed a shack, and it was decorated to appear as though a common farmhand lived there. The building's true purpose, however, was misdirection. Someone had discovered a trap door hidden inside. The short ladder below it led to a tunnel that, in turn, led to a planning room, littered with papers, maps, and other documents.

Gavin walked to the center table and started sifting through the papers he could see. The more papers he read, the more disturbing the emerging picture became.

"Mariana, is all this what I think it is?" Gavin asked, turning to her.

Mariana turned from speaking with Kiri, saying, "What do you think it is?"

"I have recruiting documents for mercenaries. I have logistical plans for moving those mercenaries in such a way as to minimize detection. I have maps of Tel Mivar and the College. Mariana, this looks like we're standing in the headquarters of a plot to overthrow the Council."

"Then, yes, it is very much what it looks like," Mariana said before she pointed to a corner off Gavin's left side. "The best part is in that iron strongbox over there."

Gavin returned the papers to the table and approached the indicated strongbox, almost wary of what he would find. The powdered remains of the lock lay at his feet when Gavin stopped in front of the strongbox and lifted the lid. More papers lay inside. Gavin started scanning them and, as he did so, stepped backward to collapse into a chair behind him. Gavin wasn't even reading the pages anymore; he just stared at them.

After what seemed like ages, Gavin heard Kiri ask, "Gavin... what is it?"

Gavin turned his head just enough for his friends to hear his words and said, "The plot is sponsored by the king."

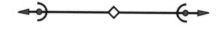

CHAPTER 39

Gavin's answer to Kiri silenced the room for some time. Everyone stood rooted to their spots, as they stared at Gavin. Their eyes were wide to varying degrees, and all of them lost a little color from their pallor.

"What does this mean?" Kiri asked, the first to speak.

Gavin sighed and stood. He placed the documents back in the strongbox and walked around the table to stand with Mariana and his friends.

"I don't know, Kiri. The big question is whether those documents are real. If they're not real, I'd say it's all part of a plot to overthrow the Council and lay blame at the king's feet...which would probably spark a civil war. If they *are* real...I don't know."

Gavin's voice trailed off as his mind sorted through all the implications he could see, and he *knew* he was missing some. Not for the first time, Gavin wished Marcus were still alive, but he didn't give voice to that thought. It wouldn't do for anyone to see his doubt.

"We must take this evidence to the Council," Mariana said.

Gavin nodded. "You are correct. That is exactly what we *should* do, but it is not what we're going to do."

"Why not?" Mariana said.

"We're going to take this to Valera. She will be able to authenticate these documents and call a meeting of the Council. I do not want to bring this before the Council as a threat from the king if it is merely an internal matter. Mariana, in the very near future, I will be facing Tauron again, and I highly doubt it will do your career any good for him to see you standing with me. You should sit this one out."

"The Great Houses of Tel stand together, Gavin," Mariana said. "They always have, and I hope they always will."

Gavin chuckled and shrugged. "Ah, well...I tried. Okay. Get your people in here to catalog this place according to proper evidence protocols. I want all this packed up and ready to take before Valera as soon as possible. In the meantime, I think I need to have a conversation with Ektor. It looks like I won't be selling this vineyard as soon as I thought, after all."

* * *

GAVIN, Kiri, and Declan traveled down the main north-south avenue in Tel Mivar, having entered the city from the north gate. Nine Battle-mages, including Mariana, rode with them in their wake. Gavin could hear Kiri, Declan, and Mariana chatting behind him, but his mind was too focused on what they had discovered at the vineyard to pay much attention to what they were discussing.

BEFORE LONG, the group entered the markets, and screams erupting from the crowd around them destroyed Gavin's focus on the evidence. In the now-open space around them, Gavin saw a woman on the ground, her hands pressed against her abdomen. Blood oozed between her fingers. A man stood over her holding a bloody dagger. A small boy started to move toward the woman, while she shouted at him to run away. The man began moving in to finish the job.

Gavin's jaw clenched at the sight. "I don't think so," he said, his tone resolute.

Gavin invoked a Word, "*Thymnos.*"

Pain savaged Gavin's guts as the invocation took hold, and the man froze mid-motion. He still breathed and could blink his eyes but not much else. A strange tattoo dominated the right side of the man's neck.

Declan eyed the tattoo and sighed, saying, "Well, damn."

"What?" Gavin asked.

Declan paid him no mind, though. He turned over his shoulder to Mariana and said, "Take the Battle-mages to the Mivar Estate, and secure the evidence there. Tell Torval this is a request from Gavin, but tell him nothing about the contents of these strongboxes. Go...now!"

"Who are you-" Mariana said, and Declan made a small gesture to direct her attention to the paralyzed man. Mariana's eyes locked on the tattoo, and the color drained from her face. "Oh, no."

"Take the Battle-mages and go," Declan said. "We'll be fine."

"I'm not leaving you guys here alone!"

"Trust me," Declan said as he slipped from his horse and handed Kiri the reins. "We're not alone."

It was clear as the sky of a cloudless day that Mariana didn't want to leave, but she knew her duty. She turned her horse toward Mivar Estate and led the Battle-mages away.

Six people in worn leather armor broke through the crowd on the far side of the tableau. They looked at the man leaning over the woman, and then, their eyes shifted to Gavin. They started to move. Declan stepped forward, drawing a dagger out of each sleeve and holding them with the point facing his elbows. Two more people in common clothing stepped out of the crowd, holding their own daggers. Declan made a point of exaggerating the motion of looking at each of the plain-clothed newcomers before lifting his left hand and waving his fingers in a beckoning gesture.

Now, the six leather-clad individuals slowed their approach, their eyes flicking between Declan and the other two. The woman leading the charge, as it were, stopped at last and stretched her arms out against her closest fellows, shaking her head. Just as they turned to leave, Gavin saw they all bore the same neck tattoo…just like the guy he had interrupted.

Town guard whistles blared nearby, and the crowd parted to let them pass. Gavin was surprised to see a healer from the temple with them. The healer went to the woman immediately and began seeing to her wound.

"All right," the sergeant said as he surveyed the scene, "what happened here?"

"Sir?" Gavin said, drawing the man's attention. "There was a scream, and the crowd parted around…well…that. She was begging the boy to run, and the man was leaning back in to finish the job. I didn't appreciate a woman being murdered on the street in front of a boy I assume is her own son, so I stopped him."

"Hey, Sergeant," one of the guardsmen said, his voice raised. "He won't drop the dagger!"

"He can't," Gavin said.

The sergeant whipped his head back to look at Gavin, asking, "What do you mean, he can't?"

"He's paralyzed. Well, all voluntary muscles are paralyzed anyway…stuff like his jaw, arms, hands, fingers, legs, feet, toes, and neck. His heart still beats, and he can still breathe; that's about it. Oh! And he can blink. I didn't want his eyes to dry out before the paralysis fades."

"That's very kind of you," the sergeant said. "So, when does the paralysis fade?"

Gavin frowned. He started to speak, then stopped. He rubbed his chin, still frowning, and started to speak again, only to stop again. He settled on a shrug, as he said, "That's a good question. I wasn't really thinking of a duration when I invoked the Word; I just wanted to stop him from murdering the woman."

"Every spell I've ever heard of fades eventually," the sergeant said. "What spell did you use?"

Gavin shook his head. "You missed what I said, Sergeant. I didn't use a spell; I invoked a Word. I'm a wizard, not a mage."

For the first time, the sergeant lowered his eyes to look at Gavin's medallion. Gavin knew the man recognized the House glyph, because Gavin watched his eyes widen and the color drain from his face and neck.

"Yes, Sergeant," Gavin said with a sigh, "I'm House Kirloth."

The man took a step back and seemed to shrink in on himself just a bit.

"Yes, well," the sergeant said, "I want to thank you for taking the time to defend the woman, milord, and while we will be in touch if we need further information, we will do everything in our power not to impose upon you. You're free to go about your business."

Gavin smiled and nodded, saying, "Thank you, Sergeant. My name is Gavin Cross, and you can find me most days at the College."

Gavin turned to resume traveling to the College and found Declan turning away from a group of five people in plain, everyday clothing. They nodded almost in unison, one of their number leaving at a brisk jog while the rest moved to surround Gavin and Kiri.

"Uhm, Declan?" Gavin said. "What's going on?"

"I'll explain once we're back at the College, but we need to hurry. I'm not sure five of us will be adequate if they come at us in sufficient numbers."

"Who?" Kiri asked. "The Lornithrasa?"

"No, but in some ways, they're almost as bad," Declan said, not slowing his pace.

A SHORT TIME LATER, the group approached the gates of the College. Declan looked at the two upper-Tier students who'd been honored as gate attendants and gestured them to move, saying, "You two, inside...now."

Maybe it was something about Declan's tone and demeanor that convinced the students to comply without hesitation, but either way, they threw the gates wide and led Declan and company into the College's grounds.

Declan stopped at the gate with his fellows, almost pushing Gavin and Kiri inside. He turned to the four who had accompanied them, saying, "You should alert the others. I don't know how this will unfold, but we should probably start preparing for a strike at the Guild. I'll send word once he has decided the course we will take."

The woman and three men each nodded once and pivoted to depart. Declan stepped inside the gates and closed them, slapping closed the latch.

By the time Gavin, Kiri, and Declan approached, a little crowd was forming on the steps of the Tower, Valera and a couple other magisters among the people.

"Gavin," Valera said as the trio neared, "what's going on?"

"He stopped a murder," Declan said. "The killer was a Shadow."

Valera let out the breath she had gathered to speak as a heavy sigh, saying, "Oh."

Every head in the crowd swiveled to look at Gavin, and it was apparent they wanted to glare.

"Would someone mind explaining why saving that woman's life was a bad thing?" Gavin asked.

Valera lifted her eyes to Gavin's and asked, "Have you ever heard of the Compact of Dakkor?"

"A few of the books I've read mentioned it," Gavin said, "but I've not read anything that says what it is."

"I see," Valera said. "Gavin, the Compact of Dakkor was nego-tiated between Kirloth and Dakkor, who was Master of the Guild of Shadows when the Army of Valthon was being formed. In exchange for the Guild's membership in the Army of Valthon, no arcanist would ever assist in the capture, identification, or trial of any member of the Guild."

Gavin looked at Declan. "I'm guessing the tattoo on his neck indicated he was a member of the Guild?"

Declan nodded.

"You were right back there, Declan," Gavin said.

Declan frowned, asking, "Back where?"

"When you said 'well, damn.'"

Declan snorted his amusement.

Valera sighed as she looked at her fellow magisters and said,

"There's nothing for it; we have to bring this before the Council…at least as many of them as are here."

They each nodded.

Valera turned to Gavin and said, "Gavin, would you please wait for my summons in your suite? We will probably need to speak with you at some point."

"House arrest, Valera?" Declan asked. "That is unlike you."

Valera started to speak, but Gavin lifted a hand, forestalling whatever she was about to say. "It's okay," Gavin said. "I'll be there."

Gavin pushed his way through the crowd to enter the Tower, leading Kiri and Declan. Valera watched him go, trying to think of how she could help her friend's former apprentice out of the situation he had created. She was not looking forward to the coming meeting at all, not that she ever did where the Council was concerned.

"Let's go," Valera said, leading her fellows into the Tower as well.

No longer having any specific events to watch, the crowd on the steps soon dispersed, though every ear on the grounds seemed cocked, waiting for word of what would happen.

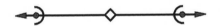

CHAPTER 40

Kiri came out of their room rubbing the sleep from her eyes to find Gavin awake, dressed, and sitting at the table. He was eating a bowl of fruit for breakfast, and he offered Kiri a bowl of her own as she approached, which she accepted.

"Think they'll summon you today?" Kiri asked.

Gavin shrugged. "I don't know, but if they tarry too long, I may just take matters into my own hands and resolve the issue myself."

Kiri placed the bowl on the table and put her fists on her hips and cocked her head to one side, asking, "Haven't you done enough of that already?"

"No," Gavin said after a slight chuckle. "Granted, I did indeed cause the situation, but there would never have been a situation to be caused if the Guild policed its people a little better. There is no reason they should've been conducting a sanctioned killing in broad daylight in a market polluted with people. Huh. Now that I think about it, that makes me wonder if the killing was sanctioned at all."

"What do you think is going to happen?" Kiri asked.

"Honestly?" Gavin asked.

Kiri looked at him in silence for a few moments before she said,

"Don't tell me anything you're not supposed to, Gavin, but I'm worried for you all the same."

Gavin thought back to the scene in the market yesterday and smiled.

"The Guild does not understand the rules of killing wizards, Kiri," he said at last. "You have no reason to worry for me. This situation will end one of two ways. First, the Society and the Guild work through the situation and keep the Compact in force. Second, the Compact is indeed no more, in which case I am free to employ my resources to see to it the Guild no longer poses a threat to the Society, and in that outcome, precious few of them will end up in prison."

"You have those kinds of resources, Gavin?"

Gavin lifted his eyes to meet Kiri's and nodded. "Yes, Kiri, I do."

Kiri opened her mouth to speak, but whatever she was about to say was interrupted by a knock at the door.

"I'll get it," Gavin said as he stood.

Gavin heard the door to the washroom close behind him as he approached the suite's door. He pulled it open to find Sera, Valera's assistant.

"Good morning, Sera," Gavin said. "How can I help you?"

"Begging your pardon, milord," Sera said, "but the Magister of Divination asked me to convey that she requests your presence in her office as soon as possibly convenient."

"Why, thank you, Sera," Gavin said. "I need to tidy up just a quick moment. If you'd like to wait, I can walk with you down to the office."

Sera nodded her acceptance, and Gavin stepped back, pushing the door wide and inviting her into the suite. He walked over to the washroom door and spoke in an elevated voice, "Kiri, Valera has asked me to speak with her in her office. I won't be here when you get finished."

"Okay, Gavin. Do you have anything you want done?"

"I can't think of a thing, Kiri," Gavin said. "You're free to enjoy your morning as you wish." Gavin turned back to Sera, lowering his voice back to normal. "Okay, then. I've tidied up; shall we go?"

"MA'AM," Sera said as she knocked on the open door of Valera's inner office, "I have Gavin Cross for you."

Valera looked up from the papers she held and smiled. "Thank you, Sera. Please excuse us, and close the door. Gavin, please sit."

"Of course, ma'am," Sera said as she bowed out of the room.

Gavin eased himself into the chair on the left from Valera's perspective, interlaced his fingers in his lap, and waited.

"Shortly after the dinner call last evening," Valera said, "three Shadows arrived at the gate under a flag of truce. It was the Master of the Guild and two associates. The Council was still in session, so they were brought before us without delay."

"Why wasn't I notified?" Gavin asked.

"Gavin, please," Valera said. "Tauron wanted to decide the matter then and there. It was an uphill battle, just to get him and those siding with him to postpone the matter until this afternoon. What I and those siding with me could not prevent was Tauron pushing this into a public session. All classes are canceled this afternoon, with the entire student body and any interested arcanists encouraged to attend. He aims to humiliate you in front of as many members of the Society as he can arrange, Gavin."

"Well, now," Gavin said, "that sounds like he's making this whole affair personal."

Valera shrugged. "I think he's still angry over the interactions following the viewing of Marcus's will."

"He was wrong then, Valera, and he's wrong now. If he wants to put on this farce in the public view, I sincerely hope he's considered the possibility of it not going his way."

"Gavin," Valera said, her voice tired, "how can it end otherwise? Most of the Council sides with him more often than not, and you would not believe the amount of negotiation I have to do just to hold some semblance of a line."

Gavin sat in silence for a few moments before he took a breath and said, "Valera, all I ask of you is that you act according to your conscience. It seems to me doing otherwise only serves to corrupt the Council."

"You need all the friends you can get right now, Gavin," Valera said. "The emissaries from the Guild want us to turn you over to them."

Gavin laughed. "I can tell you right now that won't happen. You see, I've been doing some recreational reading. According to the Arcanists' Code, a document that cannot be modified without the consent of the Archmagister, naming a wizard of the Great Houses a renegade requires a unanimous vote of the Conclave of the Great Houses…just so the Council can discuss the matter and hold their own vote. You would not like the options the Code gives the Great Houses in the event the Council chooses to carry out such a discussion and vote anyway."

Valera sagged and put her head in her hands for several moments. She said, "Gavin, you're pushing us into a civil war within the Society. We're already fragile enough as it is!"

"Valera, you yourself just said moments ago that the Council is fractured, factionalized, and fragmented. To me, that sounds like you might as well say 'ineffective,' and be done with it. Perhaps, it's time to shake things up a bit. Besides, Tauron doesn't have the conviction to carry things through to a civil war; he's too much of a coward. For that matter, I would challenge him and his cronies to duels in the arena long before anything exploded into outright fighting."

Valera rubbed her forehead with her hands for several moments, before she lifted her head to face Gavin. "The hearing is scheduled to begin at the first bell after mid-day. You should be seated in the lower gallery and wait for us to summon you to the floor."

"Thank you, Valera," Gavin said as he rose to his feet. "I'll see you this afternoon."

Gavin was just closing the door when he heard a heavy exhalation from within, followed by Valera saying, "I don't care what Tauron says; Marcus was *never* this disruptive."

ROBERT M. KERNS

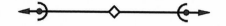

CHAPTER 41

Gavin tracked down Declan as soon as he left Valera's office. Declan was sitting in the gardens, plucking at a full-bodied lute.

"Gavin," Declan said as Gavin approached, "what do you need?"

"I want to believe the Council will do the right thing today, but I'm not confident they will. Get word to the others. I want everyone prepared to begin punitive operations against the Guild upon my order."

"Gavin, for something like this, you should not give ambiguous orders. What is your intent for the Guild?"

"If I give the order, I want them wiped out. I will not stand for them to threaten the Society—or prey on the people of Tel—any longer. If the Compact is no longer in force, I can give that order."

Declan nodded, saying, "Very well. I'll arrange for people to be in the gallery who can serve as messengers. Your word is our will."

* * *

THE MAGISTERS PICKED their seats around the table, Valera sitting at the apex of the horseshoe. The three guests sat in the first three seats of the gallery nearest the door they had entered, and Gavin saw that same row gradually empty as more and more arcanists found seating elsewhere.

The ringing of a large bell echoed through the Chamber. Valera nodded and tapped a section of the table beside her left hand. Gavin felt an instant change in the ambient power. Strong Tutation and Transmutation effects were now active. The doors leading into the chamber now had two points of red light on each of the top corners.

"It is my duty as Eldest of the Council to call this assembly to order," Valera said. When she started speaking, the rune that symbolized Divination appeared above her head. "The Council of Magisters hereby recognizes Tauron, Magister of Evocation and Chief Inquisitor."

Tauron stood. As with Valera, the rune that symbolized Evocation appeared above his head when he began to speak. "Yesterday, just shortly before the evening bell, one of our number disregarded an agreement that has protected us for ages. The Society of the Arcane now sits on the brink of a war with the Guild of Shadows, and we must deliberate before deciding what course we will take. I now call upon Gavin Cross-"

"Point of order," another voice said, interrupting Tauron. The rune of Tutation appeared above the head of the sole elf on the Council.

Tauron glared at the elf. "Yes? What is it, Kantar?"

"Is the individual not a wizard?"

"Yes," Tauron said, his teeth clenched, "he is a wizard."

"And is he not the Head of his House?"

Red began creeping up Tauron's neck as he continued to glare at Kantar. He said, "Yes, he is."

"Is it not Society policy that wizards who are Heads of their House be announced, addressed, and otherwise referred to as their House in all official circumstances?"

Gavin watched Tauron's entire face turn an alarming shade of red as the base of his neck took on just a hint of purple.

"I now call upon Kirloth to stand before the Council," Tauron said, his teeth clenched through the entire statement.

Gavin stood to the accompaniment of a rush of whispers and walked to the recessed area to stand before the Council. The moment he stepped into the recessed area, the glyph of Kirloth appeared in the air above his head. The fervent whispering in the galleries intensified.

"Well, Tauron, is this going to be a theatrical farce, or is the Council honestly interested in the truth?" Gavin asked.

Valera closed her eyes and angled her head down just a bit, and tensions were so high that no one noticed a shadow fading into existence just beside the Archmagister's dais.

"You will be silent until you are given the floor," Tauron said, spraying spittle onto the table with the force of his words. "The Council now calls the representatives of the Guild of Shadows."

The three individuals Gavin didn't recognize stood and walked down to the oval, two men and one woman. They stood a short distance away from Gavin. All three wore worn leather armor, like the would-be murderer the day before. Gavin could tell from the individuals' position and posture that the older man in the center held all the power. The woman looked just a bit envious when she looked at her superior, while the young man opposite her stared at Gavin.

"The Council has already heard a report of the incident," Tauron said, "and we are prepared to-"

"Point of order," Kantar said, interrupting Tauron again.

"Fine," Tauron said, almost spitting out the word. "Does Kirloth have anything to say regarding this matter?"

Kantar maintained his stoic composure but nodded his thanks to Tauron.

"Why, yes, Tauron," Gavin said. "I do indeed have quite a bit to say. Do you yield the floor?"

Tauron's eyes tightened, starting to speak, but his eyes flicked to

Kantar. He closed his mouth once more, took a deep breath, and resumed his seat, saying, "The floor is yours."

"Ladies and gentlemen of the Council, fellow arcanists, I do not deny that I violated the Compact of Dakkor yesterday. Knowing what I now know…if presented with those circumstances again, I would do the exact same thing."

The undercurrent of whispers increased.

"Pretty rhetoric, boy," the older man in leathers said, "but you're not protected anymore."

Gavin turned to look at the man, his expression that of granite as he said, "We may not be 'protected,' as you put it, but we are most certainly defended…but I'll get back to that. I assume you bring some kind of offer to the Society."

"Well, before your little speech, the offer was that you are turned over to us and our man be released from jail in exchange for things staying the way they've been."

"Not so bad, but you wouldn't have gotten it," Gavin said.

The old man chuckled, saying, "Don't be so sure, boy. The vote last night said we do."

Now, murmuring in the galleries took on the angry tone of disgruntled protesters.

"Oh, really?" Gavin said. "They've already voted? That certainly helps matters. You see, Articles 31 – 34 of the Arcanists' Code go into great detail about how the Great Houses of Tel and the Council relate to each other. In order for the Council to hand over anyone to whatever you call justice, they must first vote to name that person a renegade, which is a simple majority vote… except in the case of a member of the Great Houses…and here's the best part. Before the Council can even deliberate over naming a member of the Great Houses a renegade, the Conclave of the Great Houses must unanimously vote that the person in question *should* be named a renegade."

The murmurs stopped. The sudden quiet was eerie.

"Why are you blathering about the Great Houses?" the older man in leathers asked.

Gavin favored the man with a dark, almost malicious grin,

saying, "According to Article 31, the Council committed an attack upon the Great Houses of Tel by deliberating this issue and taking a vote on how to proceed, which is the first step toward the Conclave of the Great Houses assuming total authority over the Society should we choose to do so."

A graveyard at night would be noisier than the Chamber of the Council at that moment. Every magister stared at Gavin, their coloring a sickly pallor.

"I'm not prepared to go to the hassle of calling a Conclave of the Great Houses over this," Gavin said, turning to face the Guild's representatives, "as long as you answer one question."

"What's the question?" the older man asked.

"Was the murder sanctioned?"

Now, the color fled the representatives' faces. Gavin waited. Silence reigned.

"Well?" Gavin asked after a time. "It's a fairly simple question. Was the murder sanctioned?"

"No," the older man said, unable to maintain eye contact with Gavin.

Gavin took a step backward, affecting surprise. "No? I thought all activities must be sanctioned by the guild leadership. Has something changed in recent years?"

"No," the older man said, his voice almost a whisper and still not looking at Gavin.

"Forgive me, sir, but I didn't hear that," Gavin said, though the man's speech had indeed been crystal clear. "Could you please speak up?"

The man now lifted his head to glare at Gavin and spoke in a strong tone, "No."

"Well, now," Gavin said. "This is a very interesting turn of events. Sir, if the murder was not sanctioned, then did I intervene in Guild affairs?"

The older man took a deep breath and said, "No, you did not."

The woman by the older man's left side stepped forward, speaking at last, "That doesn't change anything! The Compact says that no arcanist will assist in the capture, trial, or identification of any members of the Guild or any of our holdings. One of our men is in the town jail this very moment, captured because of you! I for one am looking forward to robbing you Robes blind."

"That sounds like you came here to ensure the Compact expired, rather than be renewed," Gavin said, "but you want to be very sure that is the path you wish to take."

"What are you going to do?" the woman said. "You'll be bleeding out on our Guild-house floor."

"I don't think so, Miss," Gavin said, "and I'm finished playing in Tauron's theater." Gavin took a deep breath and, lifting his eyes to scan the upper gallery and raising his voice, said, "The order is given." Gavin turned to face the woman once more. "Within three months, the Guild will be no more. I grant you safe conduct to leave the College, but the moment you set foot on the white tiles of the market, you should run."

A stunned silence descended on the crowd. Everyone stared at Gavin, and not even Tauron had anything to say.

"Isn't that a bit drastic?" a new voice said.

Gavin turned to his right. A young man in worn leathers leaned against the pedestal that supported Bellos's statue, the very picture of nonchalance. His black hair was well-trimmed, and he wore a pencil-thin mustache.

The three Guild representatives dropped to one knee faster than the blink of an eye.

"I don't think so," Gavin said. "It seems to me they came here with the intent of delivering a demand they knew would not—or could not—be accepted, which means they never intended to negotiate in good faith. If they're so intent on the Compact's expiration, I see no reason we should just roll over and let them...what was it... oh, yes, 'rob us Robes blind.' The Society has the capability to be a very dangerous enemy, but I see no reason to mobilize the entire Society when my resources alone are sufficient to carry out the task...in three months or less."

The young man laughed and said, "I *still* remember the day your uncle walked into my Guild-house and said, 'You and your

Guild will join the Army of Valthon, or I will burn you to ash where you sit.' You remind me of him."

"I have no idea who you are or how you came to be here, but you are interfering with an official session of the Council of Magisters," Tauron said, rising to his feet.

There was a general gasp throughout the chamber.

Gavin's eyes followed the wave of gasps around the galleries, before looking at the young man once more. "I guess Tauron hasn't figured it out yet," Gavin said.

Now, Gavin turned and faced the Council, gesturing toward the young man as he said, "Ladies and gentlemen of the Council, fellow arcanists, allow me to present Dakkor, God of Thieves."

Dakkor walked around to stand between the Council and Gavin, facing Gavin. He said, "I have no wish to see the Guild exterminated. Your uncle and I negotiated the Compact once. Shall you and I do the same?"

Tauron's nostrils flared as he drew breath, saying, "He does not have the authority to speak for the Society!"

Gavin watched Valera reach over and grasped Tauron's left wrist, forcing him to sit. Gavin could tell Valera intended to whisper, but whether because of heightened emotion or the acoustics of the space, her words carried.

"Tauron, you damned fool, be silent!"

It took all of Gavin's willpower to keep his expression neutral when he heard Valera's words.

"No, Valera," Dakkor said, gesturing for her to ease back. "Tauron is quite correct. Kirloth does not have the authority to negotiate for the Society, but I have no wish to negotiate with the Society. The Society isn't a threat to my Guild. There is one certain threat to my Guild and a possible second. Kirloth is the certainty. You are the possibility."

"I don't understand," Valera said.

Dakkor turned to Gavin. "Show them, or they will never believe."

"Are you sure?" Gavin asked.

Dakkor nodded.

Gavin took a deep breath, cleared his mind of everything but his intent, and invoked a Word, "*Klaepos.*" Every nerve in Gavin's body burned as the power surged through him, and the resonance of his power slammed into the wizards present like heavy stones.

A spherical section of space a few feet above Gavin's head began to shimmer and ripple. Within a few moments, that space became an overhead view of Tel Mivar, including the Outskirts, with the edges of the image frayed like a torn tapestry. Black dots littered the image, blotting out the view of a building in some cases while many others moved like ants. There were three black dots on top of the representation of the College.

Almost all of the Chamber's occupants stared at the image in silence. Valera alone gaped at the image, her eyes wide as she sucked in a breath.

"That's a scrying sphere!" Valera said, her voice full of wonder.

"Yes, it is," Dakkor said. "Gavin, tell us what those black dots represent."

"Those black dots represent every member of the Guild of Shadows in Tel Mivar, both the old city and the Outskirts."

Dakkor directed his attention back to Valera. "Madam, you are acknowledged by the Society of the Arcane as the greatest living authority on Divination. Can you duplicate this effect?"

Valera shook her head, as she spoke, "No. There might be one or two spells capable of showing me a random Shadow, but no spell I know is capable of this. No one's seen a scrying sphere in…oh…at least a thousand years. Not since the last wizards trained by wizards."

"The Compact was never intended to protect arcanists from the Guild," Dakkor said, his gaze resting on the three Shadows present. "It was *my* price, not Kirloth's. I wanted to protect the Guild from arcanists, and back then, the only arcanists were wizards."

Dakkor directed his attention back to Tauron. "Why should I bother negotiating with an organization that's no threat to my interests? I chose to negotiate here for two reasons: one, the situation quickly escalated to a point I felt my direct intervention was required, and two, I wanted to be sure none of you interfered and caused the death of my Guild."

Dakkor turned to Gavin, asking, "Are you willing to negotiate?"

"I'm prepared for the state of affairs to return to what they were prior to this incident," Gavin said, "but I'll tell you right now the next time I see someone stabbing anyone in front of a child, I will kill whoever's doing the stabbing. I don't care if the stabbing *was* contracted."

Dakkor nodded, saying, "Yes. When I ran the Guild, there was discretion in our operations. It looks like the training has slipped over time."

"They seem to be hung up on the man in jail, who may still be paralyzed."

"He is," Dakkor said.

Gavin winced, saying, "Ouch. I didn't think the paralysis would last this long. Okay, here's my offer. The state of affairs between the Society and the Guild will return to what it was before this incident. I will see to it the captured Shadow is no threat to the Guild, and you will sort out your people. Is this acceptable?"

"It is indeed," Dakkor said, nodding.

Gavin extended his right hand. Dakkor grasped Gavin's right hand with his, and they gave each other a firm, respectful handshake.

When he ended the handshake, Gavin looked up to the gallery once more, saying, "The order is rescinded."

Dakkor turned and approached the kneeling Shadows. He said, "You will stand. We have work to do."

The three representatives stood. Dakkor led them into a shadow that had not been there before, and they disappeared.

Gavin turned to face the Council and found them all looking at him. Valera and Kantar's expressions conveyed respect. The Magisters of Interation, Transmutation, and Conjuration, and Thaumaturgy looked at Gavin with undisguised envy dominating their expressions. The Magisters of Illusion and Enchantment eyed Gavin with fear. Tauron—as always—looked at Gavin with ill-disguised hatred. Gavin invoked a composite effect, blending two

Words into one invocation, "*Zyrhaek-Othys.*" He grimaced as the pain savaged him, and the background noise from the galleries vanished.

"I have created a barrier of blurring silence between us and the galleries," Gavin said, "for what I have to say now is for your ears alone. We stand at a precipice. I am quite happy to summon a copy of the Arcanists' Code for you to review and verify my statements, but I think you know my interpretation of Article 31 is correct.

"I have more than sufficient grounds to call for a Conclave of the Great Houses and demand a vote on removing the Council, and from some of the expressions I see around this table, everyone here knows how that vote would end. The fact is, calling a Conclave is the path I do not want to take. I do not believe the Council is beyond saving. You simply followed one man in his blind headlong charge to use this latest incident to further a personal vendetta against me. The sad part of *that* situation is I don't even know why he hates me…but I'm past caring.

"It is my hope that eight of you will realize how close we have come to a situation that would spiral out of control and drive us all down a dark path none of us want to travel. It is also my hope that this will be a cautionary tale for future consideration. Now, I am going to drop the barrier of silence, make one last remark, and yield the floor. This session will then be adjourned."

Gavin stepped back out from inside the horseshoe and invoked another Word, "*Klyphos.*" A miniscule trickle of blood seeped out of his right nostril and ran down his upper lip, and the barrier of blurring silence vanished.

"I want it to be a matter of record," Gavin said, "that I do not hold the Council to blame for one man's stupidity and lack of judgment. I therefore waive the Conclave's right to Article 31 proceedings regarding this event, and I yield the floor."

Gavin turned and walked back to his seat in the gallery. As he walked, Gavin withdrew a handkerchief from the pocket of his robe and wiped away the blood on his lip.

Valera rapped her knuckles on the table, saying, "I move that this session be adjourned. Are there any opposed?"

The table was silent.

"Very well," Valera said. "By general acclamation, I hereby declare this session of the Council to be adjourned."

Valera tapped the square beside her left hand again, unsealing the chamber.

Gavin was not even sitting yet as the people began leaving the galleries. A few started to approach him, but Gavin shook his head and moved into the crowd's general motion toward the gallery door.

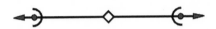

CHAPTER 42

T wo days later, Gavin and Declan arrived on the third floor and found they were not alone. Lillian, Wynn, Braden, and Mariana stood at the door to Gavin's suite, and from the way they focused on Gavin, it was obvious they were waiting for him.

"Is there some way I can be of assistance?" Gavin asked when none of them seemed inclined to speak.

They glanced at one another, and Lillian stepped forward, saying, "If you don't mind, we would like to speak with you... uhm...I'm sorry. Should we address you as Gavin or Kirloth?"

Gavin smiled. "Lillian, my name is Gavin...always has been, always will be. 'Kirloth' is just something I trot out when the occasion calls for it. Please, follow me to my suite. We can talk there."

Declan parted company with Gavin as they approached the door to Gavin's suite. Gavin removed his medallion and opened the door.

"Kiri, fair warning...we have guests," Gavin said, his voice raised just a bit as he entered the suite with the others trailing behind.

Kiri broke into a huge smile when she saw Lillian and walked

Awakening

straight to her. The young ladies embraced, and Gavin smiled when he saw how tightly Kiri hugged Lillian.

"How are you?" Kiri asked as they ended the embrace.

Lillian nodded, saying, "I'm doing well. The nightmares are infrequent, and I don't jump at loud noises anymore."

"Good," Kiri said.

"I hope that doesn't mean our talks are over."

Kiri grinned. "I hope so, too! So, what brings you here?"

"Our families want to speak with Gavin," Lillian said. "They asked us to be the messengers."

"Did they say what they wanted to speak to me about?" Gavin asked.

"No," Braden said, his deep voice rumbling throughout the common room, "but all our parents are at the Mivar Estate."

"Mother was *very* emphatic that you understand this is a request and not a summons," Mariana was quick to interject. "She said one does *not* summon Kirloth."

Gavin chuckled, grinning. "Okay. I'm not summoned. Still, though, if they're all there…I see no reason not to see what they want. Do you want to go, Kiri?"

"Unless you want me to go, I have plenty to keep me occupied here."

"Well then," Gavin said as he indicated the door, "let us proceed."

IT REQUIRED a little less than an hour to cross the city to the Mivar Estate. Several times, Gavin recognized a face in the crowd from the day he was introduced to the Wraiths, every time a different face, and he couldn't help but wonder how many of them were traveling with them unseen through the crowd. He suspected not even the King of Tel was so well guarded…but then again, Leuwyn didn't have the Lornithrasa trying to kill *him*.

. . .

259

LILLIAN WALKED AHEAD of the group to reach the bell-pull as they approached her family's ancestral home.

"Lillian, have you ever tried approaching the gate like your grandfather does?" Gavin asked.

"No, why?"

"No reason. I was just curious."

Lillian gave Gavin a thoughtful look before she turned away from the bell-pull and walked straight to the gate. When she neared it, everyone heard the lock click open just before the gate swung wide. Lillian stifled a gasp and turned to Gavin.

"How did you know?"

"I didn't, not for certain. It's just that some of my readings lately suggested that the protections are tied to each bloodline."

"Then, why doesn't it open for Father?"

"Well…he's not a wizard, Lillian. The protections have no way to recognize him."

Lillian's face fell just a bit. "Oh." She turned and led the group onto the land that uncounted generations of Mivar's descendants called home.

BY THE TIME they crossed half of the seventy-five yards that separated the manor house from the gate, Adelaide stood on the portico to greet them. She smiled as the group approached.

"It's always good to see the four of you together," Adelaide said. "I remember all the years you played together as kids when your parents came to Tel Mivar." Her eyes found Gavin, and the smile faded. "My condolences, Gavin. Torval and I regret we did not send a message at the time."

"It's quite all right, ma'am," Gavin said, "and thank you."

"Oh, my goodness…I thought we established you'd call me Adelaide after you saved Lilli," Adelaide said as she turned to lead the group into the house. "They're in the parlor."

Gavin smiled. "Yes, Adelaide."

. . .

THE PARLOR TURNED out to be a sitting room on the right side of the foyer. Gavin couldn't keep his eyes from drifting to the doors of the Conclave Hall as he followed Adelaide and wondered where Mariana and Torval had secured the strongboxes from the vineyard.

Lyssa Cothos and Sypara Wygoth shared a sofa on one side of the room, while Carth Roshan and Torval each sat in armchairs. They stood, though, when Gavin entered.

"Thank you for coming," Lyssa said. "I hope we did not disturb you."

"Nonsense," Gavin said. "My friends said you wanted to speak with me."

Lyssa, Sypara, Carth, and Torval each looked at one another, as if silently determining who would speak. Torval must've won. He gestured for Gavin to take a seat as he and his other guests did so as well.

"We've been discussing the hearing...Tauron's 'theatrical farce,' I believe you called it...and it was certainly that. We're still smiling over the memory of Dakkor not caring about the Council in the slightest." Torval paused a few moments as he looked to each of his counterparts once more, before turning back to face Gavin. "Gavin, we've spent a lot of time discussing this, and we want you to train our Heirs. We want them to be true arcanists, not empowered mages."

Gavin almost allowed his jaw to drop and looked to Lyssa, Sypara, and Carth in turn. Each nodded as Gavin's eyes met theirs.

"I don't have any issue with it, myself, but am I allowed to train people? Don't I have to be an instructor for that?"

"Not if you do with them as your mentor did with you...claim them as your apprentices as was in the old ways," Lyssa said. "Under Article 24 of the Code, that removes them from the authority of the College...and those fools on the Council."

"You really don't like them at all, do you?" Gavin said.

"Oh, Valera's competent enough, and she does what she can. I have nothing to say against Kantar, either, but they're only two of nine. They're often outvoted. Part of me wishes you had proceeded with removing them when Tauron tried to hand you over to the Guild of Shadows."

Gavin saw Lyssa's eyes tighten just a bit as she said 'Tauron,' and he wanted to know what history they had. He turned to his friends, who stood together on one side of the room.

"What are your thoughts about all this?"

Lillian stepped forward, saying, "We went to our parents, Gavin; they didn't decide this on their own."

Gavin blinked. "You did?"

Lillian, Braden, Wynn, and Mariana nodded.

Braden said, "As long as I can remember, I've wanted to create items imbued with power. I've wanted to make artifacts. No mage ever born has been able to make anything even close to the quality our ancestors took for granted, and I had to come to terms with the idea that it was beyond me, too. When I saw what you did on the Council floor, I started to hope that maybe—just maybe—I could have my dream after all."

Gavin's eyes found Mariana, and he said, "You're a graduate of the College, a *Semagus* if I'm reading the runes right. Are you certain you want to go back to school, as it were?"

"I've always felt I was just kissing the surface of what was out there," Mariana said. "Every time I cast a spell, it feels like there's something inside me trying to get out. I want to learn what I've been missing."

Gavin thought back to the reticence Lillian showed when speaking with him in the hallway outside his suite, and he frowned. "And you were afraid you couldn't come to me? I thought you knew you could come to me with anything."

"You're-Kirloth-now," Wynn said. "You-haven't-been-to-the-mentor-sessions-in-some-time. Everyone-thought-you-moved-on."

Gavin sighed. "I haven't moved on, Wynn. Events spiraled in a direction I wasn't expecting after the duel, not to mention Marcus's death. I didn't explicitly choose to stop attending the mentor sessions. Speaking of those events...Torval, where are those strongboxes?"

"They're in the Conclave Hall," Torval said. "Mariana and I felt they'd be safest there."

"Since we're all here, we'd better discuss them. Did she tell you anything about what's in them?"

Torval shook his head. "She said only that you asked me to secure them for you."

"I see," Gavin said, nodding. "Well, it's not good." He turned back to his friends. "I will consider your request and investigate whether I can do it...legally within the Code. If I can, I will. I will teach you what Marcus taught me, but first, we have a far more serious situation developing."

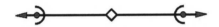

CHAPTER 43

Following Gavin's departure, Kiri puttered around the suite until the time came for her studies with Declan. She left the suite and headed to the arena, looking forward to the coming session. Declan embarrassed her less often with each passing session, but he always seemed to have some trick up his sleeve that allowed him to pass her guard with ease.

THAT SESSION, however, Kiri might as well have been a fresh student, given the number of mistakes she made, and it wasn't more than handful of minutes that Declan stopped the session and stepped back.

"Your mind is not on the moment," Declan said. "Something troubles you?"

For a time, Kiri held her tongue, saying at last, "Do you know who I was?"

"I know who you *are*, Princess," Declan said, smiling. "I recognized you the day Marcus introduced us."

"I've never asked why the world-famous bard, Declan the

Dandy, is acting as an aide and arms instructor. Believe me…I want to."

Silence ruled the space for a time until Kiri broke it again.

"Does the phrase 'Slave Queen of Vushaar' mean anything to you?"

"It does."

"Good. I want you to train me. Teach me what I need to know to be the Slave Queen of Vushaar."

Declan nodded once, saying, "I can do that, but if you know of the prophecy regarding the Slave Queen, you should also know that's only one possible outcome."

"What? What do you mean?"

"The set of prophecies surrounding the Slave Queen is one path of a forked prophecy. There is an equal possibility that it won't come true."

Kiri frowned. "I don't understand."

"Good. We try to keep it that way…*Skuv Ir Nathene*, I mean. Forked prophecies are fiendish to decipher. The base form is either 'a' happens or 'b' happens, and in this case, the text is over three thousand years old and so cryptic the ravings of a madman seem clear in comparison."

"What can you tell me about the other path?"

"The Slave Queen only rises if the broken Arrow fails to fly."

Kiri blinked. "But…but that's gibberish. How can a broken arrow fly?"

"And that's the most sensible part, with a little translation. Language has changed a bit in three thousand years. If you want to proceed with the training, I can work up a curriculum."

"I'm not sure I want to trust the fate of my country to a broken arrow flying…whatever that means. I would like to proceed."

Declan nodded. "Very well. If it does come to pass that you become the Slave Queen of Vushaar, that means Ivarson will succeed in his rebellion, and you'll be fighting a guerilla war." Declan closed his eyes and pointed his face toward the cavern's ceiling. "That means you'll need to understand small- and medium-unit tactics, logistics, basic military strategy, not to mention personal combat..." Declan's voice trailed off, and he opened his eyes, looking at Kiri once more. "That's all I can think of for now, but I'm sure I'll think of more. I'll start working up a curriculum. I won't be able to teach you all of this myself, you understand, but I have a vast network of associates from which to draw. Give me a couple days to get everything in motion, and we'll expand our training sessions."

Kiri nodded. "I'm not comfortable with this idea at all. I don't want my father to die or lose the war...but I feel I have to be prepared in case the worst happens."

"Indeed," Declan said. "Hope for the best while you prepare for the worst. As long as you follow that, very little will catch you flat-footed."

Silence dominated the arena for several moments as Kiri stared off at something only she could see. Declan stood, waiting for her to return to the moment.

At long last, Kiri directed her attention back to Declan. "How would you rate my skills?"

"When you're focused on the moment and not...other things... you're above average. You're nimble and quick. You have a subtle mind, and I've seen you come up with variations of maneuvers that others more experienced than you struggle with. I would trust you at my back in a fight."

"Can you get me armor? I can't have my left shoulder covered, because of the brand, but I want some armor."

Declan frowned. "Why do you *need* armor?"

Kiri stared at the mixture of sawdust and dirt that covered the floor, saying, "I can't shake the feeling there's going to be a battle over what Mariana discovered at Vischaene Vineyard, and I just know Gavin will insist on being out in front, leading those who oppose the traitors. I'm going to be there with him, Declan, but to do that, I'll need armor."

"You'll need more than armor. Isn't it a capital crime for a slave to possess a blade?"

Kiri shrugged. "I don't care. I'll risk it. I can't stand the thought of sitting cooped up in the suite, while Gavin and Lillian and the others go off to a fight they might not come back from."

"If the wrong person sees you with a blade, *you* might not make it…even if we win."

"And just how do you think Gavin would react to someone trying to haul me off to face the King's justice?"

Declan shrugged. "Honestly, I see it ranging from polite refusal to…well…impolite refusal, depending on the circumstances at hand."

"Exactly. So, will you get me some armor and kit?"

"I'll see what I can do."

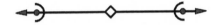

CHAPTER 44

Torval and Gavin led the group into the Conclave Hall, and Gavin saw the strongboxes sitting on a table along the wall to the right of the door. He gestured for Mariana to unlock them and turned to the group, indicating for Braden to close the doors.

"I accepted when Mariana volunteered herself and several of her colleagues in the Battle-mages to serve as my agents, and as part of her inspection of the Vischaene Vineyards, she discovered something alarming. We gathered the evidence we are about to show you and intended to present it to Valera before I violated the Compact of Dakkor."

"Evidence?" Lyssa asked. "Evidence of what?"

"See for yourself, Mother," Mariana said as she indicated the now-open strongboxes.

Lyssa pivoted and strode to the table. She moved from strongbox to strongbox, scanning their contents, and Gavin knew when she arrived at the final one. It held the most shocking evidence of all.

"Those bastards," Lyssa hissed.

"Lyssa?" Sypara asked. "What's wrong?"

Lyssa turned to face the group. Gavin expected her to be shocked, but she was not. She was angry.

"You should have let us take over," Lyssa said, glaring at Gavin. "The Council is far too incompetent to answer this threat."

"Lyssa, what's wrong?" Carth asked.

"The king appears to have sponsored a plot for his old friend, Iosen Sivas, to collect like-minded souls and overthrow the Council and Society. They're gathering troops in the hinterlands of my province. It's all there."

"What we need to verify before we go jumping to any conclusions," Gavin said, "is whether this information is accurate. Before the incident with the Guild, I was taking all this to Valera in the hopes that she would be able to verify its authenticity. I sent it here with Mariana to keep it safe until we could resume investigating it."

"We need more information," Carth said. "At what stage are they in their preparations? How many troops have they gathered? Is the leadership there with the troops, or elsewhere? That's just what I can think of now. I'm sure there's more we need to know."

"Can you get word to Garris?" Sypara asked. "Have him bring the Battle-mages back from Hope's Pass?"

Gavin frowned. "I didn't realize we had that kind of authority."

"Well," Carth said with a slight grimace, "if I sent the note, it would just be the big brother who used to thump him asking him to bring the Battle-mages home with no good reason. If he were to receive a note sealed under the Glyph of Kirloth, however…"

Gavin stared at the floor as he turned the matter over in his head. Even though the Battle-mages were nominally a unit of the Army of Tel, that was just a matter of convenience. The actual language of the Constitution was that the Battle-mages of Tel collaborated with the army upon the pleasure of the Society of the Arcane. Every Battle-mage under colors swore their oaths to the Society and the Arcanists' Code…*not* the Constitution of Tel. This would not—in most cases—be an issue, as the Archmagister was the head of the government for both the Kingdom of Tel *and* the head of the Society of the Arcane…unless there happened not to be a sitting Archmagister.

A part of Gavin wanted to keep his head down. After all, he just brought the Council of Magisters to heel in a public forum. He couldn't be the most popular individual right then. If he suborned the Battle-mages, who knew what kind of damage that would do?

On the other hand, something needed to be done…and preferably *before* a hostile army was marching on Tel Mivar. The notes Mariana had found contained battle plans for a general invasion of the capital city. Countless innocent people would be caught in the fighting, and the kinds of people the papers suggested Sivas was hiring for the army were not squeamish at all about rape, pillage, and murder.

The mental image of a woman bleeding on the street and begging for her son to run settled the matter for Gavin. He lifted his eyes to Torval.

"May I please impose upon you for writing materials and sealing wax?"

A SHORT TIME LATER, Gavin dribbled melted wax over the folded message and pressed his medallion into the wax. Once the wax dried, Gavin collected the missive and stood from the Conclave table.

"Excuse me a moment, please."

GAVIN STEPPED outside the Conclave Hall and frowned as he remembered Declan hadn't joined them for the trip to the Mivar Estate. He left the manor house and watched the gate unlatch and swing wide as he approached it and stopped just outside the gate. He lifted the sealed note so that the sealing wax with the Glyph of Kirloth impressed in it could be seen by those passing the gate.

Within moments, a young woman in the heavy leather jerkin and trousers of a courier stepped out of the traffic and approached Gavin. Her brown hair was pulled into a braid that ran down her back, and she wore several blades. Once she was close, she pulled back the left sleeve of the jerkin, revealing the tattoo of the Wraiths.

"How may I serve, Milord?"

"I need this in Garris Roshan's hands as soon as possible."

The woman nodded once as she accepted the folded parchment.

"Are you aware of what was found at Vischaene Vineyard?"

She nodded once.

"Get word to the others. I want to know everything there is to know about that as soon as possible. Both the note and the information are top priority from here on out. I'm also going to need people to move these strongboxes; I don't know where the Battlemage volunteers are, and I don't want to wait for Mariana to find them."

"I'll see to it, Milord," the woman said and turned away, disappearing back into the crowd.

GAVIN RETURNED to Mivar's manor house, and as he passed the curving staircase that led to the upper floors, raised voices faintly wafted from the doors to the Conclave Hall. The walls and doors were too thick for one to hear clearly what was being said, even if one were to press an ear against the door, and Gavin entered the Hall to find Lyssa and Torval arguing with great vehemence.

"Lyssa," Torval said, "what you're saying is almost treason. Without an Archmagister, both the Conclave's and the Council's positions in the overall scheme of things is extremely nebulous. The Conclave of the Great Houses started as an advisory body to the Archmagister, and the Council itself has no standing in the government of Tel. What would you have us do? Depose the Council? Depose the King?"

"We do whatever we must to keep those murderers and rapists off our streets, Torval!" Lyssa shot back. "I would gladly give my life if it meant this coup never happened."

"We're not doing that," Gavin said, drawing everyone's attention to him as he approached the group.

"Who are *you* to tell *us* what to do?" Lyssa said, her face flushed and her nostrils flared just a bit.

Gavin could tell that something in the discussion he missed had struck a nerve with Lyssa, and while he had no idea what it was, he also knew he didn't care.

"For one thing, it's my evidence. For another, I'm Kirloth. You said it yourself, Lyssa; one does not summon Kirloth. Why is that?" Gavin held Lyssa's gaze until the flush faded from her cheeks and she looked away; everyone in the room knew why no one summons Kirloth. People still spoke of Kirloth in hushed tones mixed with fear and awe, thousands of years after Marcus stopped using the name. "I'm not going to stand here and try to convince you that I have some kind of grand plan that will work without any effort or worry. I'm not going to stand here and tell you I have everything in hand. What I am going to stand here and tell you is that doing the wrong thing for the right reason is still doing the wrong thing. We're better than that.

"I'm going to take this evidence to Valera for verification and, then, present it to the Council. I already have intelligence-gathering operations under way to get us the information we need. I don't know how long it will be before I have a report on what's happening at the mercenary camp, but I imagine it will be sooner rather than later. I don't believe we know enough now to decide what our course should be. All I ask is that you go about your daily lives and be ready when I call you."

"What happens when doing the wrong thing for the right reason is the only option we have?" Lyssa said, her voice a shadow of its former strength.

"Then, *I* will make that decision and do what needs to be done. I was told not too long ago that's what it means to be Kirloth."

Gavin entered Valera's outer office and saw Sera working on papers at her desk. It was several moments before Sera looked up, and when she did, she froze.

"Good afternoon, Sera," Gavin said, "I need some of Valera's time."

"I'm afraid she's in a meeting right now."

"I regret that, but this is a matter of importance."

A slight smile quirked one corner of Sera's mouth before she controlled it and looked away.

"I know, I know," Gavin said, deciding on the direct approach. "Everyone believes their matter is a matter of importance. The thing is, I don't know how much time I have, so I'm afraid I'll have to be a bit rude. Either you can announce I'm here, or I'll just walk on through."

Just then, eight men carried strongboxes into the outer office. Sera looked at the strongboxes and blanched. She almost jumped up from her seat, just managing to catch the chair before it tipped over backward, and took the few steps necessary to bring her to Valera's door. She knocked twice and stepped inside.

A few moments later, she returned, saying, "The Magisters will see you now."

Gavin led his people into Valera's office and saw Kantar sitting in one of the two armchairs set aside for guests.

"What's going on, Gavin?" Valera said.

"Mariana discovered something at Vischaene Vineyard when she was acting as my agent of process in claiming all the property owned by Rolf Sivas," Gavin said and nodded greetings to Kantar before turning to the outer office. "Bring it in, please."

Gavin directed the eight men in placing the strongboxes on a table in the corner of Valera's office and accepted the keys for each one. Once they had finished, Gavin said, "I want these two rooms secured, both this office and the outer office. If anyone walks through this door, the lot of you had better be dead."

Eight heads nodded at once and left Valera's office, Gavin closing the door behind them. Gavin then went over and unlocked the strongboxes, taking the effort to rest the lids against the tabletop with as much care as possible. Then, he turned to the Magisters who sat waiting for his explanation.

"Iosen Sivas is spearheading a plot to overthrow the Council and give control of the Society to the King of Tel. If this evidence is accurate and real, I think it's a pawn-sacrifice maneuver with Iosen as the cut-out, so it doesn't wash back on the

King. Everything Mariana found is here. Look through it yourselves."

A SHORT TIME LATER, Kantar and Valera sat staring at the table that was now littered with evidence of Iosen Sivas's plot. Their expressions were vacant as they seemed to stare at something only they could see. After several moments, they turned to face each other.

"I would never have believed he would try it," Valera said.

"Who, the king?" Kantar asked. "Valera, my people have a *very* different opinion of the man who nominally rules Tel. There are factions within my people arguing for a more hardline stance against his many offenses. But that is not important to the matter at hand. We have no other option; we must call an emergency session of the Council."

"Yes, Kantar, that much we must do," Valera said and shifted her gaze to Gavin. "I need Sera, Gavin, but I don't want her killed for trying to answer my summons."

Gavin allowed his lips to quirk toward a grin for a brief moment before walking to the door and opening it a crack, saying, "Sera, the Magister needs your assistance."

Gavin opened the door for the assistant, and Sera stopped just inside the door.

"Sera," Valera said, "I need to call an emergency meeting of the Council. Will you please see to that? Use my seal, dear."

Sera's eyes widened just enough to notice, but she replied in the affirmative before departing to carry out her task. Gavin watched her go and closed the door, before turning to find Valera and Kantar examining him. Gavin raised an eyebrow in silent question.

"What are your intentions, Gavin?" Valera asked.

Gavin's raised eyebrow lifted higher. "I'm not sure I understand your question, Valera."

"There's an excellent chance the royal palace would be a pool of molten rock right now," Valera said, "if your mentor had discovered this instead of you. I want to know what you intend."

Gavin sighed and took a half-step back to lean against the wall.

After several moments, he said, "Valera, I intend to present this evidence to the Council and give the Council the opportunity to do its job. When the Council fails to do that, the Conclave of the Great Houses will step up and determine what needs to be done."

"You seem very sure of the outcome of this emergency session," Kantar said.

"My mentor never openly discussed his opinions of the Council, but by the end, I like to think I knew him pretty well. I had the impression he considered the Council utterly ineffective and a waste of time in general…if not a waste of life in some cases. Since I started reading his journals, I fear I may have overestimated his opinion, and it is unfortunate that all of my dealings with the Council have only lent weight to my mentor's view."

After several moments of silence, Kantar said, "You do not seem to mince words much."

"We all have too much to do to waste time, Kantar, even elves who live for centuries. I've already informed Torval and the others —with Lyssa fully ready to go rogue to do what needed to be done —but that's not how things are supposed to work. The Constitution of Tel charges the Council of Magisters with policing the Society of the Arcane. If I fail to give the Council the chance to discharge their duties, I am just as guilty of treason as Iosen Sivas and his people."

"If this session goes as you have predicted," Kantar asked, "what will you do then?"

"You should already know the answer to that, sir," Gavin said. "I am Kirloth; I will do what I must."

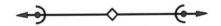

CHAPTER 45

L ater that day, Gavin once again sat in the aisle seat of the lowest row of the lower gallery in the Chamber of the Council; as he had before, Gavin chose the aisle in a direct line across the room from the doors the Council would enter soon. In a line to his left sat Torval, Lillian, Lyssa, Mariana, Sypara, Braden, Carth, and Wynn. The eight men minding the strongboxes occupied the aisle across the steps from Gavin.

The doors to the Chamber soon opened as the Council arrived. The Magisters of Interation, Transmutation, and Conjuration surrounded Tauron. The Magisters of Illusion and Enchantment walked side-by-side, but they were husband and wife. Valera and Kantar, the Magisters of Divination and Tutation respectively, chatted amiably about something as they led the procession. Drannos Muldannin, the Magister of Thaumaturgy, was noticeable in his absence.

Gavin scanned the group and saw the moment Tauron noticed him. Tauron's fists clenched, and even across the distance, Gavin could see the tension in the man's jaw. Tauron's reaction was imme-diate—almost instinctual—and Gavin shook his head and sighed.

. . .

IN SHORT ORDER, the Council seated themselves, and Valera touched the stone inset into the table beside her left hand. Red points of light appeared at the top corners of every door into the chamber, and the acoustics carried Valera's words to all occupants.

"I hereby call this emergency session of the Council of Magisters to order."

Tauron had not taken his eyes off Gavin since he sat and gestured for permission to speak. Valera nodded.

"It is most unlike you to be a scare monger, Valera," Tauron said. "I for one am very interested in learning why you've called this emergency session. I am also curious why these proceedings have spectators today."

"The Arcanists' Code grants magisters the authority to call a session for *any* reason, Tauron, and the Code further mandates that *all* meetings of the Council be open to the public," Kantar said. "Besides, I was present at the time Valera decided to call for this session, and I support her decision. I would like for Kirloth to make his presentation."

"What?" Tauron asked, his voice almost a hiss.

Before Tauron could object or recover, Valera spoke, "The Council calls Kirloth to the floor."

Gavin stood and walked the short distance to stand between the Archmagister's dais and the Council's table. He took a moment to clear his throat and began.

"Ladies and gentlemen, I declared Rite of Holsgyng prior to conducting the recent duel, and as part of that, a group of Battle-mages set out to secure various properties around the Kingdom that transferred ownership to me. One of those properties was the Vischaene Vineyard, and upon surveying the property, my agents made a rather disturbing discovery."

Gavin turned and gestured to the waiting men. Those eight men stood and carried the strongboxes of evidence to the floor. As there was no table at hand for the strongboxes, Gavin invoked a Word of Conjuration, "*Nythraex.*" A table appeared at Gavin's side, standing waist-high to him. It looked to be made of rough-cut lumber, and there were no signs of seams in the wood or any form of fasteners.

Gavin gestured for the strongboxes to be placed on the table and went about opening them.

"Beneath a shack that appeared to be a laborer's residence, there was an underground planning room with what I'm about to show you." Gavin held up a sheaf of papers. "Here, we have communications between Iosen Sivas and eight other arcanists that cover meeting times and interest in what Sivas calls the 'New Age.' These communications themselves are not very incriminating, but let's move on." Gavin returned those papers and withdrew another group. "Here, we have a detailed analysis of Tel Mivar's vulnerability to assault...written by a retired officer of the Army of Tel. He goes into significant detail about tactics for obtaining access to the city as well as force estimates if it should devolve to a siege. He concludes with a list of officers in the Town Guard who might be amenable to leaving a gate—or gates—unguarded."

Gavin returned those papers and moved to the next strongbox, withdrawing more. "These papers discuss the logistics of—and possible locations for—preparing a training camp where the mercenary army can prepare for the assault with acceptable risk of discovery. The rest of these strongboxes contain purchasing records for supplies and equipment, pay records for the mercenaries, records of bribes paid to various people, copies of potential assault plans, and many other documents. I can present each document, or you are welcome to look through them yourselves.

"This is clearly an attack on the independence of the Society laid down in the Constitution of Tel. In all truth, I'm skeptical the mercenaries would be able to defeat the defenses built into the College walls, but that just means they'd be free to rampage through the city. We must prevent this *now*...while that army's out in the middle of nowhere."

Tauron stood from his seat and walked over to the evidence. He began sifting through the strongboxes, scanning each item. He stopped when he found a document containing notes on the plan, written in what Gavin had been assured was Iosen Sivas's own hand.

Tauron stood in silence for what seemed an interminable time before he turned to face the Council once more.

"There is enough here that I feel further action is warranted, and I see there being only one response to this. I shall send a detachment of Inquisitors to summon Iosen Sivas and all those named as conspirators to answer the charges encouraged by this evidence. It could be a massive misinformation campaign to encourage us to fight amongst ourselves, but it could also be true. We must discover which is the case."

The Chamber of the Council was so silent one could've heard a mouse walking across the stone floor. Everyone but Valera and Kantar stared at Tauron, their expressions betraying shock.

"I'm impressed," Gavin said. "I thought you'd fight this evidence tooth and nail, simply because *I* was presenting it."

Tauron turned to Gavin, saying, "Don't let this admission kill you with shock, but there are people in this world I hate more than you. Iosen Sivas happens to be one of them, and I recognize his penmanship." He turned to walk back to his seat, but he stopped, turning to face Gavin once more. "Though…if you were inclined to die of shock, don't let me stop you."

THE COUNCIL AGREED that Tauron's suggestion was the proper action to take, and Tauron said he would write orders for six Inquisitors to depart at once. As the Council filed out of the Chamber, Valera held back, waiting for Gavin.

"Sera said you had two matters to discuss, Gavin. What was the second?"

Gavin was well aware he had the rest of the Conclave at his back, but he went ahead and answered Valera's question. "Torval and the others have requested I train their Heirs as my apprentices, and I wanted to ask your thoughts on that."

Valera nodded and spent a few moments apparently in thought. At last, she said, "I don't see as how you have any other option. Despite the recent cooperation, I don't think we could get you named as an Instructor at the College, and Mariana has already graduated. Yes, Lillian and the others could drop out, but they'd be forfeiting any future standing in the Society if they did so. Article 23 is your only option."

"I thought so," Gavin said and sighed. "Well, there's no time like the present. Can I ask you to serve as witness?"

"Of course, Gavin."

Gavin turned to those standing behind him and took a couple steps back. He took a breath and said, "Be it known to all persons that I claim the following people as my apprentices as was in the old ways: Lillian Mivar, Mariana Cothos, Wynn Roshan, and Braden Wygoth."

Lillian, Braden, and Wynn cheered. Mariana looked like she wanted to but was far too mature for that kind of thing. Even their parents and grandparent smiled.

"Thank you, Valera," Gavin said.

"You're welcome."

Valera stood by the Council's table, watching them leave, and her mind went back to the piece of parchment in her office desk drawer.

"'...the Apprentices shall be drawn unto him,' indeed," Valera whispered.

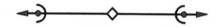

CHAPTER 46

Gavin led his apprentices down into the lower levels of the Tower. They passed the summoning rooms, where a few classes were in session, and eventually reached their destination. As they approached, the specter faded into view beside the door.

"Have you come to resume your studies, Kirloth?" the specter asked.

"Yes, I have," Gavin said, "and these are my apprentices. Is it possible for you to permit them entry to work on their lessons without my presence?"

"Of course," the specter said.

The specter turned and, as it had done so many times before, pushed its hand into the door. The sound of a massive latch releasing echoed throughout corridor, and the door began to open upward.

Once the door was high enough to proceed, Gavin started walking into the arena. The place was 'old hat' to him by now, but no matter how hard he tried, Gavin could no longer face the place as just a training venue. He still remembered the sight of Rolf Sivas's corpse laying in the sawdust outside the ring, and he was still very conflicted about it. On the one hand, he felt satisfaction that Rolf would never harm another woman, but he also felt the guilt and shame of having taken a life, especially when the Council should have done its job of enforcing the Arcanists' Code.

"Before we begin," Gavin said, "there is something I feel I have to say. I am no master of forgotten lore. I am happy to teach you what I know, but I am not Marcus. Even with everything he taught me, I feel we only scratched the surface of what he knew."

Wynn and Braden looked at each other, and Lillian broke out into a grin.

"But you are, Gavin," Lillian said. "Wizards manipulating Words of Power is the stuff of legend to us, and the entire student body saw you do it not once but twice...as if it were second nature to you. I doubt even the magisters themselves could've created that blurring wall of silence you made."

Gavin sighed, looking at his apprentices. At last, he said, "Maybe so. Still, I expect I will learn just as much from your training as you will. My learning may not be in the same subjects as yours, but I suspect it will take place nonetheless." Gavin took a deep breath and nodded. "Very well. Let us begin. We will start with the one, essential truth: the effect is shaped by the wizard's intent."

Gavin walked over to stand inside the arena's center ring.

"My research leads me to believe that the major achievement of the Fundamentals of Spellcasting class is the casting of the Light spell," Gavin said. "Mariana, is that correct?"

"I don't know that it's the major achievement," Mariana said, "but it's certainly what the instructors use as a first casting."

"Did you prepare any spells this morning?" Gavin asked.

"No," Mariana said.

Gavin smiled, saying, "Good. As I understand the Light spell, it is a simple Conjuration that produces a sphere of white light over which the caster has some marginal control. Is that so?"

"Yes," Mariana said.

"Excellent," Gavin said, and he invoked a Word, "*Nythraex*." A sphere of blazing, white light about the size of a honeydew melon appeared in the air a few feet to Gavin's right.

"But white is so boring," Gavin said. "What about green?"

Gavin invoked the same Word. The white sphere didn't even dissipate; all the other colors faded from it, until only green remained.

"Someone, pick a color," Gavin said.

"Battle-mage burgundy," Mariana said, while the others were still drawing breath.

Gavin invoked the same Word once more, and the green sphere shifted into a color that matched Mariana's mantle. Having seen him invoke Words before, Lillian, Wynn, and Braden didn't seem especially surprised. Mariana, however, gaped.

"The effect is shaped by the wizard's intent," Gavin said, indicating the sphere of burgundy light. With a thought, Gavin cancelled the Conjuration, and the burgundy sphere vanished as if it had never been.

Gavin stepped out of the ring, took a deep breath and released it. He worked his lower lip between his teeth for a few moments. His eyes went to Mariana.

"Mariana, you've cast spells before?"

"Yes, I have."

"The first time you cast, did anything untoward happen?"

Mariana frowned for a few moments and shook her head. "Not really. Why?"

"The first time I invoked a Word of Power, I fell unconscious for about two days," Gavin said. "Granted, my first invocation did a little more than create a sphere of light, but I have every reason to believe the experience will not be pleasant. I had hoped you were already past that, but perhaps it is restricted to wizardry. As much as I would like to spare all of you this, the fact is that pain is a part of who we are; it is the price we pay for what we are able to do. To begin, we will draw straws, and whoever draws the shortest straw will create a sphere of light."

As no pieces of straw were handy and Gavin hadn't thought to visit the stables for some, he cheated, focusing his mind on the image of pieces of straw of different lengths and saying, "*Nythraex.*"

As he was now outside the arena ring, the full force of Gavin's power slammed into his apprentices, visibly staggering them and leaving them breathing hard, as the desired straws appeared in Gavin's left hand. While his apprentices composed themselves, Gavin shuffled the straws and held them up so that no one could see which was taller or shorter.

"Okay then. Who wants to draw first?" Gavin asked.

The four apprentices looked to each other, their expressions making it obvious no one *wanted* to go first. After a couple heartbeats, Mariana squared her shoulders and stepped forward. She pulled the second straw from Gavin's left and stepped back. Wynn approached and drew the left-most straw. Braden drew what had been the second straw from the right, and Gavin handed the last straw to Lillian.

They held their straws up to compare them, and for a moment, Wynn looked a bit faint when he saw that his was the shortest by far. After Wynn, it would be Mariana's turn, followed by Lillian. Braden's straw served as an excellent analogy to his height, making him last.

"So, does anyone need to use the privy?" Gavin asked. "Now's the time."

No one budged, and Gavin looked to Wynn. "Very well. Wynn, step into the arena ring, please."

Wynn swallowed hard and did as Gavin said. Gavin followed him. He stopped just outside the ring and knelt, writing out the Word they would use in the common script to keep from imbuing the scribing with power.

"Now then, Wynn, listen to me very carefully. Picture a fist-sized sphere of white light in your mind. Focus on that image, and push all other thoughts out of your mind until only that remains. Whenever you feel you're ready, invoke this Word to conjure the sphere."

Wynn closed his eyes and slowed his breathing. Everyone stood silent, and Gavin wondered how successful at focusing his mind Wynn would be. The boy wasn't exactly known for calm reasoned thought, after all. After a short time, Wynn opened his eyes and dropped them to the ground where Gavin had written the Word.

Wynn took a breath and said, "*Nythraex.*"

A white sphere of light comparable to a medium-sized apple popped into existence just off Wynn's right shoulder. He didn't notice it, though, as he clutched at his midriff and collapsed to his knees, screaming in agony. Everyone winced, and for the briefest moment, Gavin relived the memory of what he had endured in the alley before falling unconscious.

Gavin stepped into the ring and knelt beside Wynn, who had yet to scream himself hoarse. "Wynn," Gavin said, "you have to master the pain. You must force your mind and body to push it away, control it, define its limits. You're more than strong enough for this, and now, it's time to prove it. Forget about me; it's time not to let *them* down."

For several moments, Gavin thought Wynn hadn't even heard him over his screaming. Suddenly, though, a shudder went through Wynn as he moved his arms away from his midriff and stood. Tears streamed openly down his face, and he didn't look that steady on his feet...but he did stand.

"Good man. The first step is always the hardest, and you've just taken it," Gavin said and leaned close to Wynn to whisper into his left ear. "Both your father *and* Roshan would be proud of you."

Wynn nodded and started walking out of the ring. Gavin walked at his side and allowed Wynn to set the pace, ever alert for the young man's knees buckling. Wynn wobbled from time to time, but he reached the nearest set of bleachers all on his own.

Once Wynn was seated, Gavin turned to face Mariana. Before Gavin could say a word, Mariana nodded, squared her shoulders, and entered the ring.

* * *

THE FOLLOWING DAY, Gavin and his apprentices were on their way to the arena for that day's studies. They passed the summoning classrooms and found a most unexpected sight before them. Valera, Kantar, the Magisters of Illusion and Enchantment, and Bella Roshan stood to one side of the corridor about a dozen yards past the last summoning room.

Gavin stopped, and the others stopped behind him. Gavin scanned the faces of those waiting for him with an appraising eye before speaking.

"In all my months of coming down here to study, I've never once seen anyone below the base-level summoning classrooms, and now, I find four magisters and the Curator of the Library."

Except for Kantar, the magisters directed uncertain glances at Valera, showing Gavin who was behind their little excursion.

Gavin smiled, saying, "Hello, Valera. Is there something I can do for you?"

"We would like to sit in on your training session," Valera said. "It's all dreadfully improper, but can you imagine the flap if four magisters and the Curator of the Library asked to become apprentices?"

Kantar sighed, saying, "The fact is, Gavin, we all want to learn from you. No wizard born in the last three thousand years has been trained as a wizard, and every wizard on the Council would give quite a bit to know how you created that wall of silence that blurred the air. If I may ask, why did you do that? Blurring the air, I mean."

"It's possible to learn to read a person's lips, so you can know what someone's saying without hearing a word," Gavin said. "When I said my words were for the Council alone, I meant it. As for 'listening in,' as you put it, I can't say as I care all that much…just remember that the instruction is for *them*." Gavin pointed over his shoulder with his thumb, indicating the apprentices.

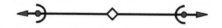

CHAPTER 47

I t was about two weeks after Tauron dispatched the Inquisitors that Declan entered Gavin's suite in the early evening. Gavin and Kiri sat at the table, talking, and Gavin looked his way.

"You don't bring good news."

Declan shook his head. "They killed four of the Inquisitors and captured the last two. One of those captured is Mariana's friend Reyna."

"Damn. Does Tauron know yet?"

Declan scoffed. "How would he? The Inquisitors rode into an ambush."

Gavin let his head rest against the high back of the chair. "Do you know where they're being held?"

"They're in the mercenary camp. As it happens, I also have a full report on that camp."

"Can we extract the Inquisitors without anyone the wiser?"

"It would be difficult, but not impossible."

"Okay. I want those Inquisitors freed as quietly as possible. Use however many people are necessary. I'll find Valera, and we'll call another session of the Council." Declan turned to leave.

"Declan," Gavin said, stopping the man at the door. "Don't go yourself on the rescue job. I'll want you here to deliver that report to the Conclave I'm fairly sure I'll be calling."

* * *

THE NEXT MORNING, Gavin entered the Chamber of the Council with Valera. The rest of the Council was already waiting.

"Good morning," Valera said as she took her seat and sat. "Gavin brought me information last night that I felt we should discuss as soon as possible."

"What now?" Tauron asked.

Valera gestured for Gavin to speak.

"My sources have informed me that your Inquisitors encountered an ambush," Gavin said. "Four were killed, and two were captured."

"How old is your information?" Kantar asked.

Gavin shrugged. "Three to four days."

"I have not received any information to that effect," Tauron said. "Are you proposing that we send another detachment without evidence of the need?"

Gavin sighed. "Tauron, I'm not proposing anything. I'm just trying to tell you four Inquisitors are dead and the other two are prisoners."

KIRI AND LILLIAN looked up when Gavin entered the suite.

"How was the meeting?" Lillian asked.

"Tauron stampeded the Council into inaction. He argued that there is no point to doing anything else until word comes in of the Inquisitors' mission, and he seemed not to regard what I was saying as word of their fate. It's a mess."

Gavin sat in his favorite armchair and laid his head against its tall back.

Lillian and Kiri let silence rule the space for several moments. At last, Lillian said, "What are you going to do?"

"I don't know," Gavin said. "I-"

Someone knocked at the suite's door.

Gavin shifted his head to look that way, saying, "I guess I'm going to answer the door."

Gavin walked over to the door and pulled it open. Sera, Valera's assistant, stood just barely closer than arm's length from the door. She held her head bowed, and she visibly trembled.

"Am I really that frightening, Sera?" Gavin asked.

Sera looked up and saw Gavin smiling. The trembling eased, and some of the tension left her body.

"People say we should be afraid of you," Sera said, her voice barely above a whisper.

"Yes, well…the only people who should fear me are the people I want to fear me. I don't want you to fear me, Sera."

"Oh."

A silence extended while Gavin watched Sera process this information. He gave her a few moments before he said, "Sera, I'm sure you're here for a reason."

Sera's eyes shot wide, and she jumped. "Oh, my! Yes! The Magister would like to speak with you in the Restricted Section of the library. I am so sorry!"

Gavin smiled once more and nodded, saying, "It's just fine, Sera. This'll be our little secret. I'll be there momentarily."

Sera nodded once and scurried off toward the Grand Stair. Gavin turned back to his suite, closing the door behind him.

BOTH KIRI and Lillian faced him. The question of who had been at the door was not so subtly implied.

"It was Sera," Gavin said. "Valera wants to see me. Would you mind gathering Declan, Braden, Wynn, and Mariana? As much as I would like to take the evening off and not think about this abysmal situation, I'm not sure we have that kind of time. I'll see what Valera wants, and then, we can get started figuring a way out of this mess."

They both nodded and followed Gavin out of the suite as he left to find Valera.

· · ·

The Library of the College was a familiar sight to Gavin. Many the hour he had spent within the space, and as he expected, the area bustled with activity. Mostly students, but a few instructors, moved through the study spaces and bookshelves. Bella Roshan stood behind the circulation desk and smiled when she saw Gavin enter.

"Good evening, Gavin," Bella said, a slight smile curling one corner of her mouth.

"Hello, Bella," Gavin said. "I've come to spend some time in the Restricted Section."

What Bella did next surprised Gavin. She handed him her key. "You know the way."

Gavin accepted the key and traversed the space to the stairs leading up to the second floor of the library. It was a short walk through the bookshelves to the entrance of the Restricted Section, and Gavin was not at all surprised to find Sera sitting at a study table a few feet away from the door. She made no reaction whatsoever as Gavin passed, not even acknowledging his presence, which only added weight to Gavin's conclusion about what this meeting was.

Gavin unlocked the door and stepped inside. His first sense was the smell of old books, but it wasn't the musty smell of ill care. His next sense came from his *skathos*; two wizards awaited him. He stepped around a bookshelf to face the study table and saw four magisters: Valera, Kantar, and the married couple. These were the four who voted to act on the news Gavin presented. Valera leaned forward in her seat with her arms folded across a book; Gavin could not read the spine, since Valera's sleeves were in the way. Kantar sat impassively straight, with his hands folded in his lap, and the married couple sat side by side, holding hands and leaning slightly toward each other.

"Well, well," Gavin said as he approached the edge of the table, "do I detect a schism within the Council?"

"'Schism' is a very strong word, Gavin," Valera said.

"We were discussing the situation," Kantar said, "and how we feel the outcome of the session is less than ideal, and we decided to make certain you are aware of all the options available to you."

"That sounds like you know something I don't…or at least think you do."

"How much of the Arcanists' Code have you read, Gavin?" Valera asked.

Gavin frowned as he pulled back a chair from the table and sat. "I've read it cover to cover, all thirty-four Articles. Why?"

Valera looked to Kantar and nodded once. Kantar lifted his hands above the table, producing a book, and passed it to Gavin. It was the Constitution of Tel.

"I thought we were discussing the Arcanists' Code," Gavin said, frowning as he read the spine.

"Read Article 3, Gavin," Kantar said.

Gavin placed the book on the table and flipped pages until he arrived at the requested topic. Article 3 was very short.

"'It is the intent of Bellos, Kirloth, and the Apprentices that the Society of the Arcane shall stand apart from the Kingdom of Tel. To this end, it is hereby recognized and decreed that any Arcanists —whether mage or wizard—answer only to the strictures placed upon them within the Arcanists' Code. No civil office in Tel shall hold any authority over them.'"

Before Gavin could speak, Valera lifted her arms and passed her book to Kantar, who in turn passed it to Gavin. Gavin turned the book to look at its spine, and his eyes widened just a bit as he read "Arcanists' Code II." Marcus's copy of the code was labeled "Arcanists' Code I," and Gavin had always assumed it was the first official copy before the print runs or something.

"Where did this come from, and why haven't I seen it before?" Gavin asked.

"There is only ever one copy of that volume, Gavin," Valera said, "and it is always kept here in the Restricted Section. Read Article 35."

Gavin opened the book and found Article 35.

"'It is hereby decreed that the Conclave of the Great Houses has the authority to act on their own, irrespective of the Council of Magisters. To invoke this authority, there must be a unanimous vote of the Conclave, with all five Houses represented, and should such a vote occur, the authority of the Conclave is absolute for a period of 60 days. Furthermore, no such vote can take place more than once every ten consecutive months.'"

"By the gods..." Gavin said, as he placed the book on the table and pushed it away. "That is terrifying...outright, absolutely terrifying."

The four magisters sat in silence as Gavin stared at the book on the table in front him.

"But why hasn't the Conclave...oh. Marcus wasn't acting as Kirloth." Gavin looked up to meet Valera's eyes. "This is the first time in so many thousand years that the Conclave has been whole."

Valera nodded. "Yes. Marcus thought his time was past and that he was a relic of a bygone age. He refused to step forward and announce himself for who he was, because he saw how the populace had turned him into some kind of amalgamation of a savior and boogeyman. You yourself have witnessed people's reaction to your medallion, Gavin."

Gavin lowered his eyes to the second volume of the Code where it lay open on the table, and he stared at it in silence for several moments.

"I do not like this option you have given me," Gavin said at last. "It is far too easy to abuse. Who all knows about this being an option?"

The four magisters looked at one another for a heartbeat, and Valera said, "The Council knows. Maybe some members of the Conclave, but I'd have to ask Bella if they've ever been in here. Bella probably knows."

Gavin reached out and closed the volume before pushing his chair back from the table and standing. Four pairs of eyes faced him.

"What will you do, Gavin?" Kantar asked.

"I don't see as how I have much of a choice," Gavin said. "If I do anything without Article 35, it would probably give Tauron leverage to try having me named a traitor. The Conclave wouldn't sit still for that, and we'd find ourselves on the brink of a civil war. I suppose I should be grateful for you bringing this to my attention, but I'm not sure I'm comfortable enough with what I must do to thank you."

Gavin picked up the second volume of the Code from where it lay on the table and left.

"Did you find what you needed?" Bella asked as Gavin approached the circulation desk.

Gavin sighed, handing her the key she gave him as he said, "We'll see, Bella."

Bella's eyes flitted to the book held in the crook of Gavin's arm for just a moment before they returned to meet Gavin's gaze. "Be careful, Gavin. Even the legal path will not be easy."

Gavin nodded his thanks and left the library. He had friends waiting for him.

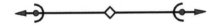

CHAPTER 48

G avin entered his suite and found Declan, Wynn, Braden, and Mariana waiting with Kiri and Lillian.

"Lillian, I want you to contact your grandfather and ask him to host another Conclave."

"When do you want the Conclave, Gavin?" Lillian asked.

"It's getting into the evening now; I see no reason this can't wait for morning, but I would like arrangements for it made tonight."

Lillian nodded.

"I would ask that you not discuss with your grandfather the nature of this Conclave. If he presses you, tell him, 'Kirloth wishes to convene a Conclave.' I would do it myself, but I don't know where I'd host it. There are no teleportation runes here in the suite."

"That's because this isn't the Kirloth Estate," Declan said.

Everyone—even Kiri—turned to look at Declan. When Declan didn't seem inclined to continue of his own accord, Gavin spoke.

"Where is the Kirloth Estate, Declan?"

"I can only guess at the reasons Kirloth had for having Mivar leave this out of his Histories, but other historians recorded it. During the early days of the Founding, this area was not completely pacified. There were roving bands of Godswar deserters and bandits, among other unsavory creatures. The Tower of the Council itself was the keep of the bandit lord who controlled this area. In order to have a secure base from which to work, Kirloth and his Apprentices created the Citadel. It wasn't until Kirloth faked his death that it became the residence of the Archmagister."

"Wait," Mariana said, holding out her hand in a 'stop' gesture. "Are you saying Gavin inherited ownership of the Citadel?"

"No. I'm saying he might have. Still, even if he did, there would be political ramifications to him using it. There is no record here in Tel Mivar of the Citadel ever being the personal residence of Kirloth, so I hope you can imagine the reaction produced by Gavin taking the Citadel for his own."

Gavin shook his head, saying, "I already have one magister who hates me; I'd rather not add the other eight. We'll proceed as we have discussed. Lillian, would you ask your grandfather if he would be so kind as to host a Conclave for me?"

Lillian nodded. "I'll go right now."

"Declan, would you arrange for her to reach her family's estate safely? I have no concerns for her well-being once she's inside that wall, but it's a long way to walk from here to there."

Declan smiled and nodded once. "I'll go myself."

"Thank you."

* * *

GAVIN STOOD before the open gates of the Mivar Estate, and like the times before, he marveled at the protections constructed into the wall surrounding the estate. Not for the first time, Gavin wished he'd had more time with Marcus; he had no idea how his mentor had even devised such protections, let alone kept them strong across six thousand years.

Torval and Lillian stood waiting on the portico. Lillian smiled to see her friends coming, whereas Torval faced the group with a sober expression.

"Do you regret not allowing the Conclave to dissolve the Council now?" Torval asked as Gavin drew near.

Gavin smiled, saying, "Not in the least, Torval. Yes, they make things frustrating right now, but in the long run, things are the way they are for a reason. Whether I know or understand the reason is immaterial to me, but that doesn't mean I won't do what I have to do to get things done."

Torval's eyes narrowed just a bit, and he acted as if he were about to speak. In the end, though, he sighed and gestured for the group to enter his family's home.

"The others will be arriving shortly. I grant thee welcome and bid thee enter, Kirloth."

Gavin nodded. "I am most grateful, Mivar."

Torval gave Gavin an almost boyish grin as he turned and led the procession into the manor house.

THE ROOM that would hold the Conclave had not changed since Gavin had last seen it, and he entered the room just in time to see the other Heads of the Great Houses arrive.

The Conclave assumed their seats around the table, and Gavin called the session to order and brought everyone current on events, including the outcome of his last visit with the Council.

"This is almost too incredible to believe," Lyssa said.

"I don't want to believe it either," Carth said as he leaned forward to rest his forearms on the table, "but what can we do? Gavin himself said the Council was deadlocked on the issue."

"Gavin could always challenge Tauron to a duel," Lyssa said. "That man has always been an insufferable ass, even when we were students together."

A laugh circled around the table among the Heads of the Houses. It took a few moments before they realized that neither their children nor Gavin was laughing.

Sypara said, "Is something wrong, Gavin?"

"I understand that Lyssa's comment was in jest, but being rid of Tauron is not worth the weight on my conscience if I challenged him. If he challenges me, that's his stupidity."

The table was silent for a time before Carth lifted his eyes to face

Gavin. He said, "I daresay you're a better man than most, Gavin. I know any number of people who would happily challenge everyone they disliked if they had your edge."

"I regret that, but it is not germane to the topic at hand," Gavin said. "You asked what we can do, Carth, and the answer is 'more than you think.'" Gavin laid a book on the table. "This is the second volume of the Arcanists' Code, containing Articles 35 through 50. Article 35 gives the Conclave of the Great Houses authority to act with impunity, should we hold a unanimous vote that such is necessary. I myself do not like that we have this option, but I see no other course of action that will protect whoever acts from charges of treason or some such."

"What does Article 35 say?" Torval asked.

Gavin opened the volume and flipped to the page in question, passing it to Torval. Instead of reading to himself, Torval said, "'Article 35: It is hereby decreed that the Conclave of the Great Houses has the authority to act on their own, irrespective of the Council of Magisters. To invoke this authority, there must be a unanimous vote of the Conclave with all five Houses represented, and should such a vote occur, the authority of the Conclave is absolute for a period of 60 days. Furthermore, no such vote can take place more than once every ten consecutive months.'"

"Well, *that* certainly isn't wishy-washy," Sypara said. "How far do you think that authority extends?"

"I'm not really sure Kirloth or the Apprentices envisioned a limit to that authority," Gavin said. "Article 3 of the Constitution of Tel explicitly decrees that the Society of the Arcane stands outside the authority of the civil government, answering only to the Arcanists' Code."

"But we're also Dukes and Duchesses," Carth said. "Isn't that a civil title? And wouldn't that give the king an avenue to attack us?"

Gavin shook his head, saying, "No. I don't think so. I'd have to check, but I believe it's Article 7 of the Constitution that establishes the Duchies of Tel. It goes on to specify that the titles 'Duke' or 'Duchess' are conferred upon the Head of each House. It's a gnarled cobweb of legalese that boils down to say each of you are

Dukes or Duchesses, *because* you're each one of the Heads of the Great Houses of Tel. Since the duchies are built upon the Great Houses, at the core of it, you're arcanists and outside the authority of the civil government."

Lyssa shrugged before saying, "I personally think the time is long past for some decisive action, and I move we vote to invoke Article 35."

"Lyssa," Torval said, "this is not a decision we should rush into making. I've never heard of any Conclave in the history of Tel *ever* voting to invoke Article 35, and that means we'll be setting a precedent...no matter what else we do."

"I agree with Lyssa," Carth said, "but with one provision. I believe we should invoke Article 35, but I also believe we should vote that Gavin be the one to wield our authority. Yes, we will counsel and advise, but Gavin has shown himself to be a man of integrity and restraint, someone who believes in the Code and the Constitution. Besides, I don't see how we can avoid an armed conflict with those mercenary soldiers, and no army run by a committee ever succeeded."

"Carth, I-" Gavin said.

"No, Gavin," Lillian said, speaking for the first time. "I agree with Carth. Someone must lead this...whatever it is...and it will have to be one of the Heads of the Great Houses. Everyone here has his or her own axes to grind, but you have repeatedly held back when everyone would support and agree with you burning Tauron down to ash. Besides all that, you're Kirloth—at least the Kirloth of this age—and you yourself have seen how everyone steps around you. People will argue and debate with any of the others; they're old friends or classmates or colleagues. When you speak, people listen."

As Lillian finished speaking, Gavin looked to each person in turn, both his fellow Heads of the Great Houses and his apprentices. Each and every person met Gavin's gaze and nodded.

Mariana was the last, saying, "Lillian's right. Everyone here is a known quantity, except you. You would not believe how often they're dismissed as relics of the past or just prestige positions, probably because the Council has nudged things that way over the last fifty years or so. I know you said you didn't want anyone to say this, but Gavin, the Council is afraid of you. They might dispute the authority granted by Article 35 if one of the others wields that power, but no one will confront *you*, not after the incident with the Guild."

Gavin scanned the faces looking his way once more and asked, "Is this your unanimous will?"

Everyone spoke their assent.

Gavin took a deep breath and let it out as a sigh. "Very well. I now call for a vote to invoke Article 35 of the Arcanists' Code."

Torval said, "Mivar votes 'yes.'"

Sypara said, "Wygoth votes 'yes.'"

Carth said, "Roshan votes 'yes.'"

Lyssa said, "Cothos votes 'yes.'"

Everyone looked to Gavin.

Gavin sighed once more and said, "Kirloth votes 'yes.' Let the record show that the Conclave of the Great Houses held a unanimous vote to invoke Article 35 of the Arcanists' Code on this day, under the stipulation that Kirloth executes the authority."

"What's our next step, Gavin?" Lyssa asked.

"We need more information and allies. If the mercenary army has built any strength at all, we do not have the resources to confront them. I think we should speak to Ovir next. He has military experience as well as the Warpriests of Tel from which to draw."

"That sounds like the best path," Torval said.

"I'll go speak with Ovir right now," Gavin said. "Unless there are any objections, this Conclave is adjourned."

CHAPTER 49

A young man sat at a desk just inside the double doors, and Gavin waited until the young man noticed his presence. The young man jerked as he saw someone standing in front of his desk.

"Oh, I'm sorry..." the young man said as he lifted his head to face Gavin, but his eyes never quite made it to Gavin's face. The young man's eyes locked on Gavin's medallion, and he froze.

Gavin smiled, saying, "Hello. My name is Gavin Cross, and I'm hoping Ovir has some time available."

The young man blinked and shook his head as if trying to clear it. "W-who?"

"Ovir Thatcherson," Gavin said. "I believe he's the Royal Priest of Tel."

Back on familiar territory, some of the young man's confidence returned, and he squared his shoulders before saying, "I'm sorry, sir, but you'll have to make an appointment to see the Royal Priest. Other clerics are available, though; perhaps, one of them can assist you."

Gavin stood in silence, regarding the young man for several moments. He considered several responses before settling on a course of action. Gavin pivoted on his heel and walked deeper into the temple.

"Sir!" the young man said. "Sir, you have to wait! Sir!"

The doors that led deeper into the temple from the vestibule opened into the Hall of the Gods. The statues represented all those who had chosen to take on the mantle of divinity after the Godswar, and they were angled so that, if a person stood on the proper spot, all the statues seemed to face him or her.

Gavin found that spot.

Even the young man from the vestibule seemed reluctant to interrupt Gavin's moment of silence as he looked to each statue in turn.

"Hello, uncle," Gavin said as he looked upon the statue of Marin.

Marin was the youngest of the three Kirloth brothers during the Godswar, and if Dakkor's information was accurate, Gavin assumed that he had descended from the middle brother, Gerrus, who fled with the refugees.

Gavin's eyes found Dakkor next, and he couldn't help but notice how real the statue looked. Gavin couldn't help but be taken aback, either, when Dakkor's statue seemed to wink at him. Not knowing what else to do, Gavin nodded once in acknowledgement.

The next statue Gavin located was that of Bellos. Gavin bowed once to the statue of Bellos before allowing his eyes to roam across the rest of the statues there. Gavin knew them all by reputation, for he had read Mivar's Histories. He allowed himself a few more moments of silence before he took a deep breath, scanned the faces once more, and said, "Thank you...for everything."

A strong, welcoming warmth suffused Gavin's entire being as he resumed his stride into the temple. As much as he would like to remain and consider those who had come before, Gavin had work to do.

Gavin stepped through the door at the far end of the Hall of the Gods and soon found himself in the concourse outside the shrine of

Valthon. Now, at last, Gavin found people. Almost thirty people occupied the space; they were separated into groups of varying sizes, and their conversations created a background noise for the room that would easily overwhelm any but the loudest voices.

Like every other room Gavin had ever seen inside the city walls, this space was lit with sconces that neither burned fuel nor radiated heat, and Gavin felt the evocation effects that powered the sconces through his *skathos*.

A door opened on the far side of the concourse, and Gavin smiled at seeing Ovir exit whatever room lay beyond. He set off at a determined gait and crossed the space in little time.

Ovir looked up from the book in his hands just as Gavin approached, and his face split into a wide smile.

"Gavin," Ovir said. "How good to see you. Tell me, how have you been?"

The young man from the vestibule skidded to a stop at Gavin's shoulder.

"Sir, please forgive me," the young man said. "This man entered the temple asking for you and walked off when I said he'd need an appointment."

Ovir's smile faded as he turned to face the young man, saying, "Acolyte, there is one man who always has immediate and unrestricted access to me. Who is that?"

"The black-robe wizard known as Marcus, sir," the young man said.

"Now, there are two. Do not hinder Kirloth's passage ever again," Ovir said. "You should return to your post. I'll distribute notification of the policy change by the end of the day."

GAVIN KEPT his silence until the young man's footfalls disappeared beneath the ambient noise. Once he had a reasonable assurance of semi-privacy, Gavin said, "I'm sorry about distressing your acolyte, Ovir."

"Nonsense," Ovir said, taking Gavin by the arm and leading him deeper into the temple. "Acolytes are made to be distressed. It teaches them fortitude. So, tell me, Gavin; what brings you here today? As much as I would like to believe so, I rather doubt it's to visit a friend of your mentor."

Gavin allowed himself a rueful chuckle before he said, "You are very perceptive, Ovir. I have a matter on my hands that might require your insight, if not your assistance."

"Well then," Ovir said as he turned a corner, still leading Gavin, "let's go to my study. Marcus and I had many weighty conversations there."

Ovir LED Gavin to the second floor of the temple and to a suite that occupied the far-right corner, relative to the main doors. The suite was well appointed, with thick carpets and tapestries depicting notable events in the world's history. The one thing that caught Gavin's eye was the Vushaari flag hanging from one corner of the suite's anteroom.

Ovir saw Gavin's focus and smiled. He said, "Does it shock you to see Vushaar's flag hanging in the residence of the Royal Priest of Tel?"

"No," Gavin said. "A man should be free to decorate his quarters however he chooses, including displaying the flag of his homeland."

"Not many people know I'm from Vushaar, Gavin," Ovir said, "though I've never tried to hide it."

"Marcus mentioned it once, but he did not say how you came to be in Tel in the first place."

Ovir laughed and motioned for Gavin to follow him.

"That is a very long story, young man," Ovir said, as he stepped through the door leading deeper into the suite. "Suffice it to say, I felt a calling to pursue membership in the Warpriests of Tel when I was but a boy, and that calling led me here."

The door leading off the vestibule allowed them entrance to a living room that felt like the common room of Gavin's suite back at the tower. Carpets lined the floor, and tapestries hung down the walls. Two sofas and several armchairs occupied the space, but Ovir didn't even slow. He led Gavin through this room to a door on the right.

Upon entering this room, Gavin found himself in what could be nothing other than Ovir's study. Bookshelves lined every wall, except two. The wall across from the door held a massive hearth and fireplace, and the north wall (to the left of the door) held a large wooden desk and a set of double doors that led onto a balcony. Two armchairs sat in front of the hearth, and a small stand stood between the two armchairs.

"Pick whichever chair suits you," Ovir said. "I shall return in a moment with refreshment."

Gavin walked across the room and chose the chair on the right, similar in placement to the chair he used in his suite. It was upholstered in a gray fabric with loops of colored thread running throughout the fabric, and Gavin seemed to sink into it when he sat; it might have even been more comfortable than his chairs.

A few moments later, Ovir carried a silver tray into the room, pushing the door shut with his foot as he passed. He delivered the tray to the stand between their chairs, and Gavin saw three decanters and an assortment of glasses on the tray.

"Tea, juice, and wine are the easiest refreshments I have," Ovir said, "and you're welcome to any or all of them. If there's something else you prefer, I'm sure it can be found somewhere in the temple."

"Thank you, Ovir," Gavin said. "These will be just fine."

Gavin selected the juice and poured a glass for himself before offering it to Ovir. Ovir shook his head and retrieved the teapot. For several moments, silence reigned as both men enjoyed their chosen beverages.

At last, Ovir said, "So, what matter weighs so heavily upon you that you would come to me, Gavin?"

"Well, it's about something that was discovered after I won the duel with Rolf Sivas," Gavin said.

For the next several minutes, Gavin outlined everything that had happened, explaining the underground room and all the evidence found therein. Throughout the whole discourse, Ovir sat in silence, sipping his tea.

"So, that's where we stand," Gavin said, concluding his presentation. "The Conclave voted to invoke Article 35 and invested me with their collective authority."

"My, my," Ovir said. "You do have yourself a bit of a problem there, don't you? Naturally, you have my full support, and you may draw upon the temple's resources however you need. This is a messy business, and this stratagem doesn't feel like something the king would put forth."

"Oh?" Gavin said. "You think he's innocent?"

Ovir chuckled before he said, "Certainly not. However, the king is by no means an intellectual giant, and he's about as spineless a man as I've ever seen. This is much too cunning a plot for his capabilities. Still...that doesn't help you resolve the situation. From the sounds of it, you're just getting yourselves organized, yes?"

Gavin nodded, saying, "That's correct. We discovered the situation once I recovered from the shock of Marcus's death."

"Very well. Continue with your preparations, and keep me informed. When you go to face down this mercenary army Sivas is assembling, the Warpriests of Tel shall march with you."

"Thank you, Ovir," Gavin said. "I appreciate your support."

Ovir smiled and said, "Think nothing of it, lad. Even if I were not a close friend of your mentor, this whole business is utter rubbish. It needs to be stopped before it kicks off a civil war unlike anything we've seen since the Godswar."

GAVIN WHISTLED to himself as he walked back to the College. After securing Ovir's support for their mission, Gavin and Ovir spent the afternoon engrossed in a conversation that ranged across a great many topics, including Marcus and Kiri. The time spent conversing with Ovir somehow lifted the weight Gavin had been feeling, and Gavin found himself relaxed for the first time in what seemed like months.

Gavin was just reaching the outskirts of the city markets when he spied the dress shop Lillian and Kiri enjoyed visiting. A dress in the window caught his eye. It was cobalt blue with forest green trim, and Gavin was turning to reach for the door's handle, intent on buying the dress for Kiri, when someone struck him from behind. The world went black.

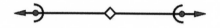

CHAPTER 50

Declan stepped out of the Grand Stair and approached the door to Gavin's suite. He pressed the tattoo on his left wrist to the metal plate, and the latching mechanism clicked open. Declan entered the suite and was just turning from pushing the door closed when Kiri almost skidded to a stop outside the room she shared with Gavin.

"What's wrong?" Declan asked.

"Is Gavin with you?"

Declan shook his head, saying, "No. We went separate ways. Why?"

"He's not home yet. I would've thought he'd be home by now."

Declan pivoted on his heel, leaving the suite and striding down the hall. He stopped at the door to the Mivar suite and applied the base of his fist to the door until Lillian opened it.

"What is it, Declan?"

"Could you please sit with Kiri?" Declan asked. "Gavin isn't home yet, and I'm going to the temple. It could be nothing, but Kiri could probably use a friend right now."

Lillian nodded, saying, "Of course, Declan. I'll go sit with her."

* * *

Ovir Thatcherson entered his quarters and began removing his vestments. Even though the shrine downstairs was open day and night, Ovir no longer had any duties. He could rest and relax at long last.

Ovir was just about to disrobe and change into more comfortable attire when a shadow beside the armoire said, "Have you seen Gavin Cross today?"

Ovir spun, his eyes searching for the source of the voice as he said, "Identify yourself."

The shadow beside the armoire moved, revealing a man in matte black leather armor. The hood and mask he wore obscured all but his eyes.

"Who I am is not important, Ovir Thatcherson," the man said. "We believe Gavin Cross to be missing, and when last he was seen, he was on his way to visit you. So, I ask you again: have you seen Gavin Cross today?"

Ovir took the few steps necessary to approach the man and reached out to pull down the neckline of the armor just enough to see the base of the man's neck. He bore no blood red symbol, and Ovir breathed easier.

"Forgive me," Ovir said as he stepped back. "I prefer not to converse with Lornithrasa. I did indeed speak with Gavin today, but it has been some time since he left. Long before the evening service, even."

Ovir closed his eyes and lowered his head, whispering the words to a prayer. In his mind, a scene played out in a hazy image as if he were watching it first-hand through fog. He saw Gavin Cross stop at a dress shop in the North Market; Gavin seemed to be looking at a dress. He saw Gavin reach for the door as two men came up behind, one striking him across the back of the head. Then, they carried Gavin's insensate form away.

Ovir took a deep breath and let it out as a sigh, before saying, "Gavin has been taken. I didn't recognize the men who did it, but I couldn't see their faces, either."

"Show me," the man said.

"I regret that I cannot. Unlike a wizard's scrying sphere, the effects of my divination spells are granted to me—and me alone—by Valthon Himself. Gavin was standing in front of a dress shop in the North Market when he was struck from behind."

The man said nothing more and stepped through the doorway of Ovir's bedroom. When Ovir followed, the man was nowhere to be seen.

Ovir smiled at the empty suite and returned to his bedroom. He crossed to an armoire opposite the one the man had been crouching beside and pulled a key from his pocket. Ovir unlocked the armoire and opened the doors, revealing the burnished armor of a Warpriest of Tel. A shield lay against one side of the armoire, and a flanged mace sat on its head in the opposite corner.

Ovir stood in silence, looking at the armoire and its contents. At last, he closed the armoire once more and locked it. Ovir turned instead to the bell-rope that hung in the corner. He gave the rope a pull and walked to meet the acolyte that would be running to answer his summons.

Ovir met the young man in the common room of his suite, and he couldn't help smiling at seeing it was the young man who'd pursued Gavin through the Temple earlier that day.

"Yes, sir?" the acolyte said.

"Summon the leadership of the Warpriests," Ovir said. "I need to see them at once."

* * *

It was a ramshackle building in the northwest corner of the Outskirts, the collection of wooden construction that had grown up around Tel Mivar over the centuries. In this section, the streets were well-trodden dirt, and the foul-smelling miasma hanging over the hovels was a cloud of despair and hopelessness few would ever escape.

A collection of men lounged around the door of the structure. They all wore faded leather in various forms, and not a one of them looked like anything other than the street ruffians they had grown up to be.

Declan scanned the small crowd and put forth the necessary effort not to sneer. There were six men he could see, outnumbering himself and his fellows two-to-one, and yet, Declan was not concerned at all as he walked up to the man closest the door.

"I've come to see the guild master," Declan said, looking the ruffian right in the eye.

"He's called the Shadow," the ruffian said, sneering, "and he don't take meetings…not with you, not with anybody."

Declan stood still, holding the ruffian's eyes with his own. There was no change in Declan's eyes, no shift in his expression. Declan's right arm was a whip, the small blade in his hand slicing the left side of the ruffian's neck just enough for the arterial pressure to spray blood across the door as well as the ruffian beside him. The sneering ruffian collapsed to the ground.

Blades appeared as the remaining five scrambled to their feet.

Declan turned to the bloody compatriot and said, "You know who we are…or at least, you should. As I told the scum bleeding out on the dirt, we're here to see the guild master."

* * *

DECLAN STEPPED over the fifth body to face the sixth guy, but before Declan could speak, this one showed some glimmer of intelligence.

"I get it! I get it!" the ruffian said, pointing at a corpse. "The key to the door is right there. The first guy had it all along."

Declan looked at the body and saw a key hanging on the corpse's belt. He returned his gaze to the live ruffian and pointed, saying, "Get it. Open the door."

"Whoa…I'm just street muscle. I rough people up. I don't have nothing to do with dead bodies."

Declan pointed at the body once more as he lifted his right hand, examining the blade he still held and running his thumb over the edge closest the hilt.

The ruffian paled, and sweat beaded on his forehead. He swallowed hard and edged closer to the corpse that had once been a colleague, if not a friend. He tried to stop his hand from shaking as he reached down and pulled the key free, fighting the urge to retch as he smelled the soiled trousers.

Declan waited until the ruffian inserted the key into the lock to say, "Stop."

The ruffian froze and turned his head to look at Declan, his eyes wide. Declan walked to him, lifting the knife. The ruffian flinched as Declan grabbed his left arm and wiped first one side of the blade and then the other on the sleeve of his leather jerkin. Declan lifted the blade to his eyes, inspecting for any hint of blood before nodding once.

"Better," Declan said, returning the blade to its sheath. "Now, lead the way."

THE RAMSHACKLE BUILDING was no more than a front and point of entry. Declan followed the ruffian into the building and down several flights of stairs to emerge in what had once been access tunnels that were abandoned following the construction of the city's sewer system. Flickering torches illuminated the hewn-rock corridors through which the ruffian led Declan, and Declan saw all manner of criminals as he followed in silence.

The Guild of Shadows had chapters in every major city and town across the known world. Whores, beggars, cutpurses, thieves, smugglers, or murderers…whatever the illicit enterprise, the Guild ran it or took a percentage for 'licensing fees.' In many ways, the world was better off for the Guild's organization; they operated under certain rules and kept things civil for the most part, and they had the numbers to ensure no rivals with less concern for the rules emerged.

The ruffian led Declan and his associates into a cavernous, dome-shaped space about sixty feet across. Many people filled the room, and one man sat on a hand-carved throne at the far back. Declan recognized him as the older man who had led the contingent to the College those weeks back.

"Beggin' yer pardon," the ruffian said, "but he-"

The seated man waved his left hand in dismissal, and the ruffian scampered to get out of sight.

"Why are you here?" the seated man asked.

Declan stepped forward to stand in the center of the room and said, "In the North Market earlier today, Gavin Cross was struck across the head and taken to parts unknown. I have come to learn what the Guild knows of it."

"You kill five of my people and expect me to help you? You're lucky I'm letting you walk out of here alive."

The left side of Declan's mouth curled in a smile that bore no mirth whatsoever, and he said, "You making a wise choice does not translate to me being lucky. Your organization has been somewhat lax in the past with its enforcement of the rules, so I see no reason not to consider the possibility that your organization is behind this...or at least some deniable assets you can throw to the wolves. Give me the information I seek, and my associates and I shall be on our way."

"Give me one good reason I don't have you killed right now."

"How much you value your life," Declan said, "because make no mistake. The moment anyone here touches a hilt, you die. There are probably sufficient people in the area to take down me and my associates *eventually*, but a great many of yours will die in the doing...not to mention all those who will die when my associates come for us. Kirloth believed we could wipe you out in three months. I believe it wouldn't take that long. Care to find out?"

A most awkward silence descended on the space as Declan and the guild master stared each other down. At long last, the guild master looked away.

"Some beggars reported seeing a couple men carrying a black-robed man into the alley beside the dress shop. I can get further information for you."

"Good," Declan said, "but while you're at it, I suggest you devote your organization's full resources to finding Gavin Cross. If I find him before you do, I'll consider the lot of you complicit in the act and respond accordingly."

Without waiting for a response, Declan pivoted on his heel and led his fellows out of the room.

* * *

Kiri looked up when she heard the suite's door open, and she started to smile at seeing Declan return. Then, she took in his expression.

"What is it?" Kiri asked, surging to her feet. "Where's Gavin?"

"I don't know, Kiri," Declan said. "He was knocked unconscious in front of a dress shop in the North Market today and taken. All that can be done to find him is being done."

Kiri turned to Lillian, saying, "You were saying how you've been studying Divination in your spare time. Can you…?"

Lillian stood and directed Kiri back to the chair. She gave her friend the best encouraging smile she could and said, "Of course I'll try."

Lillian did her best to clear her mind and focus on Gavin. She thought of his smile, his strength of will, and his dedication to helping others; in Lillian's mind, these were the foundation of who Gavin was. Her mind prepared, Lillian drew a breath and spoke a Word of Divination, "*Phezdys.*"

The invocation savaged Lillian, driving her to her knees as blood trickled out of her nose and the corner of her mouth. Lillian leaned back against the armchair she had been sitting in, gasping.

Once she regained her composure, Lillian lifted her head to face Kiri, saying, "He's somewhere in Mivar Province; that's all I know. The divination was blocked somehow; I couldn't get an exact location."

"That's more than we had," Declan said. "The two of you should get some rest. I've arranged for the Guild to assist us in locating Gavin. We'll find him soon."

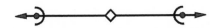

CHAPTER 51

Awareness returned to Gavin, but all he felt was pain. His head throbbed. His wrists, elbows, and shoulders ached. He could hear the slow drip of water somewhere close, and wherever he was, it was cool, almost cold.

Gavin lifted his head to the accompaniment of rattling chains, and he opened his eyes. He was in a basement or cellar, lit with burning torches that smelled foul. There were no windows or any other way to know if it was day or night. He hung from his arms, the tight manacles around his wrists biting into his flesh. The chains on the manacles were short and anchored in solid stone columns on either side of Gavin. Short chains ran from the stone columns near the floor to the shackles on Gavin's ankles. Gavin could see runes engraved into the manacles, and to top it all off, he was nude.

The sound of the door unlocking attracted Gavin's attention, and he labored to lift his head.

There seemed to be a series of locks on the door, and Gavin wrapped the chains at his wrists around his hands and pulled himself to his feet. His shoulders protested such poor treatment, but by the time the door opened, Gavin was standing on his own.

Two men entered. The first through the door was an older man;

at least middle age, he was short and wiry with dark hair and a pointed nose. A silver medallion around his neck. The second man walked behind and just to the right of the middle-aged man; a young man, maybe just a few years older than Gavin, he wore dark, matte leather overtop whatever clothes he preferred.

"Ah, good," the middle-aged man said, "you're awake. Do you know why you're here?"

"I think so, but you probably want to tell me," Gavin said with a sigh.

"I am Iosen of House Sivas, and you killed my son."

Gavin said, "Your son repeatedly committed one of the most heinous violations of the Arcanists' Code possible. I know over twenty young women who sleep better now that he's dead."

"He was my son!"

Gavin locked eyes with the man and put every bit of his contempt for the man's son, every bit of his contempt for the man, and his utter unconcern into his expression and voice. "Then, you should have raised him better…or put him down yourself."

Iosen's nostrils flared as red crept up his neck, and he said, "I'm going to enjoy watching you die."

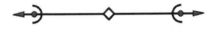

CHAPTER 52

I t was the end of the second day since Gavin went missing. Declan stood in one of the meeting rooms at the Temple of Valthon, awaiting those he had summoned. Declan chose this venue for one very specific reason, which would become apparent once he shared the information he had acquired not too long before.

This meeting room was no different than its fellows that were scattered around the upper floor of the temple. It was a bit larger, at 20 feet by 30 feet, and the table that dominated the room was a massive, oaken construct that carried the weight of its years with an understated dignity. Like all other original-construction buildings in Tel Mivar, the walls were a white, marble-like stone with strains of gray, black, and the occasional brown, and sconces that neither burned fuel nor radiated heat lit the room.

Declan stood by the room's sole window, gazing out over the city, and he turned when the door behind him opened. He watched Lillian, Mariana, Wynn, and Braden enter the room. Ovir entered after them and closed the door.

"What's going on, Declan?" Lillian asked. "Why are we not meeting in Gavin's suite?"

"Because what I have to say is not for Kiri's ears," Declan said.

"Is-Gavin-dead?" Wynn asked.

Declan shook his head, saying, "Not yet. Iosen Sivas arranged for Gavin to be taken, and he is in the process of torturing Gavin to death somewhere on his estate as we speak. Perhaps, you can see now why I did not want Kiri to know of this yet."

Lillian pulled a chair back from the table and sat, her shoulders slumped. She worked her lower lip between her teeth for several moments before turning back to face Declan.

"She'd be a mess," Lillian said.

Declan nodded.

"So," Braden said, "what do we do?"

Declan sighed and said, "I just acquired this information not too long ago, as well as independent confirmation through my own sources. The Guild was very eager to assure us that they were not involved...not even through deniable assets. As for what we do, it seems to me the only answer is we go get him."

"I have the Warpriests of Tel standing ready," Ovir said, approaching the table. "Say the word, and we march."

Declan met Ovir's gaze, saying, "I'm not sure this is something you should be taking sides in, Ovir. We have deniable assets of our own that would be far less conspicuous."

"I don't answer to you, Declan," Ovir said. "Our side is already chosen...by the only one who can."

Lillian and her friends turned to stare at Ovir, their eyes wide.

"Valthon has an interest in Gavin?" Mariana said.

Ovir gave Mariana a saintly smile and said, "Valthon has an interest in *all* of us, child. Don't you remember the clerics' teachings?"

Before anyone could respond, the door opened and swung back to slam against its stop. Lyssa Cothos, Torval Mivar, Sypara Wygoth, and Carth Roshan entered the room.

"Why are we just now learning that Gavin has disappeared?" Lyssa said.

"Mother," Mariana said, "we're handling it."

"Handling it?" Lyssa said. "Mari, aside from you, the others are all students. None of you even have the authority-"

"They don't," Declan said, "but I do."

"A traveling bard?" Carth said. "How do you have any authority, especially in something like this?"

Declan leaned forward to rest his fists on the table, and in doing so, he exposed a portion of the tattoo on the inside of his left wrist. The movement drew Lyssa's eyes, and her gaze locked on the tattoo. Lyssa stood stock still and silent for several seconds before she blinked and shook her head, as if to clear it. When she lifted her eyes to Declan once more, Lyssa's complexion had lost its color.

"You're handling it?" Lyssa asked, her eyes locked on Declan.

"Yes, Lyssa," Declan said, "*we* are."

"You know where he is?"

Declan nodded, saying, "He's somewhere at Sivas Manor. Iosen is intent on torturing him to death."

"Does anyone know if the Sivas manor-wall has embedded protections like those of the Duchy Estates?" Ovir said.

"It does not," Torval said. "By the time Sivas reached the point they could construct a manor house, no wizards capable of embedding those effects still lived...at least none who were willing to help Sivas."

"When do we strike?" Carth asked.

Declan shook his head, saying, "You're going about this all wrong. If we make a frontal assault without knowing Gavin's precise location, Iosen will have all the time he needs to slit Gavin's throat before we can reach him. We must secure Gavin, first. Then—and only then—do we conduct punitive operations."

"'Punitive operations,'" Braden said. "I like the sound of that."

* * *

A SPRAWLING DEMESNE, the Sivas Estate occupied an area twice the size of the Mivar Estate. Unlike the Mivar Estate, though, Sivas used his estate as the headquarters of the far-flung commercial interests his family had developed throughout the centuries. Large warehouses, stables, wainwrights, and blacksmiths were just some of the industries represented inside the Sivas Estate.

Declan, Gavin's apprentices, and Ovir stood inside a thick copse of trees just off the Tel Roshan road. The thick stand of trees was some seventy yards across, with trees and underbrush at the fringe more than sufficient to hide them from the Sivas' guards. They examined a sketch of the estate's layout, on which all the buildings on the diagram were crossed off, except the manor house itself.

"How did you come by this?" Mariana asked.

Declan smiled, saying, "Individuals friendly to our cause have infiltrated the estate. They have searched the entire compound, save for one location: the manor's basement. Iosen has guards at the stairs down who permit only Iosen and specific others to pass."

"That's where we'll find Gavin," Ovir said. "When do we move?"

"*We* don't," Declan said. "I will enter the estate as part of the convoys due to arrive shortly. While everyone is focused on the unloading and cross-loading of the wagons, I'll secure Gavin. You must be ready to begin as soon as my associate gives you the word."

"We'll be ready," Ovir said.

Declan nodded and, turning to Gavin's apprentices, said, "You do not need to be here. I would feel much better were the four of you back in Tel Mivar."

"We've discussed this," Lillian said. "Gavin is our mentor and friend. Our place is here. Besides, do you honestly think you can make us go back to the city?"

"Yes," Declan said without hesitation, his expression stone, "but I have no wish to explain my methods to Gavin once he learned of them."

Off to the west, a convoy of wagons and outriders crested a hill, coming from the direction of Tel Roshan. About the same time, another convoy came into sight traveling west from Tel Mivar, and these wagons and outriders found themselves escorted by the full roster of the Warpriests of Tel. A little over one thousand strong, the Warpriests of Tel rode in two columns of two on each side of the convoy.

Ovir grinned at the sight of the Warpriests, saying, "I hope those drovers appreciate our protection."

MEANWHILE, the convoy from Tel Roshan was turning onto the short road that led to the gates of the Sivas Estate. Declan moved off through the trees to a section that was closest the road, crouching behind the underbrush and waiting for his moment. Declan's moment came in the form of a group of laborers trudging alongside the wagons. No one cared enough to say anything about the new man who joined their ranks.

"HE MAKES THAT LOOK SO EASY," Mariana said, watching Declan until he slipped through the underbrush and out of their view.

A woman in matte black leather stepped up to Mariana's elbow and said, "There are many who would say he is one of the best."

Mariana jerked and turned to stare at the woman who had just 'appeared,' saying, "Where did you come from?"

The woman allowed herself a slight smile. "I have always been here," she said. "I simply chose now to be noticed."

* * *

DECLAN STEPPED inside the manor house and found it well-furnished. Tapestries hung on the stone walls, and carpets lined the wood-paneled floors. A grand staircase curved its way up to the second floor in the center of the entry hall, and windows allowed the late morning light to illuminate the dwelling. Declan could hear kitchen work—the crash of pots and pans, busy footfalls, and voices —in the distance.

Declan turned right from the main door and set off down the hallway. He arrived at a T-intersection and found the object of his search: a door flanked by two guards. The guards carried short swords and wore studded leather, and they leaned against the wall as they chatted. Neither one even looked up as Declan approached.

"Can you tell me where to find the kitchens?" Declan asked.

The two guards turned to look at him, frowning at the interruption.

"What?" one guard asked.

Neither guard had any reason to be concerned and were not watching Declan's hands. Slipping small push daggers out of concealment, Declan thrust the blades—at a slight upward angle—into each man's neck, severing their voice-boxes. Each man grabbed for the hand that held the blade, but the damage was already done. When he saw the fight leaving the man on his right, Declan took a quick moment to try the doorlatch, finding it unlocked. Declan then took each dying man in turn and pushed him backward down the stairs, and he closed the door as he descended into the basement.

Declan found himself at one end of a hallway that ran about fifteen feet before turning left. At the turn, Declan saw a door on the opposite side of the hallway.

"What was that calamity?" a voice said, drawing Declan's attention to the approaching footfalls.

Declan scooped up one of the short swords and stepped to the corner. When the footfalls were very close, Declan stepped around the corner.

"Who are-" The man's question no longer mattered; Declan opened the left side of his neck from front to back and pushed him aside to bleed out. The dying man's salt-and-pepper hair suggested he was just starting to approach middle age, and he wore blood-spattered leathers.

Declan stepped through the open door ahead of him and stopped cold. Gavin hung from his arms between two stone columns, and for all Declan could tell from across the room, he was already dead. Cuts, bruises, and burns were the most common of the many injuries that covered Gavin's body, and blood-tinged drool dripped from his jaw.

Declan crossed the room in haste and leaned close to the limp form of his friend. At last, Declan broke out into a smile. Gavin was breathing. It was faint and shallow, but he was breathing. Declan reached into the belt pouch on his right side, withdrawing a small sandstone disc. A red stripe ran across its center diameter, and he snapped it in half.

* * *

OUT IN THE copse of trees, the woman standing at Mariana's elbow gasped and clutched at her left wrist. She pulled back the sleeve of her leather jerkin and found the tattoo at her wrist glowing red. She lifted her head and spun until she found Ovir.

Ovir looked in the woman's direction as she moved.

"He needs you now," the woman said.

Ovir lifted his left arm, bringing the shield strapped there up as if to block an incoming blow. At the same time, Ovir also lifted the mace held in his right hand and struck the shield with it three times in quick succession.

AT THE GATE, the captain of Sivas's guard argued with the lead woman in the Warpriests when the sound of Ovir striking his shield echoed out of the woods. That instant, the woman snapped her fingers and gestured with her hand.

"Go!" she said. "Secure the estate with whatever force is necessary."

"What is the meaning of this?" the guard captain said, as warpriests charged onto the grounds, fanning out across the entire estate.

The woman leading the Warpriest column looked down at the guard captain, saying, "Iosen Sivas is holding someone here against their will, and we have come to secure that person's release. Valthon Himself has directed us to recover this person, and *no one* shall stand in our way."

The guard captain looked up into the woman's eyes, maintaining his silence for several moments. After a short time, the guard captain pivoted and locked his gaze on the guard standing in the watchtower on the western side of the gate.

The guard captain snapped his fingers and said, "Sound 'surrender' at once. No one is to resist the warpriests."

By now, Ovir and Gavin's apprentices reached the main gate, themselves on horseback. Ovir stopped just long enough to speak to the warpriest commander, saying, "I would prefer we find Iosen Sivas before any plain-clothed laborers or people in midnight black leather do. It will be better for all concerned if he's in our custody."

That said, Ovir nudged his horse forward to charge the fifty-plus yards to the portico of the Sivas manor house. He started the motion to step down from the horse before the mount completed its stop and strode into the manor house at a determined gait.

Lillian, Braden, Wynn, and Mariana were close behind, but Ovir had found the door to the basement by the time they caught up with him. Two men clad in the rough homespun garments of day laborers flanked the door and stopped them as they approached.

"We do not intend offense, but perhaps, it might be best for you to wait here," one of the two men said as the other lifted his left hand in a 'stop' gesture.

Lillian started to push past them, saying, "Gavin is our friend, too."

"Yes, he is, but do you want to see him naked and bleeding?"

Lillian made an abrupt stop. "Oh. No, I'd rather not."

"Thank you for helping us preserve his dignity."

✳ ✳ ✳

Ovir blanched just a bit as he stepped into the room and laid eyes on Gavin. After setting aside his shield and mace, Ovir approached the two pillars.

"Thank Valthon he's still alive," Ovir said.

"Indeed," Declan said. "I was reluctant to start releasing him until you were on-hand. It amazes me that he's still alive…in all truth."

Ovir nodded and said, "We need to get him out of those manacles, first. Do you have a key?"

Declan gave Ovir a flat look.

"Oh, of course. Sorry."

In a matter of moments, Declan unlocked the manacle around Gavin's right wrist, moving on to pick the lock of the one holding his left wrist, and Ovir took Gavin's arm to ease it down. He did the same for Gavin's left arm. A few moments more, and Gavin was free of the chains.

"Good," Ovir said. "Now, let's carry him to a clear section of floor and lay him down, but we need to lay him on his side."

Declan helped Ovir lay Gavin on the floor and looked to Ovir for the next step.

"We're going to have to do this slowly," Ovir said. "I've seen situations where healing a person this injured came with bad side effects."

In a clanking and creaking of armor and leather straps, Ovir knelt at Gavin's side. He closed his eyes and prayed. Soon, a soft gray nimbus surrounded Ovir's hands, and Ovir placed his left hand on Gavin's neck and his right hand on Gavin's waist. The soft gray radiance suffused Gavin's form, obscuring the insensate wizard from view. When light faded, Gavin's wounds looked as though they'd had about three days to heal.

For the first time since he had found Gavin, Declan saw him start to stir.

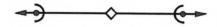

CHAPTER 53

Gavin rolled onto his back and released his breath in a heavy exhalation. For the first time in what seemed like ages, pain did not dominate his awareness. All he could remember of the recent past was pain. How long had he hung in this basement?

Gavin's memories of a time before the pain seemed faded and distant, but there was something else. The gray fog that seemed to swirl at the edges of his awareness seemed weakened, less substantial. For the first time since waking in this world, Gavin could almost grasp the memories of who he had been.

Gavin blinked open his eyes and frowned at the sight he beheld.

"Ovir?" Gavin said, his voice a fraction of its normal strength. Movement to his left caught Gavin's eye, and he swiveled his head, frowning again. "Declan?"

Gavin's head cleared, a thought floating to the forefront of his mind, and he said, "Where's Lillian?"

"What?" Declan said.

"Lillian, Declan! Where is she? Is she safe?"

Declan pointed overhead, saying, "She's upstairs with the others,

Gavin. All four of your apprentices are surrounded by warpriests and…my associates."

Gavin laid his head back and exhaled. "Good. That's good. He said he was going to take her."

"What do you remember, Gavin?" Ovir said.

Gavin rolled his head to look at Ovir, saying, "Too much."

Declan opened his mouth to speak but ultimately said nothing.

"As bad as I feel," Gavin said, "I must have been close to dying."

Ovir said, "Yes, we think so, but don't you worry, Gavin. We'll have those wounds gone in no time."

"Declan," Gavin said, "do you think you might be able to find me something to wear? Trousers of some kind, at least?"

Declan nodded once and stepped away.

Once Declan stepped through the door, Gavin turned to Ovir, saying, "I couldn't stop him, Ovir. I couldn't feel my power in those chains, and…and…I couldn't stop him from hurting Lillian."

"Lillian's safe, Gavin," Ovir said, laying his hand on Gavin's shoulder. "All this is over. Now, let's do something about those wounds."

WHEN DECLAN RETURNED, Gavin stood under his own strength. Declan could see faint tremors in Gavin's legs from time to time, though, and he presented the fruits of his search.

"I'm sorry, Gavin," Declan said as he approached. "All I could find were these homespun trousers."

Gavin laughed, a large smile splitting his face. "Those seem oddly appropriate. I wonder if I'll turn every milestone in my life wearing homespun trousers."

Gavin accepted the garment and stepped into the trousers, pulling them up to his waist and tying the cord that served as a belt.

"What's the situation up top?" Gavin said. "Did you lose many people in the battle?"

"What battle?" Ovir said. "The captain of the guard surrendered the estate to the Warpriests of Tel. There were a couple guards who didn't get the message, but none of our people were injured that I am aware."

"That's rather fortunate. I'm grateful for the rescue, and I'm even more grateful that there wasn't a pitched battle to do it."

Gavin took a moment to look around the room one last time, taking a deep breath and releasing it as a sigh. He walked to the door but stopped. Gavin turned and pointed his left index finger at the chains that had held him.

"Declan," Gavin said, "I want the manacles that held my hands and the chains that go with them."

* * *

GAVIN EXITED the manor house to a cheering crowd of Wraiths, Warpriests, and his four apprentices. Gavin couldn't keep the smile from his lips, nor the blush from his cheeks. He waved and nodded his thanks.

At last, the cheers faded, and Gavin said, "Thank you for what you've done on my behalf. I appreciate the rescue more than you know, and I shall not forget this."

Two warpriests and two wraiths pushed through the crowd, pulling two people: a man and a woman. Gavin recognized Iosen Sivas right away, and he guessed the woman's identity based on her companion.

No trace of malice or satisfaction could be seen in Gavin's expression as he faced the man responsible for his torture. In fact, Gavin spoke just three words, "Find an axe."

Four Wraiths stepped forward, presenting axes. These axes were intended for timbering, but they had been well cared-for, their blades shiny from recent sharpening.

"Kneel, Sivas," Gavin said.

Frowns and glances filtered through those closest to Gavin like a wave.

"Gavin-" Ovir said.

Gavin turned to face his mentor's closest friend, saying, "What are you going to do, Ovir? Un-heal me?"

"This is wrong, Gavin," Ovir said. "He's unarmed. He's not a threat. You're a private individual. This isn't a legal execution; it's murder."

It was then that Declan joined the group. He carried the two manacles with their chains coiled through them. Gavin didn't ask how the bard had done the job with such alacrity, but he did notice one end of a chain still bubbled.

Gavin shifted his gaze to Ovir and held the priest's eyes with his own for several moments before he said, "That man will not be alive when I leave this estate, Ovir. If you disapprove of my methods, do it yourself. Either way, he dies today."

"You're very confident with all your friends around you," Iosen said. "I'm not about to kneel before you. I demand a wizards' duel."

Gavin shifted his gaze to Iosen, his impassive expression shifting almost to a sneer as he said, "You're a traitor, Sivas. You know it. I know it. The Great Houses know it. What makes you think you have any grounds to demand an honorable duel from me?"

"Sivas is one of the most respected Houses of the Society. Besides, you have no authority to decree my execution. Duel me, or let me leave."

A hush descended upon the assembled crowd. Gavin and Iosen held each other's gaze, as those assembled looked back and forth between them.

Gavin spoke a Word, "*Thraxys.*" Iosen collapsed to the ground like a puppet with its strings cut. Iosen's wife screamed.

Gavin looked down at the corpse on the ground, his expression stone, and said, "Traitors do not deserve an honorable death."

Gavin shifted his attention to Iosen's wife. Tears streamed down her cheeks, and her jaw trembled. She closed her eyes and sank to her knees. Her knees on the grass, shaking hands reached up and pulled her lustrous, dark hair from her neck to rest on her left shoulder. She took a deep breath and opened her eyes to face Gavin.

"I had no part in what Iosen did to you," she said, "but I supported him in his plot in every way. I don't want to die, but I will not beg."

Gavin stood in silence, regarding the woman who knelt and

bared her neck for the axe. She trembled, her pallor pale, but she faced Gavin with squared shoulders.

"If you did not die today," Gavin asked, "what would you do?"

Iosen's wife blinked and said. "I...I don't know. My only child became a monster and died for it. My husband lies dead beside me. Before long, it will be known throughout the Society and the Kingdom what we tried to do. I don't know what there is left for me."

"Who managed the affairs of the Sivas commercial interests?" Gavin said.

"I did. Iosen made the deals and led his conspiracy, leaving me to pay the bills and ensure our people were fed."

Gavin nodded. After a few moments, he said, "You do realize that, after today, House Sivas is no more?"

"Yes."

"Very well," Gavin said. "You will sign over to me everything you would have inherited as Iosen's widow, and you will remain as manager of the estate and commercial interests. You will wear plain, simple clothes and sleep with the servants. I shall provide a steward to assist you and, yes, ensure your cooperation. I trust I do not need to explain what awaits you if you speak with the other conspirators or transgress further in any way?"

"I understand," she said, bowing her head. "I thank you for my life."

"Starting next month, I want all of your son's victims to receive a monthly stipend. It will not make them one of the idle rich, but I believe they are owed something. I was going to sell off all the assets I acquired through the duel and split the proceeds between them, but I think this will work out better. Besides, I'm sure there are quite a few people worried about their livelihood just now. What is your name?"

"Layla, sir."

"Thank you, Layla," Gavin said. "Go get changed."

Layla pushed herself to her feet and stripped off the clothes Lady Sivas wore. She turned and walked to the servants' quarters nude.

Once she was out of hearing range, Gavin turned at Declan and said, "Let's finish up here. Take the corpse and toss it inside the front door of the manor. Then, get everyone out of the house."

A few minutes later, Declan returned and nodded once, saying, "The house is clear, except for Sivas's corpse."

Gavin turned to the manor house where he would've died were it not for his friends. He cleared his mind of everything, except his intent. His intent a crystal-clear picture in his mind, Gavin took a deep breath and invoked a Word of Evocation, "*Idluhn.*"

The pain that tried to savage Gavin was a pale imitation of the agony he had endured, but the invocation took so much power that Gavin staggered and would have fallen had Ovir and Declan not each taken an arm.

Gavin's invocation was a complete surprise to Lillian, Braden, Wynn, and Mariana. None of them had the chance to buttress themselves against what was coming, and the resonance of Gavin's power was an abrupt, vicious bludgeon that drove the air from their lungs and the strength from their legs. They collapsed to their knees, gasping for air and their arms wrapped around their midriffs.

At first, the effect of Gavin's invocation was not apparent. Soon, though, the stone of the manor house took on a faint red glow as blue flames licked up through the wooden floors, reducing them to ash.

The group watched the flames in silence for several moments. At last, Declan said, "I'm glad the Sivas vault is under that storehouse off to the west, instead of inside the house. That could've made problems for your stipend plan until more income arrived."

Gavin blinked and looked at Declan. "You know...I never once considered where the vault might be."

More than one person within earshot looked away, hiding a smile or grin.

After a few moments more, Gavin said, "Leave some people to

be sure no one tries to go back inside, and send the steward from Kalinor's estate to keep an eye on her. Oh, and have someone strike Sivas's name from the gate. Otherwise, we're finished here. Let's go home."

As Gavin turned to find an available mount, Declan reached into a belt pouch and withdrew something, extending his hand to Gavin. Gavin looked down and smiled; a medallion of House Kirloth rested in Declan's hand, gleaming in the noon-day sun.

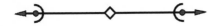

CHAPTER 54

S he floated over the city as the besiegers broke through the gates. In mere
moments, the disciplined army became a disorganized mob; the sack of
the city had begun. She flowed with the mob, witnessing their atroci-
ties...every rape, every murder. She was spared nothing.

The scene before her shifted, and she found herself at eye level with a bound
Terris Muran, King of Vushaar. He knelt before a headsman's block, and the
black-hooded man at his right shoulder held a gruesome axe. The rebel leader
stepped to the front of the platform.

"People of Vushaar, I—General Sclaros Ivarson—stand before you today as
your liberator. I have freed you from the tyrant family that has ruined your lives
for thousands of years. King Terris stands before you a captured traitor to the
spirit of Vushaar, and we are here today to see that justice is done!" The general
turned to the men behind him and nodded. "Begin."

The headsman pushed Terris down to lay his neck on the block, and he hefted
his axe and swung. The image froze with the axe at the apex of its path. A voice
resonated throughout the vision, even shaking the mists that formed the vision's fringe.

"The new year shall herald the fate of Vushaar, but should the Tiger and
the Arrow ally, as was in ages past, the Tiger shall be bloodied yet unbroken. You
shall know their victory by the golden flame."

. . .

VALERA JERKED UPRIGHT, her eyes wide and skin clammy. She gasped for breath while her heart fought to burst open her chest. She lost precious moments realizing she still sat in the Office of the Collegiate Justice. Calming just a bit, she grabbed paper and a stylus, before reaching for the ink bottle. She almost spilled the ink, but she wrote the final words of the dream, reciting them over and over so they would not be forgotten. Valera put the stylus aside and leaned back in the chair once she made sure the words were recorded.

* * *

GAVIN OPENED the door to his suite and pushed it wide. He did not see Kiri in the common room and entered the collection of rooms that had become his home, closing the door behind him. The door closed a bit heavy, and Gavin heard footfalls approaching from the room he shared with Kiri.

"Is there any word...Gavin!"

Gavin had just a few moments to look at Kiri as she barreled across the room. He wasn't sure, but Kiri just might have reached a full sprint before she skidded to slow herself and threw her arms around Gavin.

"I feared you were dead," Kiri said, her voice a whisper.

Gavin felt tears on his chest as he wrapped his arms around Kiri. He held her in silence for several moments before he said, "I almost was, Kiri, but Ovir pulled me back."

"What happened? No one would tell me anything."

"Iosen Sivas apparently took exception to his son losing the duel," Gavin said. "He had me taken off the streets and was torturing me to death."

Kiri tightened her arms around Gavin as she said, "I was so afraid you were dead; I'm so glad Ovir was there."

"I wish I could say I was afraid I was dead, too," Gavin said, "but the last few days are a bit of a haze. I'm not sure I felt much of anything."

Silence reigned for several moments.

"Please tell me that Declan killed that man," Kiri said.

"He did not. I killed him."

Kiri loosened her arms just enough to look up to Gavin's eyes.

"How? Are you okay?"

Gavin nodded and pulled Kiri across the room. He sat in his favorite armchair and pushed Kiri into the chair Marcus always used.

"I was going to have him executed on his knees. Iosen demanded a duel, and I killed him with the same Word I used on the slavers when we first met."

"And you're okay?" Kiri said. "When you won the duel, it bothered you for days, weeks even."

After a few moments, Gavin said, "I should probably be more bothered by his death than I am, but I can't bring myself to be. I don't think I'm going to start killing people every other day, but the end of House Sivas does not weigh on my conscience. I suppose that makes me a bad person."

"I'm sure there are some people who would say so, but I am not one of them."

Neither spoke for a few moments. After several moments, Kiri broke the silence.

"Gavin, there's something we need to discuss."

"That sounds almost ominous." A slight smile curled one side of Gavin's mouth.

"Is there going to be a battle with the traitors and their mercenaries?"

Gavin sighed. "It's looking that way. I personally want to keep the fight as far away from as many innocent people as possible. I'm not sure we have the numbers to do that, though. We may be forced into a defensive engagement, with us holding the city and the mercenaries besieging us."

"When you go—whether you end up manning the walls or leading the assault on the mercenary camp—I'm going with you. Declan has already provided me with armor and equipment, and he says my skills are such he'd trust his back to me in a fight."

"Excuse me?"

"I'm not going to be left here like some milkmaid to wring my hands and obsess over what may be happening to you, Gavin. I am going with you. Understand and accept that right now. Who knows…I could very well save *your* life if I'm there."

"Kiri, you have no business-" Gavin stopped as he considered what he was about to say as well as the conflicting emotions behind it. He didn't want Kiri *anywhere* near the fight, and if he were completely honest with himself, his motives had little to do with the King's prohibitions about slaves carrying blades. He wanted Kiri to be safe. He wanted her protected.

Kiri faced him in silence. Gavin took in her calm, resolute expression, and he knew she had considered all the implications of going with him. She wasn't the type to make rash judgements, and he had the suspicion she'd be at his side regardless of his response right now.

"Okay," Gavin said. "You can go."

To her credit, Kiri didn't even gloat.

* * *

THE NEXT MORNING found the Conclave gathered at the Mivar Estate once more, though with additional attendees. A large map of northern Mivar Province covered the table along with stacks of paper bearing notes and sketches. Torval Mivar, Lyssa Cothos, Carth Roshan, and Sypara Wygoth stood near their customary places with Ovir, Garris Roshan, and Declan interspersed between them. Gavin sat in the chair set aside for Kirloth, and his apprentices—the heirs to the Great Houses—stood near their own seats.

Gavin stared at the map of the mercenary compound, not giving the conversation around him his full attention. He was missing something, and what was worse, he *knew* he was missing something. Whatever that something was, though, he couldn't say; it was being very elusive, refusing to reveal itself to the forefront of his mind.

"How many warpriests do you have, Ovir?" Garris said.

"There are a little over one thousand warpriests. It's a bit of a fluid number, because the order claims members—like myself—who are not listed on the active roster or regularly participate in training."

Garris sighed, saying, "We have to face facts, people. Between the Battle-mages and the Warpriests, we might—*might*—have sufficient numbers to hold the city's walls with the town guard to help us. Declan, what are the latest reports on the mercenaries' numbers?"

"The most recent numbers I have put the mercenary army at just over five thousand, and I doubt the army will grow to more than six thousand. They've been sitting out there in the hinterlands for so long some of their people have wandered off, so the roster has been a bit fluid. With the loss of the Sivas fortune, they'd better move soon, or they'll run out of money."

Carth Roshan scanned the faces around the table. "Can't we just wait them out then? I mean, mercenaries fight for pay. When the pay chest dries up, that army will dissolve."

"Think it through, Carth," Gavin said, speaking for the first time since the Conclave began. "We don't know what the conspirators have promised those mercenaries. Do you really want six thousand—or even just five thousand—experienced fighters wandering the countryside, angry that they didn't get to loot the College or whatever? Sounds like a perfect storm for severe banditry across the Kingdom to me. No…we have to crush this army, convince them they never should've answered Sivas's call."

"And how do we do that, Gavin?" Lyssa said. "Adding the Battle-mages and Warpriests together, we only have a little over two thousand troops. Military doctrine says you should outnumber your opponent by half, or the outcome of the battle is in doubt."

"There is a way we could outnumber them," Declan said. Everyone turned to look at him. "I am aware of several units of the Army of Tel who are loyal to the Constitution and would stand with us if we only asked. If Kirloth were to issue a call to arms, I am confident we could field an army easily twice the mercenaries' number."

"I don't like that, Declan," Gavin said. "The Army of Tel answers to the King. I do not want any of those people punished for doing the right thing."

"The worst part of all this is having to split our forces between Tel Mivar and the group going out to confront the mercenaries," Sypara said. "We can't leave Tel Mivar undefended, but as it is, we barely have enough people to man the wall in a siege. The Outskirts would be lost."

Carth nodded his agreement, saying, "It wouldn't be so bad if we had access to the garrison."

The elusive thought that had been plaguing Gavin all morning clicked into place, and his eyes shot wide, jaw dropping. Gavin shot to his feet so fast, his chair tipped over and crashed against the floor, startling everyone into silence.

"I have to go," Gavin said as he strode across the room to the door. "Declan, you're with me."

At the door, Gavin stopped and turned back to the group, saying. "If you can find a way to protect those soldiers who would join us, I will issue a general call to arms before nightfall. Leave the city's defense out of the plan from here on out. It will not be an issue."

* * *

"ARE YOU SURE THIS WILL WORK?" Gavin asked between heavy breaths.

He and Declan stood near the top of the Grand Stair in the Tower of the Council, looking up at a landing with no door. They took heavy breaths, for they'd scaled the Grand Stair two—and sometimes three—steps at a time.

Declan shrugged, saying, "I have no idea. I just know how Marcus accessed the Citadel."

"I guess we're about to find out," Gavin said, taking one last deep breath before starting up the final steps.

The moment Gavin set foot onto the actual landing, a specter looking much like the Arena's Master of the Field faded into view.

"Halt," the specter said in a wispy voice. "Thou shalt go no farther."

Gavin took a moment to suppress the urge to banter with the

specter about where else he would go and, once he was sure of his composure, said, "I have not come for the Citadel, worthy watchman. I am Gavin Cross, Head of House Kirloth, and I desire an audience with Nathrac."

"Hold here, Kirloth," the specter said, "and I shall deliver thy request."

The specter faded away, and Gavin looked to Declan, saying, "Well...we're still alive."

A column of flame that neither burned nor radiated heat erupted from the landing's flagstones, leaving a purple-robed figure in its wake. The purple robe bore gold runes on the cuffs of the sleeves and the cowl of the hood, and inside the hood, a deep, impenetrable shadow obscured the figure's face. All that could be seen were two eyes the color of open flame, whose pupils were vertical slits.

"It has been some time, Kirloth," Nathrac said, and both Gavin and Declan felt the resonance of his voice in their very bones. "Why do you seek me?"

"May I still call upon that boon?" Gavin asked.

Nathrac nodded once. "You have yet to do so. How would you use it?"

"Tel Mivar needs its garrison, and if you will allow me, I will spend the boon to activate it."

"Never in the history of Tel has any provincial capital activated its garrison," Nathrac said. "What brings you to make this request?"

"That's a bit of a long story," Gavin said. "Do you have time?"

Nathrac allowed himself a brief chuckle, saying, "If you only knew how much time I have..."

"Okay, then," Gavin said and proceeded to explain the crisis the Society—and possibly the entire Kingdom—faced: the evidence of Sivas's plot, the Council's inaction, the Conclave's activation of Article 35...all of it.

Nathrac remained silent through the entire recitation, focused on Gavin's narrative. When Gavin finished at last, Nathrac said, "You would use your boon on behalf of the people? Even when that boon might very well save your life or the life of someone you love in the future? You cannot rely on Ovir always being available."

"Nathrac, these people are innocent bystanders in all of this," Gavin said and gave a light chuckle as a statement floated up out of the fog at the fringes of his mind. "They don't have a dog in this fight. The people of Tel Mivar need to be protected, and we don't have the forces to ensure the city's safety *and* meet that mercenary army in the field, well away from everyone. I need your help, Nathrac."

Nathrac stood in silence for several moments before he said, "Know this, young one. Were it not for oaths I swore in ages long ago, I would join you in the field; long has it been since I took part in a righteous battle."

Nathrac reached out his left hand to Gavin and opened his fingers. The first thing Gavin noticed was that the skin of Nathrac's hand looked more like scales than flesh, the fingernails almost scaled-down claws. In the palm of Nathrac's hand rested a tooth the size of Gavin's palm, and Declan stifled a gasp when he saw it.

"Use this to summon me," Nathrac said, "when the time comes to activate the city's garrison."

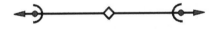

CHAPTER 55

Gavin threw open the door of the Conclave meeting room, and every head turned to look when it struck its stop. Gavin saw curiosity, hope, concern, and regard all mixed throughout the expressions that faced him. He strode across the room with Declan at his shoulder and stopped when he reached the table. He saw that his chair still lay upon its back, but Gavin didn't care; he'd deal with it in a moment.

"Well?" Lyssa asked. "We've figured out how to protect those soldiers who would follow us. It's your turn now; how will we defend the city *and* meet the mercenaries in the field?"

Gavin held out his hand, the tooth given to him by Nathrac dominating his palm. Everyone looked to Gavin's hand, their eyes widening.

"Where did you get that?" Lyssa asked. "Do you have any idea what you hold?"

"I'm pretty sure it's a tooth, Lyssa," Gavin said.

"That's not just any tooth, Gavin. That's a dragon's tooth. Where did you get it?"

"Nathrac gave it to me," Gavin said. "I'm to use it to summon him to activate the city's garrison when the time comes."

Lyssa relaxed, saying, "Ah, okay then. That makes sense."

Now, everyone else looked to Lyssa.

"How does it make sense that the Chief of the Citadel Guard gave Gavin a dragon's tooth?" Torval asked.

"Because Nathrac's a dragon," Lyssa said. "He and his hatch-mate Myrathsis led the dragon contingent of the Army of Valthon during the Godswar. He and Kirloth were close friends."

"When he gave me this, he said he'd join us in the field, were it not for his oaths," Gavin said.

"You must have impressed him to a great degree, Gavin," Lyssa said. "The dragons were known for viewing the shorter-lived races as little more than petulant children."

Gavin let that sink in for a moment before he scanned the faces at the table, saying, "Okay...now, it's your turn. How do we protect the soldiers who choose to follow us?"

"As Royal Priest of Tel," Ovir said, "I have the authority to conscript soldiers in times of crisis. The only provision is that the authority is voided if there is an Archmagister. I honestly should've thought of it sooner, but this is the first time since the Founding that the conditions apply."

"You're certain this will work?" Gavin asked.

Ovir nodded, saying, "Absolutely. Everything is spelled out in Article 12 of the Constitution of Tel."

Gavin blinked and said, "Seriously? There's an article of the Constitution that grants you the authority to conscript and field an army if there's no sitting Archmagister?"

"Yes. Do you want to read it?"

"Not at all. If I can't trust you, Ovir, I'm not sure who I could trust," Gavin said and fell silent as he ran through everything in his mind. Garrison, check. Leadership, check. Sufficient troops, check. "Well then...it looks like all that's left is to gather our forces."

* * *

DECLAN PROVIDED information on which units Ovir should 'conscript,' and Ovir, Gavin, and Declan visited the army base just north of Tel Mivar. It was a simple matter to move through the base, visiting those unit commanders they needed, and they were leaving one encampment for the next on their list when a group of about thirty men approached.

"What is the meaning of this?" the man leading the group said as he looked down at Gavin, Declan, and Ovir from atop his mount. "I have received word you claim to be conscripting units of the Army of Tel."

"You hear correctly, sir," Ovir said. "May I ask just who you are?"

"I am Derrin Cooper, General of the Army, and any such requisitions of troops must go through me."

"You are wrong," Gavin said, drawing the man's attention. "Article 12 of the Constitution grants the Royal Priest of Tel the authority to conscript entire units of the army as necessary unless the Kingdom is in a state of war. I do not recall there being an active declaration of war."

"Yes, well, I am the commanding officer of the Army; it is my-"

"Be silent," Gavin said. "I do not like your voice, and I'm tired of hearing it. Ovir does not have to ask permission or pass any conscriptions through you. You know it, and I know it. Now, turn that nag around and go back from whence you came."

A man two horses back from the general drew his sword, pointing it at Gavin as he said, "You had best get a civil tongue in your head; you address the General of the Army of Tel."

Gavin spoke a Word, "*Uhnrys*," and a tightening around his eyes was all the outward indication of the pain he felt as the invocation took hold. The general and his retinue seemed to freeze. They did not breathe; they did not blink.

"Gavin," Ovir said, "what did you do?"

"I tested a Word I discovered in Marcus's journals," Gavin said. "Marcus wrote that it was almost a forbidden Word long ago, as it allows the arcanist to manipulate time itself to some degree. I can't travel backward or forward in time—that I'm aware—but I can freeze time for myself or others. Right now, those men and those horses are in a frozen moment of time; tomorrow morning, the effect will dissipate, and we'll be gone."

Ovir and Declan stared at Gavin for several moments before they resumed their conscriptions.

* * *

HAVING GATHERED SUFFICIENT, trustworthy units from the Army of Tel, Gavin, Ovir, and Declan returned to Tel Mivar with the leadership of those units. They were going to meet with the Conclave and begin planning the assault on the mercenary camp.

The soldiers chatted with Ovir and Declan about the campaign, while Gavin rode ahead in silence. Even if Gavin hadn't casually frozen some thirty people in time, the soldiers still would've given him a respectful distance. Black-robed arcanists were such an uncommon sight people would notice them, but a black-robed wizard of House Kirloth? Probably best for all concerned to give *that* man some space…

THE CONCLAVE MEETING WENT WELL, and Gavin soon found himself stepping off the Grand Stair onto the floor where his suite awaited. All through the Conclave, a thought danced at the fringe of Gavin's awareness. There was something about armies and formations that might help in the coming 'campaign,' as the soldiers put it, but Gavin couldn't remember what it was. He did know where he'd read it, though: Mivar's Histories.

Gavin entered his suite and went to the library, where he retrieved Volumes II and III of Mivar's Histories; Gavin knew Volume I was little more than an examination of how the world reached the start of the Godswar. Pulling a chair back from the table, Gavin sat and began skimming through Volume II; Volume II ended with the Army of Valthon beginning the march to Arundel, the capital of the elf-lands in the Great Forest of the North.

Gavin set aside Volume II and began skimming Volume III, and he soon found what he sought. During the first battle on the march into the elf-lands, the Army of Valthon broke into separate formations to swarm the defenders at the Great Forest's border, and to coordinate the battle, Kirloth and the Apprentices split up among the formations. Still little more than a slap-dash affair, none of the formations had their own identity or standards yet...so Kirloth and the Apprentices gave them one each. They created massive, glowing battle standards that hovered in the air high above the formation as they marched, and the core symbols of those standards were the glyphs of each wizard's family.

Having found the object of his search, Gavin stopped skimming and read the entire section of Volume III that related to the first appearance of the battle standards. It was not uncommon for Mivar's writing to digress into a treatise on whatever arcane feat dominated the moment, but nowhere did Mivar explain how they created the battle standards that Gavin could find. Gavin glared at the book and almost slammed his fist onto the table-top. Taking a deep breath, Gavin closed the third volume of Mivar's Histories and pushed it away; besides, he still had one more place to search.

Gavin returned the two volumes to the library and walked across the common room to sit in Marcus's chair. He used his medallion to open the chest beside the hearth. The chest was half-full of journals, and Gavin began lifting stacks of journals out of the chest and placing them upside-down on the floor in front of him. Twenty stacks of journals later, Gavin took the journal at the very bottom of the chest, left side, and opened it.

"'It has been one hundred years since the death of Bellock Vanlon,'" Gavin said, reading the first line. "Damn. All those journals, and I'm only back about 500 years. This is going to take a while."

Gavin closed the journal and leaned to place it back in the chest. As he did so, Gavin saw one of the boards in the 'floor' of the chest shift a bit. The board in question had a knothole, and Gavin tried hooking his smallest finger into it and lifting the board.

In the cavity under the chest's main compartment, Gavin saw a drawstring bag made of heavy, off-white canvas. It was about the size of two men's fists pressed together. Gavin retrieved the bag and opened it, pouring out its contents into his lap. There were almost fifteen small draw-string bags made of black velvet.

Gavin chose one and opened it, upending it over his hand. A smoky-white crystal fell into his palm. It was about the thickness of two men's fingers together, and its sides were smooth. The instant he laid eyes on the crystal, Gavin knew what he had found, and he couldn't keep from breaking into a huge grin.

"Well, well...*these* will certainly be useful," Gavin said.

He returned the crystal to its velvet pouch and collected five more. The rest he returned to the canvas bag and placed the bag on the floor between the chair and the chest, before returning the board to the chest's base and filling it once more with the journals in their original order.

GAVIN SPENT the rest of the afternoon going through the six chests in Marcus's room, and as it turned out, every one of them was packed to the brim with journals. At long last, Gavin found the object of his search in the sixth—and final—chest, about a quarter of the way up from the bottom. Gavin flipped through the journal and found that Marcus hadn't just listed the Word he'd used to create the battle standards. Marcus had written out a complete diagram with annotations for each standard. Gavin grabbed a nearby journal and used it as a place-holder, before returning all the journals to their original position inside the chest.

* * *

GAVIN STOOD WITH OVIR, Declan, his apprentices, and their parents about one hundred yards northwest of the Outskirts. The army stretched out in front of them, facing north and awaiting the order to march.

It had been a grueling week between marshalling forces and the practice Gavin insisted on conducting, but the practice was paying off. Lillian, Braden, Wynn, and Mariana were proud of their work and were looking forward to showing off when the time came. Gavin was proud of them, too.

Captain Corliss approached on his horse and looked down at the group, saying, "We're ready to march. Why are we waiting?"

Gavin looked up at the captain and smiled. He said, "We—well, I—have one last thing that must be done, but don't worry. It won't take long."

Gavin withdrew Nathrac's token from inside his robe and fed it a trickle of power as he said, "Nathrac!"

A column of flame that neither burned nor radiated heat erupted from the ground in front of Gavin, depositing a purple-robed figure with gold runes on the cowl of the hood and the cuffs of the sleeves.

The assembled Dukes and Duchesses gasped at seeing a Guardian for the first time in their lives. Whatever magic hid Nathrac's form from sight apparently did nothing to hide Nathrac's scent, at least as far as animal senses go; Corliss's horse shied when it found itself so close to one of the world's apex predators, and Corliss spent the next few moments regaining command of the beast.

"Yes, Kirloth?" Nathrac said, his deep voice resonating against Gavin's bones.

Gavin sighed as he nodded and said, "The time has come, Nathrac. I desire to spend my boon to activate the city's garrison."

"Your mentor intended the boon to save your life, Young Kirloth," Nathrac said. "I respect your intentions, but your mentor was my dearest friend. I ask one last time: are you certain you wish to use it thus?"

"I have no reservations in using the boon this way, Nathrac," Gavin said. "Besides, it's the right thing to do."

Nathrac stood in silence for several moments before he said, "My friend told me once you had the potential to be his finest apprentice, and I have decided he was not wrong."

Nathrac lifted his head as if speaking to the heavens and said, "I summon the garrison of Tel Mivar!"

Those wizards present felt a surge of power as Nathrac spoke those words, and all over Tel Mivar, spectral forms rose out of the stones of the street. They were translucent at best, but enough detail existed to see they wore the arms and equipment of soldiers in the Army of Valthon: simple breastplates and helmets, short swords, shields, and a half-spear. Within minutes, the spectral soldiers lined the walls, looking out over the surrounding countryside, and there were still sufficient numbers to line the major streets and avenues of the city.

"The city is defended, Young Kirloth," Nathrac said, "and should the mercenary army already be marching on Tel Mivar and your forces somehow miss it, I myself will lead the garrison when the mercenaries arrive."

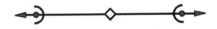

CHAPTER 56

T he army made camp about half a day's travel from the mercenary encampment. Once the tents were set, Gavin called a command conference. Ovir, his apprentices, Declan, and the officers of each unit gathered at Gavin's tent. Octagonal with a high peak, a square pavilion extended from the front some twenty feet by twenty feet, creating a shaded space much like the porch or portico of a house. The tent itself was immense and the largest on the field, which allowed for the space nearest the entrance to be a meeting area, with Gavin's and Kiri's cots in the back half.

"Good evening," Gavin said, starting the meeting. "I called this conference so that you could hear a report from one of my agents who has been involved in scouting the mercenary encampment. Unless there's a better idea, I'm thinking we'll start with the report and follow it with a question-answer session. Then, we can work out our plan. Comments?"

No one spoke up with an alternative, and Gavin nodded to a man standing to one side. He was average height with brown hair and green eyes, dressed as a common laborer. The man stepped forward and began to speak.

"The mercenary army is encamped in a bowl-shaped depression some four leagues north of us. The sides of the depression range from ten to fifteen feet in height, and they are a gentle slope that is easy to climb. The bottom-"

Mariana gasped as her eyes went wide, saying, "Lake Yortun... you're talking about Lake Yortun!"

Everyone turned to look at her, with more than one questioning expression.

"It's a dried-up lake. Up until a hundred and fifty years ago, it was fed by the Cothos River, but a rockslide from a hill about two miles upstream forced the river to change course. The outlet on the western side was filled in over time, but the lakebed itself still remains, even though it's all grassland now."

"Hold on," Captain Corliss from the Army of Tel said, making a stopping gesture with his hand. "You're saying the mercenaries made camp in this lakebed?"

The laborer nodded. "That is indeed what I'm saying."

"I don't believe it," Corliss said. "No soldier worth his salt would make a camp somewhere like that. Why, the army could be surrounded!"

"You are correct," the laborer said, "and that is not the only tactical mistake we shall discuss. You should be aware that the individuals who picked the location were *not* professional soldiers...or mercenaries. They were the arcanists spearheading the plot.

"The arcanists ostensibly leading this force were unable to keep word of Iosen Sivas's death from spreading throughout the troops, and when they noticed a tendency for those they sent on sentry duty to disappear into the night, they stopped sending out sentries at all and built four watchtowers that are manned day and night. I have confirmed reports of the discussion where that decision was made, and they felt the watchtowers would provide sufficient warning of anyone in danger of discovering the encamped army."

Corliss grimaced and put his head in hands, shaking it.

. . .

"So...THAT's the state of our opponent," Gavin said once his agent had finished the report. "I freely confess that I am no soldier to the best of my knowledge, but after hearing this same report earlier today, this is what I propose for our assault. I want to divide our forces into five formations, and my apprentices and I will coordinate them. The officers will lead their soldiers, but we will provide communication between units. Those five formations will surround the encampment during the night and march on them just as dawn is arriving. Three nights from now, there will be a new moon, which should allow us to get closer to their camp before we are seen. If this plan is accepted, from here on out, we'll do night marches only with no campfires."

"That's an excellent plan," Corliss said, "except for a couple things. First, how do you propose to coordinate between you and your apprentices? Second, how are we supposed to see on a night as dark as a new moon? We're not elves."

"The first question is easy to answer," Gavin said. "How familiar are you with the Godswar?"

Corliss frowned for a moment, lowering his eyes to the table before lifting them to meet Gavin's eyes once more. "You're talking about the Speaking Stones, but as far as I know, those artifacts have not been seen since the Godswar."

Gavin stood and walked to a chest where he retrieved a handful of black velvet pouches. Upon his return, he tossed them to the center of the table. The officer chose a pouch and emptied the crystal inside into his hand.

"I found eighteen of those not too long before we left Tel Mivar," Gavin said. "I brought six. As for seeing at night, I have an alchemical formula developed by Mivar during the Godswar for just such a purpose. Starting tomorrow night, we'll mix it with the evening meal and the water barrels for all our soldiers. It only lasts about four to six hours, according to Mivar's notes, so the soldiers will have to refresh it throughout the night."

"Will this alchemical mixture harm my soldiers in any way?"

"Mivar reported about one man in a thousand having a bad reaction, and Mivar defined a 'bad reaction' as vomiting or losing control of one's bowels. The reaction lasted the duration of the mixture but produced no longer-lasting harmful effects."

Several of the army officers winced.

"Gavin," Ovir said, "why did you bring six stones if we only have five arcanists?"

"I always like to have a spare. Why?"

"I would like to try using one, and if I can, why not have six formations?"

Gavin surveyed the others at the table, his expression inviting comment.

"Six formations would make for a more thorough trap," Captain Gartun said, "but six formations would contain fewer soldiers than five. A smaller formation might be overwhelmed more easily than a larger formation."

"How overwhelming do you expect these mercenaries to be?" Corliss said. "You heard the same report I did. They're not holding organizing drills anymore. The men are demoralized from wondering if they'll be getting paid, and no one seems to have a clear understanding of who's in charge.

"I realize you should never underestimate your enemy, and I realize they'll fight once their backs are against the wall, so to speak...but in all seriousness, what kind of fighters are they going to be?"

A three-word phrase floated to the forefront of Gavin's mind from the gray mists that surrounded his consciousness; it had been like that ever since Iosen's basement. Strange words or concepts or memories came unbidden to his conscious mind, and this phrase was no different.

"Shock and awe," Gavin said, drawing everyone's attention to him.

The army officers glanced to one another before Corliss said, "Shock and awe, sir? I'm not sure we understand."

Gavin wasn't sure he understood, either, but the meaning suddenly clicked into place like the final tumbler of a lock manipulated by skill and quality lock-picks.

"They're already demoralized, so we convince them that they

have greater chances of living if they don't fight than if they do. And here's how we'll do that. Once we're in position, we'll conjure our standards...battle standards that haven't been seen by anyone in over six thousand years. That will draw attention and, if we do it right, cause fear. Then, my apprentices will destroy the watchtowers. If you just saw the watchtowers intended to warn you get destroyed, what would you do?"

"*I* would rally the troops into a counter-charge," Corliss said, "but *they* will probably shit themselves."

THE LEADERSHIP of the army accepted Gavin's plan, and the following day, Gavin worked with his apprentices to teach them how to destroy the watchtowers. The concept of an explosion was foreign to them until Gavin thought of igniting marsh gas in a confined space, and then, they understood. That day, Ovir also tried using a Speaking Stone and found one would indeed respond to him, and the army officers devised the six formations the army would form.

The army stayed encamped throughout the following day, and Gavin and his apprentices mixed up the alchemical compound that would allow the soldiers to see at night. The first night they tested it, ten soldiers developed bad reactions and were sent to the wagons set aside for the sick and wounded.

The second night, the six formations separated and began the march to their respective positions, which were about three hours' march from the mercenary camp. They would time their approach to the mercenaries so that they were in their assault positions just as the twilight between night and day shifted to the morning dawn.

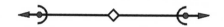

CHAPTER 57

Gavin rode at the head of his formation…Declan on his right, Kiri on his left, and a herald close behind Declan. Declan wore the matte black leather armor that was the hallmark of the Wraiths, a bow worn across his torso with a quiver of arrows strapped low on his right thigh.

Kiri herself wore matte black leather like Declan, though hers was modified just a bit. Given the peculiarities of the slave brand, it could not be covered up without causing its bearer intense pain, and so, the armor Kiri wore left her entire left shoulder bare. Like Declan opposite her, Kiri wore blades of varying sizes strapped almost to every surface of her armor where she could reach them with ease. Daggers, dirks, throwing knives, and the two short swords strapped to her back…Kiri seemed to have sufficient inventory to masquerade as a traveling blades merchant.

If anyone thought it odd Kirloth would have his slave dressed out in matte black leather armor that bristled with blades in flagrant disregard of the Kingdom's laws regarding armed slaves, those people were very diligent at keeping their opinions to themselves. By this point, everyone knew of Iosen Sivas's demise and the destruction of his manor house, and it seemed very unwise indeed to antagonize a man who could kill a man or melt stone with a Word.

"Sir, we have reached our designated position," the herald said.

Gavin nodded, saying, "Very good. Halt the march."

As the herald lifted the flag that would signal 'Halt,' Gavin said, "What's the status of the captured Inquisitors?"

"They're safely on their way back to Tel Mivar," Declan said. "They might feel a little ill-treated at their transportation, but a potato wagon was all we could find in time."

Gavin chuckled. "They shouldn't grouse too much. They're free, after all. Very well. Hand me the crystal, please."

Declan withdrew a black velvet pouch from a convenient pocket and passed it to Gavin. Gavin loosened the drawstrings and dropped the pouch's contents into the palm of his left hand. Gavin looked down at the crystal about half the size of his palm and took a few heartbeats to marvel at it.

This crystal and its fellows spread out among Lillian, Ovir, and the others were artifacts of the Godswar. Needing a way to coordinate forces spread over a large area, Kirloth and the Apprentices created what the common soldiery of the time called the Speaking Stones. The Speaking Stones looked to be nothing more than ordinary crystals...perhaps quartz or some other mostly clear crystal. However, when fed a trickle of power—whether that power came from wizardry or ordained faith—the Speaking Stones allowed their bearers to converse with each other as if they sat around a table together.

Gavin wrapped his fingers around the crystal and pushed into it a wisp of the churning cataract his power had become.

Gavin felt a faint resonance in his mind and said, "Report."

Voices sounded out of thin air as a faint light pulsed within the heart of the Speaking Stone.

"*Mivar in position.*"

"*Cothos in position.*"

"*Wygoth in position.*"

"*Roshan-in-position.*"

"*Thatcherson in position.*"

"Very good," Gavin said. "Let's do this just like we practiced. On my call."

Gavin waited a moment and said, "Wynn."

Through the Speaking Stone, Gavin heard his high-strung apprentice invoke the Word of Conjuration they had practiced both prior to the march and during it before splitting the army. At almost the same moment, Gavin felt the resonance of Wynn's invocation through his *skathos* just as the effect appeared in the air above the division Wynn led.

Fifteen feet across at a minimum, the sigil was a blazing, white light almost too bright to face and floated some thirty feet in the air above Wynn's head. It was a composite of several pieces of heraldry, but the Glyph of Roshan formed the core of the sigil.

"Lillian," Gavin said and watched another sigil appear over her division.

"Braden," Gavin said, watching a sigil appear over the division between his own and Wynn's.

"Mariana," Gavin said, and a sigil appeared over the division north of Lillian's position.

Only one remained, and Gavin himself spoke the Word. For the first time in over six thousand years, the battle standards of Kirloth and his Apprentices lit the sky.

FROM HIS POSITION between Mariana and Wynn, Ovir beamed with pride as he looked at the glowing standards surrounding him, but he was not about to be left out. Bowing his head and closing his eyes, Ovir whispered a prayer. Within moments, the glowing Seal of the Royal Priest of Tel joined the sigils of his fellows.

* * *

"YOU BETTER HAVE A DAMNED good reason for making me climb up here," Rufus said, as his head poked up through the trapdoor of the watchtower.

"Are we getting any reinforcements today?" Ackerley asked.

Rufus frowned, saying, "How should I know? They don't tell me anything, except, 'Here, take this to whomever.' Why?"

Ackerley offered his friend a hand up and pointed as he said, "Look there!"

Rufus stood up to look just as a blazing, white light erupted off to the east. Rufus was from Vushaar, so the glowing symbol over the contingent of troops to the east meant nothing to him. Ackerley, though, recognized the Glyph at the symbol's center in an instant and couldn't stop the blood leaving his face.

"Roshan," Ackerley whispered.

"What?" Rufus said, turning to face Ackerley, and saw a second symbol blaze into existence off to the west. "Ackerley, look!"

Ackerley spun and felt himself swallow hard, saying, "Mivar."

More symbols appeared, and with each appearance, Ackerley felt his fear growing. It wasn't until the fifth symbol appeared that Ackerley's fear slipped over into true terror.

"Kirloth," Ackerley said, his voice shaky. "By the gods…they've come for us."

* * *

"Braden, Wynn, Lillian, and Mariana…take out the watchtowers," Gavin said.

Gavin felt a resonance of Evocation cascade around the camp like dominoes, and four, seething orbs of blue-white fire erupted from the forefront of each of his apprentices' formations. The orbs were the size of a large man's fist, and they flew unerringly to their targets. The moment each orb reached a watchtower, they exploded, raining flaming bits of wood, sentries, and one courier down upon the surrounding area.

Gavin squared his shoulders and prepared to invoke the Word of Conjuration that would broadcast his voice across the mercenary camp. But then, Gavin froze. His eyes unfocused, and the color left his complexion. His skin turned clammy.

. . .

"I'VE DECIDED I'm going to enjoy myself with that Mivar wench before I kill her," Iosen said, whispering in Gavin's ear, "and I think I'll leave you alive to watch."

Gavin hung from the chains, Iosen's mouth so close to his ear Gavin could feel Iosen's breath. Iosen moved the red-hot iron across Gavin's bleeding form, and all Gavin could smell was his own burning flesh as he screamed.

"Gavin?" a woman's voice said.

GAVIN JERKED and found Kiri's right hand on his left. Kiri looked at him, her expression betraying her concern. Gavin closed his eyes and took a deep breath. The images and memories tried to take him again, and he clutched Kiri's hand.

"Ovir," Gavin said, his voice almost a gasp, "call for the meeting."

"I don't think anyone has noticed," Declan said, "though I'm sure some will wonder why you had Ovir contact the camp. No matter. Kiri take your hand back; you can't be seen comforting him. Gavin, for the next few minutes, you need to be Kirloth: cold, aloof, utterly confident in your plan and your people, and equally ruthless. Can you do that?"

Gavin thought back to his confrontation with Iosen Sivas outside the manor, focusing on his mindset when he killed Sivas. A calm descended over him. His breathing slowed and evened out. His jaw stopped trembling.

Declan watched Gavin, his gaze intent. A few moments later, he said, "Good. Now, hold that."

OVIR FELT those around him look to him for an explanation when Gavin called for him to contact the camp. He said nothing, even though he suspected he knew the source of the shakiness in Gavin's voice. Ovir bowed his head once more and whispered a prayer for Valthon to make his voice heard across the valley. Valthon's favor was a steady warmth rising out of the core of Ovir's soul, and he felt the effect take hold.

"Mercenaries in the camp below," Ovir said, his voice echoing across the valley, "I am Ovir Thatcherson, Royal Priest of Tel, and I call upon your leaders to confer with us under a flag of truce."

LITTLE TIME WAS REQUIRED to set up a pavilion an equal distance between the Kirloth formation and the mercenary camp. Given that snow was starting to fall, Gavin instructed the soldiers to use his pavilion that was as pleasant as a summer evening inside.

The commanders of the various units stood at the back of the pavilion. Declan stood at Gavin's right with Ovir on Gavin's left. Kiri, Lillian, Wynn, and Braden stood in a line between Gavin and the formation commanders.

As they waited for the mercenary leadership to arrive, Declan leaned close to Gavin and whispered, "There is no need to demand the mercenaries' surrender. Even without your recent acquisitions from the former House Sivas, you possess sufficient funds to hire this army yourself for several years. With the acquisitions from House Sivas, you need a guard force to maintain security at your new holdings."

"If we follow your plan," Gavin said, his voice a whisper as well, "I'd want…your associates…to serve as training cadre to whip them into shape and keep them there."

"That can be arranged."

"What are you two whispering about over there?" Ovir asked, his mouth quirking into a grin.

Before Gavin could answer, a soldier entered the pavilion and snapped to attention, saying, "Milord, your guests have arrived."

Six arcanists—a man wearing a red robe with aquamarine runes of a *Primagus*, a woman wearing a white robe with the vermillion runes of a *Semagus*, a woman in a red robe with the silver runes of a *Primagus*, a man in a green robe with the amber runes of a *Termagus*, and a woman in a blue robe with the ruby runes of a *Semagus*— entered the pavilion, followed by six men and women wearing varying armor.

Gavin ignored the arcanists completely, focusing on the armored individuals.

"You are the leaders of the mercenaries?" Gavin asked.

"Yes, we are," the red-robed woman said.

Gavin shifted his eyes to the arcanists. "I care nothing for the six of you. You traitors are the dead walking. I called for this conversation to speak with *them*." Gavin indicated the mercenary leaders.

"What do you want with us?" a woman in half-plate asked.

"How's the pay been? You looking for new employment? I can't imagine the coin has been all that regular lately."

The mercenary leaders looked to each other, their expressions thoughtful and considering.

"Now, see here! You work for us!" the red-robed man said.

"Maybe not," the woman in half-plate said, looking back to Gavin. "What's your offer?"

"I came into ownership of various pieces of property around Tel, and I find myself in need of a reliable guard force. You'll be well-paid and have a housing allowance for those posts near the more settled regions. I will provide all arms and armor at no cost to the soldier. I accept resignations, and I'll support the families of anyone who dies under my colors. But here's the thing. I expect unwavering loyalty. Anyone who takes my coin had better not betray me or those under my care." Gavin pointed to his medallion. "I trust I do not need to explain the fate traitors will face."

"How many are you looking to hire?" a man in leather armor asked.

"I'll hire everyone in the camp below who agrees to my terms. Oh...and there's one more thing. The arcanists responsible for the plot to overthrow the Council...I expect you to hand them over to me, should you decide to accept."

"You said we're under a flag of truce!" the man in green robes said, his voice a tad shrill.

Gavin turned to look at the man who'd spoken, and his expression would've instantly turned water to ice. "Have I harmed any of you? Have I attacked or threatened you in any way? No. Do not insult or question my honor again, or you will face my challenge."

"We'd like to return to our troops and discuss the matter," the woman in half-plate said. "What should we say you're offering as pay?"

"What are you supposed to be paid now?" Gavin asked.

"The common soldier gets five copper pieces per day, the average officer one silver, and commanders five silver."

Gavin directed a skeptical expression the woman's way, saying, "Lillian, do we have any copies on hand of Sivas's pay records that we took from the Vineyard?"

"I'd have to check-"

"Wait!" the woman said. "The common soldier gets one copper piece a day, the average officer five coppers, and the commanders one silver."

Gavin nodded. "That sounds much more accurate. Here's my offer. In my service, a common soldier will receive one silver, an officer five silvers, and any commanders will receive one gold piece…per day."

"Just how long do you think you can keep up that exorbitant rate of pay?" the red-robed woman asked. "They're just common thugs."

"I can keep up that rate of pay for far, far longer than you'll be alive. Perhaps, they may be common thugs, but by the time I've finished with them, I'll put them up against any army you care to name."

The mercenary leaders looked to each other again, and each nodded in turn.

"We'd like to take your offer back to the troops to discuss it."

"Excellent," Gavin said. "Braden, hand me those linen pouches, please."

Braden handed Gavin ten linen pouches, each about the size of a child's hand. In turn, Gavin extended those pouches to the mercenary leaders.

"Take these. Should you wish to accept my offer, throw them in any fire. The fire will release blue smoke to indicate your decision, and you have my word that blue smoke is all these pouches will do.

Anyone who leans into the smoke, though, will have blue skin until she or he bathes."

The woman stepped forward and took the pouches.

"Now, are we agreed that the truce ends when you reach your lines, with the provision that we will not attack you until you've informed me of your decision?"

The mercenary leaders looked to each other again, and once all nodded, the woman in half-plate said, "That's a little worrisome, but yes, we can agree to that."

"Good," Gavin said and pointed his thumb at the arcanists. "Now, please take them with you when you leave."

GAVIN WAITED for the visitors to clear the pavilion and stood. He looked to the officers, saying, "Have the troops set up camp for the night. I think minimal watch will be sufficient, but of course, I'm happy to defer to your judgment on that. I doubt they'll talk for more than a day before they accept my offer. Oh, speaking of that...I need parchment, ink, a stylus, and sealing wax."

Provided with those items, Gavin wrote out a quick note and sealed it by dribbling wax on the fold and pressing his medallion into it. Once the wax dried, he handed the note to Declan.

"Would you be so kind as to ensure the woman in half-plate receives that sooner rather than later? Just make sure they've reached their lines before you deliver it."

Declan nodded once, took the letter, and left the pavilion.

"Gavin, what was in that letter?" Lillian asked, though Gavin could see that very question written across every face present.

"I merely communicated to the woman that, on further consideration, I was willing to accept six heads at no discount or penalty, if live prisoners should be problematic."

Lillian's eyes went wide, and she opened her mouth as if to speak.

Ovir spoke first, "And by ensuring that missive arrives *after* they return to their lines, there are absolutely no grounds for claims that you violated the flag of truce. Well played, young man."

Gavin shrugged. "I can but try."

* * *

It was a little past noon the next day when the large bonfire at the center of the camp started billowing blue smoke. Gavin withdrew the dragon's tooth from a pocket and fed it a trickle of power, saying, "Nathrac, the mercenary army is no more. You may return the garrison to rest at your leisure."

The only response was the tooth crumbling away to dust.

"What are you going to do with your new army, Gavin?" Mariana asked as they watched the blue smoke rise into the sky.

"Not a whole lot, right away," Gavin said. "I'll work with the commanders to divvy them up between all my various holdings as guards and implement a training regimen. You never know, the day may come when we're glad I have an army scattered across Tel."

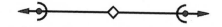

CHAPTER 58

Even with the passage of two weeks, Tel Mivar was still in an uproar. Members of the town guard stood on every street corner, while groups of three to five walked the blocks. In the space of less than one hundred yards, Gavin heard claims that the world was ending, Lornithar and his followers were coming back, and the dead were rising from their graves...just to name a few.

For once, no one seemed to recoil from Gavin's medallion. In fact, many swarmed him, asking what had happened, what those blue ghosts were, or whether he knew if the end-times had come at last. Gavin responded to each person with politeness and honesty, while doing his best to maintain forward momentum.

A SHORT TIME LATER, Gavin, Kiri, Declan, Ovir, and his apprentices rode through the College gate. Valera stood at the foot of the stairs leading up to the Tower of the Council, and stable-hands waited with her, who took charge of the horses as everyone dismounted.

"You never do anything half-way, do you?" Valera said as Gavin approached.

Gavin grinned, saying, "Why should I start now?"

"Fair point," Valera said, following it with a heavy sigh. "The Council is assembled and pretty much demanding your presence, and I have a messenger from the king cooling his heels in Sera's office. He carries a demand from the king that you present yourself before him forthwith, lest he send the Royal Guard to collect you."

"Let's go deal with the Council," Gavin said. "I'm not that worried about Leuwyn. As I believe my mentor said at one point, 'he can roast on a fiery spit in Lornithar's Abyss for all I care.'"

"Yes, well, let's not tell him that," Valera said as she turned to ascend the steps.

Gavin took two quick steps to arrive at her side and offered her his arm, saying, "Why not?"

Valera sighed once more and shook her head.

It was the matter of a short walk to arrive at the Chamber of the Council. Valera released Gavin's arm and entered on her own, with Gavin and the rest following a few steps behind. Declan stretched his shoulders and leaned against the wall beside the door; Kiri moved to stand with him.

Valera traversed the Chamber of the Council and sat in her customary place at the apex of the table, and Gavin led his apprentices and Ovir to stand before the Council.

"I hereby call this session of the Council of Magisters to order," Valera said and touched the square to seal the chamber.

Tauron lifted his hand, and Valera said, "The Magister of Evocation has the floor."

Tauron stood and turned to glare at Gavin, saying, "This city is in turmoil, and that turmoil rests at *your* feet! Give us one good reason why the Council should not declare the lot of you renegades and have you executed!"

"The Conclave of the Great Houses voted to invoke Article 35 of the Arcanists' Code," Gavin said, "and Ovir's not an arcanist, which means you can't name him a renegade to start with. There… that's two reasons."

Gavin heard suppressed snorts from opposite sides of the table, but he was too focused to see who produced them. Tauron's nostrils flared, and his hands clenched into fists.

"The fact is, Tauron, you yourself drove the Council into inaction. You have no grounds to stand there and threaten the people who were forced to act. The bulk of this crisis could have been averted, had the Council done its job…much like the situation with Rolf Sivas. I'm finished listening to you people; I answer to the Code, not the Council."

"It is sentiment like that which leads us to consider naming you a renegade might be the best course of action," said Drannos Muldannin, the Magister of Thaumaturgy.

"Then, do it," Gavin said, "and stop the threats. Be the first Council in the history of the Society to name a wizard of the Great Houses a renegade. You just better be sure that's what you want to do, because I am Kirloth. My mentor didn't train me in half-measures."

Gavin turned to those standing with him and said, "We're finished here. Let's go deal with the king."

As he reached the inclined path that led to the doors, Gavin invoked a Word of Tutation, "*Klyphos*," dispelling the magical seal on the Chamber. The red dots of light at each of the upper corners disappeared, and opening the door, Gavin left the Chamber of the Council.

Outside, Gavin waited for the door to the Chamber to close and said, "All right. That's one down. Now, we just have to deal with the king."

"Unless you specifically want me to go," Kiri said, "I'd like to head up to the suite. I'd love to get out of this armor and put on some real clothes."

"You just want to go soak in the bath for a while."

"I refuse to comment on any thoughts that may have crossed my mind," Kiri said, grinning and drawing smiles all around.

Gavin smiled. "I'll see you when we get back."

. . .

GAVIN STOPPED at Valera's office down the hall from the Chamber. He took one step into Sera's outer office, snapped his fingers, and gave the royal messenger a terse, "You...let's go."

A few moments later, Gavin and his associates mounted the waiting horses, which had been brushed down, watered, and fed by the College's grooms while Gavin visited the Council. Gavin glanced at the royal messenger and found him wearing an expression of forlorn consternation.

"What's wrong with you?" Gavin said as the last of his friends mounted their horses.

"I...I didn't ride a horse," the messenger said.

"Ah, yes; that is a problem. Try to keep up."

Scanning his associates, Gavin saw they were all mounted and waiting. He nudged Jasmine into a trot and led them out of the College grounds.

* * *

GAVIN LED his associates onto the palace grounds, and they dismounted. A nearby guard left the place where he was standing and approached.

"Who are you?" he asked.

"You know who I am," Gavin said, pointing at his medallion, "and the King wishes to speak with me."

"Yes, well...follow me," the guard said and turned to lead them into the palace.

GAVIN AND COMPANY were just stepping through the palace doors when the royal messenger staggered through the gates, gasping and soaked in sweat from running the entire distance from the College. The messenger's toe caught on the edge of an uneven flagstone, and he fell to his hands and knees. He lifted his head, and seeing the group he was supposed to be escorting entering the palace some thirty-odd yards ahead of him, he allowed himself to collapse.

· · ·

THE GUARD LED Gavin and his associates to the residential section of the palace and stopped at a door flanked by guards.

"His Majesty will receive you in here."

"Ovir, come with me," Gavin said. "The rest of you, wait here."

Inside the door, they found themselves standing in a room lined with bookshelves. An emaciated man with sandy hair sat in an armchair and stared into a fireplace with no fire. He turned at the sound of the door opening and stood to receive his guests.

Gavin watched the man rise out of the chair and realized he now faced the King of Tel. Gavin was not impressed.

"You killed my friend," Leuwyn said.

"Your friend deserved it," Gavin said.

A silence descended on the room as Gavin and the king stared at each other. After several moments, Gavin broke the impasse.

"You and I both know you sponsored Sivas's plot to overthrow the Council, but the Kingdom cannot afford the chaos and turmoil that would occur if the Conclave removed you from the throne. Ovir conscripted those units of the Army of Tel in accordance with Article 12 of the Constitution, and if I hear of anything happening to those men—even the slightest event—I will come for you. Do you understand?"

Leuwyn's eyes tightened into a glare as he said, "I want to watch you die."

"Sivas said almost the same thing; think about what happened to him."

"Get out of here," the king said. "Get out!"

Gavin nodded once, saying, "I'm glad we understand each other."

Gavin then turned and led Ovir out of the study.

In the hall outside, Ovir pulled the door closed and looked to Gavin. He said, "I think that went well."

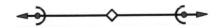

CHAPTER 59

Awareness returned to Gavin at a gradual rate. His
consciousness floated up out of the void. It was the first
night since Sivas Manor he had slept the whole night
through...without nightmares. In the wake of Sivas Manor, Kiri
argued that Gavin should take half of the bed for himself, but
Gavin maintained his stance that he wasn't about to do anything
against his ethics. He chose instead to add a few more blankets to
his space on the floor.

As he lay there, Gavin admitted that he could've moved into
Marcus's room, giving Kiri this room to herself, but the chests that
held Marcus's journals almost filled that room with little space for
anything else beyond a footpath from the door to the bed. Besides,
Gavin couldn't quite bring himself to take over that last remaining
space of what had once belonged to Marcus.

GAVIN AND KIRI entered the dining hall for the morning meal, and
they watched a wave of furtive looks progress through the room as
the ambient conversation settled to a lower volume. He could
almost feel their nervousness, or maybe it was fear. He even saw

clusters of students he had helped with their studies shy away from him, and Gavin wanted to sigh. But he did not. Without missing a step, Gavin led Kiri to the table set aside for the Great Houses of Tel.

A SHORT TIME LATER, Gavin, Kiri, Lillian, Braden, Wynn, and Mariana were sitting around the table enjoying each other's company. They were discussing everything from training to Lillian wanting to go on maneuvers with the Battle-mages.

Gavin sat with his back turned to the room, having grown tired of the furtive glances his way. He saw Lillian glance over his right shoulder. Gavin almost reacted to the threat, and it took all of his will to remind himself there were no threats here.

After two deep breaths, Gavin found himself near the calm happiness that had been his mindset just a few moments before, and he turned to see what made Lillian glance.

Sera, Valera's assistant, stood some five feet away. She worked her lower lip between her teeth as she wrung her hands. When Gavin met her eyes, Sera jerked her eyes to the floor.

Gavin sighed, saying, "Sera...I thought we were past this."

"Va—that is, the Magister of Divination—asks a few moments of your time, Milord," Sera said, still staring at the floor.

Gavin turned back to the table and said, "I should go see what this is about. Do you want to meet later, once I've had time to work up the new plan for training?"

Gavin's apprentices gave a chorus of nods, mixed with "Sure," "Yes," or "Sounds good."

Gavin stood and pushed his chair to the table before turning to Sera and saying, "After you, Sera, and my name is still Gavin."

SERA LED Gavin to the Office of the Collegiate Justice and indicated the door to Valera's office as she said, "The Magister is waiting for you."

Gavin walked to the door, knocked twice, and entered.

"At least you knock," Valera said, a slight smile curling her lips. "Marcus never did."

"Yes, well, I'm not my mentor," Gavin said.

Valera gestured for Gavin to take a seat, as she said, "Oh, yes; I'm aware. Tauron would probably be dead by now if you were."

"Don't think the thought hasn't crossed my mind," Gavin said. He moved to sit in the armchair off Valera's left. "But I don't think you asked me here to discuss whether I'm like Marcus."

"No, I did not. The Council is not at all happy with you, Gavin, but Tauron was unable to get even one other magister to support calling your bluff."

"Valera..."

"Yes, Gavin?"

"It wasn't a bluff."

Valera sighed and looked at Gavin in silence for a few heart-beats. At last, she said, "I didn't think it was, and neither did Kantar. In truth, the Council is not what's on the forefront of my mind.

"Gavin, I considered telling you a convenient fiction to explain what I'm about to say, but I need your trust...and your help. Since I was little, I have had visions from time to time. Sometimes, they are visions of the present, sometimes insights about a person, and some-times, I see glimpses of the future. I had such a vision a short time before you set out to confront Sivas's mercenaries."

Valera fell silent and looked down at her hands.

"What is it, Valera? Are you well?"

"Yes, Gavin, I am, but my homeland is not. I don't know what help you can be, but I would like for you to go to Vushaar, present yourself to King Terris Muran, and save him if you can at all. The vision...I...I saw the fall of Vushaar."

"Would Marcus have helped him?"

Valera smiled, saying, "Oh, yes. In fact, Marcus tended to watch over the Muran line, in much the same way he watched over the descendants of his apprentices. The King of Vushaar during the Godswar saved his life."

Gavin took a deep breath and let it out as a slow exhale, before saying, "Then, it looks like I'm going to Vushaar. Was there something else, or may I go prepare?"

"No, that was why I wanted to see you. Thank you, Gavin."

"You're welcome, Valera," Gavin said, as he stood. He started to open the door but stopped, turning back to face Valera. "Does he know?"

"Does who know, Gavin? And about what are you asking?"

"Does Terris know you're a blood relative to him?"

For the briefest moments, a terror Gavin had never seen before flashed through Valera's eyes, followed by sorrow.

"No, Gavin," Valera said. "He does not. All records of Muran wizards were expunged from the genealogies many years ago."

Gavin frowned, remembering a very old volume of the Muran Genealogy in Marcus's private library upstairs, and said, "If he did know about you, who would you be to him?"

Valera sat in silence, staring into Gavin's eyes for several moments. The silence dragged on until Gavin thought she wouldn't speak.

"I was his grandfather's youngest sister," Valera said, her voice soft and quiet. "He thought I was representing the Council and Society when I attended his father's funeral. I shouldn't have gone... but there was no one still alive who remembered me or what my father did."

"Want to tell me about it?"

"It was a long time ago, Gavin. It doesn't matter anymore."

"It might, if another wizard is born to the Muran line."

"I pray to Bellos every night for that never to happen again. To the best of my knowledge, he has granted my prayers thus far."

Gavin wanted to ask more. He wanted to know what Valera's father had done, but he didn't have time for that. Perhaps, he could learn more in Vushaar.

"Valera, I wish you well, and I will do what I can for Terris. I give you my word."

"Thank you, Gavin. It means a lot to me."

Gavin nodded once and left, closing the door behind him.

* * *

GAVIN RETURNED to the dining hall and found Kiri and his friends still sitting at their table. He approached and leaned on the back of his chair.

"That was fast, Gavin," Lillian said.

Gavin nodded, saying, "I'd like to speak with all of you in the suite as soon as possible. I'll be there as soon as I find Declan."

Lillian and the others frowned but nodded. Gavin turned and left the dining hall.

A SHORT TIME LATER, Gavin led Declan into the suite and found Kiri and his friends waiting, and he gathered everyone to sit at the dining table.

"What is this, Gavin?" Mariana asked.

"We're a little worried," Lillian said.

Gavin scanned the faces of the people he had come to think of as friends, and the left side of his mouth curled in a half-smile. At last, he said, "Valera has asked me to travel to Vushaar to help however I can with the situation there. I don't know what I'll be walking into, and I can't in good conscience drag the lot of you with me. We'll have to put the training on hold for a time."

"Gavin," Lillian said, "that's not how it works. We're your apprentices. We go where you go. Besides, just think of what all we'll learn and see if we're with you."

"We'll be riding into a civil war," Declan said. "Two months ago, a rebel army under the command of one of King Terris's own generals, a Sclaros Ivarson, laid siege to the capital. There are roving bands of slavers operating with impunity throughout the Vushaari countryside, and no one wears a banner to show which side he or she supports."

"Besides all that," Gavin said, "you are the heirs of your respective Houses. I don't want to risk any of you."

"Gavin," Braden said, "Roshan, Wygoth, Cothos, and Mivar were the last of their lines when they followed Kirloth to the

Godswar, and there was even less reason to think they would survive that. Our place is with you."

Lillian, Wynn, and Mariana nodded their assent as Gavin looked to each in turn. Gavin shifted his gaze to the tabletop and sat in silence for several moments. In all truth, he wanted them with him. He felt more at ease with his friends nearby.

When he lifted his eyes from the tabletop, Gavin found everyone looking at him. He turned to Declan and said, "We're going to need at least seven horses. We will leave for Vushaar once we've packed."

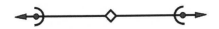

WHAT'S NEXT?

The story continues in "Into Vushaar," and it's available now!

Visit your favorite retailer and search for ISBN:
9780999201268

* * *

Want to keep up-to-date and receive exclusive content?

Sign-up for my newsletter:
kfplink.com/g8i

RATE THIS BOOK

Did you enjoy this story? If you did, please consider leaving a review.

Reviews are the lifeblood of visibility for independent authors, especially on the eBook retailers. The more reviews a book has, the more visible it will be on the retailers' sites.

I appreciate all reviews…good, bad, or indifferent.

If you would like to leave a review, visit this book's review page (http://kfplink.com/g4m).

AUTHOR'S NOTE
7 NOVEMBER 2018

First and foremost, thank you for reading…both the novel and these notes! I hope you enjoyed *Awakening*!

I first published *Awakening* on 3 April 2018, and I've been very pleased with the response I've received. One of my favorite parts of publishing *Awakening* was reading the editor's comments and feedback in the markup section of the document. I really enjoyed seeing what she found funny, what surprised her, etc. Feel free to send me a note and tell me about your experience reading the book…what you liked, what you didn't like, what made you laugh, etc.

When I first published *Awakening* in April of 2018, I had never heard of Vellum, and so, I used a formatting service to produce the formatted PDF and eBook files. They did an excellent job, but I just can't get onboard with the idea of paying someone every time I want to update the book list at the back of my novels. And besides, I really like having control over the process…or as much control as Vellum provides at any rate. :)

If you're inclined to say hello, here are the best ways to do so:

- The Contact Page of my site (valthon.net/contact)
- Facebook

- Of course, you can also send me an email: sendrobmail@knightsfallpress.com.

If you're still reading this, thanks for the dedication…or perhaps the curiosity. :) As I said above, I hope you enjoyed reading *Awakening*. Thank you.

TYPOS

Typos and little slips in grammar are the bane of any author. Unfortunately, they are almost impossible to eradicate completely. I can show you many traditionally published books—twenty years old and more—that have a 'whoopsie' here and there.

That being said, if you find a typo or something that seems to be an error in grammar, please do not hesitate to contact me at typos@knightsfallpress.com.

I will periodically collate any emails and produce an updated PDF and eBook files, and I'll make an announcement in my monthly newsletter when the updates have been published.

ACKNOWLEDGMENTS

There's an old saying: it takes a village to raise a child. I don't know if that's true or not, but it certainly seems true where publishing a novel is concerned. You would not be reading this were it not for contributions from several people.

My editor, Keri Karandrakis (kerikarandrakis.com), provided excellent feedback that made this a far better work than what I originally wrote.

Did you like the cover? The background image was created by Jakub Skop (https://www.behance.net/JakubSkop).

Two of my closest friends, Palmer Stephens and Chase Miller, provided excellent feedback on the most-recent (and final) rough draft of this story.

Another good friend who cannot go unmentioned is Dr. J. Morgan. I first met Morgan when I was working in the IT department at Glenville State College, and when I learned we share similar interests in fiction, he graciously agreed to critique an alpha version of the manuscript. This book would not be what it is without his input.

This list is not complete without mentioning Dr. Edward F. Palm. I first met Dr. Palm in English 101 at Glenville State College in the Fall of 1998, and his comment on one of my earliest writing assignments, "You write well," started me thinking that maybe—just maybe—there might be more to what I considered a relaxing hobby at the time.

Is it trite or cliché yet to acknowledge family? Without my grandparents, Bob & Janice Miller, I honestly don't know where I'd be today; my grandfather taught me to read and love reading, and my grandmother taught me to develop and exercise my imagination. This novel (not to mention my life in general) certainly would not have happened without my parents, Vernon & Judy Kerns.

ADDITIONAL ACKNOWLEDGMENTS

I've been working on this Fantasy story since the vicinity of 2000, and during that time, many people have provided feedback, thoughts, inspiration, or education in varying amounts. I greatly appreciate their time and contribution, and if you think your name should be on this list but don't see it, I truly apologize for the oversight. If you're curious, the list is alphabetical by last name.

Greg Brewster
Robert & Gayle Burkowski
Roger & Beth Burkowski
Cassie Davis
David Millard
Jon Minton
Brian Moss
Zeke Price
Aaron & Julie Radcliff
Brad & Jen Reed

THE NOVELS OF ROBERT M. KERNS

For a complete and accurate listing of all publications, both currently available and forthcoming, please visit Knightsfall Press.

Knightsfall Press - Books

https://knightsfall.press/books

SO...WHO'S THE AUTHOR?

Robert M. Kerns (or Rob if you ever meet him in person) is a geek, and he claims that label proudly. Most of his geekiness revolves around Information Technology (IT), having over fifteen years in the industry; within IT, he especially prefers Servers and Networks, and he often makes the claim that his residence has a better data infrastructure than some businesses.

Beyond IT, Rob enjoys Science Fiction and Fantasy of (almost) all stripes. He is a voracious reader, with his favorite books too numerous to list.

Rob has been writing for over 20 years, and *Awakening* is his debut novel.

Connect with Rob at knightsfall.press.

facebook.com/RobertMKerns

amazon.com/author/robertmkerns

bookbub.com/authors/robert-m-kerns